SWORDS & SIXGUNS:
AN OUTLAW'S TALE

To Phazes of
Women —

Thanks for your
support!

2021

To read more by Susan Hillwig, visit
susanhillwig.blogspot.com

SWORDS & SIXGUNS:
AN OUTLAW'S TALE

Being the First Book detailing
the Life of Richard Corrigan
(Late of America)
and his Adventures in
the Land of Arkhein,
as set down upon paper by

Susan Hillwig

ISBN: 978-1540506924

facebook.com/SwordsAndSixguns
susanhillwig.blogspot.com
swordsandsixgunsnovel@gmail.com

To Kerrie and Jennifer, for saving my life.
And to my husband, for making that life worth living.

PROLOGUE

Too long. It had been waiting far too long.

There was no sense of time passing in that place, but it knew just the same, and it was not pleased. It shrieked within its prison with a voice like sheet metal being torn to ribbons, full of insatiable fury and bloodlust, but not without direction. No, it had a target in mind: the Other, the One of the Light, who had dared to call its ways evil and then shackled it to this place, while the Other built walls around it to keep it away from the Other's precious Light. It had howled ever since then, as if sound alone could free it, but there were times when it simply had to cease its roaring, when those periods it thought of as the Low Times overtook it, and it slumbered.

It was during one of the Low Times that the holes appeared in the walls, and the Light poured in, shimmering across its drowsing senses like diamond dust, teasing, tempting, drawing it back towards consciousness. When it finally awoke, it witnessed what the Other's Light had done and was appalled, especially by the Soft Things, those little specks of Light that ran rampant outside of its prison. But it soon discovered how to hurt the Other through them, and proceeded to do so, growing stronger to the point where it thought for certain that its prison could no longer hold it. Oh, it could taste *freedom...*

But then the holes slammed shut, the darkness returned, and it began to howl even louder than before. It slept no more after that, even though the call of the Low Times was as strong as ever. It could not answer, it refused to give in, for fear that the holes would open again and it would not awaken in time. So it waited, slowly going mad from exhaustion.

It had nearly convinced itself that keeping vigil was pointless when it heard a noise, a strange echoing, cracking sound, and then suddenly the hole *was there, the* Light *was there, and it could* smell *the Soft Things and the embers of the Other that burned within them.*

And so it leapt forward from its prison, out of the Darkness and into the Light.

CHAPTER 1

Some days it just doesn't pay to rob a bank.

We'd checked out the town of Barrelhead for two solid weeks before the robbery, making sure we had everything set up perfectly. We knew who went where at what time, where the sheriff spent his off-hours, what the bank tellers ate for lunch, *everything*. Nothing, and I mean *nothing*, was overlooked. So when the whole thing got blown to Hell, we were just as shocked as everyone else in town.

The operation started out smoothly enough. Reeves and Kennedy rode into town about a half-hour ahead of me, each acting like they didn't know the other. They tied up their horses in front of the saloon, which sat right next to the bank, and mingled about the town, never wandering too far away from our intended target. Then I came up the trail just as easy as you please, no one paying me any heed as I passed on by. I'd always had the advantage of being too average-looking to notice -- having a nice forgettable face is a wonderful asset in my line of work.

I stopped my horse in front of the bank and had begun to loop my reins around the hitching post when a small voice asked, "Whatcha doin'?" I glanced over and saw a little boy of about seven or so standing next to me up on the boardwalk, bare-footed and with a carved wooden pistol tucked under the waistband of his trousers.

I turned to face him, nodding and tipping my hat as I did so. "Just passing through, sir. I don't mean to intrude where I'm not wanted." I smiled and pointed to the toy six-shooter. "You the law 'round here?" I asked jokingly.

The boy giggled. "No, that's Sheriff Walker!" He pointed down the street. "That's his office...do you want to meet him? He's fun. Gives me money for candy." He squared his small shoulders and beamed proudly. "He says I can be his deputy when I grow up."

"And a damn fine lawman I'm sure you'll make, too. Bet you can spot a bank robber from a mile away."

"I sure can, mister!"

"Listen, kid," I said, leaning over him, "why don't you run off and do a little patrol of the town? You know, look around for anything suspicious."

His eyes grew wide. "You think maybe there's some bad guys comin' 'round here?"

"Maybe. You never can tell...better keep that pistol cocked." I slipped him a wink as I pantomimed a sixgun with my thumb and forefinger.

"I sure will, mister!" He pulled out the toy gun and ran on down the boardwalk. I watched him 'til he rounded a corner, then shook my head. "Gullible little cuss, ain'tcha?" I muttered, then hopped up onto the boardwalk myself and strolled over to the bank. I soon heard two familiar pairs of footsteps behind me. *Time to get down to business, Richard,* I thought.

I unconsciously went through the motions that I'd performed countless times before. My right hand pulled the bandana tied around my neck up over my face, and my left came up to open the door to the bank, giving it a good push to clear it out of our path. Once I was through, both hands dropped to my guns: a matched set of .45-caliber Peacemakers. Reeves fell into position at my left side, swinging his Winchester up to his shoulder, and Kennedy headed up the rear, closing the door and whipping out an old LeMat. By the time I heard the door click shut, my revolvers were cocked and ready.

"Alright, folks," I bellowed, "I don't think I have to tell you what comes next!" My eyes slid around the room as I did a quick head-count. Five customers in the bank, three men and two women. Only one teller 'cause

the other one's next door having his afternoon beer --
Kennedy was already heading behind the counter to cover
him. "Check around for a gun," I reminded him.

Kennedy nodded, forced the teller to the floor, and
glanced under the counter -- his free hand soon came up
and flashed me an "okay" sign. "Good, good," I
answered. "Start filling up the saddlebag."

"Hey!" Reeves shouted. "What the Hell do you
think you're doin'?" I turned and saw that one of the men
had crept slowly towards the door. Luckily, Reeves had
caught him, and now had the barrel of his rifle pointed
right at the man's head.

"Please," the man blurted, "please don't shoot...I
was...I..."

"You was tryin' to sneak out, that's what you was
doin'!" He cocked the rifle and forced the man into a back
corner. "I oughta blow your head off right here and now
for pullin' that shit!"

One of the women on the other side of the room
began to whimper. I turned again and raised my own gun
towards her. "Don't start," I ordered. "If everybody stays
calm...and that means you too, partner," I said to Reeves,
"we'll get through this without a..."

Suddenly, the door behind us banged open, and a
voice yelled, "Alright, nobody move!"

Both Reeves and I whirled around towards the
voice and fired blindly -- our nerves had been stretched too
thin by the panicked customers to think clearly. When
you're not thinking clearly, you make mistakes. And, dear
God, we'd just made one of the biggest mistakes of our
careers.

The little boy with the wooden pistol had found
his bad guys.

The force of our shots knocked his small body into
the air, sailing out the doorway and back onto the
boardwalk. He bounced once off the slats and finally
came to rest in the dusty street not more than three feet
from my horse. The toy gun had flown forward and

landed at my feet. Everyone just stood there for a heartbeat before all Hell broke loose.

The clerk jumped up and managed to wrestle Kennedy's gun away from him, then fired it point-blank at Kennedy's face, causing the back of his head to explode outward like an overripe melon. People were screaming now, and Reeves had managed to pull himself together enough to run past me and out the door. I, on the other hand, didn't even have the strength to blink -- I just kept staring at the little six-shooter by my boot and the smear of blood on the boardwalk that led to the boy's dead body. I heard Reeves yell my name from the street, breaking the spell, but as I stepped towards the door, I heard the distinctive report of Kennedy's LeMat behind me, and felt something sharp skirt across my left temple. I suddenly found myself falling forward, my face slamming hard onto the bank floor. As my vision began to go white, I could hear people running, shouting, but I couldn't get up, couldn't move.

"Damn fine lawman..." I mumbled before I passed out. "Damn fine..."

* * * * * *

"...concussion."

"Whuh?" As I came back to consciousness, I saw an elderly man leaning over me, his eyes focused on my forehead. He reached over and touched my temple, sending a sharp, blinding pain through my skull. I yelped and swatted his hand away. "The Hell are you doing?"

"I'm trying to save your life, boy," the man answered. As he pulled me upright, I realized that I was on a cot in a jail cell, and that my torturer must be a doctor. "That bullet just grazed your skull, but it cut awful deep. You're going to have a nasty scar there...assuming you survive all this." He nodded his head towards the cell door: a good-sized crowd was gathered around the sheriff's desk in the office area, most of them yelling and making threatening gestures in my direction. The doctor ignored all the commotion and set to work, sitting beside me on the cot and swabbing the blood off my face to get a better look at the wound. "From what I've overheard," he told me, "your blond-haired friend got away easy enough, but the sheriff's got a half-dozen men out there after him, so he might wait until they drag the bastard back to hang you." He pulled some bandages out of his medical bag, then shrugged. "Or he might not. Hard to say. He ain't in all that good a mood...he really liked that boy."

I closed my eyes as he wrapped the bandage around my head, gritting my teeth against the pain his ministrations caused. "Yeah, that's what the kid told me." I swallowed hard against the double-dose of nausea brought on by the throbbing in my skull and my memories of the kid's bullet-torn body. Good Lord, I couldn't believe how badly we'd messed this job up. There was no way in Hell I was going to make it out of this town alive. It was almost funny: of all the ways I'd pictured myself dying over the years, being ripped to shreds by an angry mob had never occurred to me.

When the doctor was finished, he leaned close to me and pulled a small glass bottle out of his bag. "Laudanum," he explained. "In your condition, a dose this big would probably knock you out cold in less than five minutes. Matter of fact, you'd probably be dead of heart failure by morning." He slipped the bottle into my hand, out of sight of the angry townsfolk. "Helluva lot less painful than what *they're* planning for you."

I tucked the bottle beneath the blanket draped over the cot, then looked at him. "Why are you helping me like this? You know what I did." I nodded towards the crowd. "Why aren't you on their side?"

"Never said that I wasn't, son." He stood up, gave me a nod, and walked to the cell door.

Without looking, I placed a hand on the lump under the blanket. It occurred to me that this might be just a cruel joke, that it might only be a bottle full of water, but the man had a point: dying in my sleep was preferable to being hanged, or worse. Maybe I *should* down the stuff first chance I got. It didn't look like it'd be anytime soon with that crowd out there, though.

The doc and Sheriff Walker talked for a moment through the bars before he opened the door to let the man out. As he went to close it again, a woman rushed forward, sobbing, "You killed my son, you monster!"

"Stay back, dammit!" the sheriff ordered, and forced her away. "No one's laying a hand on this guy so long as I'm in charge 'round here!" He looked over the crowd. "I *am* still in charge, right?"

There was some nervous coughing and shuffling of feet, but for the most part, everyone settled down quickly enough. A few words couldn't dispel that look of blood in their eyes, however, and Walker knew it. He turned to one of his deputies and said, "Clear these people out of here, Grimes. I want to have a little talk with our guest."

Grimes nodded, turned to the crowd, and shouted, "Alright, you heard the sheriff. Everybody *git!*" He began to herd people out of the office amidst a lot of grumbling and dirty looks. He took the distraught woman by the shoulders and steered her out as gently as he could, though she stared back at me with red-rimmed eyes the whole time.

When the room was cleared, the sheriff sat down upon the edge of his desk across from me, lit a cigar, and looked me over. He was a tall man, about fortyish, with dark hair that showed no signs of graying, despite the obviously stressful conditions his job created. I'd even go so far as to call him handsome, but I'm not that kind of guy.

"So," I said, breaking the silence, "what'd you want to talk about?"

He puffed smoke out through his clenched teeth. "Your friend...where is he?"

"Well, unless you had someone clean it up, he's laying on the bank floor with his brains running out onto the baseboards."

"Your *other* friend, smart-aleck."

"Oh, *him!*" I leaned forward on the cot, elbows resting on my knees. "Ain't got a clue, Sheriff. Sorry." I flashed him a smile, even though my head was throbbing and my guts were tying themselves into knots. If I was going to die, I figured I might as well have some fun first.

He blew out some more smoke as he stood up. "You don't think you'll get away with this, do you? I've got a half-dozen witnesses that say you and your friend didn't even hesitate when you blew that boy to kingdom come."

The smile evaporated, and the knot in my gut tightened. "It was an accident," I said quietly.

"Yeah, you strike me as the sort of fella that's had a whole lot of 'accidents'." He pulled a sheet a paper off the desk and held it up. "You know what this is?"

I could see something printed on it, but nothing more from the angle he held it at. "Nope."

"Well, then," he said with a smile of his own, "let me read it to you: 'Richard Ashley Corrigan, alias Ashley Williams, Richard Jones, and R.A. Morgan. Age 18 to 25 years, five feet ten inches tall, average build, brown hair, brown eyes, small scar beside left eye. Wanted for murder, armed robbery, theft of livestock, and resisting arrest. Reward of two hundred dollars offered, dead or alive'." He glanced at me, and went back to reading. "'Known associates: Kyle Reeves and Joe Kennedy. Both wanted for same offenses stated above, same reward posted'." He placed the paper back on the desk and said, "Now do you see why I'm so anxious to find your friend? You two are a very valuable commodity out here, especially since being a lawman doesn't pay too well."

It appeared that the doc didn't know the sheriff as well as he thought: this guy was more concerned with lining his pockets than delivering justice. Of course, greed can have its advantages. "Listen," I said, "if you let me out of here and call the posse off my friend, I'll make sure that you get *double* that reward money within a week. What do you say?"

"Eight hundred dollars? In a *week?* Son, if you had that sort of money lying around, you wouldn't be knocking over banks." He shook his head, trying not to laugh. "Oh, and while I've got your attention, would you mind rolling that bottle of laudanum this way? We wouldn't want you to mistake that for a pint of whiskey and guzzle it on down, would we?"

I couldn't keep the look of surprise off my face. "How did you..."

"Ol' Doc Ayers has a soft spot for hard-luck cases," he informed me as he knelt down by the cell door. "He'd already helped along two or three little shits like you before I caught on. I'd run him outta town, but good doctorin' is hard to find out here." The man's expression suddenly turned dark. "Now fork over the damn bottle," he said coldly.

I cursed and pulled out my one-way ticket to oblivion, rolling it on the floor towards his waiting hand. As I watched its path, I noticed something that had escaped the sheriff's attention: the cell door wasn't completely shut. It was just slightly askew, enough to make it appear closed but not enough for the lock to catch. When you'd spent a good deal of time behind bars like I had, you knew damn good and well what a locked door looked like. Oh, I could have kissed every one of those angry townsfolk that distracted the sheriff from double-checking the lock.

As Mr. Law-and-Order looked for a place to stash the laudanum, I quickly surveyed what I could see of his office. His desk was about six feet away from the cell door, with the front door off to my right and another door to parts unknown to my left. My hat, gunbelts, and knife had been tossed on the floor behind the desk, which had the sheriff's own rifle lying across it like a huge paperweight. Walker was kneeling behind the desk at the moment, fiddling with a drawer which appeared to be stuck, judging by all the noise he was making. With him sufficiently distracted, I began to slide off my belt -- I figured the brass Union buckle attached to it could shatter his nose or wrist if I swung it about fast enough and caught him just right. I wrapped the end of the belt tightly around my fist, then stood up and crept slowly towards the door. *Just stay down for another few seconds, you sonovabitch,* I thought.

A hard slam of wood against wood, then the sheriff's head bobbed up from behind the desk looking pleased with himself. "There! That'll teach ya, you stupid..." He glanced up and saw me advancing on the cell door. "What the Hell?" he mouthed.

I kicked the door wide open, took two steps out, and swung the free end of the belt at his face. The buckle caught him near his cheekbone, snapping his head to the left and knocking him flat onto the floor. I dropped the belt and picked up the rifle, saying, "Should've taken the money, Sheriff." I walked around the desk to where he'd sprawled out. "Would've been a lot healthier for ya."

The man looked up at me, blood trickling out of the gouge on his face the buckle had made. "How in God's name did you..."

"Reckon God's on *my* side," I said with a shrug, then leveled the rifle at his head. "Tell Him thanks for me, will you?" I cocked the weapon, pulled the trigger, and was greeted with a dull click.

Empty. *Oh shit!*

I swung the rifle around and tried to nail him with the stock, but he grabbed it and used my momentum to whip me headfirst at the wall behind him. My vision went white from pain for a moment, and when it cleared, Walker was on his feet and swinging the rifle at *me.* I ducked under its arc and rushed him, slamming him up against the cell. His breath whooshed out and he dropped the weapon. I kicked it out of reach, then punched him in the gut a few times for good measure. He began to sag, but he quickly recovered and shoved me backwards into the desk. The edge of it caught me low in the back, and I crumpled to the floor as my legs went numb.

"You're *dead*, you little bastard!" Walker snarled as he kicked me in the ribs. I groaned and struggled to get up, but he shoved me back down to the floor with his boot. "By the time I'm through with you, you'll wish that you'd never been born!"

I gritted my teeth and looked up at him. "Already do...not 'cause of you, though." I grabbed his boot and yanked it to the side as hard as I could -- Walker lost his footing and landed on his ass again. As he tried to recover, I scrambled around to the other side of the desk, where my guns lay. My hand was almost on my gunbelts when Walker grabbed me by my coat collar and threw me at the cell, just as I'd done to him moments before. The back of my head whacked one of the bars pretty hard, and the world went white again for a few seconds.

Once my eyes stopped rolling about in my skull, I saw the sheriff kneeling in front of me, sweat on his face and death in his eyes. "Worthless bastard," he growled, "gonna snap your neck..."

"Not worthless," I somehow managed to say. "Two hundred dollars, remember?" I flashed him a lopsided grin. "Kill me now, and you won't get your money."

He picked me up by the front of my shirt. "Poster said dead *or* alive...and dead men don't try to escape." He drove a fist into my stomach, and I felt one of the ribs he'd loosened up with his boot give way. "'Course, that would deprive the people of a proper hanging for you, and we wouldn't want to disappoint them, would we?" He was grinning himself now. "Hell, we haven't had a good hanging for going on six months now," he said as he drove his knee into my crotch. I howled and sagged into his arms, all the fight draining out of me.

The cell door still stood open, and he dragged me back inside. "There, that should keep you quiet for a while," he said as he let me drop to the floor. He shook his finger at me, as if scolding a child. "Now I want you to sit here and think about what you did," he smirked.

I coughed and turned over onto my side. Though my body hurt like Hell, my tongue was a sharp as ever. "Gonna fucking *kill* you," I groaned, "just you wait and see..."

"Oh, give it up already!" He staggered out of the cell, closed the door, and gave it a few good rattles to make sure it was locked tight this time. He leaned on one of crossbars and looked down at me. "Face it, kid: *you lost.* I don't know how long you've been at this, but you've finally hit the end of the line. Trust me, you're not the first snot-nosed kid to end up in here, and with my luck, you won't be the last. You're nothing special, you're just another dumb shit with a gun." He straightened up, gave the cell door another good shake, then turned away from me. "Now why don't you get some sleep? Don't want to die tired, y'know." He began to laugh at that, a cold, merciless laugh that had no humor in it at all.

"Go to Hell," I whispered hoarsely, then shut my eyes so I wouldn't have to look at him anymore. I could feel myself drifting along the edge of consciousness, and I didn't fight it. I was too damn exhausted to fight anymore...just needed to rest a minute...catch my breath...I'd get even with the bastard later...right after I...
...I...

* * * * * *

Darkness. Totally black, couldn't see, couldn't hear...tried to yell, but I had no voice. Hands tied behind me...something around my neck...where was I?

"You're at death's door, Richard," the sheriff's cruel voice whispered in my ear.

After he spoke, I could see the world again with frightening clarity: I was standing in the middle of Barrelhead, surrounded by screaming townsfolk. Sheriff Walker stood next to me with a rope in his hands -- on the other end of it was the noose wrapped around my neck.

"Let's go, dead man!" He yanked on the rope, tightening the noose around my throat. I had no choice but to walk forward with him, towards the gallows that stood in the town square. I heard someone shout my name, and as I turned towards the speaker, I saw that it was the woman from the sheriff's office. She held the boy with the toy gun in her arms, and they were both covered in his blood. "I hope you rot in Hell!" she spat at me.

I opened my mouth to tell her I was sorry, that it was an accident, but no sound came out. The sheriff tugged at the rope again. "Quit stalling and *move!*" he ordered. He pulled me up the steps leading to the gallows and looped his end of the rope over the wooden beam above our heads.

My heart began to thud loudly in my ears, and my legs felt as if they were about to buckle beneath me. *Oh God,* I thought, *I don't want to die like this...please don't let me die like this.*

"Murderer!" the crowd screamed at me. "Wretched thief! Burn in Hell!"

No, you don't understand, I tried to say, but I couldn't form the words. *I wasn't always this way, I'm not...*

"You're nothing," Walker said to me, and placed his hand on the trapdoor lever. "Always have been, always will be."

I tried desperately to work my hands free, to slip out of the noose, anything I could to avoid what was coming, but it was no good. *Dear God, please help me, somebody help me...*

"Do you truly wish to live?" a softly-accented voice asked. I turned and saw someone standing next to me on the gallows platform. He was slightly taller than me, and dressed all in black, with a hooded cloak hiding his face. He looked like Death itself.

"Who...who are you?" I whispered, my voice having somehow returned.

"Someone who has been down the path that you are about to set foot upon," he answered, "assuming that you *do* wish to live."

"Why wouldn't I?"

He held up a black-gloved hand, saying, "Does this look familiar?" He was holding the bottle of laudanum. "You probably would have swallowed this if the sheriff had not taken it from you, correct? Nor would it be the first time you tried to..."

"Alright!" I interrupted, turning away from the figure. "I know that I haven't always been very...stable in the past, but..."

"Your stability is of the utmost importance to us." He cupped my chin in his hand and turned my face towards his -- I could vaguely make out his features beneath the hood, but nothing specific. "We need to know that you will be there when the time comes."

"When the time comes for what?"

"That does not matter yet. All you have to remember is to go south...until you find that." He pointed down the street, past the crowd which was now as still and silent as a photograph. Beyond them, I could see a black, octagon-shaped object laying flat on the ground. It appeared to be a large stone slab, about eight feet across, with strange markings all over its surface.

"What is that?" I asked the hooded figure, unable to take my eyes off of the object.

"The end of one life, and the beginning of another." He placed a hand gently on my shoulder and leaned close to my ear. "You are a *n'toku-rejii*, Richard Corrigan, and your destiny lies south."

"What's that supposed to...?" I began to say, only to realize that the man had disappeared. "Hey! Where'd you go?" I yelled. "Aren't you going to help me?"

Then I heard something click, and the trapdoor beneath my feet opened. For a moment, I was suspended in midair before gravity took hold of me once again. The rope went tight, snapping my neck like a dry twig, and blood began to pour out of my mouth, my nose, my ears...

I woke up screaming. It took a moment for me to realize that I wasn't dead, but that didn't really help my state of mind. I lay on the floor of the jail cell, shaking, sweating, trying to reassure myself that it was all just a dream, but I wasn't easily convinced. I could swear that noose was still around my neck, choking me until...

"What's the matter, boogeyman jump you?"

I yelped and looked up to see Sheriff Walker standing at the cell door. At least I *thought* it was the sheriff: it had become too dark to see clearly. "Sunlight," I mumbled, "where'd the..."

"It's *two* in the ever-lovin' *morning,* you *idiot.* Sun's been down for hours." I caught the vague impression of him shaking his head. "Christ, I messed you up worse than I thought. Too many blows to the braincase, I reckon."

I nodded unconsciously in agreement. Yes, that explained it: the doctor told me I had a concussion, it must've been causing me to hallucinate, that's all.

Then I saw something move in the darkness behind the lawman...something in a long dark cloak. The scream left my mouth before I even knew it was there. I pulled my battered body as far away from the cell door as I could, hollering, "Stay the Hell away from me!"

The sheriff just stared at me. "Now what's wrong with you? Dammit, I'm never gonna get any sleep if you keep..." Before he could finish his complaint, the thing in the dark lifted something, then slammed it against the back of the sheriff's head, smacking him face-first into the bars. The sheriff fell to the floor and lay there, limp as a rag doll. The thing knelt down, looked him over...then it looked up at me.

A sound somewhere between a moan and a whimper came out of my throat as I pressed my backside into the corner of the cell. My heart was pounding fit to burst out of my ribcage, and I shut my eyes so I couldn't see what was coming for me. "Oh God," I whispered, "I want to wake up, I *want* to *wake up...*"

I could hear the key turn in the lock, and the door swing open. "Corrigan?" a voice said, but I didn't answer, I didn't look. Boots scraped against the wooden floor, ever closer, then I felt hands on my shoulders. I cried out and tried to push them away, but they wouldn't let go. "Corrigan, *stop!*" the voice ordered, and a hand slapped me across the face. "*Wake up*, dammit! It's me...it's Reeves!"

I stopped struggling and cautiously opened my eyes. Sure enough, it was Reeves, his long duster spattered with mud -- in the dark, it had looked just like the cloak I'd seen in my dream -- and the rifle he'd used to clock the sheriff with slung over his shoulder. I slumped forward into his arms, feeling exhausted as the tension faded from my body. I tried to speak, to tell him what I thought I saw in the darkness, but the words in my head were all jumbled together. "Good Lord," Reeves whispered, "what did they do to you?" He slipped his arm behind my back and pulled me to my feet. "Just put one foot in front of the other, okay? I've got you if you slip."

I nodded, and he half-guided, half-dragged me out of the cell. "Almost didn't make it back," he told me. "That damn sheriff's got men posted at both ends of town...had to inch along in the shadows for a good hour or so before I could duck in here." He lowered me to the floor near my belongings. "Gonna be Hell getting back out of this place. Think you can do it?" he asked, kneeling beside me.

I didn't respond right away, my mind was still clouded over with images from my dream. Instead, I reached over with a trembling hand and pulled one of my guns from its holster. I held it loosely, feeling the weight of the iron, the smoothness of the worn wooden handle.

This was real, not that freak in the Grim Reaper outfit, and certainly not that overgrown black tombstone I saw. Those were just figments of my imagination, strange images conjured up by my overtaxed mind...they meant *nothing.* "Gimme a couple of minutes," I finally answered, "I need to get my head on straight."

"Okay. In the meantime, I'll take care of this guy, then we'll head on out." He stood up and walked over to where the sheriff lay, grabbing the unconscious man by the shoulders and dragging him into the cell -- a little extra security while we made our escape. I slowly got back to my own feet and looked around for the belt to my trousers. I found it on the desk, and as I picked it up, I spied that damned wanted poster lying beneath it. Whoever had sketched the picture of me on it was a terrible artist: he made me look closer to forty than twenty. I crumpled it up and shoved it in one of my coat pockets, figuring on burning it later out of spite.

"Hey, you done woolgathering?" Reeves asked. He'd plopped the sheriff down onto the cot and pulled the blanket over his head. Except for a slight difference in height, you couldn't tell that it wasn't me passed out beneath it. "Got him trussed up like a Christmas goose under there," Reeves told me. "I think we'll be safe for a while." He locked the cell and dropped the keys into a spittoon next to the desk, where they made a sickening *splut.* "Ready to go?"

"In a minute." I buckled on my gunbelts, slipped my knife back into my boot sheath, then settled my hat back onto my head, mindful of the bandage. "Out the back way?" I asked.

"No, out the front, so's they can shoot our heads off." He slapped me on the back and stepped towards the mystery door. "'Course, for you, they'd just be finishing the job they started earlier."

"Not funny," I said, and followed after him. The door led to a back alley running behind most of the main buildings. Getting away wasn't as tough as Reeves made it out to be, but I'd had better times. The worst part was spending ten minutes under a horse cart, waiting for some idiot deputy to finish suckin' on his brain tablet before we could cross one of the streets.

"Damn," Reeves muttered, "that cigarette looks good right now."

"We get out of this, I'll buy you a pound of tobacco. Now *hush!*"

After the deputy moved on, we bolted. We finally reached Reeves's horse about a half-hour after we started. It protested a bit when we doubled up on it, but we were more concerned about a clean getaway than the animal's comfort. Reeves took the reins and led us off into the night as I concentrated on staying in the saddle behind him.

I didn't even notice until an hour later that we were riding south.

CHAPTER 2

We stopped riding about an hour shy of sunrise. There had been no sign so far that we were being followed, so we decided to let the horse rest a bit. Reeves led the animal over to a patch of dry grass to feed while I sat on a rock and dug through his saddlebag, looking for a bottle of anything. I found a half-full, unlabeled pint, took a swig, and deemed it good. "How long you think before they find out I'm gone?" I called over to Reeves.

"Don't know. Maybe now, maybe by breakfast." He walked over and sat down on the ground next to me. "Speaking of which, I've got some jerky in here somewhere." He began to look through the bag himself. "You hungry?"

"I'll stick with the booze. I need something to numb the pain in my head."

"You're lucky you still *have* a head." He stopped rummaging for a moment, staring off across the open plain. "Christ, I still can't believe Kennedy's *dead*. We messed up real bad this time, Corrigan. If Carson was here, he'd..."

"Carson's *not* here," I snapped, "and he's *never* gonna be here again. It's been three years, so get used to it already." I took a long pull off the bottle. "I'm sick to death of you dredging up his name every time we make one little mistake."

"But this wasn't just any mistake, we..."

"I don't want to talk about it."

"Fine," he said, and went back to looking for the jerky. He finally found it, and the silence stretched out between us while he ate and I drank. I knew that the alcohol wasn't the best thing for me at the moment, but I was in so much pain that I didn't give a damn.

After a few minutes, Reeves got chatty again. "So, which way do you think we should head?" he asked.

"Anywhere but south."

"But we've *been* goin' south. What's wrong with it now?"

"I just don't want to go any further that way, alright?" I knocked back some more liquor. "Dammit, Reeves, do you have to have a reason for everything?"

"In this case, yeah. I think that bullet knocked your brain for a loop, Corrigan. You've been actin' strange ever since I busted you out."

"I'm just tired and hurtin' and sick of your whinin'. Leave me be."

"Richard..."

I realized then that he wasn't going to let the matter drop. We rarely called each other by our first names -- old habit. "I had a really weird night before you showed up, Kyle," I said as I placed the pint on the ground. I hesitated a moment, then began to tell him about the dream I had, the things I saw...or rather what I *thought* I saw. He just sat there and listened to me spill my guts. When I finished, I turned to him and said, "Well? Have I finally gone 'round the bend or what?"

Now it was Reeves's turn to take a swig off of the bottle. "I don't know," he said after a moment. "The whole time we've known each other, you've always had bad dreams, but nothin' so out of the ordinary. I mean, you don't believe all that shit was *real* or anything, do you?"

"Hell no! But all the same, it was damned disturbing at the time, y'know?" I gazed up at the pre-dawn sky -- most of the stars had disappeared from view, but I could still make out one or two in the growing light. "I've dreamed before about dying, even wished for it quite a few times when I was awake, but this time...I was afraid, Kyle. Afraid of death, of that guy in black, of that...that *thing* he showed me. I just wanted him to shut up and let me go, but he kept on talkin' and talkin'..." I closed my eyes and rubbed my hands over my face. "It *felt* real, every bit of it, maybe even more real than talking to you right now does."

"Maybe we should quit," he said after a while.

I dropped my hands to my lap and looked over at him. "Come again?"

"I said we should quit. Look, I don't think you're nuts, but you're definitely starting to crack under the pressure. It was hard enough on you last year when Stewart died, but now Kennedy's gone too, and…"

"Don't…you…dare…" I held up a finger. "Don't you dare drag Stewart into this."

"I'm just saying maybe it's finally time for us to walk away from all this, try and have a normal life."

"And what makes *now* any different from last year? You didn't even want to talk about it back then." I stood up, telling him, "Matter of fact, you called me a damn fool for bringing it up. Now *you're* the fool."

Reeves stood up as well. "Hey, hold on, that *was* different."

"No, it wasn't. I told you that I'd had enough, but you wouldn't let me leave, not even after…after we lost Stewart." My face felt hot, and I turned away from him. "I finally got the message then: we're stuck in this business until the day we die."

"That'll be a lot sooner than later, the way you're going at it. Y'know, for somebody who just admitted that he's afraid to die, you sure are doing your damnedest lately to get planted in the ground."

"So maybe I am crazy, then," I muttered. "Maybe the only way to make sure I stay alive is for you to stick around."

"Richard, I'm serious."

"So am I." I turned back around enough to look at him, waving a hand at the endless expanse surrounding us. "I don't know where you plan on running off to, anyhow. You know as well as I do that it doesn't matter where we go, we're still criminals. It'll catch up with us eventually, so why even bother tryin' to get away from it?"

He tried to stare me down, but he slowly began to see the truth in what I said. And why not? He'd told me nearly the same thing a year ago. "Alright," he said with a sigh, "I'll stay."

I bent over and picked up the pint. "That's good to know," I said, then took a drink.

"You gotta do me a favor, though."

"Sure thing. What is it?"

"Number one: Stop drinking." He plucked the bottle out of my hand. "Number two: We keep going south, strange dreams or not."

"What the Hell for?"

"Because you need to see a damn doctor, that's what for." He jerked a thumb southward. "I remember somebody in Barrelhead saying there's another town a few hours away. I know it's a risk and all, but you look like Hell, partner. You need some rest, I need some rest…maybe we'll get lucky and somebody'll be willing to hide us for a couple of days."

I scoffed, but he had a point: alcohol would keep the ache in my head and ribs at bay for only so long. Still, I couldn't shake the fear that dream had put in me. *It's nothing,* I told myself, *you just had a nightmare, same as you have damn-near every night. This one was just a mite scarier than usual, that's all. You can't keep hesitating like this.* "Damn it all to Hell," I muttered, and rubbed my eyes.

"Come on, Corrigan," Reeves said, "the only way you're gonna get over this whole thing is by facing your fear."

I grunted in frustration, then said, "Fine, let's get moving. Daylight will be here before we know it."

We saddled up again, same as before, and continued heading south. I shaded my eyes from the growing dawn from time to time, peering first behind us to check for any signs of a posse, then ahead to where this town was supposed to be. For the first fifteen minutes or so, I saw nothing but desert and scrub brush in either direction, but soon I began to make out a few squareish shapes to the south. I thought I saw a gleam that might have been sunlight bouncing off glass or metal, but it was too indistinct at that distance. I did point it out to Reeves, however, and he urged the horse to move a little faster.

As we got closer to the town, I could feel that knot in my stomach return with a vengeance. Neither one of us saw anything moving, nor could we hear anything besides the soft jingle of our gear and the horse's hoofbeats on the hard New Mexico plain. Not very encouraging, to say the least. About a hundred feet or so from the first building, we stopped at a billboard covered in signs and adverts for the various goods, services, and nostrums this particular town could provide you with. Barely visible beneath all this nonsense was a wooden placard declaring:

Welcome to
HADLEY
God Bless You All!

At least that's what it must have originally said: somebody had taken some red paint and written *"SAVE"* in huge letters, obscuring the word *"Bless"*. Religious nut, probably. I looked past the sign at the town itself. The buildings seemed well cared for, but there appeared to be no life in or around them -- not so much as a fly buzzing a manure pile, even. "You sure those folks in Barrelhead weren't talking about a ghost town?" I asked Reeves.

"Pretty sure," he answered, but I could hear the doubt in his voice. "Maybe this is an ambush, you know? Maybe that posse chasin' after me last night headed up thisaway."

"If that's so, they sure are bad at being nonchalant about it." I pulled one of my guns and told him to go forward.

The horse, unfortunately, had other ideas. When Reeves tapped it in the side with his spurs, it refused to move. He gave the reins a tug and tried again, but the dumb thing just shook its head and whinnied. "What is this, you on a lunch break or something?" Reeves said. "Get moving!" He dug his spurs in, and the horse got moving alright: it reared up, screaming and kicking its front hooves in the air. Not sitting in the saddle proper to begin with, I flew right off and hit the ground butt-first. I scrambled away on my hands and knees, trying to get as much distance as I could between me and the horse, while Reeves hung on for dear life and struggled to get it under control. The two of them danced around for a minute like some crazy rodeo act before Reeves gave up and jumped off the horse. The moment he left the saddle, the horse broke north, back the way we came, foam flying off its muzzle. We just sat there and watched it go, helpless to do anything but choke on trail dust.

After a minute or so, I got up, walked over to where my hat landed when I fell, and picked it up. I whacked it against my leg a couple times to knock off the dirt before putting it back on, saying, "Well, at least now we know there ain't no ambush, 'cause if there is, they missed a perfectly good opportunity to blow us both to Hell and gone."

"I don't know what happened," Reeves said, gesturing in the direction our ride went -- he was still sprawled out on the ground. "I've never seen a horse go crazy like that for no reason."

"Maybe it just got sick of us riding double." I looked down the main street of Hadley. "There'd better be somebody here," I said, "or else we are in serious trouble." I began to walk into the town proper, revolver out and cocked. Reeves followed a moment later, pausing only to collect his Winchester which, thankfully, had fallen out of the saddle holster before our mount took off. The town was small, but it appeared to be prosperous, despite being in the middle of nowhere. I noticed that many of the doors and windows were boarded up (from the inside, no less) and drifts of sand had formed on parts of the boardwalk, but otherwise, it looked inhabited.

There were just no people.

Reeves stepped up onto the boardwalk and poked his head into one of the few open storefronts: a tailor and dressmaker's shop, according to the sign above the eave. "Hello?" he called out. "Anybody in here?" No one responded, but he went inside anyways. I continued on down the street, searching for any clue as to why this place was deserted. As I approached the first cross-street, Reeves shouted my name. Fearing the worst, I turned around and ran back to the shop. When I got there, I found him leaning against the doorway, his eyes wide and face pale.

"What is it? You find somebody?" I asked as I hopped up onto the boardwalk.

"Sort of. You'll see." He nodded towards the shop, then pulled the bandana hanging around his neck up over his mouth and nose before heading back inside. I followed a few paces behind him, taking in the scene: the whole store was in disarray, with everything that wasn't nailed down tossed about. Bolts of cloth and pieces of garments were strewn across the floor, and a dressing dummy had been knocked over in one corner, the fabric-covered chest shredded open. "What the Hell happened in here?" I wondered aloud. "Indian trouble, you think?"

"This is nothing," Reeves said, a slight tremble in his voice, "you gotta see the upstairs." He led me to a stairway at the back of the shop, paused, then turned to me and tugged slightly at his bandana. "You might want to do the same."

I didn't get what he meant until I noticed the smell: a gut-twisting, rancid stench, like a carcass left out in the sun for a few days. I had an inkling of what Reeves had found and pulled up my own bandana to stifle the smell. He led the way up the stairs, and I followed with absolutely no desire to see what the source of the smell was. At the top was an open door, cracks in the wood near the handle and hinges from Reeves forcing it open, and bloody scratches all over the surface from someone -- or something -- that tried to do the same before him and failed. Beyond the door, the second floor opened up into one huge room which, going by the furnishings, must've served as the home for the shopkeeper's family. There were a couple of beds along one wall, a table and chairs along another...and about ten dead bodies. They were scattered all about the place, some lying on beds, others sprawled out on the floor, but they all looked the same: skin shriveled and turning black, eyes bulging from bloody sockets, and expressions of pure terror carved into every face. I staggered back slightly, fighting the urge to throw up. "Sweet Jesus," I whispered, "what did this?"

"I was hoping you might know," Reeves answered. "The door was blocked from the inside, but it gave way after a couple shoves. There's no wounds that I can see, no signs of a fight." He threw his hands up in exasperation. "These people barricaded themselves in here and just *died.*"

I took off my hat and waved it in front of my face to disperse the stench a bit. "Maybe there was an epidemic, like typhoid or cholera...they could've been quarantined up here."

"Then why was the barricade on the *inside* of the room? It's like they were hiding from something."

"Yeah, but what? And for how long?"

Reeves shrugged. "Got me. These people could've died yesterday or a month ago for all I can tell." He walked over to one of the bodies laid out on a bed: a man, judging by the clothes, but that was the only distinguishing feature left of the original person. The skin on the face had stretched tight in the dry heat, giving it a leering, skull-like appearance. Its milky-white eyes stared up at the ceiling, and a few wisps of hair still clung stubbornly to the peeling head. Reeves leaned over for a closer look, muttering, "Hell, could've been a *year* ago..."

Suddenly, the corpse reached up and grabbed Reeves by the arm, then sat up straight. "Warm..." the thing hissed out from between its cracked lips. "You're warm...so cold down here..."

Reeves screamed hysterically and tried to push it off, but it wouldn't let go. I just stood there watching the whole thing, too much in shock to scream myself. The thing managed to get to its feet, then yanked off Reeves's bandana and wrapped its bony arms around his waist -- it looked like it wanted to kiss him. "*Shoot it!*" he ordered as he forced the thing's putrid face away from his own.

"I can't! I might hit *you!*"

"Do you really think I care about *that* right now? *Shoot* the damn thing!"

Without thinking twice about it, I brought my gun up and fired. The bullet neatly pierced the corpse's skull and embedded itself in the wall behind them. The corpse stiffened for a moment before slumping to the floor, lifeless again. Once it was down, Reeves began to stomp on its head until it split open. The blackish ooze that splattered all over his boot was like nothing I'd ever seen before, especially not coming out of some guy's head. Reeves barely took notice of it, he just kept kicking and stomping on the corpse, snapping brittle bones and ripping open dead flesh. Throughout it all, Reeves's face was locked in a tight grimace, his breath whistling in and out from between his gritted teeth.

"Reeves, it's *dead*, stop it already," I told him, grabbing his arm. He just shook me off and kept on kicking. "Reeves...Kyle, stop it!" I shouted, this time taking him by the shoulders and pulling him away from the body. He stared right through me for a moment, the expression on his face probably quite similar to the one I'd had when he broke me out of jail the night before. I'd only had a really bad dream, though, while what he'd just experienced was much more horrifying than anything I'd gone through in that cell.

"Corrigan?" he said after a time.

"Yeah?"

"You can let go now."

"Huh? Oh, sure." I took my hands off his shoulders, and he stepped away from me, his hands trembling slightly. I couldn't blame him. "C'mon," I said, hitching a thumb towards the door, "let's get the Hell out of here."

"No!" He shouted so loudly that I jumped back a little. Frantically, he slipped his rifle off his shoulder. "We've got to get the rest of them!"

"Rest of...Reeves, they're dead already, remember? You checked them yourself."

"I checked *that* thing too," he answered, pointing at the mangled corpse that had attacked him, "*but it wasn't dead.* Leastways, not all the way dead." He cocked the rifle. "I'm not taking any chances with the rest of 'em."

"Christ, Reeves," I muttered, then reached out and tried to pull him towards the door. As my hand came towards him, though, he pointed the rifle straight at me. He said nothing aloud, but I could read the look in his eyes well enough: if I tried to stop him, I'd get a bullet in my own head for my trouble. I'd never seen him act so crazy before. *Yeah,* I told myself, *like you've been a perfect example of sanity lately.* I swallowed hard, then said quietly, "I'm going downstairs. You've got five minutes to do whatever you want up here, then we light out of this place. Okay?"

"Okay," he replied, but he didn't lower the rifle. I stepped backwards through the doorway, then turned and went down the stairwell, half-expecting Reeves to take a potshot at me behind my back.

The first shot went off as I reached the ground floor -- I flinched at the sudden roar that shattered the dead quiet. "Just save some bullets for the posse, Reeves," I mumbled as I pulled down my bandana and took in a lungful of fresh air. It tasted good, and I leaned against the shop's counter to drink it in. My head was beginning to pound again -- coupled with that stink upstairs, it made me feel like I might puke for sure. God, I needed some sleep. That, and some real food and some decent doctorin', and I'd be right as rain. But with a posse potentially on our asses, no horse, and Reeves trying to kill dead people, it didn't look like I'd be getting any of that anytime soon.

As I stood there listening to Reeves's intermittent rifle shots, I spied a notebook of some sort lying on the floor. Needing a distraction, I picked it up and began to flip through it. The notebook contained nothing terribly interesting at first -- records of payment, measurements, idle sketches -- but the last entry definitely caught my eye: "*Aug. 24-74: blue Gingham dress, Mrs. D. Foley - $2.00*". It wasn't the merchandise so much as the date that held my attention. Unless I had my days mixed up, we were already two days into September, which meant this entire town had quietly dropped dead within *nine days.* That didn't seem possible, especially with Barrelhead being only six hours away at most. The whole time we'd been checking out the town for our bank job, I hadn't heard a peep about an epidemic or Indian attack or *anything* happening right down the road. I sure as Hell didn't hear about any walking corpses, either.

I walked out of the shop and back into the street, anxious to find some more clues to clear up this mystery. It wasn't as easy a job as I'd hoped, for I soon discovered that most of the other buildings were boarded up pretty tight. When I could get into a place, I found nothing other than more dead bodies -- luckily, none of them moved. I was about to give up and head back to Reeves when I spied some piles of dirt and lumber near the edge of town. Probably some sort of mass grave, I figured, but I decided to check it out anyway. As I got closer, I could see that it was some sort of shallow pit, no more than four feet deep, and I realized that it was the beginnings of a cellar -- someone had started work on a new building before the whole town kicked off. No big mystery about that. I stepped up to the edge of the pit and looked in, and that's when I saw the black object from my dream lying right in the middle of the cellar pit.

My blood turned to ice as I stood there, rubbing my eyes and hoping it would disappear. It looked just like I remembered it: a pitch-black stone, about eight feet across and eight-sided, and every inch of its surface covered in strange symbols. *Oh, God, this can't be real*, I thought, and tried to shout for Reeves, but my voice was gone, just like in my dream. Before I even realized what I was doing, I jumped down into the pit and approached the thing slowly, stopping a few feet away from it, a sickening feeling of dread filling my gut. The stone stuck up out of the earth about two inches, and it appeared that someone had attempted to pry it out even further with a couple of crowbars, which were wedged beneath one end of the massive slab. In the center was a fist-sized hole, the same shape as the stone itself. That hole seemed important, but I couldn't remember if I'd seen anything in there in my dream.

But it was only a dream, I thought, *how in the world can this be possible?* Then again, I'd also just seen a corpse get up and attack my friend -- up until we got to this place, I wouldn't have thought that was possible either. Were the two things related somehow? Hell, I was just a bank robber, what did I know about crazy things like this?

My ruminations were cut short by a quick, sharp crack of thunder. I looked up and saw ugly black storm clouds rolling in from the west, which was puzzling, as the sky had been mostly clear when we'd arrived. I dug out my pocket watch to check the time, and realized that I'd been so focused on checking out the town that I'd lost a half-hour. I cursed myself for not paying closer attention. In our situation, rain was a mixed blessing: it'd cover our tracks if we fled across the desert, but we'd also get soaked to the bone. I decided to go find Reeves and weigh our options, not that we had many. As I walked back to the edge of the pit, I caught a sparkle of something out of the corner of my eye. Curious, I bent down and pulled out of the dirt a bluish-green shard of what I thought might be some kind of crystal, about three inches long and as thick as my thumb. The colors within appeared to swirl and pulse with warmth in time with my heartbeat as it sat in my palm, which struck me as rather strange. Even stranger still, the feeling of dread inside of me seemed to pass the longer I held onto it. I ran the pad of my thumb along the shard, and as I did so, I noticed the edges of it were jagged, like it had broken off of a larger object. I glanced back at the black slab, thinking perhaps that this was what went in the hole, but if that was so, then where was the rest of it?

Thunder rumbled overhead again, bringing my attention back to the more pressing problem. After tucking the crystal into my shirt pocket, I climbed out of the pit and continued on my way back to the shop where I'd last seen Reeves. I was halfway there when I felt the first droplet hit my cheek, then another and another as the clouds ripped open over the wide New Mexico plain. The main street quickly began to turn into a muddy mush that sucked at my boots with every step, and the rain rolled off the brim of my battered hat like a waterfall. *Slogging across the plain in this mess isn't going to be much fun,* I thought.

I found Reeves outside the shop, sitting on the edge of the boardwalk with his head hanging low. His Winchester was lying beside him, inches away from being soaked by the downpour. He didn't even look up when I hopped up onto the boardwalk and approached him. "Reeves? You okay?" I asked, but I got no response. I knelt down beside him and went to touch him on the shoulder, then stopped when I saw that his entire body was trembling. "Reeves...hey, c'mon, you're scaring me."

"I g-g-got 'em," he finally stammered. "They're all dead now, th-that's for sure." He then looked up at me, and I could see that his face was slick with sweat, coupled with a pale, feverish complexion.

"That's good to know," I answered, but inside I was panicking. Reeves was in no shape to travel, and I had a horrible feeling about what the cause might be. "You feel alright, partner?"

"S-sure!" he said, suddenly perking up. "Just a little tired, that's all...just need to r-r-rest a bit..." His voice trailed off as his head dropped low again.

Oh God. "Kyle, listen to me: that stone in my dream that I told you about, it's *here,* I'm not foolin'. I don't know what that means, but I doubt it's good. You understand me? *We can't stay here."* He nodded, and I breathed a sigh of relief. "Good, then let's get moving before this storm gets any worse." I slipped a hand under his armpit and tried to pull him to his feet, but he was nothing but dead weight. "Come on, dammit!" I yelled, but once again, he didn't respond. I managed to drag him away from the edge of the boardwalk, but when I let go, he merely laid there on the planks, breathing shallowly and moaning, "I'm c-cold," an eerie echo of the corpse-thing's ramblings.

This wasn't right. Hell, this whole damn *town* wasn't right. Berserk horses, dead people who didn't stay dead, a disease that crippled you within an hour of catching it, things seen in dreams becoming real...what in the world had I walked into? I gazed out over the dead town, watching the sky light up in jagged patches from lightning, then shake from the deafening crack of thunder. One thunderclap seemed to go on forever, but then I recognized it as the sound of horsehooves slapping the ground. I jumped off the boardwalk and into the street, staring towards the north through a sheet of rain. I couldn't tell how many were riding our way, but they were coming in way too fast to be casual visitors. "Reeves, get up! We've got company!" I scrambled back to where he lay and tried to pick him up again, this time succeeding in getting him to his feet. He mumbled something, but I couldn't make it out. "Look alive, pal. It's time to show that damned sheriff why we're worth two hundred apiece."

I slapped his face a couple of times in an effort to rouse him some more, but all he did was loll his head back.

The posse was nearly close enough to see us by now, so out of desperation, I hauled him into the shop and dumped him behind the counter. Unfortunately, I didn't have time to go pick up his rifle before the newcomers rode up the main street, their mounts bucking just as wildly as our own had done. I managed to shut the door before they passed in front of the shop, but between Reeves's rifle and my muddy footprints, it wouldn't be long before they figured out where we'd holed up. "Search every damn building!" I could hear the sheriff shout over the horses' strangled cries. "Shoot those bastards on sight!" I hunkered down behind the counter, my pistol in hand as I stared hard at the door. The first one of 'em that dared open it would get a bullet for his troubles.

"We're gonna die, aren't we?" I turned and saw Reeves attempting to sit up. His eyes were glassy, but he seemed coherent again.

"Nonsense," I replied, "we'll be fine. This is just like that time in Saundersville."

He coughed, making a thick, phlegmy sound. "Carson *died* in Saundersville."

"Yeah, but *we* didn't," I answered sharply, then asked, "Did you see a back door in this place?" He shook his head. "Damn, that means we'll have to run out the front. You up for some runnin'?"

"I...I don't think I can do it, Richard. I keep...I'm not sure what it is." He stared down at his shaking hands, saying, "It's like I black out or something." Somebody outside started yelling -- I suspected that they'd found one of those dead bodies -- and Reeves tried to stifle another cough. "Forget about me, get your own ass out of here," he told me once he had his coughing fit under control. He couldn't do anything about the look of fear in his eyes, though.

"No way. You didn't leave me to die in Barrelhead, so what makes you think I'd abandon you here?"

"I'll slow you down." We could hear more yelling, then a gunshot. "Besides, it'll be easier if we split up. We can meet up somewheres later when it's safe."

I thought about it for a moment. "You remember that old hidey-hole in Texas? By the river?"

"Of course."

"Alright then, let's both head there. If one of us doesn't hear from the other in a month..." I let the thought trail off.

Reeves smiled. "You'll make it, partner."

"And so will you." I stood up, saying, "Stay low for a little longer. Maybe I can take a few out before you go." I made ready to run, opening up the door a crack to peer outside.

"Corrigan?"

"Yeah, Reeves?"

"You...you weren't kidding about that stone, were you? Finding it here, I mean?"

I looked over at him crouched behind the counter. "No, I wasn't kidding." The expression on his face went from fear to utter disbelief when I said that. He opened his mouth, as if he had one more thing to tell me, but I didn't bother to listen: I'd seen a chance to run and jumped out the door.

The posse was clustered around a building that I'd passed over. Sheriff Walker had brought five men along with him, all loaded for bear, and one of those men was currently kneeling on the ground, clutching his arm in an odd way and yelling. I suspected that he'd had a run-in with one of those corpse-things. All their backs were turned towards me at first, so I was a good amount away from the shop when they finally spotted me. Bullets whizzed by inches above my head as I dove behind a nearby horse trough. I laid there in the muck and mud for the longest time, waiting for the shooting to stop. As soon as it did, I popped up and fired off my whole cylinder. I clipped two of the men, and caught another in the head, but the sheriff still stood. He fired his rifle as quick as lightning -- I didn't even have a chance to duck -- and I felt bullets rip through my right shoulder and my left side, just below my already-busted ribs. I collapsed back into the mud again, my gun hand growing numb from the pain. I'd barely managed to holster the empty pistol when Walker was on me, grabbing the front of my shirt and pulling me to my feet.

"Hello, you little bastard," he sneered at me. "Thought you could get away from me, didn't you?"

I tried to blink the rain out of my eyes -- my hat had flown off when I'd keeled over. "Hi, Sheriff. That's a nasty cut on your face...you get it last night while you were in jail?" Even now I couldn't help but be mouthy.

He didn't like *that* at all. "Where's your friend hiding, smart-aleck?"

"Didn't we already play this game?"

"Give me a straight answer or I'll rip your worthless head off!" he roared.

Lucky for me, there was no need: in the confusion, Reeves had recovered his own rifle and was proceeding to take potshots at the sheriff's men from the safety of the shop's doorway. As Walker turned his head to see where the shots were coming from, I brought up my good arm and boxed the sheriff's ear. He loosed his grip on me from pain and surprise, and I whirled and ran as fast as I could away from the posse's blazing guns. My heart thudded in my ears and my body was wracked with pain, but I didn't slow down. I'd leapt beyond thought, beyond reason, straight into blind terror. I wasn't even paying attention to where I was going, just ducking down alleys at random, my eyes fixed behind me more than ahead. If I *had* been paying attention, I probably would have been able to stop myself from falling right down into the cellar pit. I must've sucked up a gallon of water when I landed face-first, muddying up whatever parts of me weren't already

filthy. I managed to roll onto my back to keep from
drowning, but that was about all I *could* do: my shoulder
and side were screaming in agony from the gunshots, and
my vision was starting to turn black around the edges as I
stared up at the stormy sky.

I heard a far-off voice telling me to get up, the
sheriff's voice, but I couldn't do it. I wanted to...I wanted
to run, but there was no strength left in me. A boot
connected with my side, right where the bullet had gone
in...Jesus, it hurt so much. Dragged through the mud, my
head slammed against something hard and flat, bloodying
my nose...must've been my tombstone, I could feel my
name engraved on the smooth surface...slight vibration
running through it, like a steel rail when a train's on the
way. My injured arm wrenched behind my back, don't
scream, don't...sheriff's voice in my ear, saying he's going
to tear me apart, then cold laughter...fingers clutching at
my hair, blood pouring down my face as he smashed it
against my tombstone again...no, wait, it wasn't
my...something else, something important, what was...no
use, couldn't think anymore, reality crumbling beneath my
fingers.

My fingers. I felt the vibration growing beneath
my fingers...roaring in my ears, like a hard desert
wind...sheriff stopped laughing, started screaming. The
stone felt hot, burning my hands...going deaf from the
noise...what's happening, so bright...blue-white light,
engulfing me, swallowing me whole, and a
darkness...hungry darkness, everywhere, pulling at my
wounds, my chest burning...no, please...darkness and light,
swirling around me, churning black white black white
blurring into gray...oh God, what was this, I didn't want to
die, didn't want to...falling so far, so fast...please, God, just
let it end, I wanted it to end...end over end, falling...

...falling forever...

CHAPTER 3

Voices.

I could hear voices trickling down a long tunnel of darkness...faint whispers, what...words didn't make any sense, not English, not Spanish...*Who's there?* Couldn't speak, couldn't move, body felt numb...hard to breathe, head spinning, throbbing...*Oh God, am I dead?*

Arms around my shoulders, lifting me...white-hot needles ripped through my arm, my ribs, everything was on fire...tried to scream, release the pain, nothing but a squeak came out...sucking in air, tasted so cold. More talking, more movement, no sense...sound of boots scraping against a wooden floor, doors opening...someone pulling off my wet clothes, wrapping me in dry warmth. *Who are you? What happened to me?* So many questions locked within me, no way out.

A woman's voice nearby, soft, gentle. A hand brushed against my cheek, then slipped behind my neck, slowly raising my aching head. Mouth of a bottle pressed against my lips, sour liquid pouring down my throat, dowsing the fire in my wounds...laudanum, must have been...could feel myself losing consciousness again, sliding back down into the cool darkness...if I fell asleep now, would I ever wake up again? Didn't know, didn't care...

Find out later...

* * * * * *

Drip...drip...dripping...raindrip? No, no, rain*drop*...still raining...still *alive*...at least I think so...

The fog in my brain slowly cleared up: Yes, I *was* still alive and kicking, but at the moment, I wasn't sure how that was possible. The last thing I could remember with any clarity was being shot and having my guts pounded in, both courtesy of Sheriff Walker. After that...Lord only knows.

I struggled to open my eyes -- none of my muscles were in the mood to respond. When I finally managed to, I found myself staring at a candle burning on a small table beside me. After a moment, the rest of my surroundings came into focus: I was lying on a bed in a small, shadow-filled room, the only window covered by a heavy blanket. The dripping noise I heard wasn't rain, but a leak in the roof -- a wooden bucket sat beneath a wet patch on the ceiling, catching the steady drip-drip-drip of water.

"Where the Hell am I?" I whispered hoarsely, my throat feeling like I'd swallowed a bucket of sand. A groan escaped my lips as I pushed myself up to a sitting position, every nerve in my body screaming in protest against the maneuver. The last time I felt that bad, I'd begged God to kill me, but I'd soon learned that He doesn't do requests, least not for me. I pushed back the blanket covering me so I could check the gunshot wounds to my shoulder and belly, and saw that someone had bandaged them up nicely, and it felt like they'd even changed the dressing on my head wound. But who exactly was "they"? Did Reeves somehow manage to eliminate the posse, sheriff and all? That didn't seem likely, considering Reeves's condition when I last saw him, but I knew for damn sure that Walker would've rather shot me dead on the spot than drag me back to Barrelhead to be hanged.

I could see a closed door in the dim light. I called out towards it, but gave up after a minute or two, my throat too raw to produce any sound loud enough to carry outside the room. Realizing that I wasn't going to get any answers lying around like that, I gritted my teeth and slowly eased my battered body out of bed. My legs wobbled, and I could feel a busted rib or two shift around beneath the bandages, but I felt alright after a moment. The room was freezing, compounded by the fact that I wasn't wearing a stitch of clothing -- whoever rescued me had been kind enough to remove my rain-soaked clothes, but had neglected to give me anything dry to wear. I soon spied my things laying on a chair in the corner, and hobbled over there so I could get dressed. As I picked up my shirt, I noticed that the bullet holes had been neatly patched up, and most of the blood scrubbed away. The same had been done to my coat and trousers, and even my boots looked cleaner than they had in months. *Not bad,* I thought, *looks like the only things they missed are my longjohns and my guns...holy shit, where are my guns?!?*

I shoved the chair to the side and checked the floor. Nope, not there. Not *anywhere,* as far as I could see. Oh, this was *not* a good sign: Reeves would know better than to take my guns away, which meant that my unknown benefactor was most definitely not him. I hastily began to pull my trousers on, wishing that they *had* sewn up my longjohns -- I hated not having anything between me and that chafing denim. Strangely enough, my knife was still in its sheath. Why in the world would somebody take the guns but leave a Bowie knife? I didn't know, but I planned on making somebody real sorry for their slip-up. Once I was dressed, I pulled out the knife and carefully cracked open the door.

I soon discovered that whoever built that house wasn't too good of a carpenter: the doorway was so low that the top of my head brushed against the frame. Beyond, it opened up to a short hallway, and I could see firelight flickering at the end, where the hallway connected to a larger room. There were couple of doors on either side of the hall, but I didn't feel much like exploring at the moment. I slid quietly down the corridor, my mind and heart racing. The smell of meat cooking reached my nostrils, and I licked my lips -- I honestly couldn't remember the last time I'd eaten. When I reached the end, I peeked around the corner to find a dark-haired woman kneeling by a fireplace, her back to me as she tended to a pot of something hanging over the crackling logs. I saw no one else in the room, and she seemed harmless enough, so I lowered my knife and walked into the room proper. Before I'd taken more than three steps, the lady turned, took one look at me, and let out a scream that was so high-pitched I jumped back and yelped as well. I guess I'd given her one Hell of a scare, 'cause her face was completely ashen. She got up and backed away from me, babbling in some language that sounded vaguely familiar, but I couldn't place it.

"Lady, please, calm down! I'm not gonna hurt you," I said as I walked towards her, but she wouldn't stop, the words didn't even seem to register with her. "*Silencio, señora!*" I tried again in Spanish, but that didn't work either. "Dammit, woman, will you shut up before I give you something to scream about!" I hollered, and brought the knife up to her face. I had no intentions of using it on her, but she didn't know that.

The lady stopped screaming, thank God. She'd backed herself up against the wall, and she just stood there, motionless, staring at me with the bluest eyes I'd ever seen. "*Hu nee vist za,*" she whispered.

"What?" Now it was my turn to stare as I tried to puzzle out what she'd just said. I never got the chance, though: I heard hinges creak, and we both looked in time to see a small trapdoor open up in the floor behind me -- I'd stepped right over the thing without realizing it. A man poked his head up through the opening, saw the two of us, and gasped.

"*J'nath!*" the woman cried out. I didn't have a clue what that meant, but it made the man jump up out of the trapdoor in a hurry. Then I saw that he had one of my guns in his hand. I didn't know if he intended to use it, but I wasn't about to stick around to find out. I grabbed the woman by the arm, shoved her towards him, and made a break for what I hoped was the front door. Remembering to duck a little so I wouldn't whack my head, I banged the door open with my good shoulder and ran out into the snow.

Snow?

Snow?!?

I slid to a stop about twenty feet from the front door, unable to comprehend the fact that I was standing in nearly three inches of snow. *Where the Hell did all this come from?* I thought as I gaped at the unfamiliar landscape. *How long was I out for?*

Someone behind me shouted, but I decided that I didn't want to stand around and chat. I saw the edge of a forest not too far from me, so I headed that way as fast as I could manage. I was nearly within the tree line when a shot cracked out, the bullet burying itself in a nearby tree. I thought it was a little too close to be a warning shot, so I ran even faster, jumping over deadfalls and dodging branches. For the life of me, I couldn't recall there being any forests in this part of New Mexico, yet here it was, just like the snow.

After a few minutes of going flat-out, I collapsed in a small clearing, my left side feeling like it'd been ripped open. When I looked down, I saw that my shirt was soaked in blood -- all that running had reopened the gunshot wound. Oh, this was *not* good. I scooped up a handful of snow and packed it against the wound in a vain attempt to slow the bleeding. "C'mon, Richard, hold it together," I muttered, "things could be worse." I leaned against one of the trees, shivering from pain, cold, and confusion. "Least you're still alive." Sunlight shone down on me through the winter-bare trees, and I tuned my face up towards the inviting warmth.

That's when I first noticed that the sky was *purple.* Not a deep purple, mind you, but more like that lavender color you sometimes see at dusk, except the sun was at about the high-noon position. Good Lord, *the sun*...it was a red-orange *fireball!* I shut my eyes and shook my head in disbelief -- I was seeing things, I had to be -- but when I looked up again, all that madness was still there. "Oh dear

Jesus," I choked, "what's going on around here, this can't be real..."

Just then, the man who'd popped out of the trapdoor stepped into the clearing. Despite the cold, there was no color in his face at all, it was the same ash-gray as the woman's. He didn't appear to have my gun anymore, but looks can be deceiving, so I held up my knife, trying my best to keep my hand from shaking. "Stay the Hell away from me," I warned.

The man stood there for a moment, brushing his long black hair from his eyes, then said, "*Nee*...thou not *kedda*...I am friend." His voice had a flat quality to it, and his pronunciation was all sorts of messed up -- it was like he'd never spoken English before. He began to approach me, saying, "Come with me, I explain..."

"I don't care who you are, I said stay back!" I slashed the air between us with the blade. "I've seen a lot of weird shit lately, fella, and I've had *enough*. You can keep my guns, just *leave me alone!*" I stood up and was about to head off deeper into the woods, but my knees buckled before I could take another step, the knife dropping from my numb fingers and landing in the snow. The man rushed to my side in an instant to catch me. "Don't touch me!" I hollered as I swatted at his gray-skinned hands, trying to push him away, but I felt so weak.

"*D'hojek*, please, lay still," he said in that strangely-flat accent. "Thou hast lost blood, thy wounds were deep..."

The world was turning black, but I wouldn't stop fighting, not this time. "Go to Hell," I said, but my voice sounded so far away.

"Please calm thyself, thou art safe here."

Liar. Don't know who you are, but you're a liar.

"*D'hojek*, I beg thee."

So dark, so cold, just leave me alone.

"*D'hojek?*"

Dark...so dark...

* * * * * *

When I woke up again, I was back in the room and sprawled out on the bed, bare-chested. Thankfully, they'd kept my trousers on this time. A woman was leaning over me, but not the same one I'd seen before. That lady had been dark-haired and young, while this newcomer looked at least fifty with silvery-white hair, all piled up on top of her head and held in place with these chopstick-lookin' things like I'd seen Oriental ladies use before. Her skin was just as ashen as the other two people I'd seen. I felt pressure around my middle, and I looked down and saw that she was applying a fresh bandage to my wound -- her gray hands looked so strange next to my battered pink flesh. I tried to sit up after she'd finished, but she pushed me back down and said something in that strange language. "Back off, lady," I told her, "I'm gettin' out of here."

"*Z'kira* Kali wishes thou to stay in bed and rest," a voice beside me said. I looked over and saw the man from before standing near the bed. "Thy wounds need time to heal."

"They'll heal just as well someplace else," I answered, and tried to get up again, but the lady still wouldn't let me. She turned to the man and -- going by her tone -- began to berate him for my disobedience. The man tried to defend himself, and there was much shouting and waving of hands, but I didn't understand a damn word of it. After a minute or two of being argued over (literally), I sat up and snapped, "Look, either make up or take it outside. I'm supposed to be *resting*, remember?"

They both stopped and stared down at me, as if to say my welfare was none of my business. The man then motioned to the older woman, and the two of them moved a bit closer to the door, talking in much more civil tones. She finally left a few minutes later, and the man shut the door behind her and leaned his head against it, looking very tired all of a sudden.

"What's the matter? Having a rough day?" I quipped. "Trust me, it's probably nothing compared to how my life's been lately. Matter of fact, why don't I do us both a favor and get the Hell out of here." I swung my legs over the side of the bed.

The man whirled around. "Thou *will* stay in bed!"

"Look, just leave me be. I don't take orders from anybody, especially gray-skinned freaks that talk like they're in a Shakespeare play." I picked my shirt up off the floor, then dropped it back down when I realized it had become little more than a blood-soaked rag. I moved to get hold of my coat instead, but the man grabbed my wrist with a strength that contradicted his slender build. He was a few inches shorter than me, and he gazed up at me with eyes just as oddly colored as the dark-haired woman's.

"Art thou not aware of what has *happened* to thee?" he asked. "Art thou so *blind?*"

"What're you talking about?" I said. "I got shot, got a little banged up, then I woke up here."

"But *where* is *here?* I saw the way thou stared at the snow, and at the sky...thy world is quite different from mine, *kai?*"

"You're crazy, let go of me!"

"Name the land where thou art standing at this moment. If thou art correct, thou may leave."

"I ain't playin' this game..."

"Name it!"

I blew air out of my nostrils, frustrated, then said, "New Mexico. I'm in New Mexico." I tried to pull free of his grip, but he didn't let go. "C'mon, I answered your damn question..."

"And thou answered *wrong,*" he told me.

I could feel all the blood drain out of my face. The way he said that last word, the certainty of it, wasn't helping my state of mind. "Texas, then? This is..." I let the sentence trail off, but he still held on. "What the Hell do you *want* me to say? I'll name off every damn state in the Union if you want, just let go of me!"

After an eternity of silence, the man looked me straight in the eye and said, "Thou art near the village of Betedek, in the kingdom of Taorin, and is part of the land my people call Arkhein." He then let go of my wrist. "Now dost thou *kedda* why thou cannot leave?"

I backed away from him, clutching my arm as if he'd broken it. I couldn't help but gawk at the man: what he was suggesting in his strange, flat-toned voice was completely beyond my realm of comprehension, as if he'd just told me that two and two now equals seventeen. I shook my head in denial, unable to accept any of the weirdness I'd seen since I woke up. Hell, even *before* that, the world wasn't making a whole lot of sense. Ever since I'd been shot in the head...

Yes. Yes, that was *it*. That was exactly, precisely *it*. I laughed nervously at my revelation, the tension bubbling out of me in uncontrollable giggles. The man stared at me, afraid to approach. "*D'hojek?* Dost thou feel well?" he asked.

"I'm dreaming!" I answered, laughing. "My concussion is probably so bad that I never woke up in the first place!" I reached up and brushed my fingers against the bandage around my temple. "Lord, it's hard to believe that one little bullet can cause so much damage...I wonder how long I've been out? Reeves seemed pretty real, but the rest of it..." I sat down on the edge of the bed. "This certainly explains that stuff in Hadley, that's for sure."

The man muttered something that made no sense to me, but I didn't care, none of it was real anyways. Sooner or later, I'd either wake up or die, and at that point, either one was welcome. Anything to end the madness around me. "Why dost thou doubt all of this to be true?" the man asked me after a time. "Everything I have told thee, thou denies. Every movement made, thou perceives as a threat." He walked over to the chair in the corner and slumped down into it. "So many centuries of studying, preparing, hoping...none of it matters if thou refuses to trust me."

"Why *should* I trust you? Why should I believe *any* of this is real?" I waved my hand about the room. "The sun, the sky, the snow, *you*...not to mention that corpse I saw get up and..."

What little color was in the man's face suddenly drained out, and he nearly leapt out of the chair. "Thou hast *broken the seal?* In Avisar's name, thou cannot truly be *that* ignorant!"

"Hey, it's not *my* fault! They were all dead when I got there!"

I don't think he bought my excuse, though, because he just glared at me like I had shit for brains. "Stay here!" he barked, then rushed out the door, slamming it behind him with such force that I thought it would fly off its hinges. I think I sat there for a full ten seconds before I decided it was time to get out of this freakshow.

My knife was nowhere to be seen, so I wrote it off as a loss and pulled my coat on over my bare chest as I walked down the hall, back to the main room. The dark-haired woman was standing by the open front door and saying something to someone outside, I couldn't see who. A boy was standing next to her -- he looked to be a few years younger than me, and his coloration was just as strange as the other folk. He saw me first, and tried to block my path. "Oh, please," I snorted, and shoved him out of the way so hard that he hit the floor. The woman ran to his side to help him up, then she looked up at me and said something, but it didn't make a lick of sense to my ears. *God, I can't wait until this nightmare is over*, I thought as I stepped out into the yard. It was a little dimmer outside, and a bit colder, too. *For a dream, this sure feels real,* I thought with a shiver, and held my coat shut as best I could. *I'm getting chilled to the bone out here.*

"What art thou doing?" the man called out from the far end of the yard, opposite the way I'd run earlier.

He was kneeling in front of something half-buried in the snow. "Thou should stay inside. In thy condition..."

"I ain't got a 'condition'," I said, "this is all just one big hallucination." I took a few steps towards him, a smirk on my face. "Hell, I don't even know why I'm bothering to argue with you. You're about as real as...as a..." The smirk fell off my face the closer I got to the man and the object on the ground behind him. From a distance, it appeared to me nothing more than a patch of black earth, but as I closed in, I could make out the strange markings on its surface, and the vague impression of its octagonal shape beneath the snow. "No...no, it's not real," I moaned, staggering back from the sight of it. "None of this is real, can't be real, it can't..."

The man stood and said something to me, but I couldn't hear him, my mind was filled with a hideous roaring. I threw my hands up over my ears and squeezed my eyes shut in a vain attempt to block out all this madness, only to be greeted by the sight of hungry red eyes in a sea of black, staring through my soul. *Go away!* I tried to shout, but the roaring drowned out my voice and drilled straight into my brain, obliterating every last bit of sense that I still possessed, tearing away all hope of escape from the horror before me. The world was gone, there was only darkness and death and oh God please let me wake up wake up wake up...

"Wake up, please!" The man was talking to me, shaking me. "Can thou hear me? Wake up!"

My eyes snapped open. I'd collapsed in the snow, my hands still clasping the sides of my head. My throat felt raw again, and I soon realized that I'd been screaming at the top of my lungs through the whole episode. My breath raced in and out of me in hitching gasps. "What was that?" I choked. The man was kneeling beside me, and I reached up and clutched at the front of his shirt like a drowning man. "For God's sake, what's going on around here?"

The man placed one hand over mine, then another upon my shoulder. "Calm thyself, *d'hojek,* all is well here," he said, then turned his head towards the house. I followed his gaze and saw the woman and the boy standing not too far away, looks of concern on both their faces. He said something to them in that strange language before returning his attention to me. "I think that, when thou saw the stone, it...forced thy mind to remember thy journey here. The shock of crossing over must have been too great to bear, but thou art safe now." I shook my head in denial, but he insisted that the danger had passed. "Will thou trust me now?" he asked quietly.

"Yes." As an afterthought, I added, "I'm sorry."

The man smiled at me, a fairly warm smile considering all the grief I'd given him. "Thou art forgiven, *d'hojek,*" he said, then helped me to my feet and led me back into the house.

*   *   *   *   *   *

I was pretty numb between the ears for a while after that. My mind was still trying to piece all of this into something I could recognize and understand. The best I could arrive at was that I wasn't dreaming, I wasn't dead, and I was a damn far cry from New Mexico. I knew for sure that the black rock I'd found in Hadley had something to do with all of this, but every time I tried to recall the memory that had come to me in the yard, a wave of terror would wash over me with such force that I felt like I might throw up. I eventually gave up and decided to concentrate on thoughts that *didn't* make me sick.

My host gave me all the time I needed to compose myself. He sat me down near the fireplace, provided me with some food to fill my empty belly, and even scrounged up a spare shirt for me to wear, though it looked strange to me: it was bit longer than normal, and there were no buttons, save one near the throat. The man and the boy both appeared to be wearing something similar, so I just slipped it on without question. I told him my name when he asked, my brain too muddled to even think of using an alias. In turn, he informed me that he was J'nath Bannen, and that the young woman was his wife, Nina Kandru. The boy I'd knocked over was their son, Pietruvek. I nodded and said hello, but I didn't attempt to repeat their names, the words being so foreign to my ears that I knew I'd butcher them. J'nath was having a hard time with my first name as well: he kept slurring it in the middle, so "Richard" kept coming out "Reshard". I was too damn tired to correct him.

I got the impression right off that his wife didn't like me much...not that I could blame her, I'd been acting like a complete jackass. She kept pulling J'nath aside and talking to him in sharp tones, and even though I couldn't understand the words, I figured it to be something along the lines of, "This guy's nuts, can't you get rid of him?" The boy, however, seemed to have the opposite opinion about me: the look of curiosity on his face was hard to miss. He sat far enough away to be unobtrusive, but close enough to watch every move I made. Though what he found so fascinating about a beat-up Irishman eating a bowl of stew was beyond me.

When J'nath began to ask me questions, he thankfully kept them simple: where I was from, how I'd been injured, what I'd seen in Hadley, pretty basic stuff. I did quite a bit of lying, of course: this guy didn't appear to suspect that I was a criminal, so I wasn't about to tell him that I'd nearly had my head blown off during a bank robbery. I quickly spun a yarn about me and my friends being ambushed by bandits on the trail, and taking refuge in that dead town, completely unaware of what lay in store for us. There were a few holes in my story, but he didn't seem to notice.

After a while, I worked up the nerve to ask him the question that I was afraid to have an answer to: "How exactly did I get here?"

J'nath gazed into the fire for a moment. "The explanation is...difficult," he said, not looking at me.

"Give it a shot."

He sighed. "It may be easier if I showed something to thee." He stood up, gesturing for me to do the same, then walked over to the trapdoor set in the floor and pulled it open. Nina began to say something, but J'nath gently cut her off and started to descend the ladder beneath the opening, the woman still looking worried.

"Trust me, I won't lay a hand on him," I reassured her as I slipped through the trapdoor myself. "Of course, if he pulls anything first..." I muttered under my breath. I descended into the darkness, my ears picking up a strange chinking noise, like something being scraped, and I recognized it as flint and steel scraping each other. "Hey," I called out in the blackness, "I've got matches in my coat if you need a...oh my God, where did you get all of this *junk*?" The flint and steel had finally sparked, lighting a small oil lamp and revealing to my eyes an array of items that should've been in a museum, not some guy's root cellar. The dim light flickered across dozens of books, fraying scrolls, small trinkets sealed in glass cases, ancient-looking metalworks, and some things that I just plain couldn't identify. Pieces like these were way out of my field of expertise, but I knew enough to realize that these people had a fortune in antiques stashed away like fruit preserves. On a nearby shelf sat a small, milky-green statue, no more than five inches high, depicting a man in robes sitting cross-legged with a serene smile on his face. I picked it up so I could get an idea of the weight -- unless I missed my guess, the thing was pure jade.

J'nath hung the lantern from a chain dangling down from the ceiling, then came up beside me. "That is a statue of *Gautama Buddha*...a holy man on your world, I believe. This and all the other artifacts you see have been in my family's possession for over five hundred years."

"Five hundred...you've got to be kidding me." I waved a hand around the room. "Do you have any idea what this stuff's probably worth? I wouldn't keep it, I'd sell it."

He shook his head. "Is that all thou sees here? Money? That is a fleeting thing compared to the knowledge all this contains."

"Knowledge of what?"

"Thy world." He took the statue from me and placed it back on the shelf. "Had it not been for my family, all of this would have been long forgotten, and thou would have woken up in Arkhein quite alone."

"Whoa, hold on. That's the second time you've said 'thy world'. What exactly are you talking about?"

"Thy world and mine are...counterparts to one other. They exist separately, but they touch together in some places. In those places, one can cross over from one world to the other." I must have still looked pretty confused, because he soon changed his tactics. "Think of a pond in winter," he ventured. "Thou stands upon the ice and it remains firm, unyielding. Thou looks about and sees the land, the sky, the trees, all the things that make up thy world. Now, picture a hole in the ice. Thou looks through it and sees..."

"Frozen fish?" I guessed.

He shook his head. "Another sky, different trees, a completely new shoreline. Two worlds, totally unique, but forever connected." He then gestured in the general direction of that weird rock. "When thou passed through the Crossroad, it was if thou had fallen through that hole, and now thou art standing on the other side."

I ran a hand over my banged-up, grizzled face. What the man said was a bit hard to swallow, but it made sense when compared with all I'd seen so far. Not *much* sense, mind you, but things were becoming clearer. "So, basically you're telling me that I fell though some sort of rabbit hole? And now I'm on a whole 'nother *planet* or something?"

A broad smile spread across his face, and he clapped me on my uninjured shoulder. "*Kai,* now thou begins to *kedda*...to understand."

"Oh, I'm a long way from understandin' all of this." I glanced around the room again, and this time spied my guns and knife lying on a table near the center of the room. A lot of the tension in my body washed away at the sight of those familiar items. I strolled over and immediately began the ritual of inspecting my weapons: checking the barrels, reloading the cylinders, that sort of thing. J'nath stood silently by as I went through the whole operation, watching me with the same look of fascination on his face that his son had when we were upstairs. Strange folks. "So what's that rock out there for?" I asked as I strapped my gunbelts back on, finding comfort in their weight on my hips. "A marker or something?"

"That," he answered, "is thy 'rabbit hole'. The Crossroad -- the path between our two worlds -- does not lie open naturally. But if the proper sigils are placed upon it..."

"'Scuse me? Sigils?"

"Signs, markings, writings. If one finds the proper combination, the Crossroad can be opened permanently, and one can pass back and forth with ease."

I frowned at what this guy was suggesting. "You're talking about magic, ain'tcha? You've been dabbling in some kind of hoodoo, and those folks in Hadley..." My hands slid over to my guns. "I may not have been to church for a while, but I don't cotton to anybody who deals with the Devil."

"*Nee!* Thou art too quick to judge." J'nath held out his hands in a pleading gesture. "These magicks were used only for good, not for evil intents. My ancestors meant no harm at all."

My eyes narrowed. "I'm not talking about your great-great-granddaddy or whoever, I'm talking about *you.*" I poked my forefinger at his chest, saying, "*You're* the one who brought me here, and for all I know, *you're* the reason that whole town's dead."

"*Nee*, I am merely a...a caretaker for these artifacts. The Arkans who built the Crossroads are long gone."

"Uh-huh. So how do you explain this mess? Somebody forget to close the door on the way out?"

"Please, a moment..." He cast his eyes about the room, tugging unconsciously at his bottom lip. "There is a scroll," he muttered, "very old...it can show thee...ah, here it is!" He gingerly removed the yellowing paper from its place on the shelf. "This was written by my ancestor, Aranath Bannen, over five centuries ago. He helped build the Crossroads...and he was witness to the Fall." The last words he said with a note of sadness in his voice. He cleared off a spot on the table and began to unroll the ancient document, which consisted of a mixture of crude illustrations and line after line of vaguely Chinese-looking markings. "He detailed here how the Crossroads were discovered in the year 2777 by..."

"Wait a minute...*what* year? The last I checked, it was 1874!"

"*Ke?* Oh, I had forgotten: our method of recording time is different than on thy world. For example, according to our calendar, we are nearing the end of the year 3294." He tugged on his lip again. "I believe our year of 2777 corresponds with...on the Christian calendar it would around the early 1300s, and the Hebrew would be..."

"Close enough, pal."

"Good, good. Now, at that time, the discovery of thy world was just as shocking to my ancestors as thy arrival has been to thee. Thy world was called Tarahein -- the Shadow-Land -- and was believed to be filled with nothing but demons and spirits. But they soon discovered thy people." He gestured towards the items scattered about the room, saying, "Thou art so...so different from us. So many languages, and cultures, and...and this!" He reached out and grasped my hand in his. "Thy people and mine look alike physically, but thy pigment is so varied compared to ours. Pinks and reds and browns...fascinating..."

"Uh, yeah, I'm flattered." I jerked my hand away. "I still don't see what this has to do with how I got here."

"Patience, Reshard Corrigan." He opened the scroll a bit more to reveal two rough maps. One of them looked like a child's attempt to draw a map of the world...or rather, *my* world: the shorelines were all off-kilter, and whole pieces of some continents were missing. The second was completely unfamiliar: it showed an enormous continent that vaguely resembled South America in shape, but with the bottom tip cut off and a few smaller islands of varying size scattered about it. I assumed that it must be a map of this world, Arcane or whatever it was J'nath called it. "There were originally twelve Crossroads," he explained, indicating tiny triangular marks upon each map. "Six in my world, corresponding with six in thine." The marks on the alien map formed a rough circle around the continent's perimeter, but the ones for my world seemed scattered at random across the Northern Hemisphere -- there was one in the States, of course, and the other five landed in the general area of South America, Great Britain, Europe, and East Asia, the latter claiming two all to itself...assuming that I'd interpreted the sprawling mess before me correctly.

"You said there *were* twelve. How many are there now?" I asked.

"Only two." Again, his voice sounded strange, almost pained. He'd been making motions over the scroll, following the marks on the maps, and now his hands had stopped, his forefingers coming to rest over the Stateside triangle (presumably the location of Hadley) and one situated near the southwest corner of the alien continent (presumably, again, my current location). He looked down at the pair of symbols, saying nothing for a minute or two, then told me, "My ancestors explored thy world for five years, observing, learning, collecting artifacts. At first, they did not know what to make of thy people: in one land, thou would look and act in one manner, while in the next, all they had learned suddenly ceased to matter, for thou would be so different in this other land. For a time, they believed that the Crossroads opened to *six* separate worlds, not one. It confused them, but fascinated them as well." He lowered his head. "If thy people had not been so enigmatic to my ancestors, then perhaps...perhaps..."

"Perhaps what?" But J'nath didn't answer, he'd shut his eyes and turned away from me slightly. "Hey, what's the matter?" I asked, and jostled his shoulder.

He looked at me, and in his eyes I could see...something. Something bad. "Please, my English words are not good. I have read them many times, but to speak them..." He shook his head. "Can thou forgive me if I ask to continue this on the morrow? This day has been long for us both. We should rest, it will give me time to think of the proper words to tell thee."

The man was stalling, that was obvious, and not for the reasons he was giving, either. But he did have a point: I was just about done in from the shock and excitement, and the thought of getting a good night's sleep in an actual bed for a change sounded wonderful. "Fine," I answered, "but tomorrow you have to spill your guts out about the rest of this."

J'nath's face went a bit pale at my phrasing, but he must have realized that I didn't mean what I said in a literal sense when his color returned to "normal". He nodded, saying, "*Kai*, we shall speak of this later, I promise."

We ascended the ladder out of his hidden museum, and after mumbling a half-hearted goodnight to him and the others, I retreated to my room. Heh...*my room*. Like this was a hotel or something. I closed the door and wedged the chair under the handle as best I could -- I didn't want "room service" to come in while I was asleep,

I'd had enough of that while I was unconscious. I wondered how long I'd been out for anyways: with all the madness going on around me, I'd forgotten to ask. More questions for tomorrow, I supposed.

I lay down on the bed, boots and guns still on, and smoked a cigar I'd scrounged from one of my coat pockets, lighting it with the candle still burning beside the bed -- it tasted stale, but I didn't really notice too much. As I blew a few lazy smoke rings, I could hear J'nath and his wife talking down the hall -- I thought I heard my name mentioned a couple of times, but I couldn't tell for sure -- Nina didn't sound too happy to have me in the house, that much I could discern. I figured I'd try and apologize to her tomorrow for my behavior, but I didn't have the slightest idea how I'd do it, as she didn't appear to understand English. I wasn't too sure about the boy, either: he'd barely said a word, alien or no.

After a time, I felt myself getting drowsy. I stubbed out my cigar on the bedside table and closed my eyes, my mind constantly drifting back to what J'nath had told me earlier:

Thy world is quite different from mine.
How much different?
How much?

CHAPTER 4

Back in the darkness again, smothered by it. I could feel something in there with me, a deeper dark, reaching out for me. I tried to get away, but it was everywhere, digging under my skin, ripping open my wounds until blood poured out of me in rivers. The dark poured in to replace it, engulfing my soul in a deathly chill. I cried out in pain, but no one heard me. I was alone, always alone, abandoned and forgotten by the world so long ago, left to the mercy of the dark.

Then I saw a light, small at first, but quickly growing in intensity until it drove away the darkness. I threw my arms over my head as the light burned into my eyes and through my skull, but it didn't help, it didn't stop, it dug into my soul just as easily as the dark had, drowning me in endless white. *This is worse*, I thought, not knowing why. *Please, just go away, make it all go away, no more dark, no more light, please...*

Slowly, the light began to fade, and I found myself lying on my side in front of that strange black stone...but not the one I saw half-buried in snow. I sat up and whipped my head around, immediately recognizing the cellar pit I'd found in Hadley. "I'm back," I whispered, then leapt to my feet and ran to the edge of the pit. "Oh God, it really *was* all a dream," I said in relief as I climbed out, "it was all just one big, crazy dream." I was about to start running back to the shop where I'd last seen Reeves when I happened to glance down at my clothes: I was wearing the shirt J'nath had given me, the one that was too long and had the single button at the collar. "What in blazes..." I muttered, and slipped a hand beneath the shirt. Sure enough, my fingers brushed against the bandages around my shoulder and midsection. I groaned at the realization that this was yet another dream -- chances were, I was still in that *other* world, fast asleep. *I can't take much more of this*, I thought. *I don't know what to believe anymore...*

"What you believe now is not important," a voice told me. "When you are ready, you *will* know the truth."

I looked up and saw the mystery man from my other dream, his face still obscured by a black hooded cloak. He stood before me as if he'd been there the entire time, watching me. "Who *are* you?" I spat at him. "What are you *doing* to me? First I'm in one place, then another, I'm dead one moment and alive the next, and now you've dragged me back here and *why don't you just leave me the Hell alone!*" I kicked a clod of dirt at him like a child having a tantrum. I suppose that I *was*, but I reckoned that I was entitled to one little outburst, considering.

"I am afraid I cannot do that," he said, acting as if I *hadn't* just screamed at him like a madman, "you are needed far too much. We understand that you need time to adjust to this new situation, but we trust that you will adapt very well, despite the obstacles. That is one of your unique talents."

"Yeah? Well, let me show you one of my others," I growled, and drew my guns. I figured a couple of bullets sailing past the man's cowl might put an end to his riddles, but when I tried to pull the trigger, both guns refused to fire. "What the...what did you *do*?" I kept pulling, but to no avail, the mechanisms were frozen.

"This is not why we called for you," he answered, then stepped forward, placed his black-gloved hands over my pistols, and forced them down until they pointed straight at the ground. "You think with these guns first, and with your fists, but rarely with your *mind*. You are capable of so much more than you can imagine, yet you would rather throw bullets at every problem before you."

"Best way to solve most of the problems I run into."

"That will not always be so." He let go of my guns and took a step back. "You have to abandon what you think of as 'right' and embrace a new way of thinking. All you need concern yourself with is your role as a *n'toku-rejii*. Beyond that, nothing else matters."

"The Hell it doesn't! You turn my life upside-down, and you don't even have the common courtesy to tell me *why*?"

"The answer would hold no meaning for you at the moment, nor will it ever so long as you cling to old habits." He gestured to the guns still in my hands -- I shoved them back into their holsters and folded my arms across my chest, but that didn't seem to satisfy him. "Tell me, why are you so quick to label me your enemy?" he asked.

"It ain't obvious?" I snapped. When he didn't answer, I continued, "Why do *you* think that I should *trust* you?"

He gave me a slight smile from beneath his shadowy hood. "Because the moment you do, most of my work shall be done."

"Well then, you've got a damn long way to go yet, especially with you talkin' backwards all the time."

"I tell you what I think you are ready to hear...and at the moment, that is very little." He began to circle me, and I turned to keep facing him as he did so. "As time passes, you will hear more, and most of what you will learn will not be from me, but from the world. You could hear it now, if you chose."

"All I hear right now is you runnin' your mouth, and that ain't tellin' me shit," I said. "Stop being coy and spill it."

"One step at a time, that is the best way for you to progress. And until you learn to trust, it is the *only* way."

"What do you want me to do, throw my arms wide and yell, 'Boy, it sure was stupid for me to question a *total stranger*! I may only understand one word out of seven that he says, but golly, I'm sure I'll puzzle him out sooner or later!'" I gave the mystery man a shove and started to walk away from him. "Do me a favor and go to Hell."

"Your denial will change nothing," he called after me. "You are a *n'toku-rejii*, you always have been."

I stopped walking and spun around. "And what the Hell is *that* supposed to mean? It's just a damn nonsense word, it doesn't make a lick of sense to me."

The man stood silently for a minute before answering, "If I show you, will you listen to what I have to say?"

"Dunno. Show me first, then I'll decide."

He sighed, then approached me, his body moving with an unnatural fluidity. "Pay attention," he told me as he reached a black-gloved hand up towards my face. "Remember how it *feels*, the way it *moves*."

"What are you..." I started to say, then his fingers brushed my cheek, and my brain exploded. Countless voices spoke in my head all at once, and images flew past my eyes at dizzying speed. I couldn't take it all in, it was too much, far too much. Somewhere in that maelstrom, I managed to put together one thought, one word, and I held onto it as tightly as I could, concentrating on it until I had the strength to scream it with my very soul:

"STOP!!!"

Remarkably, it worked. In the space of a heartbeat, I went from standing in the middle of a deserted New Mexico town to lying in bed in a land whose name I couldn't pronounce. I clutched at the blankets, trying to fight off a bad case of vertigo -- it felt like someone had tipped the room sideways, not to mention the screaming headache I suddenly had. *Good Lord, what's happening to me?* I thought, and gingerly touched the bandage around my head, afraid that the pain was from the gunshot wound. All seemed well there, however, and the headache soon began to fade, leaving me with foggy impressions of what I'd seen and heard when the mystery man touched me. None of the images were coherent enough for me to make out now that I was awake (not that it really felt like I'd been sleeping during that whole thing), but something I'd heard stuck with me. A single word, one that I'd never heard before, but there it was, lodged in my mind...and I didn't have the slightest clue how to pronounce it. I laid there in the dark, my hand pressed to my forehead, and did my best to say it aloud, but I just couldn't manage it. The closest I could get was "hell-land", and I *knew* that wasn't right, but I didn't know *how* I knew. All I knew for sure was that I didn't want to experience whatever that was ever again.

I sat up in bed, wincing at the sharp pain in my side. The last couple of days had been far too strange for my tastes, and it didn't look like things would be getting back to normal any time soon. *Why me?* I thought. *Why does all the bad shit happen to me?* All I wanted at that moment was a stiff drink and an express ticket back to New Mexico, preferably both, so I could forget all about this crazy place...not that I could have either. I was a *n'toku-rejii*, whatever the Hell *that* meant. "Sucker", probably. I decided to settle for the cigar I'd stubbed out earlier, and rooted around my coat pocket for my matches, the candle on the bedside table having gone out in the night. As I did so, my fingers brushed against a crumpled piece of paper. I couldn't recall what it might be, so after I relit my cigar and the candle, I pulled it out, looked it over, and cursed.

It was the wanted poster from the sheriff's office. With everything that had happened to me, I'd forgotten all about grabbing it. *Oh, this is bad,* I thought, and began to pace the room. *If J'nath sees this, I'm done for.* I could feel a wave of panic rising inside me: I had no clue how to get home, so I was completely dependent on J'nath and his family until I did, and nobody wants to help a cold-blooded killer. *Maybe he hasn't seen it yet. Yeah, it was all the way at the bottom of my pocket, easy to miss...but if he HAS seen it...*

"Dammit, Richard, stop being stupid," I said under my breath. "If he knew who you really are, do you think he would've let you live?" I looked back down at the paper, staring into the hard, dark eyes that some unknown artist had decided to give me. Without thinking, I pushed my thumb through the drawing, obliterating my "face" -- I couldn't stand seeing it anymore. I knew I had to get rid of the thing, just to be safe, so I touched a corner of the paper to the lit candle. The flames hungrily lapped up the yellowing sheet, devouring my name, my crimes, everything that was *me*.

Now, if I only could have burned away the feeling of doom inside me just as easily.

* * * * * *

I barely slept the rest of the night, pangs of worry eating at my guts the whole time, not to mention the fear that, once I closed my eyes, the crazy dreams would return. I gave up around dawn and stumbled half-asleep into the main room of the house, lured by the smell of breakfast and the sounds of conversation, though both were alien to me.

J'nath greeted me with a cheeriness that made me want to go back to bed. "Reshard! Thou was beginning to worry me: it is long past First Light, and thou was still slumbering." He gestured towards the room's lone table, where Pietruvek sat wolfing down what looked like flat biscuits smothered in purplish applesauce. Nina knelt by the hearth, fixing a pot of tea. "Come eat," J'nath said, and pulled out a chair for me. "Nina has made some *milhafi*. The taste is quite sharp, but I think thou will enjoy it."

"Hold that thought," I told him as I spied a wash basin by the door, with a small, polished-metal mirror hanging above it. "I think I'll get cleaned up first, this beard's starting to itch." A puzzled look crossed his ashen face, but he let me go about my business. When I first got a glimpse of myself in the mirror, I almost couldn't believe it was me: in addition to a few days' growth of whiskers, my face was covered with cuts and bruises from my scuffle with Sheriff Walker. They were healing up quite nicely, though, and I had to admit, I'd looked worse in the past. I couldn't find a straight razor anywhere by the basin, so I just wet my face down and began to shave with my knife -- it was clumsy, sure, but I'd managed to do it before without any grievous injury. By the time I was nearly done, I noticed that the room had become rather quiet. I turned around and found everyone staring at me, as if I'd just finished relieving myself on the floor. "What's the matter?" I asked.

"What...what art thou doing to thy *face*?" J'nath said breathlessly.

"Huh? Did I cut myself real bad or something?" I started to run a hand over my face, then I took a second look at J'nath's own baby-smooth cheeks and chin, and the reason for their distress became quite clear. "You, um...Arkans...you don't grow beards, do you?" He just looked at me blankly, so I pantomimed stroking my now-nonexistent whiskers. "Y'know, hair on your face? Arkan guys don't have to shave?"

He shook his head. "I have never seen anyone with a hairy face before. What thou did with thy knife...it was shocking, but I am glad thou cut it off. It made thee look...like an animal."

His words took me aback slightly. For the first time, I realized that *I* was the one who was different around here, not everybody else. I tried to imagine for a moment what I looked like to them with my unruly brown hair and pale-pinkish skin...in their eyes, my appearance might have been downright appalling.

My self-abusive ruminations were cut short by a knock upon the front door. I flipped my knife back into its sheath and wiped stray hairs from my shirtfront as Nina opened the door to greet our early-morning visitor: a man of about J'nath's height, with a slightly heavier build and a fading hairline. Like J'nath, this newcomer wore a single-button shirt with a sleeveless tunic pulled over it and belted at the middle, coupled with loose-fitting trousers and leather boots. Over all of this, the man had draped a fur-lined cloak that reminded me of the ones sometimes worn by women back on my world -- he shrugged it off and handed it to Nina after he entered, then he started talking to J'nath almost immediately. I couldn't understand a word they spoke, of course, but I could read their body language well enough to figure that this guy was important in some way or another. The reason he was here was pretty obvious, too: that lady I'd seen the day before had probably spread the word that I'd regained consciousness, and this fella was stopping by to check me out.

After a moment, J'nath called me over and said, "This is Yaved N'dahl, one of the elders of Betedek. He has come here to properly welcome thee."

"Figured as much. Good morning t' you, sir." I flashed him the warmest smile I could dredge up that early in the day and stuck out my hand. Instead of shaking it, though, Yaved stared at me for a moment, then said something to J'nath, who blanched and forced my hand back down to my side. "What? I'm just trying to be friendly," I told him.

"What thou did with thy hand was...rude," J'nath replied. "It resembles a gesture people make when asking for money. It makes thee look like a beggar."

"Well, then, what am I *supposed* to do?"

Without a word, he brought my hands up to chest level and showed me how to clasp them together with the thumbs and index and middle fingers sticking outward. "Now bow slightly," he told me, "and say, '*Dandoa, d'ho-N'dahl.*'"

I felt like a damned fool, but I did what he told me to do -- I mispronounced the words a bit, but I think I got the point across. Yaved smiled and returned the gesture, saying "*d'ho*-Corrigan" instead of his own name. He then began to speak in a manner that seemed a bit rehearsed...I guess he'd memorized some sort of speech. Too bad it was all lost on me.

"The people of Betedek extend...hospitality to thee," J'nath translated. "Thou art a very special visitor to our land and, though our village is small, every effort shall be made to accommodate thee. The *tehr-hidmon* can arrange to provide nearly anything thou may need."

"I don't understand. What's a *tehr-hidmon*?"

"It is...ah...a group of elders, shopkeepers. They make decisions for our village."

"Like a town council."

"*Kai*, a council. If thou needs anything, simply ask one of the *tehr-hidmon*." He paused to listen to Yaved. "In addition, *d'ho*-N'dahl would like to formally invite thee to the Feast of Halitova three days hence. He hopes that thou accepts, for all of the village is eager to make thy acquaintance."

"Um...sure, I guess." I didn't know what else to say: it didn't seem right to turn down the invitation, but I sure as Hell didn't plan on sticking around this place for three more days. "I hope it's not a real fancy party, 'cause I forgot to bring a change of clothes with me," I joked.

J'nath translated my answer for Yaved (including the joke, presumably), and Yaved looked at me strangely for a moment before he burst out laughing. It put me a bit more at ease to hear that, but when he clapped me on my injured shoulder in a gesture of friendship, I had to bite my lip to keep from hollering. Nobody noticed. J'nath himself was grinning from ear to ear, obviously happy that I'd hit it off so well with this guy. Personally, I couldn't have cared less, but I smiled and nodded my head as Yaved babbled on like we were old pals.

I endured about ten minutes of unintelligible chatter before Yaved decided he had to be on his way, thank God. After he left, I turned to J'nath and asked, "What the Hell did I just agree to?"

"The Feast of Halitova welcomes the coming year." J'nath walked over to the breakfast table, where

Nina and Pietruvek were finishing their meal. He bent down and kissed his wife on her high, ashen forehead before sitting beside her. "There is food, dancing, music. Except for harvest-time, it is probably the biggest festival of the year."

I took a seat at the table myself, with J'nath on my left and his son on my right. "You mean it's some sort of New Year's party? But it's the beginning of September, you're four months early."

"On thy world, it may be, but here, it is the last month of the year, so..." He spread his hands wide and smiled. "*Filal Halitova.*"

"Same to you, pal." I put some of the soft, flat biscuits on my plate and spooned the purplish stuff -- which was some kind of tart fruit preserves -- over the top of them like the others had done. "I don't see why everybody's making such a big fuss about me anyways," I said around a mouthful of biscuit. "I mean, I'll be heading for home just as soon as I've rested up a bit."

J'nath's boy looked up from his breakfast, an expression of shock on his face. I guess that he *could* understand English, but I couldn't fathom what I'd said that would get that sort of reaction. He whispered something to his father across the table, to which J'nath simply waved his hand in dismissal. Even his wife was beginning to give him a disapproving look. "What? What's wrong now?" I asked.

J'nath stared down into his tea. "I cannot send thee home," he finally answered. "I am sorry if I misled thee, but..."

I felt like I'd been punched in the gut. "You're *sorry*? You drag me out to God-knows-where and the best you can say is *you're sorry*?"

"Reshard, please listen..."

"Listen to *what*? You haven't told me one damn useful thing *yet*!" I stood up, knocking over my chair, then grabbed J'nath by his long black hair and pulled him to his feet. My gun flew into my free hand as I growled,

"You're gonna show me the way back home, right now, or so help me, I'll..."

"Thou does not *kedda* the danger," he told me as calmly as he could. "Traveling through the Crossroad nearly *killed* thee. Thou spent over four days on the verge of death...thou could never survive the journey back."

"Quit lying to me!" I began to raise the gun towards his face, but Pietruvek rushed over and grabbed my hand.

"Please, *d'ho*-Corrigan," he begged, "*Padra* speaks truth." The boy's accent was worse than his father's -- that certainly explained why he hadn't spoken English earlier.

I stared at the two of them, looking for any hint of deception but finding none. Slowly, I let go of J'nath, then holstered my gun and turned away from them, trying to rein in my anger before I did something stupid. This was getting to be too much to handle: the dreams, the dead town, this strange place...just one damn thing after another, and now I had to deal with the possibility of being exiled here forever. "Why didn't you tell me this last night?" I asked, my back still to them.

"I...I wanted to give thee time to adjust," J'nath stammered. "Thou was already quite confused. I thought in a day or two, perhaps, thou would *kedda* my words more easily."

"Yeah, well, you thought wrong."

"Please forgive me, Reshard. I did not wish to deceive thee, I only wanted to do what I thought was best for thee."

I turned around and stepped towards J'nath so fast that he backpedaled right into Nina. "Then quit holding shit back from me."

"*Ke?*"

"Tell me *why* I can't go back home. Tell me what scared you so bad when you were talking last night that you wouldn't finish your story."

Pietruvek said something to him, and once again, J'nath tried to dismiss it, only now Nina joined in on her son's side. The two of them looked at J'nath expectantly, urging him to make a decision in (I presumed) my favor. After a moment, he nodded and spoke to them in Arkan, then cautiously approached me and took me by the arm. "Come, we will step outside," he said, "for privacy."

The morning air was crisp and cold, but I noticed that the snow appeared to be melting in some places. It almost smelled like Spring, but the idea wasn't sitting right with me, as my brain and body still thought of it as being late Summer. The red sun was hanging low in what I assumed was the east, casting long shadows across the yard. Unconsciously, my gaze wandered off towards where the Crossroad lay, black and glaring in the purity of the snow. In the morning light, however, I noticed something that had escaped my attention the other day: while the fist-sized hole in the center of the stone in New Mexico was empty, this one held a larger version of the strange bluish-green crystal I'd found lying in the pit. *So it* was *part of a bigger stone*, I thought. *But if that's the case, how come I only found that little shard?*

"Does thou remember what we spoke of last night?" J'nath asked me after a time. "About how my ancestors discovered the Crossroads and journeyed to thy world?"

I nodded, never taking my eyes off the crystal. It seemed to absorb the sunlight, causing it to glow from within.

"For five years, they explored Tarahein...thy world...trying to learn all they could about thy people," he continued. "Unfortunately, they soon became too focused on the knowledge, and could not see that the Crossroads were beginning to kill both of our worlds. It was not very evident at first, just an isolated death here and there, but always near where a Crossroad lay. Then the deaths began to grow, and spread away from the portals. They soon became too numerous to count. Funeral fires burned day and night in an effort to eliminate this unknown plague that had fallen upon us, but to no avail. Some people began to say that they had seen...they had seen some of the dead rise up and kill those who were still living." He swallowed hard, as if trying to hold back tears. "No one knew, no one even *suspected*, that the Crossroads were the source of all this misery until it was too late. Within two years, nearly every Arkan was either dead or dying -- there were only a few thousand left alive, all scattered across Arkhein, every isolated group thinking it was the last of our race. From millions of people to a handful in *two years*..." He fell silent again, just as he had the night before, those strange blue eyes staring down into the snow.

I could see now why J'nath was reluctant to talk about this: what he described sounded a thousand times worse than what Reeves and I saw in Hadley. Oddly enough, something about his story seemed familiar, like I'd heard it somewhere else before. Then it hit me like a freight train: a few years back, me and the boys had ended up in a town that had an outbreak of cholera, and the local doctor checked us out to make sure we hadn't contracted it. During my examination, the doc told me about some of the nastier epidemics he'd read up on -- not the sort of thing you want to hear about in that state -- and one of the nastiest he'd come across had been something called the Black Death. It had gotten so out of control, he said, that it wiped out nearly half the people in Europe and Asia...over five hundred years ago.

It's just some sort of sick coincidence, I thought, and shook my head in denial. I didn't care that the time and circumstances matched, or that the locations of most of the Crossroads were on those continents. If I acknowledged all that as true, it just made this whole situation more *real*. "It doesn't make sense," I told J'nath. "You said that the Crossroads *caused* all of this death, like it was consciously killing people, and that it almost killed *me. It's just a damned rock.*"

"That is what my ancestors thought as well." He looked back up at me, a somber air about him. "But there is a legend, one of the oldest told, that speaks of a creature that ruled the universe long before our god, Avisar, created the world. It was called Beterion, and it lived only to destroy, crushing anything that brought order to that maddening void. When Avisar came, they fought, and Beterion was defeated. From its body, Avisar made the world, so that this creature of death would finally bring about life. But Beterion's spirit, its *kahn*, could not be destroyed, so the legend says that Avisar sealed it away in the realm between Arkhein and its shadow." As he said those last words, his gaze shifted over to the Crossroad. "The passage is vague, unless one considers Tarahein to be the 'shadow' referred to."

"Th-that's crazy, what you're saying...I can't believe this." I pushed my hands up through my hair. "The fact that this place *exists* is too much by itself, but *this*...are you telling me that I literally went through *Hell* to get here?!?"

J'nath shook his head. "It is not thy world's idea of Hell. It holds a devil, *kai*, but that was meant to be its only occupant. When my ancestors opened the Crossroads, however, they gave Beterion a way to pull in the spirits of others, to feed off of them, and grow stronger. What my people now call the Fall or the Great Plague was actually Beterion's *kahn* invading the bodies of the innocent, tearing each of them apart from the inside out and twisting their *kahn* for its own use."

"Dear God." I crossed my arms over my gut as I recalled my dream from the night before: the darkness I couldn't escape from, and the pain that it wrought. "That's what it tried to do to me, isn't it? And Reeves...oh my God, that thing's going to kill Reeves!" Without thinking, I began to approach the Crossroad.

J'nath grabbed my arm. "I am sorry, but...thy friend is most likely already dead. Most people succumb to Beterion's madness within a few days -- thou hast been here for nearly five days now."

"But what about *me*? It didn't kill me, so maybe Reeves..." My voice trailed off as I saw the look of pity in his eyes. He pointed to the crystal in the center of the Crossroad, and part of me realized what he was going to say before the words left his mouth.

"The central stone," he told me, "is called the Heart of Avisar. By some miracle, my ancestors discovered that it could drive back Beterion, and even help those stricken by the Great Plague. Unfortunately, only a few stones existed, so the two largest were placed in the only pair of Crossroads located in then-uninhabited regions. Once in place, Beterion was trapped once again, for the remaining portals were destroyed. The plague dissipated not long after in this world, and obviously in thine as well."

"Until some moron accidentally broke the damn thing," I muttered.

J'nath nodded, saying, "So long as the Heart remains intact and in place, neither Beterion nor its plague shall return to Arkhein. Unfortunately, it appears thy Crossroad had no one to safeguard it like this one. From what thee described, the forces of God and Nature must have buried it over the centuries." He shook his head. "It never occurred to me that thy people would not know what it was."

"Just my luck, eh?" I shook my own head, thinking that was indeed luck that I'd snatched up the one thing that could help me survive my little trip between worlds. "So the only reason I didn't get slaughtered was that shard of crystal in my pocket? If that's the case, why can't I use it again to get back home?"

"Because it barely helped thee survive the first time. The Heart's strength lies in its size: the larger the piece, the more power it holds. The ones placed in the Crossroads were flawless and vastly powerful -- more than enough to keep Beterion at bay. Once the Heart in thy world was shattered, however, most of its power was lost immediately. The shard thou found would have protected thee from the plague, but when exposed directly to Beterion, what little power it still contained was quickly used up. When thou arrived, all that remained of it was a handful of slivers...useless." He gently placed a hand on my shoulder. "I am sorry, Reshard, but without a large enough piece of the Heart, there is no way to send thee home unharmed."

"Then *find* one, dammit!" I yelled, jerking away from him. "Or find a way to go *around* that fuckin' thing, *something*. I can't just *sit* here while it rips my best friend to shreds, not to mention the entire New Mexico Territory."

"We have tried...for five hundred years, we have tried." There was a hint of exhaustion in his voice. "Aranath Bannen, my ancestor, spent his entire life trying to find an alternate way to Tarahein, or something that would protect just as well as the Heart. So did his son, and *his* son, and on down the line to myself and *my* son. Over twenty generations have lived and died here, only to discover the same thing: *There is no safe passage back to Tarahein.*"

I stared deep into his eyes, trying to discern whether or not he was telling me everything. All I could see in them was concern...and pity. I couldn't stand it, and turned away from him again, my hands clenched into fists, feelings of anger and loss tearing my insides in two. I wanted to scream at the world, to pound that damned stone into powder, to do *anything* but stand there helplessly while some ancient monster prevented me from ever going home again. "So what am I supposed to do now, just lay down and die?" I muttered.

"Thou will stay with us," J'nath answered. "Our home shall be thine for as long as thou wishes. It would be thoughtless to do otherwise." He paused for a moment, then asked, "Does thou have family, Reshard?"

"What?" I turned back towards him.

"Family...parents, siblings...a wife, perhaps?"

"You mean is anybody gonna miss me, don't you?"

"I...*kai.*" He quickly became very interested in the tops of his boots.

"And what would happen if I said 'Yes'? You gonna suddenly conjure up a way to get me home?" I let that hang between us for a moment before I went on. "No, I don't have any family, haven't for a long time. The closest thing I have to family right now is Reeves, and he's...my God, Reeves..." The full implications of what J'nath had told me finally sank in. The idea of Reeves being dead, while awful, was still palatable, but the notion that his very *soul* had been consumed by some demonic *thing*...and that it had tried to do the same thing to *me*...

I fell to my knees, a shudder running up my spine. While my memories of coming face-to-face with that Beterion creature were still fragmented, I could recall enough to know that it wasn't the sort of thing I'd like to experience for all eternity. That's what was happening to Reeves, though, and all the people in Hadley, and countless others before them. "It's too much," I whispered, and put my hands over my face. "It's too damn much to take in."

J'nath knelt beside me and placed his hand on my shoulder again -- I didn't shake him off this time. "This is why I was afraid to tell thee so soon," he said. "Thou art still too close to it. The more time passes, the easier it will be to face, and the pain in thy heart will lessen."

"No, it won't," I answered, and even as I did so, the mystery man's voice from my dream bubbled up in my memory: *We understand that you need time to adjust to this new situation, but we trust that you will adapt very well, despite the obstacles.* I tried to block out the words, but I couldn't.

And that scared me more than anything.

CHAPTER 5

"Table."

"Table...um, *nuhr*."

"Cup."

"*Ulum*."

"*Nee, ulum* means 'to drink'. What does thou drink *from*?"

"Alright, give me a minute...I don't remember."

"Thou was close. *Ula*."

"Okay, 'oola', whatever." I leaned back in my chair, crossing my arms over my chest. I was sick of practicing, sick of talking in general. For the past two days, most of my time consisted of J'nath alternately pumping me for information about my world and struggling to teach me Arkan. I did my best to be helpful with the former, but the latter was like pulling teeth: I quickly discovered that some words which rolled off J'nath's tongue with ease just clunked around in my mouth, not to mention that Arkan had absolutely nothing in common with English. I'd picked up Spanish a helluva lot faster than this nonsense.

J'nath shook his head. "The word is *ula*...thou keeps making the words too round," he chided me. "Sharper, faster, *that* is the proper way."

"I'm *trying*, dammit. Y'know, I really don't see what the big deal is, especially since you don't exactly speak proper English. All of them 'thees' and 'thous' and shit...nobody talks like that anymore."

He nodded in agreement, saying, "So I have noticed, but thou art still aware of the meaning, despite that. If thou mispronounces an Arkan word, it is quite a different matter. Now, we will try again."

"Later," I replied, "I need a break." I got up from the table and walked over to the ladder leading out of the cellar. We'd spent a great deal of time down there among the relics from my world as I practiced Arkan, and I was beginning to feel like the walls were closing in.

"Reshard, thou needs to work more on thy lessons. The Feast of Halitova is tomorrow evening and..."

"I know, I know. Christ, can't you back off for a few hours and let me have some time to myself?" Moving up the ladder, I pushed the trapdoor open and popped up into the main room of the house, then glanced back down at J'nath. The look of frustration on his face was fairly obvious. "When I'm ready to make a fool of myself again, I'll come back," I said, letting the trapdoor fall shut before he could object. Frankly, I didn't want to hear it: I was tired of listening to the man, and tired of being cooped up in the house. Physically, I was doing a lot better than when I'd first regained consciousness a few days before, but J'nath kept treating me with kid gloves. The time had come to break out, so to speak.

Nina sat near the hearth sewing something, and she'd put it aside when I came up from the cellar. While she couldn't understand what I'd said to her husband, she could read my mood well enough. *"Rhe nuktvei neda?"* she asked. Unfortunately, the only part of that I understood was *neda*: "wrong". Not really enough to get the gist of the sentence. She spoke again as I approached the front door, but the meaning was still lost on me -- I figured she was probably wondering where I was going, and responded appropriately.

"I'm running away from home," I said in English. "Don't wait up." I stepped outside into the warming Winter-to-Spring air and drew a deep breath. *Better, much better*, I thought, and started walking around the yard, the early-afternoon sun shining down on me. I really had no plans of running off -- where the Hell was I going to go? -- I just wanted to blow off some steam. It wasn't just the language problems that had me riled up: I'd had difficulty sleeping the last couple of nights, with most attempts ending with me sitting bolt upright in bed, a feeling of absolute dread constricting my chest. Other than a sense that these nightmares were worse than the usual ones I suffered from, I had no recollection of what they were about, though I was oddly certain that none of them involved that mystery man in black.

The other thing that had me on edge was the stuff J'nath told me about my new "home". The more I learned about Arkhein, the bleaker my future looked: the whole country, it seemed, was smack in the middle of the Dark Ages. No steam power or trains. No telegraphs. No gaslights. No industry of any sort. From the sound of it, J'nath's people had lost more than their lives to the Great Plague...they'd lost hope. In the centuries between the Fall and my arrival, nearly all of the original cities had crumbled to ruin, and basic knowledge of many things was forgotten. Most Arkans seemed to have acquired an innate fear of discovery, preferring to rely upon tried-and-true (and usually very simplistic) methods rather than experimenting and risking another disaster. Those same fears kept them confined to Arkhein's mainland (which, if I understood correctly, wasn't much bigger than the United States, territories and all), though a few islands no more than a couple of weeks from the coasts had been colonized.

Needless to say, J'nath was absolutely stunned when I told him what life was like in my world these days. He could barely conceive of some of the everyday things that I took for granted. It was strange to watch his reaction as I tried to explain what exactly a photograph was, or how a person could send and receive a telegraph message over hundreds of miles almost instantaneously. Sometimes I got the impression that he thought I was lying.

Two things that he had no doubt about, however, were my guns. While Arkans had developed gunpowder, no one had taken it any further than simple cannons or small fireworks, so my Peacemakers were unimaginably unique in this world. That fact also led to a sheepish confession on J'nath's part: the potshot he'd taken at me in the yard a few days before was actually an accident. He'd been studying my gun when he heard the commotion upstairs, and hadn't thought to put it down when he went to pursue me. Consequently, he'd slipped on a patch of ice and fallen, causing the gun to misfire when it hit the ground. Once the shock of the whole incident had worn off, J'nath christened my weapons with an Arkan name: *trit bakido*..."hand cannon." He also wisely decided to never touch them again.

Those guns were strapped to my hips as I paced around the yard, tapping my fingers against the worn grips in a nervous gesture. I'd become too accustomed over the years to always being on the move, so just sitting around like this was torture for me. I wanted to jump on a horse and ride away from there, no destination in mind, just movement...but once again, where the Hell was I gonna go in this world?

From the far end of the yard, a voice called out, "*Dandoa, d'ho*-Corrigan!" I looked over and saw the boy, Pietruvek, coming around the side of the house. In his hands was a large wooden bucket brimming with water -- I supposed that there must be a well of some sort behind the house. "No more *khimbol* today?" he asked.

"Beg pardon?" I replied, walking over to where he stood.

"*Khimbol...Padra* and thee speaking, so the words become part of thee. *Kedda?*"

I stared at the boy for a minute, trying to puzzle out what he was saying. Unlike his father, Pietruvek's English was pretty fractured. He could read and understand it fairly well, but he spoke it only marginally better than I spoke Arkan. That sometimes made our conversations a tad labored, like right now. "Teaching? Learning? Is that what you mean?"

"*Kai. Padra* speaks of Arkhein and thou learns, and *Padra* learns when thee speaks of Tarahein. No more today?"

I shrugged. "Maybe later, I've had enough *khimbol* for right now." Gesturing to the bucket, I said, "You need a hand with that, kid?"

"*K'sai, d'hojek*...the door." He nodded towards the nearby barn, and I stepped over and opened one of the wide front doors. The familiar smell of dry hay wafted out, along with an animal-like odor I couldn't place. The boy slipped in and I followed, leaving the door open so as to provide some light. The interior looked more or less like any barn back home, with a low-hanging loft and various tools and farm implements placed along the back wall. One side of the barn was outfitted with a wood-slatted cage about six feet long and three deep, a small flock of dun-colored birds fluttering about inside. Pietruvek rapped a knuckle against the slats, making a "kek-kek-kek" noise with his mouth as he did so. The birds clucked back in kind.

"So what do you call these things?" I asked. "They look like chickens."

"'Shikkens'? *Nee*, they called *m'rivek*...'dust-bird', for the color." He reached through a slot in the cage and pulled out a tin pan of water that had been sitting on a shelf. After dumping it out, he refilled it with fresh water and slid it back into place -- one of the *m'rivek* immediately flew up to the shelf to take a drink.

"Hell, I wish I'd known these guys were out here. I've been hankering for some fried eggs the last couple of mornings."

Pietruvek had picked up the bucket again and began moving towards the back of the barn, but he stopped and looked back at me after I'd spoken. "Eggs? Thou means..." He formed a circle with his thumb and forefinger, like an "okay" sign, then pointed at the cage, his eyes wide the entire time.

"Yeah, eggs. Crack 'em open and fry 'em up in some bacon grease...Lordy, that's Heaven!" My mouth watered at the thought of it.

"Tarans eat...*eggs*?" The boy was looking more disgusted by the second. "Unborn *vekaiben*?" At first I thought the kid simply didn't like eggs, then I suddenly realized that he was seriously offended by what was, to me, the best damn breakfast I could think of.

Great, Arkans have some sort of religious aversion to omelettes, I thought, but said aloud, "Naw, I'm just pulling your leg, kid. Had you going good for a minute, eh?"

He just nodded, looking like he didn't believe me one bit, then continued on with his chores. There was a stall about midway back, and Pietruvek unhooked a latch and stepped inside. When he did so, I saw what looked like a horse's head pop up for a moment. "Hey, I didn't know you guys had horses," I said, and approached the stall. I soon realized that, whatever the thing was, it certainly wasn't a horse. While it was roughly the same shape and size of one, the general structure of the head was more like an elk, though instead of antlers, it had a bony, serrated plate that ran from just above its nose all the way up to between its eyes. The animal's deep brown coat was much thicker than I'd ever seen on any horse either, with a ring of longer, lighter-colored hairs running from its withers down over its throat, neck, and breast in lieu of a mane. I was about to ask Pietruvek if you could ride the thing when the animal suddenly reared up, its large, split-toed hooves striking the stall's gate. I jumped back with a yelp as the boy grabbed hold of its long throat-hairs, speaking softly to calm it down. "What the Hell was that about?" I asked once he had it under control.

One hand still holding onto the animal, the other scratching behind its ear, Pietruvek simply responded, "Thou smells."

"I *smell?* Well, pardon me...what with all the excitement the last few days, I kind of forgot to take a bath."

He leaned his head against the animal's neck and laughed. "*Nee...nee,* thou smells *different.* It upsets her."

I nodded. It made sense, what with me not being native and all. "Hope it gets used to me, 'cause I ain't walking everywhere. That *is* the local transportation, right?"

"Trans...*kai,* we use *vessek* for riding, for pulling wagon and plow." He gave it a final pat on the neck before exiting the stall, the bucket now empty. "When thou art healed, we will have *khimbol* for riding," he said.

I wrinkled my nose at him and said, "I *know* how to ride, and I'm damn good at it too. Trust me, kid, there ain't nothin' new you can show me 'bout that."

He fell quiet for a moment. I thought perhaps I'd said that last thing a bit too harshly, but then he looked at me and asked, "What is 'kid'?" Actually, he said it more like "keed", as if he'd spent too much time south of Texas.

"Huh? Oh...it means child, youngster...y'know?" I shrugged. "You're obviously younger than me, and..."

"Only a little younger, it seems," Pietruvek replied, and pulled at a lock of hair curling against his shirt collar. "See? *Padra* already gave me his blessing, even though I will not be fifteen until mid-*Bensela.* Thy own looks about the same."

I shook my head, saying, "I already went though this the other day with your father: we don't do that where I come from." J'nath had been confused as to why a man my age only had hair long enough to cover the back of my neck -- it turned out that all Arkan adults grew their hair long as a sign of maturity. "But you've got a point. You're not gonna be a kid much longer, so I'll try to stop calling you such. Reckon I'll have to think of something else, then."

"Why not call me by my name?"

"Well, to be honest...I can't say it right. Believe me, I've been trying like Hell, but...I don't know, I keep tripping over it."

"It is easy name, simple name," he said as he walked over to a squat wooden bin. After trading his water bucket for a dry one, Pietruvek opened the lid and began sifting through the feed grain inside. "*Thy* name is not easy. Family name is easy, but first name..." He shook his head.

"What's wrong with 'Richard'?"

"Nothing wrong with thy name, just the middle noise is too..." He gestured at the empty air between us, as if trying to pluck out the right word. "It is too *Taran*. Arkan does not have that noise."

I didn't understand what he meant at first, then I remembered his odd pronunciation of "chickens" a few minutes before, and that J'nath had slurred a few other English words from time to time during our talks. Arkans apparently didn't have that *ch* sound in their language, so they kept substituting a *sh* sound instead. "*That's* why y'all keep calling me 'Reshard'?" I said, laughing.

Pietruvek nodded. "I cannot make it come out the way thou does...perhaps we have *khimbol* for that?"

"Yeah, sure, I'll *khimbol* the Hell outta you," I answered, "but that doesn't solve my end of the problem. Don't you have a short version of your name, like a nickname or something?" His brow furrowed slightly as he puzzled out what I meant, but before he could, I thought of a solution: "What if I called you 'Peter'?"

"'Peter'...a Taran name?"

"That's right. I used to have a friend named Peter. He was about a year or two older than you, actually, before he...before he died." I stared down at the barn floor, feeling suddenly embarrassed at the memory. I'd yelled at Reeves that last day for bringing up Peter Stewart's death, and here I was doing the same damn thing with a near-stranger. "Peter was a good kid," I told him quietly, "you would've liked him."

"Thou wishes to honor his memory, then? By passing his name on?"

"Yeah, I suppose. Mostly I thought of it because it sounds a little like Petru...Pit..."

"'Pietruvek'."

"Yeah, kind of like that."

"Then thou may call me 'Peter'." He smiled, then said, "Perhaps we should give thee an Arkan name."

The last thing I need is another alias, I thought, then began to say aloud that I'd stick with the name I already had, when the boy suddenly dropped the bucket, crying out something in Arkan. "What's the matter?" I asked, approaching the grain bin.

Pietruvek muttered a bit more in Arkan -- I think he was cursing -- then pointed to a dark lump in the grain. Actually, there were three or four lumps. "*Zemezi*...vermin," he explained, "all dead."

"It's only a few, the feed's probably okay." I pulled on a pair of worn leather gloves that I had in my coat pocket and pushed aside a handful of grain, revealing about a dozen more of the things laying beneath -- they looked like tailless squirrels. "Christ, did you folks put out some poison 'round here?"

"*Kai*, some small bags of *agiri* powder, but not near food. Be *bruhzod* to do that."

"Maybe they ate it before getting in the bin, then dropped dead. Best chuck all this to be sure."

The boy sighed and shook his head. "A waste."

"I know, but you don't want to poison the livestock by accident, kid...Peter." I shrugged. "Forgive me, I'm in a transitional period."

He nodded and said with a smirk, "In punishment, thou has to help carry this." We each grabbed hold of the chest-high bin and moved it outside to a trash pile behind the barn, upending it to dump out the questionable grain. I counted at least thirty dead *zemezi* as they tumbled out, their furry stomachs bloated from their last meal.

*   *   *   *   *   *

A few hours later, I had myself a visitor: the doctor (or *z'kira*, to use the Arkan term) who'd bandaged me up a couple days before stopped by to see how well I was healing up. Her name was Beva Kali, and to my dismay, her bedside manner hadn't improved since I'd last seen her. She had a tendency to poke and prod and do whatever she damn well pleased in her efforts to cure whatever ails you. Lucky me.

Despite her rudeness, she was surprisingly capable. I'd never been looked over by a lady doctor before, and that made me a mite wary, but I must admit that she put most of the men that had patched me up in the past to shame. J'nath told me that, in Arkhein, the healing arts were primarily performed by women, and ol' Doc Kali had me thinking that maybe it wasn't such a bad arrangement. As she changed the bandages, I could see that my wounds were coming along nicely, though they remained a bit raw and jagged around the edges, as if something had been digging at them once the bullets had passed through. I had an idea of what the cause was, but I didn't even want to think its name.

After she redressed my wounds, I sat on the bed while *Z'kira* Kali threw a seemingly endless barrage of questions at me. Apparently, she'd given me a thorough check-over while I'd been unconscious, and the physical differences between Arkans and myself had fascinated her so much that she'd concocted some really weird theories about Tarans and why we were the way we were. Most of the questions she asked me were pretty bizarre, and I began to wonder if J'nath was omitting parts when he translated them for me: "How did thy hair and eyes become brown?" "Why dost thou have four extra teeth in the back of thy mouth?" "Is all that hair growing on thy face and body to keep thee warm?" A few questions were so embarrassing that I began to flush red, and I was surprised she didn't ask me any questions about *that*.

The only thing I flat-out refused to talk about was my scars. I'd collected my fair share during my life as an outlaw -- a bullet hole here, a knife wound there -- plus there were others I'd acquired long before then. They covered my back and shoulders, with a few more on my arms and upper legs, and one that ran down beside my left eye, thin and white. Each time she reached out to touch one of my scars, I twisted away from her, but that only made her more persistent. It finally reached a point where I grabbed her by her wrists and shoved her away from me. "That's it, we're finished," I snapped. "No more questions, no more poking and prodding. Get her out of here, J'nath."

Z'kira Kali looked from me to J'nath, puzzled. The two of them talked for a moment before J'nath said, "Reshard, she just wishes to know what happened to thee. I *kedda* that it is making thee uncomfortable, but..."

"But nothing. I'm *done*." I grabbed my shirt and pulled it on. "I've put up with this for long enough. I ain't got no problem with her changing bandages, but if she wants to ask me a bunch of annoying questions along with that, then forget it." I looked straight into the doctor's eyes. "Leave...*adai*. You get me?"

J'nath spoke softly to her, glancing at me occasionally out of the corner of his eye. After a minute or so, she left my room, and J'nath closed the door after her. Once that door was shut, he let loose on me, saying, "What is the matter with thee? She has done everything in her power to help thee, and thou does nothing in return but show hostility. She is only curious about thy scars...and to be honest, so am I."

"I don't give a damn. It's something I don't talk about, so don't ask. *Ever*." I turned away from him and stared at the wall, trying to ignore the throbbing pulse of pain coming from the wound on my left temple.

"Why?"

Without thinking, I reached up and rubbed the two-inch-long scar by my eye with my fingertips. I could feel a vague sensation of pressure, but for the most part, the area was numb. It hadn't changed in over ten years. "Let's just say that I had a really lousy childhood," I answered, still staring at the wall.

J'nath had no response for that. I think I'd scared him, which was fine by me, so long as he left me alone about it. Maybe someday, I'd tell him, but not now.

It wasn't the sort of thing you could get out of a person by pestering them.

* * * * * *

I had a harder time than usual getting to sleep that night. I just laid there, wide awake, more than a little scared at the thought of going into the village the next day for the Halitova party. I had the same knot-in-the-gut feeling that I always got before pulling a job, a nagging sensation that it wouldn't work, that it would all just get blown to Hell. Of course, it didn't help that the last time I'd gotten those feelings, I was *right*.

My thoughts kept wandering over that day again and again, one of the last sane days in my memory. They flitted from the boy with the toy pistol, to the old doctor with the laudanum, to the people screaming for my head, to that damned sheriff, then back to the boy again. It occurred to me then that I didn't even know the boy's name, and it bothered me. I'd killed lots of people before without knowing their names, but this time it wasn't right, he shouldn't have died unknown like that. "He shouldn't have died at all," I whispered to the darkness, the knot cinching tighter within me.

I eventually drifted off to sleep, but it sure as Hell wasn't easy.

CHAPTER 6

The day of Halitova was the warmest yet: nearly all the snow had melted, and some of the trees near the house were beginning to show the tiniest amount of bluish-green buds. If I closed my eyes, I could imagine that I was standing outside my boyhood home in New York on a pleasant April day, a clear blue sky overhead and a soft breeze tousling my hair. But when I opened them again, blue skies gave way to pale violet, and I suddenly didn't feel so warm inside.

J'nath and his family began preparing for the festival early on in the afternoon, with Nina putting the finishing touches on a dress she'd made especially for the day, while Pietruvek and his father coached me through a bit more Arkan. At one point I shook my head and declared their little crash-course useless. "People are probably going to be firing questions at me too damn fast for me to understand," I said, "and if you guys aren't with me, I won't even be able to tell them so."

"I can help that," the boy replied. "Say this: *Nee kedda.*"

"Um...*nee kid*...no, no...*kedda. Nee kedda.* Okay, what did I just say?"

"'I do not understand.'"

"You had me say the word, but I don't know what..."

J'nath began to laugh and waved a hand to cut me off. "That *is* the word, Reshard. '*Nee kedda*' means 'I do not understand.'"

"Now why the Hell didn't I think of that?" I muttered. I'd run into a few foreigners in the past that were in the same position I was now, and sometimes the only comprehensible words *they* knew were "No speak

English"...short, clear, and to the point. Patting him on the back, I said to Pietruvek, "My boy, you're a genius."

When Nina was done with her dress, she modeled it for all of us to see, and I couldn't help but stare. While it was rather simple, the neckline on it plunged down lower than I was used to seeing respectable women wear. "Um, shouldn't that be a bit higher?" I asked, and held my hand up to the level of my Adam's apple. "'Bout to here, maybe?"

J'nath looked, but apparently saw nothing wrong. "It seems fine to me," he answered, then stepped behind her and slipped his arms around her waist with a smile. She laughed a little and turned her head to give her husband a peck on the cheek.

"But I can almost see her...you know..." I could feel myself blushing -- I wasn't exactly a prude, but there's some things you shouldn't blurt out regarding a man's wife, especially with their son standing right next to you. J'nath still didn't get it, so I let it drop and did my best to not let my eyes linger.

Nina had another, more tame surprise just for me: since my original shirt had bit the dust not long after I'd arrived, she copied the general pattern of it and made me a brand-new one, even going so far as to salvage the buttons from the original. The overall result was an interesting blend of Arkan and American. I was rather touched when she gave it to me, especially considering that we'd exchanged very few words so far due to the language barrier -- unlike her husband and son, Nina spoke no English at all. "Thank you...I mean, *k'sai*," I said, catching myself and saying the phrase in proper Arkan, then went to change into my new duds.

We left the house not long before sunset in a horse-drawn wagon...or rather, *vessek*-drawn. I tried to help J'nath as he hitched it up to the wagon, but the animal kept swinging its head at me, nearly cutting me once or twice with the plating on it snout. Guess it hadn't gotten used to my smell yet. Even with me sitting as far back in the wagon as I could, the stupid thing snorted and shook its head the whole time.

The village of Betedek, on a whole, was rather unimpressive. The buildings were mostly stone, with a few wooden additions tacked onto them. They all had a worn-out feel to them, an ancient look that I'd never seen in any place back home. Actually, there was very little that I could compare to any town I'd seen before. Sure, they had a blacksmith and a livery, but the majority of the storefronts left me scratching my head. Maybe if I could've read the signs, it would have made more sense, but at a glance, I couldn't tell one from another.

The people, of course, were beyond comparison. Everyone I spotted had the same gray, ashen complexion, although there were a few lighter or darker variations -- perhaps the Arkan equivalent of tanned skin, I couldn't say for sure. Just as I was checking out the locals, however, they were most certainly checking *me* out: more than a few heads turned as we trundled by in the wagon, and after a while I started feeling like a geek in a carnival sideshow. I scrunched down and turned the collar of my coat up, and if I'd still had my hat, I would've jammed it down past my ears for good measure. Pietruvek, sitting beside me, couldn't help but notice me trying to hide, and asked if something was the matter.

"I don't think I want to do this anymore," I told him, still scrunched down.

"Getting nervous?"

"As a matter of fact, yes."

"Why? This is party. Have fun!"

"How the Hell am I supposed to have fun with everybody staring at me?"

"Should have thought of that before we left home," he replied, smiling.

We left the wagon near the livery, then walked to the main square, which was ablaze with torches and paper lanterns, even though there was still sufficient light in the sky to do without them. People were laughing, talking, drinking, and having what appeared to be a glorious time.

That all stopped the moment I entered the square: every conversation ground to a halt, every cup raised to lips dropped down, and every eye in the place focused straight on me. Needless to say, I wanted to crawl into a hole and pull it in behind me. Then a murmur started up through the crowd, and I shot a quick look to J'nath standing beside me, silently pleading for him to take some of this pressure off. Lucky for me, he got the message, and stepped forward to speak to the crowd. He talked for a few minutes, gesturing towards me once or twice -- I picked up a little on what he was saying, but not much -- then he looked back at me and cocked his head in the direction of the crowd, as if to say, "Okay, Richard, it's your show now."

My legs felt like jelly when I stepped forward. Good Lord, even robbing banks didn't make me this nervous. *What the Hell am I supposed to do?* I thought. *I'm just an outlaw way out of his element, not a politician. I can't even think of anything to say that they'd understand.* I could feel time ticking away as I stood there, and pretty soon, that murmur started up again. *You're losing them...do something, you moron!*

I straightened up my backbone as best I could, clasped my hands together the way J'nath had shown me when I met Yaved N'dahl, and bowed deeply. *"Dandoa, Betedek,"* I called out as clearly as my bone-dry throat would allow, then paused as I tried to construct a sentence in my head. It seemed best to at least thank them for inviting me to the party, so in halting Arkan I said, *"K'sai a zii abahnum,"* which I realized as soon as the words left my mouth translated to, "Thank you for my coming." Not the most intelligent-sounding phrase I'd ever spoken, but Hell, I was operating with a handicap here.

There was no reaction at first, until a woman about twenty feet away from me returned the gesture. *"Dandoa, Reshard Corrigan,"* she said to me, smiling. From there it went like a wave, spreading out until nearly everyone had bowed and welcomed me to the village, their words spoken with much more precision and clarity than my own. They began to come towards me after that, smiling and pulling me into their celebration like I was an old friend, not a stranger with odd clothes and an even odder vocabulary. I turned my head to check and see if J'nath or Pietruvek was there to play translator, and was relieved to see that the boy was right at my elbow. He grinned and clapped me on the back, saying, "Not so bad, *kai*?"

"Yeah, Peter, maybe it isn't so bad as I thought. Still not totally relaxed, but not so bad."

The night soon became a whirlwind blur of activity: people pulling me around the village to show me this and that, talking to someone or another with Pietruvek or his father sandwiched between us translating as fast as he could, food and drink of all sorts being offered up for me to sample...my head was spinning after a while. Everyone I met was quite cordial, and though a few people seemed to do their best to keep their distance, it appeared that my fears of someone giving me trouble were unfounded. I was surprised at the curiosity shown by those who did approach me, considering what J'nath had told me about most Arkans' fear of the unknown. I'd show them some little trinket that crossed over with me, and they'd run off to fetch somebody else so they could see it, which would start the show all over again. The guns, obviously, were a subject of fascination, as was my pocket watch -- Arkans didn't have clocks, instead getting a general reckoning of time by the position of the sun, so explaining what a watch was for took a while -- but the thing that held their attention the most was, of all things, my hair. Virtually every Arkan I'd seen that night had either black or whitish-blond hair (though I did spot a few fiery redheads scattered in the crowd), and judging by *Z'kira* Kali's questions the day before, that was about as varied as they got. People kept coming up to me and running their hands through that unruly brown mess on top of my head, and one woman even wanted to cut off a lock, but I refused. I didn't want to be bald by the end of the night.

A few hours into the party, someone asked if I could demonstrate my guns. I was hesitant at first, not wanting to waste precious bullets on target shooting, but enough people kept insisting that I gave in to their request. We set up a bench along a stone wall for safety's sake, then laid out some small clay pots on it. I stood a good fifteen feet from the targets, hands dangling beside my hips. My shoulder wound was aching a bit, but I didn't think these folks would notice if my fast draw was a mite slower than normal. "Okay, folks, this is gonna be loud...and for the love of God, stay back," I said, waving at a few onlookers that kept creeping in for a better view. J'nath translated the warnings for me until they sunk in, and then gave me a nod. I nodded back, saying, "Alright then, on three: one...two...*three!*" I slapped leather, both guns whipping up and barking off three shots apiece. More than a few people screamed and clapped their hands over their ears -- Hell, I tried to warn them -- and once the smoke cleared, they could see the results of all that noise. We'd lined up six targets, and while I only managed to hit four, the whole spectacle was impressive enough for the crowd to let out a cheer and stamp their feet. Their admiration was beginning to give me a swelled head, and I twirled my guns a couple times before returning them to their holsters. Not far away, J'nath was grinning like a proud papa.

As some folks picked up the remains of my demonstration (and made souvenirs of those potshards, I'd wager), a wiry man sidled up to me, gesturing over to another part of the square and talking at a pace I simply couldn't keep up with. I finally got him to pause after a minute of two so I could wave J'nath over, then let him start up again. Turned out the man wanted to know if I'd like to try my hand at a different sort of target. "There is a *faask* board set up over there," J'nath explained, pointing in the direction the man indicated. "It is a very simple game, just..." He pantomimed tossing something with the flick of his wrist.

"Sure, sounds like fun." I began to follow the man, while J'nath got snagged into a conversation with someone else -- no big deal, I figured, a translator wouldn't be necessary for this. There were already a few guys playing when we got over to the other side of the square, and they stopped to wave me over the moment they saw me. The game itself looked simple enough at first glance: a wooden board with geometric patterns of varying shapes and sizes painted on it was nailed to a post, and upon my approach, one of the men had been throwing small, dagger-like objects at the shapes. "It's like darts, right?" I asked, then realized that they couldn't understand me, so I picked up one of the daggers that had been embedded in a nearby stump, hefted it a little to get a feel for the weight, then threw it at the small square in the center of the board. "Alright, bull's-eye on the first shot!" I crowed, but quickly discovered that it must not be the object of the game, as my hosts were laughing and shaking their heads. Another man removed the dagger from the target, then shooed me back a couple of feet so he could take his shot. His toss hit a triangular mark near the top of the board, which made the other men groan -- I thought he'd made a mistake as well until I saw the smug look on the man's face. He then proceeded to throw one dagger after another, hitting the board in what looked like, to me at least, a totally random pattern. "I am definitely not getting this," I muttered as I stood on the sidelines, hoping that the object of the game would eventually come clear.

In between their turns, the men drank from some wooden mugs sitting nearby, and after standing around them for a bit, I noticed it smelled kind of like beer. "Hey, where'd you get that?" I asked one of them, a heavyset gentleman with thinning black hair. "*Vahd rhe ulum*?"

He cocked an eyebrow at my butchered Arkan, then flashed a grin and handed me his own mug -- guess he had no qualms about drinking from the same glass as me. I took a sip, and discovered that the reddish beer didn't taste as familiar as it smelled. There was a strange bitterness to it, as well as something else I couldn't identify. Not necessarily unpleasant, but certainly not what I was expecting. I was about to hand the mug back when I noticed how intently the man was watching me, along with a few others standing near us. "*Ulum, d'ho-*Corrigan!" one of them called out, raising his own mug.

I glanced down at the beer. "Well, when in Rome...or Arkhein..." I said, and proceeded to knock back the whole thing. That got a cheer out of them. My drinking buddy waved to a girl passing by with a round-bottomed pitcher, who promptly refilled my mug. I knocked that one back with even more gusto than the first -- after the initial taste, the bitterness became less noticeable. Coupled with the fact that I'd been dying for a drink the past few days, that beer was the best thing about the night so far.

Midway through my third mug, the men let me have another go at the game. I'd been watching intently, and thought for sure that I had the rhythm of it down, so I was eager to show them what a fast learner I was. It seemed to depend on what shape you hit first, so I picked up a few daggers and tossed them in a pattern I'd seen one of the other men make. The more I threw, the louder the shouts from my fellow players became, and by the time I'd let the fifth and final dagger fly, my drinking buddy was clapping me on the back in approval. "Yes! I got it right!" I yelled, and threw my hands up in the air...then fell flat on my face as my knees suddenly buckled. A couple of people laughed, but I didn't find the situation very funny: it felt like all the strength had run out of my body. They managed to pull me to my feet, but my legs were wobbly, plus a thin sheen of sweat was forming on my skin. "Too much excitement, I guess," I mumbled as they tried to make me sit down. Truth to tell, I didn't want to sit: the crowd in the square was beginning to feel a mite thick to me, and I just wanted to get away from it.

Shrugging off my helpers, I walked away from the party, thoughts of heading back to J'nath's house on my mind. Trouble was, I couldn't recall just how to get back there from where I was. I stripped off my coat as I wandered down a deserted avenue, confused and overheated, and eventually stopped and leaned against one of the stone buildings, the wall feeling gloriously cool though my sweat-soaked shirt. I could see the edge of the square from where I stood, but I was too tired to walk back.

After a while, I saw a young woman with vibrant red hair leave the party and come my way, a concerned tone in her voice as she approached -- I guess I looked as out-of-sorts as I felt. "I'm alright, honey, don't worry," I said, and stood up a little straighter to emphasize it. She didn't appear to believe me, though, because she reached up and pressed a hand to my cheek. When she did, the top of her dress shifted slightly, letting just a bit more skin show. That's damn-near scandalous, you know that?" I said, unable to take my eyes off the small amount of cleavage laid bare before me. As she continued to touch my flushed face, talking in soft, alien tones, I began to feel a different sort of heat rise up within me. "You Arkan women...y'all ain't got no sense of decorum, I swear. Where I come from, women got to stay covered up, top to bottom...'less they want something..." I dropped my coat and leaned close to her, my stubbly cheek brushing against her smooth, ashen skin, then kissed her gently just below her ear. She gasped and tried to pull away, but I grabbed her by the shoulders and brought her even closer. "Shh, it's alright, honey. I won't hurt you," I whispered in her ear as I played with her hair -- she reminded me another redhead I'd known, the memory of whom just served to stoke the flame higher. "Just stay with me a few more minutes, that's all I want." I tilted her face up towards mine and kissed her, then slid my hands from her shoulders and down her back. "Been a long time..."

The woman pushed against my chest, sobbing, struggling. "What?" I snapped. "Why are you crying? Do you think I'm ugly or something? Huh?" I gave her a good shake. "Well, *tough shit*! You shouldn't be walkin' around dressed like that if you don't want men like me to notice ya!" She tried to twist out of my grip, but only succeeded in ripping her dress, exposing even more flesh for all the world to see. "That's enough! Stop!" I said, trying in vain to remember the Arkan equivalent. She ignored me, and instead began to pound on my chest, screaming something unknown as she did so. It made no difference to me until her fist connected with my injured shoulder, sending white-hot needles of pain shooting through my arm. I let go of her as my right hand went numb and began to spasm. She recoiled from me, a look of pure revulsion on her face as I cradled my arm against my chest. "*Zo rihn tu m'taka*!" she spat at me, tears in her eyes, then ran back towards the square. I watched her go, the lust I'd felt moments ago slowly twisting into anger and hate. Sweat was rolling down my face now, stinging my eyes. I wiped it away without a thought and began to stagger after her.

Just as before, all eyes were upon me when I stepped into the square, but I thought I could see something new in those eyes: fear, disgust, hatred. I just shot it all back at them and looked around for the woman. I finally spotted her on the far end of the square, huddled in the midst of a few other Arkans, including J'nath. He caught sight of me before the others did and approached me, saying, "What in Avisar's name is wrong with thee? Ari says thou attacked her, tried to force thyself upon her..."

"Little bitch asked for it," I growled back.

"I doubt that she did...as would her husband, I am sure."

"Well, *obviously* her man ain't providin' for her, or else she wouldn't be paradin' around dressed like a whore when the cowhands are in town." I looked at her when I said it, and while the words may not have been clear, the woman's aforementioned husband must have picked up on my meaning well enough, because the next thing I knew, I'd been knocked on my ass by a very pissed-off-looking man. He stood over me, his long white-blond hair falling over his face, and goaded me to get up. I obliged him, putting up my fists and setting my feet into a boxing stance. "You wanna dance, you bastard?" I taunted. "C'mon, let's go!"

J'nath stepped between us, yelling something in Arkan. He then talked to the man for a moment before turning his attention to me. "Reshard, thou art acting like a madman. I think thou may be ill, thy face is..."

"I'm fine. Leave me be." My fists were still up, ready to fight.

"*Nee*, we are going to find *Z'kira* Kali so she..."

"What, so she can poke at me some more? To Hell with you, I'm not going."

"Reshard, I heard about thou collapsing not long ago, and the way thou art acting at the moment, I am afraid something may be very wrong with thee." He reached out to force down my fists. "Please, we should..."

"I said...I'm...*not...GOING!*" I pulled my fist back and gave him a hard left to the jaw. J'nath didn't even see it coming. Drops of spittle flew from his lips as his head snapped to the side. He stumbled and fell to the ground, sprawling out on the cobblestones paving the square. Staring down at him, I was soon aware of how quiet it had become, and I could feel all those alien eyes staring at me, burning through me. "*What the Hell are all you people looking at?*" I screamed at them, blood pounding behind my own eyes.

One of the men nearby helped J'nath to his feet, a deep-purplish bruise already forming on his jawline. "Reshard, calm down," he pleaded. "I know that..."

"Like Hell you do! A few days ago, I woke up on another goddam *planet*, J'nath! You don't have the slightest clue what it's like to know that you're *completely alone* in the world, or to have people constantly staring at you and thinking, 'Dear God, would you look at *that* freak!'" I waved my hands at the crowd surrounding us. "Is this what I have to look forward to for the rest of my life? Huh? Being the main attraction in a carnival sideshow?" J'nath opened his mouth to speak, but I cut him off. "*No!* No more lies, no more fancy talk! I'm *sick* to *death* of hearing it! You and your damned Crossroad *ruined my life.* You took my whole *world* from me, just when I thought I had nothing left to lose! You...y-you..." My hands clutched at my suddenly-rolling stomach as I fell to my knees, my jaw clamped tight against the pain. A hand reached out to me, but I jerked away, yelling, "Don't touch me! I swear to God, I'll *kill* the next man that comes near me!" I glared at the crowd, my soul brimming with anger. "Do you really think some goddam *party* is gonna make up for me having to spend the rest of my life with you backwards people?"

J'nath gawked at me, his mouth moving, but no intelligible sound came out. I sneered back at him and said, "What's the matter? Did I dare to *offend* you? Well, let me remove myself from your sight before you decide to make my life any *worse!*" I staggered to my feet and did my best to exit in a dignified fashion, despite the agonizing pain in my guts. The crowd parted before me like the Red Sea, afraid to come within arm's-length of me -- they may not have understood a word I'd said, but screaming is screaming. That, and I *did* deck J'nath.

I was out of sight of the square by the time I collapsed on a bench out front of some shop, my legs shaking too damn much to go any further. I lay down, arms crossed over my gut, and stared up at the unfamiliar stars. Before long, they began to waver as my eyesight kept slipping in and out of focus. I blinked, rubbed my eyes, blinked again...no good. Coupled with the pain I was in, I was beginning to become a little concerned. "It'll pass, it'll pass," I mumbled, "just need to relax, not have people...*touching* me all the time..."

A noise echoed down the empty street, but not from the end leading towards the square -- it sounded like boots scraping against the cobblestones. I leapt to my unsteady feet, heart pounding, and stared into the darkness. No one was in sight. "Hello?" I called out, then thought, *Shit...wrong word, jackass.* I tried again in Arkan, "*Dandoa*? Who's there?" All the while, my hands slid shakily down to my guns.

More noise, this time accompanied by a hint of movement, then I saw a dark figure step out of the shadows, his features hidden by a black hooded cloak. "I'm dreaming again, that's got to be it," I reasoned, but I wasn't as sure as I sounded: this newcomer may have been dressed like the mystery man, but his posture was definitely different, more tense. The man called out to me in Arkan and began to approach, but I threw up a hand and said, "Hold it right there, fella." It didn't occur to me that he wouldn't know what those words meant any more than he'd know "Hello", but that didn't stop me from continuing. "Look, whoever you are, just stay back, okay? You picked the wrong time to mess with me."

Without any hesitation, the man repeated whatever he'd said before and pushed aside his cloak, revealing a massive sword hanging from the left side of his brown leather belt -- he rested his hand on the pommel as he barked something unintelligible at me. My blood turned to ice at the sight of the thing, and the ground felt like it was swaying beneath my feet. "Don't come any closer!" I hollered, making no attempt to keep the panic out of my voice. He kept coming, of course, now reaching across with his right hand to grasp the sword's handle and slowly draw it out. *Looks like I'm not gonna get anywhere by talking,* I thought, then drew one of my pistols and fired.

The sound of the gunshot echoed off the buildings around us, the muzzle flaring bright for a moment as the bullet screamed out of the barrel and plowed straight into the stranger's left shoulder, the force of it knocking him flat on his back. I waited for the guy to get up, move, do *something*, but he just lay there like he was dead. Admittedly, I didn't know much about Arkan anatomy, but I wouldn't have thought a shoulder wound could kill one. I steeled myself and approached the body, my gun still drawn. The cloak was splayed open now, revealing what might have been a uniform: a thick black tunic belted over a matching shirt, brown leather bracers covering the shirt cuffs, a fine pair of black boots, and blue-gray trousers with a brass-colored stripe running down both legs. A second belt ran from his right shoulder to his left hip, presumably to help support that monster of a sword -- there was an emblem of some sort affixed at the shoulder, but I couldn't tell if it was a badge of office or merely a fancy buckle for the rig. The hood still obscured part of his face, so I knelt down and pulled it back. The man was a dark-haired Arkan (no big surprise) with red, raw-looking scars carved into the left side of his face, radiating from the eye socket. Thankfully, he wore an eye patch that obscured most of the damage. "Damn, boy, what did you do to deserve *that*?" I said to his motionless form.

That's when he opened his good eye and saw me. His face twisted into a snarl of anger as he chopped the edge of his hand into my Adam's apple. I fell backward, clutching my throat with my free hand and gasping for air. He was on me a second later, knocking the gun from my grasp as I tried to raise it, then yanking its mate from the holster and tossing it aside -- both weapons went skittering across the cobblestones, far from my reach. Before I knew it, he was sitting on my chest and drawing out his sword fully this time -- it was a double-edged nightmare in black metal that looked like it could cleave me in two easily. Pressing the blade against my throat, he leaned down towards my face and growled something that I took to be a threat of bodily harm if I moved, then eased back and hollered, "*Tehr-hidmon!*" He waited a moment or two, then yelled something else. Just what he was saying didn't matter to me at the time, I was too busy trying to draw breath. Between him crushing my chest with his weight and his sword coming close to slicing my jugular open -- not to mention my guts twisting painfully -- I thought for sure I'd be dead before anyone answered the man's call.

The sound of approaching footsteps caught my attention. "Help," I wheezed, "this crazy bastard's trying to kill me..."

"*Het!*" the stranger ordered as he pressed the blade down harder -- a trickle of blood ran down the side of my neck, and my throat felt suddenly cold. I could see nothing but the man sitting on me, but judging by his expression and what I could hear around me, I figured quite a few people were now clustered around us. Someone began to speak, and I recognized the voice as belonging to Yaved N'dahl -- made sense, he had been shouting for the *tehr-hidmon*, though I didn't know why. He and the stranger conversed for what seemed like forever before I heard another familiar voice chime in. "J'nath!" I shouted as best I could, not giving a damn anymore about my throat getting cut. "Oh God, J'nath, please help me!"

"Reshard, for once, wilt thou please *be quiet*." His words were tinged with a note of anger that I'd never heard come from him before, and I was suddenly glad that I couldn't see his face clearly. I did my best to lie still and be patient as J'nath spoke to my captor, confident that this mess would be cleared up in a few minutes. Sure enough, the man soon removed the blade from my throat and stood up, stepping back to give me room to get to my feet as well.

"About damn time," I said to J'nath as I rubbed the spot where I'd been cut -- it wasn't deep, but it hurt like Hell, the blood trickling between my fingers for a minute before it finally clotted. "What took so long?"

J'nath glared at me. "Dost thou remember when I told thee about the Kana-Semeth?"

"You've told me about a lot of things, I don't remember them all. What the Hell's a Kana-Semeth?"

"They are soldiers...constables. They travel the across the land enforcing the Laws." Someone behind me grabbed my wrists and quickly bound them behind my back. "And thou just shot one."

All the blood drained out of my face as what he was saying sank in. I twisted my head around and saw Mr. One-Eye standing behind me with a very satisfied look on his face, both of my guns tucked beneath his belt. I whipped back around to J'nath, saying, "Aren't you gonna talk him outta this? I thought he was *attacking* me, I didn't know he was a lawman! It was a mistake!"

"A *mistake*? Was *this* a mistake as well?" He gestured to the ugly lump I'd put on his jaw. "Thou hast made a *bruhzod* of thyself tonight, and shamed both myself *and* my family. I told these people that thou art a good man, and thou hast made a *liar* out of me in front of the entire village!" His cheeks took on a violet-red tone as they became flush. "Were I vengeful man, I would not have told the Kana-Semeth to be lenient when he decides upon the proper punishment for thee."

Punishment? Visions of dancing on the end of a rope filled my head as I pleaded, "For God's sake, you can't just *leave* me with this guy!" I tried to twist my hands free of the bindings, but it was no use. J'nath ignored me and spoke with the lawman for a moment more, then turned away from the two of us and began to disappear into the crowd. I saw Nina and Pietruvek join him before I completely lost sight of the man -- I called out to them, begging for help, and the boy actually hesitated for a moment, but his father took him firmly by the arm and pulled him away from me. The milling people soon swallowed them up, and I was alone with a very angry lawman.

The Kana-Semeth snapped something at me and gave me a shove from behind. I stumbled forward on wobbly legs for a few feet, then collapsed to my knees as the ever-present pain in my stomach became blinding, my thoughts quickly turning from death by hanging to being torn apart from the inside out. I could hear the people around me talking in worried tones as I knelt there, head hanging low and sweat pouring down my face. The lawman must have thought I was faking, though, because he reached down, grabbed my shirt collar, and gave me a good shake.

Big mistake. My guts suddenly seized up, and I emptied the contents of my stomach all over the cobblestones. The sight and stench of my own bile was enough to make me puke once more before I thankfully passed out cold.

CHAPTER 7

I awoke the next morning feeling as if I'd been dragged a hundred miles behind a freight train: my skin felt blistered and raw, and the pain in my gut had spread out to encompass my whole body, from my burning eyes to the soles of my feet. Both my brain and my joints were filled with ground glass, and I could feel my heart straining with every beat. At first, I couldn't remember what had happened the night before, then I recalled my little run-in with the local law, and I quickly realized that I was in a heap of trouble.

Slowly, I opened my eyes and saw that I'd been laid out on the floor of a stone-walled room, a thin blanket spread out beneath me. I guessed that I must be in what passed for a jail cell in Arkhein. The room was empty save for myself, with a heavy wooden door reinforced with iron bands standing between me and freedom -- a small barred window was set in it near the top, allowing the morning light to pour in. I half-wished it wasn't there, because the light clawed at my eyes every time I looked in the door's general direction. *Dear God,* I thought, *I've never had a hangover like this before.*

I spied a bowl of water within arm's reach, and carefully pulled it towards me with shaking hands, afraid that I'd spill it all over the floor before I drank any. Once I had a good hold on it, I gulped it down greedily, eager to wash the sour taste out of my mouth. After about three or four swallows, however, my stomach rolled violently and I puked up every last drop. When there was nothing left, I began to dry-heave so hard I thought I might cough up my liver. Mercifully, the spasm didn't last for too long, but it left me feeling even more wasted than I'd been beforehand.

I lay on the floor in a stupor, barely noticing when the cell door opened not long after. The lawman entered without a word, crossing the small room in two quick strides to kneel down beside me. I stared up at him with glassy, half-closed eyes -- I suppose I must have looked dead, because he soon leaned close to my face to see if I was still breathing, then fumbled around my neck for a pulse. "I'm alive...barely," I somehow managed to tell him, although my voice was almost inaudible to my own ears.

"*Hu zo kef vahd zo rihn?*" he asked. I just stared at him blankly, not entirely sure of what he'd said. Undaunted, he tried again: "*Hu zo kirved ke mihrrud urt abir?*"

"I don't speak Arkan very well," I croaked, trying to sit up. "*Nee kedda Arkan.* If you want to talk, get...guh...*AAAGH!*" My guts suddenly felt like they were being yanked out through my navel. I curled up on the floor, my knees almost touching my chin, and prayed to God to make it stop. The Kana-Semeth spoke rapidly to me as I tried to ride out this new wave of agony, but the meaning of his words was lost on me. He must have finally realized that talking was useless, for he fell silent and began to act upon me without warning or apology: he untucked my shirt and proceeded to jab me below the ribs with his fingers, as if searching for something. All I got out of it was more pain. When his probing reached the small of my back, it felt as if I'd been stabbed with a jagged piece of glass, and I let out a scream so loud that the lawman jumped back a bit, spitting out what definitely sounded like a curse. I didn't really care about that at the moment, I had my own problems. Christ, what was wrong with me? I hadn't felt this bad since I'd arrived in this crazy place...

Sweat broke out on my forehead anew. Oh my God, it couldn't be that...as long as that stone's in the Crossroad...no, please, God, no... "Gotta get outta here," I gasped. "The doctor will know, or J'nath...I gotta get out..." I struggled to stand up, to reach the open door, but I barely had the strength to crawl. The lawman jabbered something, probably trying to figure out why I'd become so animated, then he grabbed my arms and pinned me to the floor with minimal effort. "No, you don't understand," I said to him, "the plague...I've got the plague..." I didn't know if that was true, but what else could it have been? I remembered how pale and shaky Reeves had become before I'd left him, and I certainly felt as bad as he'd looked then.

"*Narras, Taran,*" he told me, the second word coming out full of hatred and derision. I'd heard that tone of voice from men with badges countless times before, and it was a weird sort of comfort to know that some things never changed. He stood up, wincing a bit and rubbing his left shoulder -- I'd briefly forgotten that I'd shot him the night before -- then glared down at me one last time before exiting the cell, the door slamming shut behind him.

"Come back...please...don't let me die in here..." I stretched an arm out towards the door as I begged, but there was no answer, just dead silence. I had to get out of there somehow, but I felt so tired, so sick...just had to rest a moment, then I'd...I didn't know, but I'd think of something.

Just a moment, that was all I needed.
Rest up, and then...
Then...

* * * * * *

"*Aivit, Taran.*"
Huh? Whozat?
"*Zo git za, m'taka? Aivit!*"
Speak English, dammit. Ain't makin' no sense.
"Hmph...*zo sanrud a jad...*"
"*GAAH! FUCK!*" I sat bolt upright as the lawman dumped a bucket of cold water onto my head, shocking me back to full consciousness. I coughed and gagged until I

thought my head would split, while he crouched beside me with a smug look on his face as I tried to pull myself back together. Aside from being soaked to the bone, I felt slightly better than before, and I glared at him through strands of wet hair. "You treat all your dying prisoners like this?" I gasped, then propped my back against the cell wall. "Need a doctor...*z'kira*...not a bath." I had to admit, the cold water did feel good on my sweaty, feverish skin. I let my eyes slip closed, concentrating on that coolness as it quickly evaporated off of me.

Thinking I was drifting off again, the lawman lightly slapped my cheek. I grunted and pushed his hand away, so he decided to pull my eyelids open instead. "Alright, okay," I said, then pushed back the hair from my face and glared at him. "The Hell do you want?"

He got up without a word and walked back to the cell door. There was a small wooden bowl sitting next to it, which he picked up and brought back to me. "*Adem*," he ordered, handing me the bowl. *Eat.*

I stared down at the bowl. The stuff inside looked vaguely like greenish-yellow clam chowder and smelled worse. I set it on the floor beside me, telling him, "I'm not hungry." It was a lie, but I knew that if I couldn't keep water down, *that* crap would be an even bigger problem.

The Kana-Semeth wasn't about to take "No" for an answer: he knelt down in front of me, picked up the bowl once again, and scooped up a spoonful of...whatever. "*Adem*," he said again, and shoved it in my face. As soon as I began to turn my head away, he put down the bowl, grabbed me by the jaw, then forced my mouth open and proceeded to shovel it down my gullet. *Oh, Christ, it tastes like manure*, I thought. *Hell, it probably is manure.* I gagged and threw the stuff back up -- at least the lawman had been kind enough to pull over the empty water bucket for me to puke in *before* he fed me that crap. My head hung low for a few minutes as I waited for the sick feeling to pass, and when I finally sat back up, that sadistic bastard was waiting with another spoonful. "Aw God," I groaned, "why are you doing this to me? I *need* a *doctor*! *Z'kira*! Don't you *get* it?"

"*Adem*" was all he had to say about my request.

I could tell by the look in his eye that he wasn't going to quit until I'd polished off the whole thing. "Why can't you let me die in peace?" I muttered, taking the bowl from him. It took two or three more spoonfuls before I could manage to keep the stuff down, and every bite tasted worse than the last. The lawman just sat there on his haunches the whole time, watching me gag on every last bit of it. When I finally finished, I chucked the bowl across the cell as hard as I could. "There," I grunted, wiping some of the vile concoction from the corner of my mouth. "You happy now?"

He glanced over to where the bowl landed, looked back at me, then grabbed me by the front of my shirt and hoisted me off the floor. I yelped as my feet left the ground, the toes of my boots brushing against his knees. He slammed my back against the wall, and I suddenly thought of my tussle with Sheriff Walker, which now seemed like it took place a thousand years ago. *Jesus, I don't think I can survive another fight like that,* I thought, *not in this condition.* I carefully looked down at the lawman, my heart thudding even harder than before. He met my gaze with an expression of pure *hate*, his ashen lips pressed together until they became a thin white line, a muscle along his jawline quivering as he bit down on the pain that *had* to be screaming out of his injured shoulder. I braced myself for the blows that I knew would come soon, but he simply stood there and watched me squirm. I felt like a bug in a bell jar.

To my surprise, he soon let me drop with as much warning as he'd given me when he picked me up. I stumbled as my feet touched the ground once again, but I managed to stay upright. His one icy-blue eye remained locked upon me, pinning me to the wall with nothing more than a glance. He then brought his right fist up, lightning-fast, and I did something that I'm not particularly proud of: I flinched.

The lawman smiled, a very disturbing smile to see on a face so scarred -- I think he actually enjoyed scaring the piss out of me -- and he lowered his fist. *"Bruhzod Taran,"* he scoffed as he turned away from me, heading for the door.

I've had more than one person tell me that I didn't have enough common sense to know when to shut the Hell up, and I once again proved them right by muttering, "I've got a name, you ugly sonovabitch."

He stopped dead in his tracks and turned back towards me slowly, shooting me a look that surely would have killed me had I been any weaker. Good Lord, I could *smell* the hate pouring off of him. I thought for sure that he was going to jump on me again, but he didn't move at all. *Well, Richard,* I thought to myself, *you got his attention, now what the Hell are you going to do with it?*

I wiped the sweat from my boiling forehead, tapped myself on the chest, and said as clearly as I could, "Richard Corrigan." He frowned, his eyebrows knitting together as he tried to puzzle out what I was trying to tell him. I decided to help him out: I pointed to him, saying, "Kana-Semeth," then pointed back to myself and repeated my name.

Realization began to dawn in his eye -- he wasn't an idiot, after all, he just didn't speak English -- then he smiled again, a sort of "Oh, I get it" smile. "Richard Corrigan," he repeated, my name rolling off his tongue with a precision no other Arkan had been able to manage yet. He tapped himself on the chest. "Jamin H'landa," he told me, then pointed at the two short, brass-colored stripes stitched onto the left side of his tunic, draping over the shoulder -- I could plainly see the hole my bullet had made between the two stripes. *"Lermekt* Jamin H'landa," he added in a "And don't you forget it" tone.

It took a moment for the information to filter through my brain, but when it did, my jaw dropped open.

The man's last name matched up with the half-remembered word from my dream a few nights before, the one that I thought sounded like "hell-land". I was suddenly struck with a feeling of *déjà-vu*, for with the name now came a memory of this very moment, of the lawman standing before me with the very same look on his face -- it had been jumbled up in my head all that time, just another piece of information among countless others forced upon me in a flash by the mystery man. It occurred to me then that it had been the same way with the Crossroad: an image presented to me without reference, something totally without meaning until I was face-to-face with it.

"Jamin H'landa," I echoed hollowly. The lawman nodded, and I could tell by the way he looked at me that he couldn't figure out why I was staring at him with my jaw agape. He shook his head and waved his hand at me in a gesture of dismissal as he left the cell.

I slid down the wall as the door shut, barely noticing when my butt hit the cold stone floor. This had to be a mistake, I must have heard him wrong. How could I have known his name three days before I'd ever met him? How come I kept seeing things in my dreams before I saw them when I was awake?

God help me, I think I'm losing my mind, I thought.

* * * * * *

The day seemed to crawl by as I did my time in total isolation. I heard a door close somewhere not long after the lawman left the cell, and after that, nothing. No sounds filtered in from the outside world, and had it not been for the sunlight shining through the cell door's tiny window, I would have thought that I might be underground. Now, I'd done time before, and while it's never a walk in the park, it is a bit easier to handle when you don't feel like you're dying by inches. The pain in my guts would fade for a time and the sweat on my brow would cool and evaporate, but it would soon come crashing back again in all its stomach-churning, dry-heaving glory. Not for the first time in my life, I considered committing suicide just to get away from this particular Hell. Unfortunately, I didn't have anything to do the deed with: the lawman had not only stripped me of my gunbelts and knife while I was unconscious, but also my coat, the belt to my trousers, and the spurs off my boots. The man wasn't taking any chances, that was for sure.

After what I judged to be an hour passed by with no sign of the lawman's return -- and I felt that my guts weren't going to rebel against me -- I attempted to break out of my cell. I staggered over to the door and peeked through the opening, which was at about the level of my chin... fine for most Arkans, but I had to stoop a little to get a good view. The room beyond looked vaguely like many other constable's offices I'd seen over the years: a desk of sorts with a couple of chairs to my left, and a rack of weapons against the wall to the right (instead of guns, it held some short swords and daggers and some contraption that looked like a rifle stock with a small bow tacked on the end). A cot of sorts lay on the far side of the room -- I figured that these Kana-Semeth must use this place as their living quarters when they were in town, because it definitely looked slept in. Above the cot was a barred window made with what looked like clear glass, which wouldn't have seemed too out of place back home, but here in Arkhein, it was the first glass window I could recall seeing. In fact, it was one of the few glass objects I'd seen outside of J'nath's little museum. The weapons rack had a glass front as well. "Well, whoever these suckers are, I reckon they've got money," I muttered.

Another potential sign of wealth hung behind the desk, directly across from the room's only door (except for the cell door, of course). It was a banner or tapestry of some sort, about the same shape and size as an American flag hung sideways, although this thing tapered off to a point about a foot or so from its bottom. The background was the same blue-gray as the lawman's trousers, with more of that brass-color piping running along the border. At the center, a large hawk or eagle had been embroidered, wings spread and a crown of feathers rippling back on its head. It was familiar in a way that I couldn't pin down, then I remembered the lawman had a similar emblem attached to the shoulder guard on that rig he wore.

I did my best to look downward, but the bars on the small window prevented me from getting a good look at the front of the cell door. I thought I'd heard a bar or bolt sliding back and forth whenever the lawman shut the door, and I wanted to find out if I was right. I couldn't *see* it, though, so that meant I'd have to *feel* for it. I began to reach between the bars with my right hand, then remembered my own shoulder wound and switched to my left -- it was my stupid hand, but I'd have to make do. I squeezed my body up against the door as best I could while I groped blindly for the bolt, hoping that I didn't pop my arm out of its socket in the process. I was rewarded a few minutes later when my fingers brushed cold iron. It felt like a metal plate about a foot-and-a-half long, with a long, meandering groove cut into it and a short metal bar sticking out one end. I grabbed the bar and juggled it back and forth for a moment, then managed to slide it into the groove. I got it to move a few inches before it jammed for no apparent reason. I felt around a little more, confirming that there was nothing blocking the path of the bar, then I reached down a little further and felt a second groove below the one I was working on, and a third below *that*, with small channels running back and forth between them all. I groaned as I realized this was more like a puzzle than a simple slide-bolt: I'd have to switch from one groove to the next in order to avoid the hidden dead-ends like the one I'd just run into.

Rosy light passed slowly across the walls as I cursed and sweated and yanked that damn bar around, my left arm throbbing from being in such an awkward position for so long, not to mention the waves of pain that still rippled through my guts from time to time. I was on the verge of giving up when I heard a loud *chunk* and the door swung open a few inches -- I was so stunned that I just stood there for a moment or two with my arm still thrust through the bars. When I regained my senses, I entered the Kana-Semeth's office proper, fighting the urge to start whooping and hollering over my little victory. Still, I had a ridiculously-huge grin on my face, despite myself.

Okay, first order of business: find my guns. I was all ready to tear the room apart when I realized they were lying in plain sight on top of the desk. "God, I really *am* sick, ain't I?" I mumbled. I reached over to pick them up, but stopped cold when I took a closer look at them.

That sonovabitch had *disassembled* one of my guns, right down to the last spring and screw. He'd even cracked open one of the *bullets*, for Christ's sake. All the pieces were lined up neatly on the desk atop a hand-drawn diagram of my revolver, with little notes written in Arkan here and there. I shouldn't have been surprised -- such a weapon would give a lawman one Hell of an advantage in a world like this -- but now I was worried that it may never work again once it was put back together. I was about to try and reassemble it myself, but one look at my trembling, sweat-slick hands told me that I was in no shape to do that sort of work. I couldn't even trust the seemingly-intact gun, since I had no way of knowing if the Kana-Semeth had taken that one apart as well. I picked it up and turned it over slowly in my hands, looking for anything unusual or out-of-place, but I just wasn't sure.

My ears pricked up as I heard movement outside the main door. My grip tightened on the gun's handle -- perhaps I couldn't trust it for firing, but I could still use it to cold-cock somebody. I scrambled over to the door, standing so it would block me from view when it opened. It occurred to me then just how stupid this was, and that I'd probably be back in the cell by sundown, but dammit, I had to try: the sonovabitch would probably keep me locked up until I died if I didn't make a break for it.

The door opened slowly, and I could see the edge of a dark-haired figure emerging from behind it. As quick as I could, I yanked the door open the rest of the way and brought the butt of my gun down hard on his head. Unfortunately, I realized too late that the "lawman" was about a head shorter than he used to be, and the person I'd just whacked was actually Pietruvek.

The boy crumpled to the floor with a groan. I dropped my gun and knelt beside him to see if he was alright, saying, "Oh, Jesus...can you hear me, kid? What the Hell are you doing here?" Dazed, the boy stared up at me, then his eyes fixed on something just past my shoulder and opened a little wider. Before I even had a chance to turn around and look, I was grabbed by the back of my shirt and literally hurled across the room. I skidded to a halt upside-down in the cell, my head pointed towards the door and my feet propped against the wall. I looked back out into the office to see the lawman, topsy-turvy, about ready to run into the cell after me. He roared what I was sure were Arkan obscenities at me, a high reddish-purple color in his cheeks. I couldn't figure out for a moment why he was just standing there, but then I saw that Pietruvek had grabbed him by the arm and was trying to calm him down -- my continued existence likely depended on the persuasiveness of a half-conscious fourteen-year-old boy.

I turned myself upright as the lawman vented, only to have that sick feeling grow in my guts again. I sat as still as I could, both to calm my insides down and to not give that man any more reasons to kill me. After a few minutes of talking to him, Pietruvek managed to get the lawman's temper down to a low boil. He turned away from me with a scowl and proceeded to make sure Pietruvek was alright -- the kid seemed a little unsteady on his feet, but he was toughing it out quite well. You had to admire that. The two of them conferred together for a

time, one or the other glancing over to me occasionally
(the lawman's was more like a glare), then they entered the
cell. The boy took a seat on the floor near me, while Mr.
One-Eyed Ugly stationed himself in the doorway, feet set
firmly and a hand on the hilt of his sword.

I smiled weakly at Pietruvek and said, "I don't
know if this'll make you feel any better, but I meant to hit
that guy." I pointed at the lawman.

"Figured that." He rubbed the lump on his skull
with a wince, then leaned close to me, saying in a serious
tone, "I do not *kedda* what thy plan was, but I would not
try again. The Kana-Semeth are not a joke. He can keep
thee here until all thy brown hair turn white!"

"Just let him try. When J'nath gets down here,
he'll..."

"*Padra* not coming."

"*What*?!?"

Pietruvek seemed genuinely surprised by my
response. "Thou forget last night?" He pantomimed
getting decked. "*Padra* not forgive easily. Maybe in a
few days he come here, but now..." He shrugged. "The
Kana-Semeth even tried to force *Padra* to come here, to
translate. No good."

"So he dragged you down here instead?"

"*Ke*? Drugged?"

I rolled my eyes. "*Dragged*. He brought you here
unwillingly."

"Ah. *Nee*, he asked, so I came." The boy paused.
"Thou truly thought *Padra* would come here?"

"Well, sure. After all, I just gave him a little
whack. Nothing serious." I closed my eyes and tried not
to think about the glass grinding once again in my belly.

Pietruvek made a noise which I took to be a grunt
of disbelief. He then spoke to the lawman in Arkan, who
responded by letting out the scariest laugh I'd ever heard.
"What's so damn funny?" I asked the kid, opening one
eye.

"Thou, um, did more than hit him." He then began to relate to me last night's performance, of which I could only recall tiny shreds. I didn't know what shocked me more: my behavior or the fact that I could barely remember it. "Maybe it's because I'm sick," I ventured. "Yeah, this fever must be frying my brain."

The boy shook his head, saying, "Thou not sick."

"What, you think this is *normal*?" I wiped sweat off of my face. "I've been pukin' my guts up all day, Peter. At first, I was so out of it that I thought I might have the plague, but I figure I should be a lot worse by now if it was that. All I know for sure is that this sonovabitch here won't bring the doctor over to see me." I looked up at the lawman, glaring at him as I told the boy, "All he's done is toss me around the room and make me choke down a bowl of yellow shit."

"But thou not sick, not as thou thinks," Pietruvek insisted. "Thou hast poison in thy blood."

I sat up a little straighter when he said that. "I was *poisoned*? But how...who did this?"

He smiled sheepishly. "Did it to thyself." He gave me a moment for the shock to wear off, then continued, "Last night, when thou was drinking...*Padra* did not *kedda* this, or he would have stopped thee..."

"What? Spit it out, son."

"In the ale thou drank, there is something that makes Tarans sick. It gets in the blood, makes thee sick in brain and body...it will not hurt Arkans, but it is *poison* to Tarans." I could see concern in his eyes. "Thou could have died last night."

"Still feel like I might," I replied, trying to swallow -- my mouth had suddenly gone dry. Christ, no wonder I felt so awful. "So, is this permanent damage?"

He conferred with the lawman again, then shook his head. "*Nee*. Three, perhaps four days, and the poison should be out of thee. The medicine thou took will help clean thy blood."

"What medicine? I told you, the doctor hasn't been by."

The boy looked confused. "The Kana-Semeth say he gave it to thee this morning. He say it taste bad, so he mix it in some mash *pirril* so thou could swallow it better."

My eyes slid over to the corner of the cell where the wooden bowl had landed, a small yellow-green smudge on the wall above it. "You mean he was trying to *help* me by force-feeding me that slop? Why the Hell didn't he...oh, wait, I guess he *couldn't* tell me, could he?" I turned back to Pietruvek. "But how'd he figure it out -- the poisoning, I mean -- if it doesn't have the same effect on Arkans? Did he talk to the doctor or something?"

"I...I do not know." I could tell by the look on his face that it hadn't even occurred to him to question what the lawman had told him.

Before Pietruvek could clear up that little mystery, however, the lawman stepped forward, snapping something unintelligible at him. I guessed that he was tired of waiting for us to finish our conversation. "Back off, pal, and wait your turn," I growled at the man.

The Kana-Semeth turned to me, all that hate showing on his face once again. I knew he didn't understand what I'd said, but the tone I'd used made him aware that it wasn't nice. "*Irrel*," he ordered, making an upward motion with his hand.

"He wants thee to..."

"I got the message, kid. I'm not *that* dumb." I stood up in front of the lawman on wobbly legs, my body aching, cold sweat running down the back of my neck, while he slowly looked me over. I think he was waiting for me to make another snide remark. When he saw I wasn't about to give him the satisfaction, he stared dead into my eyes and began to talk, pausing only briefly here and there to give Pietruvek a chance to catch up on the translation:

"Hear me well, Taran. I think we both *kedda* that we do not like one another. That is no matter. But *kedda* this: I will make the pains thou feels at the moment seem like bliss if thou does not begin to cooperate with me. Thou will answer my questions truthfully, and obey any order that I may give thee, until I believe that thou hast served enough penance for thy crimes."

"And what if I don't cooperate?" I asked Pietruvek, who translated the question for the lawman. The answer was swift: Fifty days in the cell. No visitors. No medicine to help me recover from the poison. And when he finally decided to let me out, *no guns* -- I'd be thrown out into this alien world without my only advantage to whatever terrors might be lurking out there. Basically, this was outright blackmail, but what choice did I have? I decided to play along for now until a better opportunity presented itself. "Alright," I said, "I'll behave, but he has to promise me something in return."

"What is that?" the boy asked.

"He has to stop throwing me around. I'm not exactly in what you'd call the picture of health right now."

The Kana-Semeth flashed that disturbing smile of his again after the translation. *"Kai,"* he replied.

CHAPTER 8

That bastard lawman lied to me: it took nearly a week for me to fully recover from my little drinking binge. Hard to believe that chugging a couple mugs of ale could so easily lead to endless bouts of puking, sweating, and crippling muscle pain. I wasn't always in such dire straits, but usually when I was, I'd swear very loudly (and quite truthfully) to God that I would never, *ever* drink again. The lawman's "hangover cure" (as I so fondly called it) took most of the edge off, but the twice-daily doses of that lovely greenish glop were about as pleasant as the spasms they prevented. I couldn't wait for when I was well enough to eat normal food again, as opposed to that pissed-in chowder.

At least I had some company while I recovered. Pietruvek came by every day like clockwork to act as both interpreter and moral support as *Lermekt* H'landa interrogated me. I'm pretty sure that, on more than one occasion, the kid's presence was the only thing that kept me from being run through with that sword the lawman constantly kept by his side. I never seemed to be able to read anything more than contempt in the man's eye as he made Pietruvek translate the same questions over and over again: "What is thy real name?" "From which of the Seven Known Lands dost thou come from?" "Who made all those strange devices thou carries?" "Why dost thou refuse to speak Arkan properly?" "Dost thou know of any others who are deformed like thee?" It was always that last question that made me want to punch him out. *Deformed.* Like I had a crippled hand or a gimp leg instead of just different-colored hair and skin. The scary thing was, from his point of view, I *was* deformed: the man kept insisting that I was nothing more than an unusual-looking Arkan with a good story, and that J'nath and his family were in on the whole scheme. The fact that J'nath refused to come see me reinforced the theory for the lawman somehow. At the same time, though, he acknowledged that what I said was true: he usually referred to me as "the Taran", he memorized quite a few English words so that he could talk with me easier (even going so far as to use the more-modern idioms that I preferred), and of course, he gave me medicine for a supposedly "Taran-only" ailment. How he'd figured *that* one out was still a mystery.

The man himself was a bit mysterious as well. I questioned Pietruvek about the *lermekt* during one of the lulls in my interrogation: I'd gotten the idea that the man's name might hold some significance about him since it had stuck in my head so easily. Unfortunately, the most the boy could tell me was that "*h'landa*" was an old Arkan term for a stranger or traveler, and loosely translated into English as "One who is far from home" -- "*H'landa* would be a good word to describe thee," Pietruvek observed. The lawman's first name proved to be elusive, however, as the boy had never heard it before, but he also noted that the lawman himself didn't appear to be local (apparently, most of the Kana-Semeth spent a lot of their time moving from one village to the next, like circuit judges or something), so we both shrugged it off.

Luckily, Pietruvek did find out why H'landa was so insistent on discovering who (or what) I really was: the lawman had let slip at one point that word of my arrival had reached the capital of Taorin, which was the country I'd landed up in. The folks there were curious about me, so they'd sent the lawman to Betedek to check things out. *Well,* I thought after learning this, *I'm glad I went out of my way to make such a good first impression on him.*

That little bit of information did make me wonder if that was why I'd heard H'landa's name in my dream: was that man in the cloak trying to warn me about the lawman like he'd warned me about the Crossroad? I didn't know, and I had no way to ask, for while I was still having difficulty sleeping, that cryptic bastard had yet to rear his hooded head in my dreams again. I was beginning to wish that he would just to get it over with, especially since my patience with the lawman had worn thin. Even though we'd more or less agreed to not make this situation any more painful than it already was, we both managed to find ways to poke at each other. We couldn't help it, really: he obviously hated me, and I wasn't fond of being locked up, so we each took jabs here and there just to drive the other nuts. My personal favorite involved waiting until H'landa had fallen asleep, then singing as many raunchy ditties as I could think of. Actually, it was more like yelling. I knew that he couldn't understand all the words, but it was more than enough noise to wake him up. One thing's for sure, it was a good way to learn Arkan cuss words.

He always had the upper hand, though, being the jailer and all. The man had the option of walking away when he didn't want to deal with me, while I was stuck in the cell. That's not to say that he never got even with me. On my second or third day in his custody, I kept interrupting the interrogation by complaining about the scenery. "I'm getting a little sick of seeing nothin' but this cell and your ugly face," I told H'landa. "Maybe if I could see some sun other than that little bit through the door..." He was obviously getting annoyed by all this, so I kept pushing until he couldn't take it anymore.

"No more questions!" he said in Arkan. "We are finished for today!" He got up out of the chair he'd brought in with him, grabbed Pietruvek by the arm, and left the cell, slamming the door shut behind them. I was sorry to see the kid go, but at least I'd have some peace for a while.

About maybe a half-hour had passed by when H'landa came back into my cell. "*Irrel, Taran*," he said, then told me in English, "Have surprise for you."

"Aw, gee, and it ain't even my birthday." I stood up and let him lead me out the office door and into the room beyond: it appeared to be a meeting hall of sorts, with two rows of benches facing a podium or dais, and a set of heavy wood doors directly opposite the office door at the back of the hall. All the walls save the back one had tall, narrow windows set in them, filling most of the room with rose-colored sunlight. "Now this is much better," I said to him.

He smiled and pulled me over to a back corner, probably the darkest spot in the whole room, then I saw that he'd attached some shackles to the wall there with an iron spike. We grappled for a moment, but he eventually managed to cuff me, and he even slapped a collar with a short chain around my neck so my face was barely inches from the wall. I couldn't see him, the sunlight, nothing. It was so dark in that corner that I couldn't even really see the *wall*.

The lawman clapped me on the back. "Enjoy your sun," he said in English, and disappeared back into his office.

"Very damn funny!" I hollered, tugging at the chains. "All right, H'landa, I'll behave...now come unlock these things!" But he didn't come back out. I clunked my head against the wall in frustration -- I couldn't believe how easily I'd been tricked by the man. Hours passed as I stood in the corner, unable to kneel without choking myself, and wondering if anyone was peeking in the windows to witness my humiliation.

The lawman came back around the time the light began to fade from the room. "Had enough?" he asked.

"Yeah...*kai, kai...*" I'd been fighting against a wave of nausea for at least an hour, and needed to sit down before I fell down and hung myself.

He must've been able to tell that I wasn't doing so good, because he leaned close to my face and asked in English, "What wrong? Gonna fuckinpuke?"

I tried not to laugh when he when he parroted my oft-repeated phrase -- I knew that he only had a vague idea of what it meant -- instead telling him that I just might, and he graciously undid the shackles and collar. The moment they were off, I sank to my knees, rubbing my throat and trying not to "fuckinpuke".

"I am not cruel by nature, Taran," he said in Arkan after a moment or two. He spoke slowly, giving me time to translate the words as well as I could in my head -- the best thing to come out of his constant interrogations was that my grasp of the language was improving. "I am only returning to you what you give to me. Your lies and your childish actions only hurt yourself."

Oh, please, I thought. I'd lost count of how many lawmen back home had said nearly the same thing to me, and I certainly wasn't going to take it from *this* guy. "Perhaps if you were not such a...such a *dirruk*...I might be nicer," I spat back in my own hackneyed Arkan.

H'landa looked puzzled. Not exactly the reaction I'd expected: I thought that I'd just called him (judging by some of the rants I'd heard him go on) something pretty damn nasty. I was about to repeat the insult when he began to laugh. "I am...I am a *dirruk*," he managed to get out. "A *dirruk*..."

"What's so damn funny about that?" I snapped in English.

He snorted, then started to get himself under control. "*Kirruk*," he corrected. "I think you mean *kirruk*. A *dirruk* is...it is..." He couldn't finish his sentence: it just degenerated into laughter again.

"Oh, yeah. Ha-ha, real funny. Everybody laugh at Richard's pidgin Arkan." I got to my feet. "Just you wait 'til you mess up, I'll be all over your ass."

I could tell by his expression that he barely understood what I'd said. No big deal, *I* knew what I'd said and I meant it. As he led me back to the cell for my evening bowl of shit, I wondered how long I'd have to wait before I caught him making any sort of mistake.

I had no idea at the time that I'd get my chance for revenge rather quickly.

* * * * * *

I awoke on the fifth day of my incarceration with my stomach growling. This certainly wasn't new, but I didn't usually notice it right away because I was too busy being sick. This morning, however, I felt perfectly fine. I sat up carefully, sure that the pains would start up again the moment I began to move around.

Nothing. Not so much as a twinge. After nearly a week of Hell, this was almost disturbing. Just to be sure that my ordeal was indeed over and done with, I pressed my fingers into the small of my back, around by my kidneys (for some reason, the poison in my body had made them extremely tender to the touch). Other than the normal pain you'd get from jabbing yourself in the guts, everything seemed right as rain. "Thank you, God," I whispered, leaning back against the wall. "Believe me, I'll remember this the next time they pass around the plate in church." I sat there for a few minutes, just relishing the fact that I felt *good*, until my stomach began to growl a little louder. I needed some food in me, *real* food, like a ham steak and a mess of scrambled eggs, or whatever the Arkan equivalent was. I got up and stretched, popping my spine like a string of firecrackers -- sleeping on a cold stone floor with nothing but a blanket beneath you is not the best thing for your back. Judging by the scant amount of light in the cell, it seemed a bit early for breakfast, but I didn't care: I was a well man once more, and if I interrupted the poor *lermekt's* beauty sleep with my demands, he could just lump it.

I walked over to the cell door, rubbing sleep from my eyes and trying to think of a good way to rouse the lawman this morning. My plans were abruptly cancelled, however, once I looked through the cell's window.

H'landa had awakened before me and was finishing up getting ready for the day...by shaving.

There was no mistaking it. He stood in front of a small mirror he'd tacked to the wall, and was carefully cutting away the stubble on his face with a palm-sized, curved blade. The short, dark hairs were barely enough to give him a five-o'clock shadow -- I personally wouldn't have even bothered with it until they were at least twice that long, but then again, I wasn't trying to pass myself off as a naturally clean-shaven Arkan. It took more willpower than I knew I had to keep from screaming at him at that moment. It didn't appear that he'd noticed I was awake yet, so instead I forced myself to settle back down in the corner of the cell and wait.

About ten minutes later, he entered the cell to wake me up -- I'd been feigning sleep the whole time just in case he peeked in on me. He knelt down and gave me a shake, saying in Arkan, "Get up, Taran. Sun is up, you should be as well."

"Don't feel so good," I told him in English, my voice muffled by the blanket I'd pulled over my head.

"Still? You seemed better yesterday." He began to pull the blanket off of me. I grabbed his hand, yanked him forward, and socked him hard in the jaw. It all happened so fast, he didn't even have time to make a fist.

"You lyin' sonovabitch!" Twisting his arm behind him, I slammed the lawman down on the cell floor face-first. "All this time, you've been calling *me* deformed, when *you're* just as much of a freak as *I* am!"

"*Ke?*"

"*You're human!* Or Taran, or whatever the Hell you want to call it. You ain't totally native, that's for damn sure. I saw you this morning, shaving off those whiskers...you been doin' that the whole time I've been locked up in here?"

He turned his head as best he could to look at me, his expression somewhere between extreme anger and complete embarrassment. "I am *nothing* like you."

"Yeah, right. You looked in the mirror lately, cousin?"

He growled and swung his foot up. Despite his awkward position, he managed to crack me real hard on my elbow. I yelped and loosened my grip, inadvertently giving him a chance to free himself. He then flipped onto his back and slammed his feet into my chest, knocking me onto my ass.

"Not so sick anymore, *kai*?" he said in English, getting to his feet.

I flashed him a grin. "Nope."

"Good. Will not hold back anymore." He lunged at me, but I rolled out of the way, sweeping my leg into his. He stumbled and hit the floor hard, stunning him just long enough for me to make a mad dash out of the cell. I slammed the door behind me and rammed the locking bolt into place as best I could -- it wasn't perfect, but it would keep H'landa in there.

"Unlock this door, Taran!" He tried to kick it open, but the bolt held fast.

I regarded him for a moment through the cell window, well out of arm's reach. "Not until you answer *my* questions for a change," I said in Arkan. "Why did you lie?"

"I do not know what you are talking about."

"Sweet Jesus, what is it with you?" I lapsed back into English. "I caught you dead to rights this morning, so quit covering it up. Why didn't you tell me you were a Taran?"

The lawman's gaze met mine -- I could still see the anger simmering in his good eye, but it didn't seem to be directed at me anymore. "Were you a good child, Richard?" he asked in Arkan.

I was taken aback, both by the question and the fact that he addressed me by my name, as he rarely bothered to. "What do you mean?"

"Did you obey your *padra* and *maia* always? Did you ever doubt the words they spoke to you?"

"I suppose there may have been a few times when I did not believe them, but I..."

"Once," he interrupted. "Only once did I doubt my parents. I never before had a reason to." A smile drifted across his face, briefly softening those hard-edged features. "My *padra* was a Kana-Semeth as well. He taught me more about what that meant than any trainer after him. Every word he spoke was law, no question. Do you *kedda* so far?"

"Yeah, sure," I muttered in English.

"When I was about Pietruvek's age, my *maia* woke me early one morning and led me to the parlor. *Padra* was there, tending the fire -- I had not seen him for many months. I rushed up to greet him, but he held me away and told me to sit, for we had many things to talk about. 'What do you know of Tarans?' he asked. I thought this was a strange question to be woken up so early about, but I answered him as best I could. 'They were supposed to be people from another world, back before the Great Plague,' I said. 'I think they all died.' He then asked, 'Do you know the tale of the Taran man who fell in love with an Arkan woman, and how he turned his back upon his life in Tarahein to stay in Arkhein with her?' I said I did, for he was the one that told me, long ago.

"*Padra* fell silent for a time, then said, 'My son, what I am about to tell you is not easy, and you may think me *bruhzod* for saying it. But it is the truth, and I would not say such things if I did not love you.' He told me that the Taran who stayed behind...that he was the founder of the H'landa bloodline, a direct ancestor of both myself and my *padra*. He explained that, though many Taran traits had fallen away over the centuries, a few remained, and now that I was approaching adulthood, they would become more evident, and I must prepare for that. My *padra* then produced a leather pouch, which contained the cutting blade you saw me using this morning. I did not know at first what it was for, but when he leaned forward to give it to me, the firelight struck his face so that I could see the hair on his cheeks -- he had not cut it off yet that morning."

The lawman paused for a few minutes, one hand propped against the cell door while he rubbed the back of his neck with the other. I shuffled nervously from one foot to the next -- with the door and its tiny window between us, I felt like I'd snuck into the church confessional. Just when I thought that he wouldn't (or couldn't) go on, he picked his head up and continued:

"I called my *padra* a liar for the first time that morning. 'I am an Arkan, just like you, and just like *Maia!*' I shouted at him. He tried to calm me, but I would not listen, not anymore. I ran out of the house, still in my bedclothes, wanting nothing more than to get away from *Padra* and his terrible lies. What he said *had* to be lies, of course: Tarans were not real, they never were, so how could I be a Taran? The idea that there was something unknown inside me, something beyond my control...it frightened me." The lawman said the last thing with obvious distaste. "I hid in the forest near our home as I tried to sort out in my mind what *Padra* had told me, and eventually I accepted it as truth, for I could find no reason for him to make up such a thing. When I returned home, my *maia* tried to comfort me, but my *padra* would have none of it: he said I was no longer a child.

"*Padra* taught me many things about my Taran heritage after that day, including how to cure that blood poisoning like you had...but he never taught me how to *live* as a Taran, how to cope with being different from every other Arkan. So I now became the liar, telling myself that there *was* no difference, even as I cut away the hair from my face every morning. I was an Arkan, nothing more, and Tarans did not exist, they had *never* existed..."

"And then you heard about me," I interjected. "That is the *real* reason you came to Betedek, is it not? No one sent you at all."

"*Nee*, I was sent here, I did not lie about that." He flashed that disturbing smile of his again. "I do not think my superiors know of my...experience with Tarans, however. I was simply the only one available."

"Hell of a coincidence," I muttered in English.

"*Ke?*"

"Nothing, nothing." My thoughts drifted once more to that mystery man: he'd tried to send me a message about H'landa in my dreams, but it had become garbled. Had *this* been what he was trying to tell me, that I'd soon cross paths with someone who might be the only part-human Arkan in this whole strange world? And if so, what of it? It wasn't exactly like H'landa was fond of that fact. It just ended up being another unanswered question, and things like that were really beginning to stick in my craw, especially since I couldn't really talk to anybody about it without sounding like a complete madman. Maybe if I had some actual proof of any of it instead of a lot of sleepless nights, I could make some headway, but all I had at the moment was my word, and that's never been very good.

"What are your plans now?" the lawman asked, bringing me back to reality. "Will you run off, tell all of Betedek my secret?"

"Why would I do that?"

"Revenge."

"Hell of a good idea...but I think I'll pass for now," I said in English, and unbolted the cell door. He hesitated, probably thinking that I would pull something as soon as he came out, so I stepped a few feet away from the door. He eventually stepped out, looking confused. "I understand why you hate me now," I told him. "I don't like it, but I understand it. I also don't care, but that doesn't mean I'm going to let you keep treating me that way you have been."

He folded his arms across his chest. "So, the prisoner makes demands now?"

"Just one: pretend for a moment that I'm not a Taran."

"What do you mean?"

"Think about all the grief you've given me for the past week, all the times you've nearly crushed my skull. Now, tell me the truth: would you have done *exactly* the same things if I was a normal Arkan?"

"No...I would have already given you a trial, convicted you, and probably sent you off for a few months in the workhouse as well." He took a step closer to me, staring me square in the eye -- unlike most of the other Arkans I'd met, he and I were nearly the same height, a fact that did intimidate me a little. "I have not done those things because you were ill, although you now seem fit to stand before a council of law."

"Oh, so it's standard Kana-Semeth practice to chain a prisoner -- a *sick* prisoner, at that -- so that his face is jammed in the corner for hours at a time? What kinda store y'all runnin' here?"

"Speak to me in Arkan," he snapped. "Your Taran chattering hurts my ears."

I closed the gap between us and leaned close to his ear. "I don't give a damn," I said to him in English. "What you're hearing is *what I am*. It's what *you* are, too, under this uniform, at least partially." I reached up and tugged on the front of his tunic. "I also don't give a damn if you hide behind this thing for the rest of your life. Myself, I prefer hiding in a bottle...but I guess that option's no longer open to me, is it?" I pulled back a little, then said, "Look, H'landa...Jamin...my point is, I'll forget that *you're* a Taran if you can forget that *I* am. Just leave your grudge with my whole world at the door and maybe...this is a *huge* maybe...we can keep from trying to kill each other all the time. Deal?"

He stepped away from me and circled around behind his desk, mulling it over. "You are still in my custody. This...this thing between us does not change that." He paused. "And do not call me by my personal name. You have not earned the right. You will address me by rank and with the respect that is due a Kana-Semeth."

I bowed slightly, saying, "*Kai, Lermekt* H'landa.*"

He looked me over, trying to discern whether or not I was serious. "I will admit," he continued, "that I let my anger regarding Tarans affect my actions, but you have done very little to show me that you do not deserve that anger. If you can convince me that you can be trusted, I will release you. No trial, no fine, nothing. I will even give you back your *trit bakido*. Just show me that you can live by the Laws...like a normal Arkan."

"I will try not to disappoint you, *d'ho-lermekt*."

* * * * * *

Pietruvek showed up about an hour later to perform his usual middleman/translator duties. When he opened the door to the office, he stopped short, unable to believe the scene before him: H'landa sat hunched over his desk writing out reports, while I sat in a chair near the wide-open cell door scarfing down my second helping of *milhafi*. The boy stood in the doorway for a minute or so, just looking at me, then at the lawman, then back at me again, before asking in Arkan, "What happened?"

H'landa looked up from his paperwork. "What do you mean?"

"This," he said, indicating the two of us. "This is all wrong."

"The *lermekt* and I have come to an agreement," I told him.

"*Kai*, an agreement," H'landa agreed. "If *d'ho*-Corrigan can behave himself for the next few days, I will let him go."

"You will?" He looked us both over again. "This is a joke."

"What, you don't think the two of us are capable of sitting down together and having a nice, civilized conversation without you around?" I asked him in English. "I'm shocked, Peter, really shocked. I thought you had more faith in me than that."

"I do, Reshard, but..."

"Hey, you want this last biscuit?" I held out the plate towards him. "I guess I don't have as much of my appetite back yet as I thought."

The boy picked up the biscuit and looked at it like he had no idea what it was. "I must have missed something big," he muttered in Arkan. "This is definitely not the same room I stood in yesterday."

The lawman smirked as he rolled up the papers he'd been working on and slipped them inside a slim metal cylinder. It had something etched in Arkan on the side, along with the Kana-Semeth emblem. "Pietruvek, do you know of anyone who travels to Dak-Taorin regularly?" he asked.

"*Nee*, I cannot...wait, *d'ho*-N'dahl sometimes goes out there to visit his brother, I think."

"Find out when he will be heading that way again." He capped off the cylinder, dribbled some wax over the seam, and pressed a brass seal into it. "If it is more than five days, then find someone who can deliver this sooner. Promise them ten *kepa* upon their return."

He handed the cylinder to Pietruvek, who took it with his eyes wide and his mouth agape -- I had no idea how much a *kepa* was worth in American dollars, but ten of them must have been a helluva lot. "The message...what..." the boy stammered.

H'landa glanced at me, still smirking, and said, "It is a letter to my superiors in the capital, telling them that the rumors of a Taran in Betedek are true, and that I wish to know how to proceed." The smirk faded. "Now go on, boy. That is an order."

Pietruvek looked over at me, as if he were afraid to leave me alone with the lawman -- he probably thought this was all an act for his benefit, and that we'd be at each other's throats the minute he left. "You heard the man," I said in English, and waved a hand at him. "Beat your feet, Pete."

That seemed to break him out of his trance. He nearly bolted for the door, the now-forgotten biscuit squashed in his fist. I waited until I heard the meeting hall doors shut before I said to H'landa, "So, what did you tell them about me?"

"Only what they needed to know."

"How long 'til you get a response?"

He shrugged. "Ten days. A month. It depends on how much importance they place upon it."

"They thought it was important enough to send you here in the first place. Why would that change now?"

"I think you frightened them."

"What do you mean? Do they think I'm a threat or something?" I leaned forward in my chair. "Did you tell them that I'm *not*?"

The lawman turned away from me, becoming suddenly interested in the dust motes floating in the early-morning light that poured through the window. "I only told them what they needed to know," he repeated.

CHAPTER 9

"Do you see anything?"

"*Nee*, I think this one is...ah, found one."

"Is it bad?"

"Bad enough. Hand me the paint." H'landa passed up a small clay pot. I dipped my already-stained finger in, using it to draw a deep red 'X' on the window panel. The glass pane was small, only about six inches on each side, but it had cracked so badly that I could feel the wind outside pass through it. "Well, that's it up here...comin' down, boss," I said in English, and began to climb down the ladder.

"Fine. Two more windows and we will be done." He took a look around the meeting hall, surveying all the work we'd already finished over the last two days. The lawman had gotten the idea that, since he had an able-bodied prisoner, he may as well put me to work. That was fine by me, I felt like I was going crazy from being cooped up in a cell for so long. He wouldn't let me leave the building, but there were so many little things to take care of inside, I barely put up a fuss. Matter of fact, since our tussle a few days before, we'd barely done so much as raise our voices at each other. There were still times when I wanted to sock him (and I'm sure he had the same problem) but now that I knew his secret, I almost felt sorry for him.

Almost.

"So, once we have all the busted glass marked, what do we do?" I asked as I maneuvered the ladder over to the next window. Each one started a couple of feet above the baseboards and went up about five feet, all made up of two columns of glass panels. That's a lot to check.

"I will probably have to send all the way back to Dak-Taorin to replace them. This village seems too small to have a glassmaker." He frowned. "I do not think I have enough money to fix every one of them. Perhaps only the three worst we find."

"You mean all those things we fixed up so far -- the loose floorboards, that broken bench -- you had to pay for all that out of your own pocket?"

"That was nothing. A few nails, some wood...this is *glass*, Richard. You could probably buy my *vessek* with six of these panels." He tapped the window we stood next to with his finger. "I have to pay for them because no one in this village can spare that much money just to fix a *window*. Why do you think so many are broken?"

"Hadn't thought about it like that." I'd gotten the impression that glass was a bit more of a luxury item in this world, but this was nuts. A good horse back home cost...what, fifty, maybe sixty dollars? "If the cost is so dear to fix this much glass, why did they put it all in to begin with?" I wondered aloud.

"They did not. This hall was built by the Kana-Semeth." He pointed to a small, dull brass plate placed over the main doors, engraved with the Kana-Semeth symbol and something in Arkan. "The plaque says this was built nearly two hundred years ago. Back then, the people needed to be shown that civilization still existed, and that the Kana-Semeth could give it back to them, so they built places like this in some villages." The lawman smiled, saying, "I suppose they thought all this rare, expensive glass would convince the people of their sincerity."

"Well, they should've realized that these things wouldn't hold together forever." I made sure the ladder was secure and was about to start climbing when I casually looked out the window, which faced the main square, giving me a view of the whole area. The paper lanterns of Halitova were long gone, but there were still quite a few folks coming and going across the cobblestones, and only one of whom I actually knew.

J'nath stood at the opposite end of the square, talking with someone leaning in the doorway of a shop and completely unaware of me watching him. Hell, after what I'd said to him, he probably didn't even care if I still existed. I rested my head against the window frame and asked H'landa in Arkan, "Have you ever regretted doing something so deeply that you would give anything to take it back?"

"A few things." He was looking out the window now as well. "Neither *d'ho*-Bannen nor his son told me exactly what you two came to blows about, but judging by his attitude when I asked him to help me with you, it must have been quite bad."

"I was sick," I muttered, "I was not thinking straight, I can barely remember what I said...and I do not think he will ever forgive me."

"Are you sure?" I was about to ask him what he meant by that when he stepped away from the window and stretched. "I think we should take a break," he said. "I have some work to finish up in my office. You can lay on one of the benches and rest out here if you like." He started to walk up the aisle, then stopped and told me, "You know, with that door closed, I can hardly hear a thing." He looked back at me with this odd little smile on his face before continuing up the aisle.

It took a few seconds for me to realize what he was getting at -- I had to admit, this was the last thing I expected from him -- but I soon got the message. Once he'd entered his office and closed the door, I casually strolled over to the hall's main doors, opened them up, and stepped outside. No one said a word to me as I walked across the square, making a beeline for J'nath. That's not to say that I wasn't noticed: quite a few people saw me, but I reckon they were all too stunned or too scared to say or do anything about it. That bothered me a little, but their unease with me was not my concern at the moment. I had something more important to take care of first.

I came up behind J'nath and laid a hand on his shoulder. He turned around, and I could tell by the look on his face that I was the last person he expected to see standing there. His eyes widened slightly, and he took a couple steps away from me. I couldn't figure out why he did that at first, then I saw the shadow of the bruise I'd given him skirting across his jaw, and I felt my face flush.

About a thousand years passed between us as we each waited for the other to speak first. I wanted it to be me, but all the things I'd thought to say on my way across the square had flown out of my head. J'nath's friend in the doorway had ducked inside, and I could see out of the corner of my eye that people had begun to gather around us at a safe distance, waiting to see what happened next. It suddenly occurred to me that I'd somehow been sucked into one of those middle-of-the-street standoffs that they always wrote about in those stupid dime novels. *Like I really want an audience for this*, I thought.

J'nath was the first to find his voice. "I...I did not know the Kana-Semeth was releasing thee today, Reshard," he said in English. "Pietruvek told me that thou might be out soon, though."

"Actually," I said after a moment's hesitation, "I'm kind of on parole. He only let me out long enough to see you."

"Ah." He probably had no idea what "parole" meant. "Thou looks...better. And thy wounds, have they all healed?" He pointed to my forehead -- the bandage I'd worn since I arrived in Arkhein was gone.

"Oh, yeah, I forgot about that. I took it off yesterday...figured I'd healed up enough to get rid of it." I pushed the hair away from my left temple to show him the pinkish scar. "Itches like Hell. My shoulder's doing pretty good, too. 'Bout another week for that, I think."

"That is good." He tried to smile, but it didn't work. It was obvious that my showing up the way I did made him uncomfortable. Maybe he thought I'd attack him again if he said the wrong thing. Going by what Pietruvek had told me about my behavior that night, I couldn't blame him.

I took a deep breath, then all the words I'd been holding in came tumbling out. "You probably think I'm a real jackass, don't you?" He opened his mouth to respond, but I held up a hand. "It's alright, you're not the first...and you're right, I *am* a jackass. But I'm also a *scared* jackass, I have been ever since I got stuck here, which means I'm twice as likely to do something really stupid. And that stuff I did during Halitova, the things I said to you...well, that was about as stupid as it gets." I shoved my hands into my pockets. "I know saying I'm sorry doesn't change a damn thing, but I *am* sorry. Hell, I'm probably the sorriest guy in this whole world. I just...I'm not asking you to forgive me, but I...I don't know. I really don't know." I turned away sheepishly, thinking, *Why the hell did I come out here? Did I really think I could fix this mess with a couple of words?* I shook my head and began to walk away from J'nath. "I should go. This...it was a mistake."

He took hold of my arm. *"Nee*, it was not," he said. "At least, it was not thine."

"What do you mean?"

"I abandoned thee. When thou needed me most, I turned my back on thee. I had no right to do that."

"J'nath..."

"I swore to my *padra*," he continued. "When the Crossroad became my responsibility, I swore to him that I would protect it *and* the artifacts *and* any Taran that may come through, no matter who or what they might be. But when thou became too difficult for me to handle, I gave thee up to the Kana-Semeth. Nina and Pietruvek have been trying for these past days to talk me into at least visiting thee, but I would not. I felt there was no hope for thee, that thou could not be redeemed." He stared down at the ground. "But now thou art here before me, ready to accept blame without being asked, and I see how wrong I truly was about thee."

Don't be sure on that, I thought, then said aloud, "Y'know, considering that we've both been messing up left and right since I arrived in this place, I don't think we've done too bad a job."

"How so?" He picked up his head slightly.

"Well, we haven't killed each other yet." I smiled. He didn't. "That was a joke."

"Ah," he answered, still not smiling. "That is not very funny."

I shrugged. "Sorry, I've been sick."

That did the trick: J'nath tried to hold the laughter in, but it was just too much. I found myself also trying to stifle a few giggles before I finally said to Hell with it and let go. Some of the people in the square were now staring at us like we were nuts, but neither of us cared. I think the last week had been as humorless for him as it had been for me, and we both needed the release.

* * * * * *

H'landa didn't seem too surprised when I returned with J'nath. He simply ushered us into his office and began talking about the terms of my release like he'd planned it this way from the beginning. I wasn't getting off that easy, though: the lawman made it clear that if I slipped up again, I'd be tried just like any other Arkan, no more favors. He also made J'nath my *gama*, or legal guardian, which meant that he'd be held fully accountable for my actions. I didn't like the idea that J'nath could be punished for my mistakes, but then again, I didn't plan on *making* any more of them, so I guess there was nothing to worry about.

There was still the matter of the letter, as well...or rather, the lack of one. H'landa was still waiting for a response from his superiors in Dak-Taorin, and he wanted my assurance that I would cooperate with whatever

mandate the Kana-Semeth passed down when word finally
came. I reluctantly agreed, making a mental note that if
their response included anything that sounded even
remotely like "incarceration" or "execution", I'd run for it
and take my chances.

Once all matters had been settled and all the
legalities gone over, there was only one bit of business
left: the return of my Peacemakers. I'd expected some sort
of double-cross on this, but the man was true to his word.
I asked H'landa about the one he'd taken apart, and he
reassured me that every piece had been put back just the
way he'd found it.

Mental note number two: disassemble and clean
both guns *thoroughly* as soon as possible.

"Do you promise to keep those things sheathed
from now on?" the lawman asked me in English as I
strapped on my gunbelts.

"Holstered," I corrected him. "You holster guns.
And yeah, I'll keep my hands off 'em so long as things are
quiet."

"Oh? Do you expect trouble?"

"You never know."

"I do not *kedda* why you would need to have such
a powerful weapon, anyway. Is life in Tarahein that
dangerous?"

"Well, back east, it's pretty safe," I told him.
"Most people aren't walking around New York with Colts
or Smith & Wessons strapped on, but out west...I can think
of a few nasty fellas that you wouldn't want to run into
without a sixgun at your side." *Like myself, for example*, I
silently added.

"So a *trit bakido* is used to protect yourself from
other Tarans?" H'landa asked. "To kill them?"

I didn't like where this conversation was going.
"Well, sometimes, but not..."

"Have *you* ever killed anyone with those things,
Richard?"

I ran a dry tongue across my lips. "No," I lied. Aw, Christ, this wasn't happening. I was so close to getting out of here, *so damn close*. I did my best to remain calm as I waited for him to call my bluff.

"We should go now," J'nath interjected. "I told Nina I would not be gone for long, and it is already long past midday."

"*Ke?* Ah, *kai*, I suppose you are correct." The lawman turned towards him, saying, "You may take him now, but remember: he is free only so long as he behaves."

"Of course." He clasped his hands and bowed slightly. "*K'sai, d'ho-lermekt*." When he straightened up, he nudged me with his foot.

"Huh? Oh yeah, thanks...er, I mean *k'sai*." I did a hasty little head-bob and turned to follow J'nath out, but I was stopped by the lawman's hand falling on my shoulder. *Dammit all to Hell...*

"You will remember?" he asked. "What we spoke of a few days ago?"

I was about to tell him that I didn't know what he was referring to, then I saw him rub his smooth chin with his free hand. "Oh, that," I answered, mimicking the gesture -- the week-old stubble on my face rasped beneath my fingers. "Not a word, I promise."

He visibly relaxed a bit when I said that, then he let go of me, putting his no-nonsense Kana-Semeth face back on. "Well, off with you, then."

"Yessir." I smirked and left the office. J'nath was waiting for me by the main doors.

"What was that about?" he asked as I approached.

"Nothing important, really. He just wanted to remind me of something." I pushed the doors open and stepped out into the sunshine. It felt good in a way that you just cannot imagine unless you've ever been a prisoner. "By the way, J'nath, I owe you one."

"Owe me one what?"

"Forget it. Let's go home."

* * * * * *

"He set Reshard free? How did you manage that?" Nina was looking at me as she spoke in Arkan, but the words were directed at J'nath. While she'd been stunned silent when I walked into the house, it didn't take long for her to find her tongue again. Once she got going, though, it took me a minute to get the gist of the conversation.

J'nath smiled and shook his head. "Actually, I did nothing," he replied. "Reshard somehow managed to do it all himself."

"He did?" She finally turned towards her husband. "But he cannot even speak Arkan, how could..."

I couldn't hold back any longer -- I'd been silent ever since I'd entered the house. "That is not so true anymore," I said to her in Arkan.

The expression on her face was priceless, even better than the one she had when I first entered. Pietruvek, who was standing nearby, bit his lip to keep from laughing -- I guess he hadn't told his mother that I was getting a better handle on the language. "You..." she started to say as she gave me a hard whack on the arm. "Why did you not *say* anything?" She sounded mad, but she was smiling when she hit me. "You made me stand here like a *bruhzod*..." She whacked me with her palm again.

"Speak slower, I...*ow!*...I am still learning," I said as I tried to protect myself. "J'nath, your wife's beating me up!" I yelled in English.

He held his hands up. "I am sorry, this is thy fight."

"Best to just stay still and take thy punishment," Pietruvek added, laughing.

Nina stopped and turned towards them. "What are you two saying?" she asked in Arkan. "I always feel like you are telling secrets to each other whenever you speak Taran."

"They are telling me to ask forgiveness from you," I said to her, hoping that my words didn't sound as clumsy as I thought they did. "I should not have tricked you like that."

"*Nee*, you should not have, and you had best not do so again." She smiled again and, putting her hands on my shoulders so she could boost herself up a bit, kissed me on the cheek. "Welcome home, Reshard Corrigan."

"*K'sai*, Nina Kandru. After what I have been through, I am glad to be welcomed *anywhere*."

*   *   *   *   *   *

That evening seemed like a dream to me: after being cooped up for so long, it just didn't seem possible for me to be free again. But there I was, sitting in front of the hearth with J'nath and his family, eating, talking, laughing. I brought out a deck of cards that had crossed over with me and tried to teach Pietruvek how to play poker. It was probably the best night I'd had since arriving in Arkhein.

When I went to bed, however, the dream ended and the nightmares began.

The robbery, the getaway, the dead town, the Crossroad...I watched it all happen again and again, and I was powerless to stop it. The bullets shattered Kennedy's skull over a dozen times. Reeves, half-dead and fever-slick, endlessly telling me to leave him. Sheriff Walker's hand wrapped around my throat, then it turned into a hard black *thing* somewhere between a claw and a tentacle, then it was Walker's hand again, then the blackness, until both were choking me to death as the rain pours down and the light pours up and Jesus Christ please I just want to *WAKE UP!*

I snapped awake in bed to find myself curled into a tight ball, my every breath coming in and out of my lungs in a pitiful, choked scream, as if my vocal cords were paralyzed. I don't know how long I laid there, eyes wide, heart racing, just wanting the memories to go away. I kept expecting someone to knock on the door and ask if I was alright, why was I screaming, but no one did. It was a good thing, too, because if anyone *had* knocked, I probably would have jumped out of my skin.

I wanted a drink so badly, but I couldn't have one without killing myself, and just sitting still was making the craving worse. I got out of bed and dressed in the dark -- my hand hesitated for a moment over my gunbelts hanging on the chair, then I went ahead and grabbed them anyway. I left the house as quietly as I could, not caring where I was going, just so long as I was moving.

There was no rhyme or reason to my movements at first, just aimless pacing in the moonlit front yard. Before I knew it, I'd picked a direction and was heading away from both the house and Betedek. The land was just open fields to begin with, but then it thickened into a copse of trees, gently sloping upward. I occasionally caught glimpses of little rodent-like things scurrying through the underbrush, probably scared to death of this big monster tromping though their territory in the middle of the night. *Sorry, kids,* I thought, *you're just gonna have to deal with it for now. I've got to blow off some steam.*

The slope of the hill became steeper, the trees stouter, until it finally leveled off into a forest proper. Most of my anxiety had burned off by then, but my legs ached too much to walk back right then and there, so I made myself comfortable at the base of one of the trees, figuring on resting for a few minutes before heading back down. My little excursion must have worn me out more than I thought, however, because I fell into a deep sleep not long after my back hit the tree trunk, and I stayed out until the rosy dawn began to seep in through my eyelids.

I was a little puzzled when I woke back up -- it took a minute to recall just how I got outside -- then I rubbed my eyes and looked up through the trees at the lightening sky. I remembered the first time I saw it, cold and confused and hurt. How different it looked to me now...it wasn't scary anymore. I got up and hobbled over to a thinner part of the woods on stiff legs. I could see Betedek at the bottom of the slope, small and still in the morning light, with the sunrise just beyond the rooftops giving everything a rose-colored glow. I stood there for quite a while, taking it all in, really *looking* at this place as if for the first time. As I gazed out over the landscape, I began to realize the unique opportunity this strange world had given me: the chance to honest-to-God walk away from my old life and start over. Unfortunately, I was still the same arrogant jackass I'd always been, and I'd already messed up any chance I had of beginning this new life with a clean slate -- *Lermekt* H'landa could attest to that. I sagged against a nearby tree, reflecting how I'd been acting around everyone for nearly two weeks now: rude, sulking, hollering about how much I wanted to go home, but now...now this *was* my home. It suddenly hit me that I'd referred to it as such yesterday, and so had Nina. Good God, when was the last time I could honestly call any place "home"? I could barely remember.

I looked down at the guns on my hips. H'landa had asked me earlier why I needed them, and I had given him a flippant answer. And now, standing on that hillside overlooking Betedek, I asked myself the same question, and I couldn't think of a good reason at all, not in this place. Those Peacemakers used to mean the world to me, but now they just seemed too heavy a weight to bear. I felt like they were just going to keep dragging me down, crushing me until I'd ruined my life here as badly as I had on my world. *I can't let it happen again*, I thought, and began to head back down the slope. *I have to try and stop it before it gets any worse, I have to try.* A few more steps, and I soon found myself running, the sky above me turning violet as the sun rose higher. *Please, God*, I thought as I got closer to the house, *I mean it this time, I want to do this, let me do this...*

Everyone was already awake and getting ready for the day when I opened the front door, out of breath.

"What...when did you...is something wrong?" J'nath stammered in Arkan. He looked surprised to see me, as did the others -- I guess they all thought I was still asleep in my room.

I swallowed hard. "Never mind," I told him, "it is not important." Then, before I could think twice about it, I began to unbuckle my gunbelts.

"Reshard, what are you doing?"

"Put these somewhere safe." I handed the belts over to J'nath. "Stick them downstairs with the other artifacts, hide them under your bed, I do not care. Just make sure they are safe."

"But why? These are yours. *Lermekt* H'landa gave them back to you. Why are you giving them up?"

Because I quit. "Because I should not need them anymore. Not here."

"*Nee*, these are yours," he insisted, trying to hand them back.

"If I need them, I will ask for them, but for now..." *For now, I don't even want to look at the damn things.* "Please, J'nath."

He must have seen the distress in my eyes, because he finally agreed. As he went down to the cellar to store them away, I slumped down into a chair at the table, head cradled in my hands. Nina asked me if I was feeling sick again. I lied and told her I felt fine. Pietruvek, who'd seen me at both my best and worst, let me be.

I'd never given up my guns voluntarily before. *Never.* But I had to do it. No matter what happened to me down the line, no matter what the consequences, I had to do it. And it wasn't just for me: I was doing it for Kyle Reeves, for Joe Kennedy, and for Peter Stewart...*especially* for him.

You hear me, guys? I silently called out as I stared at the tabletop, fingers pushed deep into my hair. *This is for you. I'm walking away from it all because you guys can't. The outlaw life killed you, but I won't let it kill me any more than it already has.*

Because I quit.

CHAPTER 10

I wish I could say that becoming an honest man was easy, that I just turned away from my old life and never looked back. I'd tried to do it once before, and hadn't lasted very long, but I thought it could be different this time. For one thing, I didn't need to steal to pay for food and shelter, I already had those things. Nor did I have to worry about bounty hunters or Pinkertons or whoever else driving me out of hiding, obviously.

My biggest problem turned out to be me...or rather all the lessons that had literally been beaten into me since I was thirteen. Carson had been a ruthless taskmaster when we were young, using fear, pain, and hunger to get us to do whatever he wanted. After a while, it just became second nature: You see something you want, you take it, and if someone tries to stop you, you kill them. Conditioning like that cannot be broken overnight, no matter how badly you may want to stop. I'd walk into a shop in Betedek and catch myself counting exits like I was planning to rob it, or I'd unconsciously palm some little trinket and slip it into my pocket, then come to my senses a few minutes later and have to sneak it back to its proper place. After a while, I started to walk around with my hands shoved deep in my trouser pockets, my eyes focused on the ground. People began to think I was either shy or sulking, but it seemed the only way to keep myself out of trouble.

It didn't take J'nath long to figure out something was the matter, and he asked me about my behavior one night at the family's evening meal. "I just...I do not know what to do with myself here," I told him in Arkan. That seemed the best way to put it without blurting out the truth.

"Are you bored?" Nina asked.

"*Nee*. I need a distraction, I think." I idly pushed my spoon around in my soup bowl, trying to sink a chunk of some bitter yellow vegetable in there. "Just something to help take my mind off...other things."

"Still no word from Dak-Taorin?" J'nath ventured.

"Not so far as I know," I replied. It had been fifteen days since H'landa had sent the message to his superiors. I had to admit, their silence wasn't exactly helping my state of mind. What were they waiting for? "Maybe they decided I am not that important."

"Then they should at least tell *Lermekt* H'landa to return," J'nath said. "A village this small has no need for a full-time Kana-Semeth."

"I saw *d'ho*-Kinik talking to him the other day," Pietruvek added. "She wanted him to arrest little Mazad for spilling a sack of dried beans in her store."

Nina's eyes widened. "Arrest a two-year-old boy?"

"*Kai*. She said if his parents were going to let him run wild in the square, then it was up to the Kana-Semeth to stop his rampage."

I could picture the lawman trying to wrestle a toddler into the cell -- he didn't strike me as the type that liked kids. "Well, did he do it?" I asked.

Pietruvek laughed. "Of course not! He told her if the Kana-Semeth locked up every child that misbehaved, there would be no room in the workhouses for the adults."

"He should have locked *her* up for suggesting such a thing." Nina pronounced as she got up from the table and went over to the hearth to get some more tea. She began to pour some into her cup, then paused and said, "Although, I must admit that boy does cause quite a bit of trouble sometimes."

"So you think Mazad *should* be locked up," I joked.

"*Kai...nee*...I mean...why do you always play with my words like that?" She came up to me and cupped my chin in her free hand. "I think you are learning Arkan *too* well, Reshard."

"Not as well as I pretend to," I answered. "I still guess at what people say many times."

"Despite that, you seem to be improving with every passing day. Do you not think so, J'nath?"

"Hmm?" He'd been staring off into space, hands clasped together before him. "I am sorry, I was thinking..." He turned to me. "Reshard, I want you to come with me to Betedek tomorrow morning. I may have a distraction for you, at least for a while."

"What did you have in mind?"

"I am not sure, we shall see tomorrow."

I leaned close to him, saying, "You know I hate it when you keep secrets. Just tell me now."

"Fair enough," he said with a smile. "One of the villagers near the south end began rebuilding his barn a few days ago. Unfortunately, two of the men helping him have fallen ill suddenly. You told me that you helped the *lermekt* make a few repairs to the meeting hall, so..."

"But those were small things, I am not a...um, a..." I drummed my fingers on the table, trying to think of the proper Arkan word, then gave up and reverted to English. "I'm not a carpenter, J'nath. I wouldn't have the slightest idea where to start on something that big."

"I do not think they will make you do the job by yourself," he said in Arkan, "but they would probably appreciate an extra pair of hands." He looked at me, eyebrows raised. "Well? Do you wish to try?"

I shrugged. "I suppose so, if you can spare me. I have been helping Peter with the chores lately."

"He did well enough by himself before you came, he can manage to do them again without you for a while."

"It will not be half as fun, though," Pietruvek muttered.

I reached over and mussed the boy's hair, smiling. "I will hurry back, I promise."

* * * * * *

I got a pleasant surprise the next morning when I met my new employer. While most of my memory of the Halitova party was still hazy, I recognized the man right away as my drinking partner from that night. The first few minutes of reintroduction consisted mainly of him apologizing for nearly killing me (his words, not mine), and me trying to reassure him that I was fine, no permanent damage done. Once that was out of the way, we got down to the business of what I was to do around there.

The man, whose name was Dimidev ("But call me Dimi," he insisted, "everyone calls me Dimi."), was a bit stout for an Arkan, but he moved quickly for a man his size. He kept pulling me around his homestead, introducing me to his wife and daughters, showing me the partially-constructed barn, and talking, always talking. "Oh, it was terrible," he told me when I asked what happened to his old barn. "Early last Winter, I was in there, feeding the *h'ruuniben*...do you know what those are?"

I nodded. A *h'ruun* looked like a cross between a cow and a camel, with a shaggy pelt Arkans would shear off to use like wool.

"Well, I was feeding them, and I saw one lying on its side, making that awful wet coughing noise that they do. So I lit a lantern, went into the stall to see if it was sick, and do you know what it did? It kicked me! I fell flat, the other *h'ruuniben* tried to trample me, and the lantern fell on some dry hay. By the time I got up, half the west wall was on fire." He shook his head. "Got most of the animals out, but the whole barn was gone by nightfall. And you know the funny part? The *bruhzod h'ruun* that kicked me lived through all of it! I decided then that those things were more trouble than they were worth. Sold the whole herd five days later." That was a typical exchange between the two of us: him talking a mile a minute and me doing my level best to keep up.

When he finally put me to work, it was *work*: I cut lumber, hauled stuff up ladders, drove nails, just put myself through paces like I'd never done before. Hell, I'd never had a real *job* before, but despite the inexperience, the other men helping out with the construction were pretty fair to me when I messed up. In fact, only one guy gave me any trouble, but it had nothing to do with my work ethic. I'd only been on Dimi's property for a few hours, and was just beginning to get my hands dirty, when one of the workers threw down his tools and stormed over to Dimi, yelling something and pointing in my direction. Dimi tried to calm him down, but that only seemed to get the guy more riled. While I couldn't understand every word shouted, it was obvious enough that I was the main subject, so I put down my own tools and went over, saying to them in Arkan, "Did I do something wrong?"

Without even acknowledging my presence, the man said to Dimi, "Either that thing leaves or I will."

Dimi held up a hand. "I know you are angry, Noren, but you should not hold onto your anger. At least give Reshard the opportunity to apologize to you and Ari."

When Dimi said that, another hazy memory from Halitova surfaced: the man before me knocking me down, livid because I'd made a drunken pass at his wife. I felt my face turn red -- Lord, how many mistakes did I make that night? -- and tried to make amends right then and there, but before the words even had a chance to leave my mouth, the man turned towards me and spat in my face. "Come near me or my wife ever again," he said evenly, "and I will put you down like the animal that you are." He shoved me aside and stalked off, all eyes in the yard following him.

I wiped the spit off with surprising calm. Inwardly, I wanted to jump on the guy's back and bash his head in with a rock, but that certainly wouldn't sit well with *Lermekt* H'landa. "Forgive me, Reshard," Dimi said,

"I did not expect Noren to react like that to your presence."

"Not the first time I have been spit upon," I replied, "and considering what I did, I suppose he is justified."

"But there are better ways to resolve this than threats and insults. You are a part of this village now...does he expect to hate you forever?"

I watched Noren as he left Dimi's property. "Reckon it looks like he's gonna try," I muttered in English.

* * * * * *

Despite that rough first day, the experience overall was uneventful: I showed up in the morning every day, did my share, and went home around mid-afternoon. The only thing of note were the spectators that followed me around *everywhere*. It wasn't the adults, mind you -- most of the wonder about me had worn off for them -- but the kids in the village still found me terribly interesting. I'd catch them out of the corner of my eye, hiding behind trees or buildings, looks of fascination stamped on their faces. Whenever I returned their stares, they'd all fly off, screaming and giggling. I thought it was kind of funny the first couple of days, albeit weird: I just couldn't figure out what it was about me that kept bringing them back.

Eventually, two of the boys in my "audience" worked up the courage to approach me while I was taking a break one day. I was sitting under a shade tree when I saw them creeping up on me, each one advancing by prodding the other in my direction.

"You ask him," said one. "*Nee*, you do it," the other countered. "It was *your* idea," the first one insisted.

"Can I help you boys?" I said to them in Arkan. They froze in their tracks, looking guilty for no apparent reason. "Well? You had something you wanted to ask me?"

They looked at each other, at the ground, anywhere but at me. Finally, the younger of the two blurted out, "Can we see your tail?"

"*What?!?*" I exclaimed in English so loudly that the sound of it alone scared them.

"It was his idea!" The little guy pushed away from the other. "He thought we should ask you and I did not want to but he brought me out here..."

"Liar! You said you wanted to come with me!" the older boy said.

"Did not! I said I wanted to *see* it, but I did not want to come over here."

"Whoa, hold on a minute." I held my hands up, hoping the kids would stop hollering, then switched back to Arkan, "Who told you I had a tail?"

"My friend Riner," the older boy said, cautiously. "He heard that Tarans have long hairy tails, but he said *d'ho*-Bannen makes you keep it tucked away so you look more normal." He took a few steps closer to me. "Looks like he made you file down your teeth as well."

"My teeth are *supposed* to look like this," I answered, "and I *do not* have a *tail*."

"He made you cut it off?"

"I *never* had one!" I rubbed a hand over my face as I tried to regain my composure. Good Lord, kids and their overactive imaginations. "You two heard anything else about me?" I asked, not really wanting to know the answer.

"You can spit fire."

"You tore the door off the cell in the Kana-Semeth's office with your bare hands."

"You hunt down animals in the woods and eat them raw."

"At night, your eyes glow in the dark."

"You can make..."

"Stop, stop, that is enough." I said, rolling my eyes. "Look, I hate to disappoint you, but none of that is true. I am just like you or any other Arkan. I just look a bit different. I am not some sort of animal, and I do not have any strange powers, *kedda*?" They nodded, looking absolutely crestfallen. "Good. Off with you, then. And be sure to tell your friends what I told you." I made a shooing gesture, and they slunk back the way they had come, heads down and feet dragging.

The next day, I spotted twice as many kids watching me. So much for brutal honesty.

* * * * * *

About five days after I started working for Dimi, one of the men I'd replaced died. Heart attack or something in the middle of the night. The guy had been about forty or so -- well into middle age for an Arkan, as I understood it, but not *that* old. J'nath told me that the man had a weak heart, and was always getting sick. "Darus should not have been helping Dimi," J'nath said, "at least not with a strenuous task like that, but I guess he owed Dimi a favor."

The village almost completely shut down the next day for the funeral. I attended more out of curiosity than sympathy: I'd never seen anything resembling a graveyard within Betedek's borders, and death wasn't exactly a subject that Arkans were eager to talk about. The funeral procession began in the front yard of Darus's house, with his family carrying the shrouded body out the front door on a wooden stretcher. Once they had passed everyone gathered in the yard, the mourners fell in line behind them, two by two. I waited until everyone else had begun to follow before joining them -- being still, in my eyes, a stranger in this place, I didn't feel right taking a position closer to the front. I found some company at the end of the line, though, for as I began walking along, H'landa fell in step beside me. "What are you doing here?" I asked him in English.

"I was wondering the same about you."

"I *live* here now, remember? I have to be social to some degree. What's your excuse?"

"This, as always." He tapped the buckle-emblem near his right shoulder as we walked. "It is common Kana-Semeth practice to acknowledge all customs and events wherever one happens to be stationed."

"Shouldn't you be up near the front, then?"

"I prefer not to be around the dead."

"I can understand that." The procession had been heading down the main road leading out of the village. After a short ways, it began to turn right onto a narrow path into the woods, flanked on either side with short, thick shrubs. I could see people reaching out and snapping off branches from the shrubs here and there. The lawman did the same, the branch making a dry crack. "What's that for?" I asked.

"The *idiayo*. You toss these in as a symbol of your loss, like you are giving up a part of yourself to the deceased." He pulled leaves off the branch, explaining, "This is *kahufilk*...bloodwood. At the beginning of the world, Avisar cut down a great red tree and used the wood to carve the first Arkans. The shavings became bloodwood bushes." He plucked off a small purplish-red berry from the branch in his hand. "Here, eat this."

Cautiously, I put the berry in my mouth and bit down on it -- it was hard, with a strange coppery aftertaste. "This is disgusting," I muttered. "It tastes like blood." I tried to spit the rest out without anybody noticing, only to get sticky red flecks of the stuff on my bottom lip, which then got smeared on my hand as I wiped my mouth. H'landa smiled, doing his best not to laugh out loud. "Oh, you think it's funny? You have some, then." I tried to rub my ruddy hand on his uniform.

He grabbed my wrist. "Stop it. I think we have reached the *idiayo*." A clearing lay ahead of us, but there were too many people in front of us to see anything.

"What does *idiayo* mean, anyways? 'Church'? 'Graveyard'?"

I could tell by the look on his face that he didn't understand me. "You *kedda* what *idi* means, *kai*?"

"Yeah, that's like 'fire' or 'flame'. But I still don't..." I stopped talking when we'd come close enough to the clearing to see the *idiayo*. It was a rectangular metal frame, about six feet long and more than three feet tall. They'd placed the body, stretcher and all, on top of it, and about twenty or thirty fresh-cut logs had been laid over the pile of ash beneath the frame. "They're gonna *burn* the body?" I asked the lawman incredulously under my breath.

"Of course. How else can you rejoin the Light if your body still ties you to the physical world?" He snapped the branch he'd been holding in half, then handed me a piece. "Take this, and remember to say a prayer for the dead before tossing it in." He then walked into the clearing, towards Darus's body. A few others were already standing closely around the *idiayo*, heads bowed and hands clasped in that odd Arkan gesture. When each one finished praying, they'd toss their pieces of *kahufilk* onto the logs -- one more little maroon stick amongst dozens of others -- then join everyone else on the edge of the clearing. I stood apart from the group for a minute or two, thinking about how I sure as Hell didn't want to be set on fire when I died, then finally worked up the courage to approach the body.

Darus's family had wrapped his body with a single piece of finely-woven white cloth. The shroud was so tightly-bound that it outlined his entire body, even his face. On his forehead, just above the two round hollows that marked where his eyes were, someone had drawn a symbol:

It looked to me like an upside-down Ace of Spades. I'd never seen anything like it before, but figured it was the Arkan equivalent to a Cross. Something about that symbol wasn't sitting right with me, though: looking at it gave me a weird crawly feeling on the back of my neck. I wanted nothing more than to get away from Darus's corpse, the sooner the better, but I couldn't, not until I did my thing with the stick. I clasped my hands and rattled off in English, "Our Father, who art in Heaven, hallowed be Thy name, Thy kingdom come, Thy will be done, on Earth as is in Heaven. Give us this day our daily bread, and forgive us our trespasses...and I don't remember the rest. Amen." I tossed the branch in and walked over to where J'nath and his family stood, glad to be done with it.

When all the mourners had finished, Darus's relatives gathered 'round the body, one of them holding a small lit torch. He touched it to the kindling, quietly saying in Arkan, "Avisar, Bringer of the Light, we ask that You welcome the *kahn* of Darus Mederi into Your arms. We thank You for letting us know him, and we forgive You for taking him away. As we come from the Light, we must return to the Light."

The phrase echoed through the crowd, some people struggling to get the words out without breaking down in tears: "*Ven z'ro abahn sho va Kana, z'ro dima efana u va Kana.*" I fumbled my way through the words as best as I could, even though they meant nothing to me: I didn't feel bad about the guy dying, and I'd never even met him before as far as I was aware. To me, he was nobody.

The flames rose up to claim the body, the white shroud quickly turning black. The logs and bloodwood branches gave off a pleasant aroma as they burned, but it wasn't strong enough to completely cover up that *other* smell. It brought back memories of Hadley, of all those bodies in that little room...my throat clenched up at the thought of it. I pulled out my bandana and held it over my mouth and nose as I tried to breathe normally and think of other things, but I couldn't, I just couldn't. Dead bodies, all over town, mummifying in the dry heat, and they all smelled the way this funeral pyre smelled, and...and I...

One of the mourners caught me as my knees buckled, black spots swimming in my vision. *"D'ho-*Corrigan? Are you ill?" I heard someone ask. I tried to focus on the voice, but when I turned my head towards it, all I saw was the bloody, blackened face of a corpse. I tried to scream, but I could barely draw enough air to breathe. I turned away from it, and then realized that I was surrounded by dead bodies...only they weren't completely dead. They reached out towards me, razor-sharp claws ripping through my shirt and drawing blood. A hand closed around my throat, cutting off what little air I could suck in. I did my best to fight them off, but it was no use, there were too many...so many hands, pulling me down, smothering me...oh God, I've got to get out of here...can't breathe, choking, get up get up get out...

"Get off of me!" I shoved at the bodies around me as hard as I could. A woman standing beside me fell to the ground, crying out in surprise. The man who'd caught me let go and backed away. I whipped my head around, looking for more walking corpses, but there weren't any, just a bunch of villagers who were likely now convinced that I was crazy, and I couldn't exactly disagree with them on that point.

The crowd parted before me as I made my way out of the clearing and back to the path. Once I got there, I fell to my hands and knees, still shivering with terror. *What the Hell happened back there?* I wondered. *Everything was fine, then BANG, I fall asleep standing up or something and have a godawful nightmare. Doesn't make sense.*

I heard movement behind me, so I scrambled to my feet, fists clenched, then relaxed when I saw it was J'nath. "Art thou kay-oh now?" he asked in English.

"'Okay', the word's 'okay'...and yeah, I'm fine, I guess." I rubbed a hand over my face.

"Thou does not sound very sure."

That's 'cause I'm not. "No, I'm sure. Don't worry about me. Go back and do...whatever." I waved him away and sat back down on the ground, but he didn't budge.

"Something frightened thee back there. I can still see it in thine eyes," J'nath said. "I do not think I should leave thee alone."

"I said don't worry. I'm just gonna sit here, alright? I don't need to be watched every damn second."

"Art thou..."

"*Adai*," I snapped in Arkan. I almost made a crack about how he should go help barbecue his friend, but wisely held it back. He turned away from me without another word and headed back to the pyre.

True to my word, I didn't move an inch. I just sat on the path and idly drew patterns in the dirt with a stick. One I kept repeating over and over was the symbol on the shroud. I didn't get that weird crawly feeling looking at it now like I did the first time, but I just couldn't get the image of it out of my head. There was something about it, digging at my mind in a way I couldn't explain.

When the funeral finally ended, I dragged my foot through the drawings, just in case they might offend somebody, then fell in beside J'nath when he passed by. He glanced at me uncertainly, but neither one of us said a word about the strange way I'd acted.

* * * * * *

H'landa flagged me down the next day as I headed home from Dimi's. The lawman had a bounce in his step that I'd never seen before. "How goes the barn-building?" he asked in English.

"Right as rain. Tomorrow should be the last day...and one of the other men wants me to help him with another job. A *paying* job." I grinned and held my palm out and up, waggling my fingers -- an Arkan gesture I'd learned for money or payment.

Grinning himself, he answered, "I am afraid you will have to turn him down." Before I could ask him what he meant by that, he held up a metal cylinder...a very *familiar* metal cylinder.

I stopped dead in my tracks, my eyes wide. "Is that...did they...holy shit..." I took it from him and turned it over in my hands. Sure enough, there was the Kana-Semeth emblem, with *TAORIN ~ BETEDEK* etched below it in Arkan. I also noted that the seal had already been broken.

"A *karrel* delivered it just a little while ago," he explained. "I had to send him back immediately with an answer. You should feel honored, Taran. They do not usually turn three-stripers into errand boys." I gathered that a *karrel* must outrank a *lermekt* in the Kana-Semeth hierarchy.

"Well? What's going on? What does it say?"

"It says I should get another stripe for putting up with you," he said with a smirk, taking back the cylinder, "and I think we should have *d'ho*-Bannen present before I tell you the rest."

"*What?* What's going on, dammit!" I pestered him the whole way home, but he refused to say a word until J'nath, Nina, and Pietruvek were gathered around the hearth with us. Only then did he finally read aloud the letter that I'd been waiting nearly a month for.

"'To *Lermekt* Jamin H'landa, Betedek Station Officer: Despite precautions, knowledge of the arrival of the Taran Richard Corrigan has become widespread. Both the Taran and J'nath Bannen are to be brought to Dak-Taorin immediately. Neither is to be considered a prisoner...'" He glanced up at J'nath and me when he read that part, then continued, "'...but no delays of any sort are to be tolerated. Signed, *H'drek* Triaal Sela.' She was the one who originally sent me here," he explained.

"And that is all she had to say?" I asked in Arkan.
"A bit short, considering she took so long to respond...and
what is that 'prisoner' remark supposed to mean?"

"I told her about my having to arrest you. Perhaps
she thought I may still have you locked up."

The lawman handed me the letter, not that it did
me any good: aside from my name (written as *RESHARD
KORRIGAN* in Arkan) and a few other words, I couldn't
make head nor tail of it all. I handed it off to J'nath, who
looked it over and asked H'landa, "This letter makes it
sound like the Kana-Semeth were trying to hide Reshard's
presence here. Why?"

"As I told Richard before, I think my superiors
were a bit frightened by his sudden appearance in our
world. There were so many different ways this incident
might have turned out, especially if I was not...if someone
else had been sent in my place." H'landa caught himself
just in time. "They were expecting a threat, an invasion,
something dangerous, so aside from myself and a few
others, no one else was told about this." He began to pace
a little, saying, "When I sent word back, I told them not to
worry, that the Taran was harmless...well, *mostly* harmless.
I thought that would be end of it. It never occurred to me
that they might want to bring him in, regardless."

Bring him in. That wasn't exactly a phrase I was
comfortable with. "You know, when you stopped me
earlier, I had the impression that this was *good* news."

"It is neither good nor bad." He took the letter
back from J'nath. "These are *orders*, Richard, not
explanations. Those are in Dak-Taorin. Tomorrow, the
three of us will leave to find out what those explanations
are."

"Tomorrow?" J'nath echoed. "But that gives me
no time to prepare." He stood up and began to pace as
well. "All those Taran artifacts, the manuscripts, the
maps...what do you think your superiors would be the
most interested in?" He spun around to look at H'landa,

then turned away before the lawman could answer, muttering to himself.

Nina, who was sitting near me, leaned over with a smile as I watched J'nath's suddenly frantic behavior. "He acted like this the first day you were here. Just running around nonstop, like no one else was in the house."

"So he *will* settle down eventually?" I asked.

"Eventually."

H'landa apparently didn't want to wait: he reached out and grabbed J'nath by the nape of his neck, which managed to snap him out of it. I had to admit, it was amusing to see someone besides myself get throttled by the Kana-Semeth. "I will give you a satchel," he told J'nath, still holding onto him. "You can fill it with whatever useless things you deem 'important', but once it is full, you are done packing. *Kedda?*"

"*Kai.*"

"Good." The lawman let go. "I was ordered to bring back two men, not a museum."

J'nath backed away from him a couple of steps, rubbing his neck. "If I may, *d'ho-lermekt*," he said hesitantly, "I am sure it would be easier for me to decide what is and is not important if I had more time."

H'landa made a noise somewhere between a grunt and a growl. "Fine...we will depart the day *after* tomorrow." He then pointed at Pietruvek, saying, "And you make sure he does not drag his feet to get an extra day out of me." The kid grinned from ear to ear at the prospect of bossing his father around.

I stood up and approached H'landa, asking in English, "Can I see you outside for a minute?" He nodded, and we stepped out into the yard. Once I thought we were far enough from the house, I turned to him and said, "Okay, let's see the rest."

"The rest of what?"

"The letter. C'mon, I know you've gotta be holding something back."

He squinted at me. "Has anyone ever told you that you are a very *zoggoth* man?"

"If that means 'suspicious', then yes, I am...especially when my ass is potentially on the line." I pushed my hands through my hair. "Look, you said it yourself: your superiors thought I might be dangerous. For all I know, they might still think that, despite what that letter says. We could arrive in Dak-Taorin thinking everything's fine, and J'nath and I might end up being executed on the spot."

"Exe..."

"*Killed*, cousin. You *kedda* that word, you one-eyed wonder? They kill me to eliminate any potential threat that I might become, and they take out J'nath because he basically owns the Crossroad that brought me here."

A look of disgust crossed the lawman's face. "What kind of a world do you come from?" he breathed, then he composed himself and said, "The First Law, the one every Arkan is expected to obey above all others -- and I am surprised that you Tarans do not know -- is also the simplest: 'No life shall ever be valued over another, and no death shall ever be acceptable.' Do you *kedda* what that means?" I shook my head, and he continued, "It means that *every* life is sacred, including the lives of 'potential threats'. It would not matter if you killed a hundred people, the person that took *your* life would be equally guilty. No exceptions. Even the Kana-Semeth must obey the First Law."

"And what happens if somebody *does* break the First Law?"

"It depends. If the death was accidental, the Laws allow for mercy to be shown. If it was not, then...we take their life from them."

"You mean you kill them."

"No," he said in the tone one normally reserves for small children, "we take their *life*. We lock them away from the world: no sunlight, no people other than guards, just a small, barren cell and their own guilt....usually until Avisar sees fit to end their sentence."

I swallowed hard. Life in a box, basically -- it made hanging seem almost desirable. At least that way would be quicker. "So you're reasonably sure that your superiors aren't going to cut our heads off or anything when we get to Dak-Taorin?"

"*Kai.*"

"And there aren't any sort of little loopholes to this whole 'No killing' rule?"

"Well, there is one..." the lawman began to say.

"Dammit, I *knew* it! We're gonna die!"

"But," he continued, "unless you consider yourself an invading force intent on overthrowing the ruling family and bringing harm to the country's citizens, I do not think you have much to worry about." He cocked an eyebrow. "Well? Do you?"

I could feel myself turning red at how he had pulled my leg so easily. "Go to Hell," I muttered.

CHAPTER 11

"Leaving? Why?" Dimidev and I stood out in the yard, in the shadow of his new barn. Some of the other men were still milling about, collecting tools, checking the structure...and eavesdropping, of course.

"*Lermekt* H'landa was ordered to take me and J'nath to Dak-Taorin. I have no choice." I looked about the yard. "I do not see *d'ho*-Gorin today. Could you tell him I am sorry, but I cannot take the job he offered? I am not sure when I am coming back."

"Of course, Reshard." He clapped me on the shoulder. "Do not look so sad, my friend. I will explain you meant no disrespect to him."

"It is not that. I...I cannot explain it." Despite H'landa's reassurances, I still wasn't too keen on the trip. That old knot-in-my-gut feeling had returned: something told me this was going to be like Halitova all over again. "Have you ever been to Dak-Taorin, Dimi?" I asked.

"Once, but that was years ago...before Pera was born, even." He shook his head. "Too big, too noisy, thieves everywhere...you had best watch out while you are there."

"I will, do not worry," I told him, smiling. "I should go home now, finish getting ready. The *lermekt* wants to leave at First Light tomorrow."

"Of course...oh, wait a moment." He began to turn towards the house. "Stay there, I have something for you."

I did as he asked, saying my goodbyes to the other workers in the meantime. When Dimi came out a few minutes later, he took my hand and dropped some coins into it. "This is all I can spare," he told me. "I would give you more if I could, but..."

"Dimi, you do not have to give me anything." I looked at the coins: a couple of silver, squarish *kepa* pieces, and a few red ring-like ones that I wasn't familiar with. "I did not expect to be paid for helping you."

"It is not payment, it is a gift." He wrapped my fingers around the coins. "If you are going to Dak-Taorin, you will need money. How did you expect to pay if you wanted something, hmm? Would you try and use some of that Taran money like you gave my girls?"

The man had a point. A few days before, I'd shined up some old dimes and given one to each of his three daughters because, as currency, they were completely useless in Arkhein -- the only value they held was in the silver itself if melted down. "Fine, you win," I said, and put the money in my pocket. "But if there is any left when I return, I am going to give it back to you."

"Then you had best make sure that there is none left," he answered. I smiled and told him I would try, at last taking my leave of him.

When I got home, Nina was still busying herself with gathering supplies for the trip. Traveling to Dak-Taorin would take about two or three days, so we had to pack accordingly: some food, a few cooking utensils, blankets, and a couple other odds and ends. With J'nath and Pietruvek down in the cellar and me wrapping up my own affairs, Nina had graciously begun to pack up what we needed.

"That did not take very long," she said when I came in. "Did you talk to *d'ho*-Gorin?"

"No, I could not find him, but Dimi will let him know." I waved my hand over the supply-laden kitchen table, asking, "How is all of this going?"

"Just about ready to pack it all up, I think. Will two blankets each be enough?"

"More than enough. Let me see how J'nath is coming along, and then I will help out with the packing." I walked over to the cellar's trap door, which had been left open for convenience. "Hello down there, anybody home?" I called out in English.

Pietruvek came into view. "Hallo y'self," he answered, trying to copy my American accent and failing miserably.

"You got room down there for one more?"

He nodded. "Mind thy step, it is a bit messy."

After I'd descended the ladder, I saw that the boy wasn't kidding: it looked like a tornado had torn through the place, tossing papers and artifacts all over the floor. I carefully pushed some of the debris aside with the toe of my boot just so I'd have a place to stand. "Doing a little redecorating?" I asked J'nath jokingly.

He either didn't hear me or was ignoring me. J'nath was standing at the table in the center of the room, shuffling through a pile of books heaped upon it. I watched as he picked one up, looked it over, and casually dropped it on the floor.

"Don't you want to be a little more careful with this stuff?" I said as I crossed the disaster area laid out between us. Once again, there was no response from him. I reached out and waved my hand in front of his face. "Hello? Is there anybody home?"

J'nath jerked his head up, like someone waking up from a bad dream. His eyes seemed a bit unfocused, with dark circles beneath them, and I noticed that he seemed a bit flushed. "What...Reshard, when did thou come back?" he asked, staring at me as if I'd materialized right in front of him.

"Just a few minutes ago," I said, putting my hand on his forehead -- he felt a bit too warm for my liking. "Pardon my saying so, but you look like Hell."

"I do?" He backed away from me, his own hand reaching up to massage his temple. "I feel fine. A little tired, perhaps, but..." He abruptly stopped talking and let out a wet, hacking cough, his body rocking back and forth with the force of it.

I turned to look at Pietruvek and asked, "He been doing this all day?"

"Off and on. I have been coughing a little myself. It gets dusty down here." The boy ran his finger across a nearby shelf, leaving a clean stripe in his wake.

"Who made this mess?" J'nath bent down and picked up the book that he'd just tossed aside. "Pietruvek, I have told you before to not be so rough with these things," he said in Arkan. "They cannot be replaced."

"Um, J'nath, you did that yourself," I said.

"I did no such..." He paused as another string of coughs escaped his throat. "I did no such thing."

"You have been doing it all day, *Padra*." Pietruvek replied, exasperated. "I have been trying to pick up after you, but you seemed too distracted to even notice."

My brow furrowed at this new piece of information. Nina had said that J'nath could get a little self-absorbed when it came to the Crossroads and such, but this struck me as rather extreme. "J'nath, perhaps we should go upstairs for a while," I told him. "I think you have been down here too long."

The man shook his head at my suggestion, and stared down at the jumble of artifacts on the floor. "I do not remember doing this. I would never treat these things with such dis..." He paused again, the hand at his temple moving over his eyes now. "I would...not..." His whole body shuddered for a moment, then he dropped like a puppet with its strings cut. Luckily, I managed to catch him before he could smack his head on the table.

As we sank to the floor, Pietruvek plowed through the mess between us as best he could, panic in his eyes. "*Padra? Padra*, please answer me," the boy said as he gently slapped his father's face. The whites of J'nath's eyes were visible beneath his half-closed lids, and a thin sheen of sweat was building on his brow.

I put a hand on Pietruvek's shoulder and tried to shove him away from the two of us. "Go get the doctor, Peter," I ordered in English.

"No, I do not want to leave him."

"Better you than me. Now *move it*!"

He hesitated for a moment, but then headed up the ladder, leaving me and J'nath alone in a pit full of useless relics.

*   *   *   *   *   *

Pietruvek brought back *Z'kira* Kali in record time, and even managed to snag *Lermekt* H'landa in his wake. Not that the lawman's presence made much difference: he just ended up standing in the hallway along with me and the kid as Nina and the doc hovered about an unconscious J'nath in the bedroom. He did help out with getting J'nath out of the cellar, though, for which I was grateful.

"Have you noticed anything else strange before today?" the doctor asked Nina. "Dizziness, chills, any sort of complaint?"

"He kept getting headaches, for the last four or five days, but he seemed fine this morning. A bit distracted, perhaps, because of the trip..."

"Nothing more?"

"Not until he collapsed." Nina sat down on the edge of the bed, gently picked up J'nath's hand from off the blanket, and kissed his knuckles. If her husband felt it, he made no sign. "What is wrong with him?"

"I am not sure. It looks merely like a case of Winter's chill, but that should not cause him to lose consciousness." The doctor took a bottle out of the wooden box of medical supplies she'd brought along, and tapped some of its contents into a little envelope. "I will consult my books and see what I can find. In the meantime, this should bring his fever down." She gave Nina the envelope, saying, "Two pinches in a thin broth, no more than three times daily."

"*K'sai, d'ho-z'kira,*" Nina replied, her voice quiet.

"Please, do not worry about this so much. He probably just overtaxed himself. Let him rest."

She nodded and looked to her son. "Pietruvek, will you show *Z'kira* Kali out?" she asked. As he and the doctor went up the hall, Nina stayed at the bedside, her hand still clasping J'nath's.

"Well, I suppose the trip is off now," I said in Arkan.

"What do you mean?" H'landa asked.

"We cannot go if J'nath is sick. What, were you planning on lashing him to a *vessek* or something?"

"I do not see anything wrong with you, Taran. If *d'ho*-Bannen must stay behind, then so be it." He took a couple steps closer to me. "You and I, however..."

"I am not going *anywhere* alone with you, especially unfamiliar territory."

"You are not being given a choice."

"Stop it! Both of you, just *stop*!" Nina stepped into the hallway and shoved the two of us apart. "You are no better than *children* around each other, sometimes." She turned to H'landa, saying, "I hope the Kana-Semeth do not encourage this sort of behavior." I made a face at him over the top of Nina's head, but she caught it somehow and snapped, "As for you...my son looks up to you, in case you had not noticed. You could try and set a better example for his sake, at least. Now, if you two want to continue arguing, I am going to have to ask you to leave my house. Is that understood?"

"*Kai, d'ho*-Kandru," the lawman answered, rather sheepishly. I echoed his reply, and she seemed satisfied with that. With her husband ill, she needed as few worries as possible.

"And as far as this trip goes," she continued, "whether J'nath is sick or not, you still have an obligation to fulfill, Reshard."

"But I do not..." I started to whine, and Nina shot me a look. My mother used to give me looks like that.

"What about me?" Pietruvek asked as he came back towards the bedroom. "I can go, I know nearly everything *Padra* knows."

"How long have you been listening?" Nina said.

The kid rolled his eyes. "This is a small house. I could hear all of you arguing from the front door."

"Actually, it does not sound like a half-bad idea," I said. "If he was good enough to be a translator for me, why not a Crossroads expert?"

"That is not the same thing," she said. "Besides, he is too young to make the trip by himself."

"We *will* be with him during the trip, Nina. I swear, nothing will happen to him."

"Most of his time will probably be spent at the main Kana-Semeth station," H'landa added. "You could not ask for a safer place."

She looked from the lawman to me, saying, "You mean the two of you actually *agree* on something?"

H'landa shrugged. "It happens. And the boy is correct: he seems to know quite a bit about Tarahein and the Crossroads."

"Please, *Maia*," Pietruvek said to her, "I may never get to do something like this again. I am almost fifteen, anyways...you have to start letting me make my own decisions sooner or later."

"I know, I only wish that it was later. *Much* later." She put her hands on either side of the boy's face. "You were always in such a hurry to grow up, Pietruvek Bannen," she told him, then kissed him on the forehead. "Fine, you can go off and be a man for a while...but I still expect you to be my little boy when you get back."

* * * * * *

No one got much sleep that night, between the excitement about the journey ahead and J'nath's coughing fits. "Winter's chill" or no, he definitely wasn't going to be able to travel any time soon. Nina said that he'd woken up once or twice, but he wasn't very coherent -- whether it was from the medicine or the fever, she wasn't certain. "Are you sure that you still want us to go?" I asked her during breakfast.

She nodded and said, "There is nothing you can do here. What happens now is up to the *z'kira*, J'nath, and Avisar." She then placed her hand on mine. "I have a feeling that your future in our world depends heavily upon this journey. J'nath would not want you to throw that future away just for his sake. I know you are afraid of leaving the safety of Betedek, but you must face that fear, get past it."

I couldn't help but laugh a little at that. When she asked me what was so funny, I said, "The last time somebody told me something like that, I ended up here."

The lawman arrived just as Pietruvek and I were getting ready to saddle up our mount. His family only had one *vessek*, so the two of us would just have to double up in the saddle and hope the animal could take it. I also hoped that it would tolerate my presence during the journey: while it seemed to have gotten used to whatever alien smell I must put off, it would still sometimes swing its head at me in a definite "back off" gesture whenever I entered the barn...and now I had to spend two whole days on the back of the damn thing. Wonderful.

To add insult to injury, the *vessek* loved H'landa. While Pietruvek strapped down our gear, the lawman stroked its muzzle and talked softly to it, and the animal just ate it up. "Treat her well, and she will treat you well," he told me as he scratched it beneath its chin. "You can start by removing those spike things from your boots."

"Like Hell I will. The first time it acts up on me, it's getting one of these in the ribs." I tapped the toe of my boot against the ground, causing my spur to give off a soft *p-ching* sound.

"Very well, but if she dumps you on the ground and stomps on your head after you do it, try not to act too surprised."

Finally, with the last strap cinched and buckled, and the last rope knotted, it was time to depart. I adjusted my gunbelts for the thousandth time: despite my promise to myself, I wasn't about to head out into the wilderness unarmed, and had rummaged through the mess J'nath had made of the cellar until I found where he'd stashed my Peacemakers. Besides, what else would I use if there was trouble? A sword? I'd probably end up stabbing myself in the leg the first time I tried to use one.

Nina kept fussing over her son before we mounted up. "I want you to behave yourself," she said in Arkan as she smoothed down a few wild locks of hair on his head. "This trip is very important for Reshard. You obey him and *Lermekt* H'landa the same as you would your *padra* and myself."

"*Kai, Maia.*"

"I mean it. This is not another little village you are going to. This is Dak-Taorin, the King's city. A certain level of behavior is expected."

"Do not worry, I will personally beat him over the head if he gets out of line." I lightly rapped my knuckles on Pietruvek's noggin. He tried to duck away, but I threw an arm around his neck. "Oh no, Peter, you don't get away that easy!" I told him in English, and proceeded to grind my knuckles deep into his hair. Nina just shook her head at our horseplay.

H'landa swung up unto his saddle, saying, "Are you two through wasting time? I would really prefer to spend only *one* night sleeping on the ground."

"Alright, hold your water." I let go of the kid, who laughed and gave me a quick punch on the arm. "It looks like we have to leave now," I said to Nina, switching back to Arkan.

"It certainly does." She wrapped her arms around her boy and kissed his cheek. "You remember what I said, and be careful."

"I will, *Maia.*"

They hugged again before Pietruvek went over to the *vessek,* then Nina looked up at me, saying, "You be careful as well."

"Kai, Maia," I said jokingly. In a lower, more serious tone, I added, "If anything happens with J'nath, please send word to me."

"Everything will be fine," she answered in an almost-convincing way, "you worry about yourself for now." She then took a few steps back and bowed slightly. "Have a safe journey, and may Avisar guide your path."

I mounted the *vessek* and pulled Pietruvek up into the saddle, seating him in front of me. We rode out of the yard, the lawman in the lead, and headed towards the road that would lead us to Dak-Taorin.

* * * * * *

We rode along in silence for the first hour or so, but for different reasons. H'landa had seen it all before and seemed a bit bored with the scenery, while Pietruvek and myself had never strayed more than a few miles from Betedek's borders and were too busy taking it all in to talk.

The woods that lay along the northeast edge of the village ran on for a couple miles, thinning out in places where someone had cleared enough land for a farm. About five miles from Betedek, the trees gave way completely to open fields as the land became dotted with small hills. Whoever had originally plotted the road managed to avoid the steeper grades, but we still found ourselves with an unusual view of the landscape: high enough to see for miles sometimes, flanked by grassy slopes at others. The population soon dwindled along with the trees. The road and surrounding lands became so empty that we could have been the only people in the whole world -- it reminded me of riding on the open plains back home. After a long stretch of nothing but swaying grasses and the occasional bird, I asked H'landa if we'd pass any other villages on this road.

"Not on the road directly," he replied, "but there is a crossing about three *kalem* or so from here. Follow it west, and you will reach Vel K'noshiben Hala...Three Brothers Valley. That is not along our path, though." He pointed north, towards a dark patch of landscape a couple of miles off. "The road we are on passes through that wood up ahead, and will lead us to Dak-Taorin. Once we enter, we will not see another village until we come out the other side."

"We're probably going to be sleeping in there, aren't we?"

"Better under the shelter of trees than on open ground." He signaled his mount to move faster, saying over his shoulder, "If we pick up our pace, we can be halfway through the wood by nightfall." He rode up a small rise and disappeared down the other side as the road took a sudden dip.

Pietruvek twisted in the saddle to look at me. "I never slept outside before," he said.

"Aw, it's no big deal, I used to do it all the time. Just keep the fire stoked, put a decent layer of blankets under you, and sleep with your boots on." I gave the *vessek* a nudge so we could catch up with the lawman. "Trust me, once you're asleep, you won't know the difference."

The sense of isolation I'd felt out in the open increased tenfold once we entered the woods. The road narrowed, and the forest canopy blocked out most of the sunlight, giving the path a very claustrophobic feel. After a while, the sound of water reached my ears, and I could see a small stream flowing in from the east, bending through the wood until it ran parallel with the road, sometimes no more than ten feet from where we were riding.

When what little light that passed through the foliage began to dim, we decided to make camp for the night. We found a well-cleared spot beside the stream, one that had probably been used as a campsite before, judging by how free of rocks and small plants it was. As H'landa and Pietruvek unloaded the packs, I worked on getting a fire started. "So, what would you folks like for dinner: dried meat or dried meat?" I joked as I tried to coax the kindling to light.

"Actually, I was thinking of something a bit fresher." H'landa unfolded a bundle from his pack and began to assemble a contraption which I soon recognized as that bow-and-rifle stock thing that I'd seen in the weapons case.

"What the Hell is that thing for?" I asked.

"Hunting, of course." He snapped the final component in place. "It is a *gautteng*." When this got no reaction from me, he turned to Pietruvek and asked, "How do you say *gautteng* in Taran?"

"I do not think it translates," the boy replied, "but I remember a drawing of something similar in one of the old texts...larger than a *gautteng*, though. A crossbow, I think it was called."

"Never heard of it." I fanned the flame until the wood caught fire sufficiently.

"You should try it," the lawman replied, smirking. "You might like it better than your *trit bakido*."

I laughed. "Oh, I seriously doubt that. What are you planning on using it on, anyways?"

He slung a small leather bag over his shoulder. "I saw a *lissur* or two in this area when I was riding into Betedek. Too much meat for one person, but for three, it will make a fine meal."

"Would you mind some company?" He said he didn't, so the two of us headed off into the deeper part of the woods across the road, leaving Pietruvek to tend camp. I'll admit, I had no idea what we were looking for -- I wouldn't have known a *lissur* if it had literally come up and bit me on the ass -- but H'landa seemed to know what he was doing, so I just followed his lead.

After a few minutes of walking through countless thorny vines that kept pricking at my trousers, the lawman's hand came up, stopping me in my tracks. "Up ahead and to the right," he whispered.

I squinted at the dense shrubbery. "I don't see...oh." It took a moment to make out the shape of the animal: while it had the general look of a deer, its dark brown fur was broken up by tan stripes across its back and legs, making it hard to distinguish amongst the foliage. H'landa pulled a lever on the crossbow to cock it -- the sharp click it made caused the animal to look up, its long, donkey-like ears pricking up and pivoting. Luckily, it didn't notice us, and went back to its business of nibbling at some wildflowers. The lawman waited a moment, then reached into the bag he'd brought along. He pulled out a short but thick-shafted arrow, which he laid into a groove along the top of the stock. Bringing it to his shoulder like a rifle, he sighted along its length with his good eye. We both held our breath.

He pulled the trigger, and the arrow flew towards its target, sinking into the meaty part of the *lissur's* foreleg -- a decent wound, but far from a killing blow. The animal bleated as it turned and ran deeper into the woods. While H'landa cursed and loaded another round, I was already drawing my pistol and had scrambled around the cover between myself and the fleeing animal so I could get a clearer shot. I snapped off three quick rounds -- the *lissur* jerked back and collapsed as one of the bullets connected with its skull. The other two went wild, but no big deal...until I heard a metallic *clang* somewhere off in the wood. I'd been starting to walk towards the carcass when I heard it, so I stopped and cocked my head, waiting for the noise to repeat. It didn't.

H'landa came up behind me. "Something wrong?" he asked.

"I thought I heard one of my bullets ricochet off something," I said in English, then realized that he didn't know that word. "Ricochet...bounce off...you know..." I flicked my finger and made a little "pee-yow" noise, but that still wasn't getting it. "Bullet hit metal, make noise. *Kedda?*"

"How could you hear anything over all that thunder you made?" He went over to where the *lissur* lay and lifted its head. "That was quite a shot."

"Uh-huh." I was still looking off where the stray bullets had gone -- I thought I could see something large beyond all those trees, but I couldn't tell what. "I'll be back in a minute," I told him, and walked off to take a look. The underbrush in that area was just as thick and thorny as the rest of the woods, but here and there I saw bits of stone peeking their way through the green, and in a fairly regular pattern. *Something used to be here,* I thought. *Something man-made...or Arkan-made.* As I got closer to the large object I'd spotted, I could make out its edges more clearly: it seemed fairly square, about twenty feet wide and nearly as tall. The same growth that covered the forest floor had taken root all over it, obscuring most of the surface from view. Had I not been looking right at the thing, I probably would have never seen it.

"It appears to be a building of some sort," H'landa said behind me. I spun around at the sound of his voice, and saw him kneeling to examine some of the stones. "I hear of people finding things like this from time to time: pieces of Old Arkhein that were abandoned and forgotten." He waved his hand to the left, then to the right, saying, "Whatever this was, it looks like it had a wall around it. Not too high, though, or else more might still be visible."

"'Old Arkhein'? You mean from before the Fall?"

"*Kai.* This...whatever it is has probably not been touched for over five hundred years." He stood up and approached the building, and I joined him, grabbing a handful of the vines and creepers that covered it in an effort to get a better look at what was beneath. The vegetation clung stubbornly to the surface, though, so I pulled out my knife and hacked it away. Beneath it all, pockmarked with age, lay a large bronze panel, and a few more swipes revealed an engraved symbol. To my surprise, it was strikingly similar to the one I'd seen on the funeral shroud a few days before:

"Hey, *lermekt*, take a look at this." He came over to where I stood, and I said to him, "I think I figured out what my bullet hit, but what the Hell is this?" I tapped the symbol, which was nearly as big around as a dinner plate.

"It is a *kahn*," he said matter-of-factly.

"Wait, I thought *kahn* meant like your soul or spirit."

"It does. This is a symbolic representation of a *kahn*." He traced his finger over the design. "The center line is for your life now, your path, guided by the Light of Avisar within you. The left line is your old paths, circling back through time and adding strength to your current life. To the right is your future, and the paths you are forging now, though you cannot see them."

"Sort of an Arkan Trinity," I ventured. "Like the Father, the Son, and the Holy Ghost."

He furrowed his brow. "Just once, I would like to hear you say something that makes sense." He took out a knife of his own and began to cut away more vegetation from the panel, saying, "I wonder why someone would put a *kahn* on a building."

"Maybe it's a church."

"There you go again."

"Oh, come on, you know what a church is. It's a building full of priests and stained glass and holy water. You go in and talk to God and toss a little money in the collection plate."

"Why would you need a building to talk to God?" H'landa stopped cutting when he came across a seam splitting the bronze panel in two. "I think this may be a door. The handles must have fallen away long ago." He ran his fingers along the seam, then said, "What do you think: push or pull?"

"With no handles, I hope it's push."

He agreed. We set our feet, put our shoulders to the panel, and shoved as hard as we could -- ancient hinges screamed, reverberating through the metal. Once we'd made a gap wide enough to squeeze through, H'landa slipped inside, and I followed after.

The size of the chamber once again made me think of a church: its length was more than three times its width, with a high, vaulted ceiling (or what was left of it) and what appeared to be a stone altar at the end. The floor was littered with debris and more plant life, and I could see a couple of small animals rush away as we began to move about. "It looks like this entrance was originally blocked, judging by what is left," H'landa said as he checked out some items piled behind the door. He picked up a long chunk of wood, still mostly intact. "Bring me one of your fire-sticks, Richard."

I pulled out my tin of matches, lit one, and held it to the moss-covered wood 'til it caught. The light it gave off wasn't much, but it helped supplement the waning light coming through the holes in the roof. The lawman held the torch high over his head as we proceeded to the far end of the chamber, trying to avoid the chunks of masonry in our path as best we could. The walls, from what we could see, appeared to be fairly intact: vines slithered down from the remains of high-set windows, winding around small statues set in niches, their eroded faces and broken limbs peering out of the choking green. When I pointed them out to H'landa, he shrugged and said he had no idea who or what they might have been. "Perhaps they are more of your 'church' things," he suggested, pronouncing the double *ch* sound more precisely than most Arkans could.

"You really don't understand what I'm talking about, do you?"

"Do I ever?" He stopped suddenly and knelt down, picking up what at first looked like a bit of debris. Then he brought the torch closer, and I could see a couple of teeth sticking out of it. "Part of a skull," he said, stating the obvious. "Quite old, from the look of it." He glanced around the decaying structure and nodded. "It fits: the forgotten places usually have the remains of the dead scattered about. We have probably been grinding the remnants of old bones into the ground with every step." He gently placed the skull fragment back where he found it, then proceeded on.

A cold sweat trickled down the back of my neck as my eyes searched for more bones, half-expecting some grotesque skeleton to rise up out of the shrubbery now. "I don't think we should tell the kid about this place," I said. "He probably wouldn't be able to sleep tonight if he knew about it. Hell, I don't think *I'll* sleep."

We found another surprise when we reached the altar. Draped over the top was the tattered remnants of a robe, with what little remained of its owner lying both in and beside it. H'landa's reaction upon seeing this was a little bizarre: he thrust the torch into my hands, grabbed the robe, and lifted it off the altar. The fragments of bone inside the robe fell out and shattered to powder as they hit the floor. H'landa didn't seem to notice. "Christ, man, have a little respect for the dead, will ya?" I muttered.

"You claim to know what this place is," he said, his tone dead serious. "So tell me: is this another 'church' thing as well?" He shoved the robe very nearly in my face.

I pulled away to get a better look at it. Most of it had disintegrated, but enough remained intact to get a general idea of what it once looked like: a long, black cassock with a broad gray stripe that ran down the length of it, both front and back, and wide enough to cover the entire chest area. "I guess it looks a little like a priest's vestments," I told him finally.

"'Priest'?" he echoed.

"Yeah, a priest. Somebody who, um...who speaks for God, you know? To the masses."

He silently looked at the robe for a long time. "Somebody who speaks for God," he eventually said, echoing my words. A cold smile came to his lips. "*Kai*, of course he is," he said in Arkan, as if to himself. "He speaks for God and expects everyone to listen."

The lawman's behavior was beginning to disturb me. "What are you talking about?" I asked.

"Nothing that concerns you." He dropped the robe and began to walk away from the altar. "We should get back to camp. The boy is probably worried about us."

The man says that I'm *hard to understand, and then* he *goes and does something like that?* I stood there for a moment, trying to puzzle out what I'd just witnessed. *Forget about it, Richard*, I told myself. *Is it really that big a deal if the two of you don't see everything the same way?*

I shrugged and followed the lawman out of the church, mindful the whole way of where I stepped.

* * * * * *

Pietruvek wasn't worried, but he did question us about the strange noises he'd heard echoing out of the wood. We just played dumb until he stopped pestering us, and hoped that he wouldn't go exploring in the middle of the night.

We feasted that evening on roasted *lissur* meat and dry biscuits, gorging ourselves like it was our last meal ever. It reminded me of many nights I'd spent under the stars with my friends -- the landscape and the company may have changed, but the feeling was the same. Not long after our meal, the boy's head started to droop, and before we knew it, he'd fallen asleep sitting up. I walked around to his side of the fire and gently guided him down to a more comfortable position. He made a little noise in the back of his throat when I did so, but otherwise he didn't stir at all.

"You two really are close," H'landa commented. "I did not notice until *d'ho*-Kandru mentioned it."

"He just reminds me of somebody I used to know, that's all." I pulled Pietruvek's blanket over him. "Besides, he's a good kid." I stepped back over to my own bedroll and, after sitting down, picked up my coat and fished out my last cigar. As far as I could figure, there was no such thing as tobacco in this world, so I'd been rationing out the couple of cigars that had crossed over with me. I used a small twig from the campfire to spark it up, then laid back on my bedroll and gazed up at the stars peeking through the trees, wanting to savor the very last smoke of my life.

"What in Avisar's name is in your mouth?" I heard H'landa say after a minute.

I twisted around to look at him. "Huh? Oh...it's a cigar." I popped it out and held it towards him, saying, "You wanna try it?"

He took it from me, holding it between his fingers like it was a dead mouse. "What do you do, just put it between your teeth?"

"No, you've got to breathe in a little...here, give it back, I'll show you." I took a couple puffs and blew them out. "See, you hold the smoke in your mouth, then let it out slow. C'mon, give it a shot." I passed it back again.

The lawman hesitated, and finally brought the cigar to his lips. As soon as he breathed in, he started coughing and sputtering, with little clouds of smoke spurting out of his mouth -- I had to bite down on my knuckles to keep from laughing. When the fit passed, he asked with a wheeze, "Why would you do such a thing?"

"To relax," I deadpanned, then took back the cigar and clamped it between my teeth. "Guess Arkans don't have anything like this, huh?"

"Not that I have seen."

"Reckon this really is my last one, then." I blew a couple of smoke rings, which made H'landa cock an eyebrow. "No booze, no tobacco...I'm gonna have to find a new way to unwind."

The lawman poked at the fire with a stick for a minute, then said, "*Kuat* root."

"Come again?"

"In Ikara, I recall some of the rural folk chewing on smoked *kuat* root...chewing only, not swallowing. It releases an oil of some sort. I have heard the effect is very relaxing."

"Huh. I'll have to look into that." I took another puff, then asked, "Ikara's the country north of here, isn't it?"

"*Kai*, very north. Take you at least two months of hard riding to reach the border from here." He smirked. "A long way to go to relax."

"Well, it can't be that hard to reach. I mean, it sounds like you've been there."

"I have been to six of the Seven Known Lands," he said. "Here, of course, and my birth-land of Nevasile, as well as Gobaira, Ikara, M'salnek...I even went to Keto once, but that place barely counts."

"What's the seventh? Why haven't you been there?"

His mouth twisted. "Haru-D'keng. No one goes there, especially Kana-Semeth."

"Why not?"

"That country is full of madmen. Their idea of 'order' and the Kana-Semeth's have very little in common." He poked at the fire some more. "The borders between Haru-D'keng and the rest of Arkhein were set long ago. As long as we each stay on our own side, all is well."

"Oh, come on, how bad can the place be?"

He gave me a sideways glance. "The less you know, the better you will sleep at night. Trust me."

"Fine, forget about it." I took a few more puffs off my cigar, then bid it farewell as I tossed the remaining stub in the fire. "How about your home, then? What's Nevasile like?"

"Quite different from Taorin," H'landa said, a wistful look in his eye. "Not as much woodland, for certain. Low plains in the south, and high rocky hills in the north. You can be six *kalem* from the shore and still smell salt in the air." He smiled. "I have never seen another land like it."

"Why did you leave?"

All the joy that had lit up his face suddenly dimmed, until you couldn't even tell it had been there in the first place. "I had something important to take care of," he said quietly, then tossed the stick into the fire, sending up a small burst of hot embers. "We should be getting to sleep. We still have a long way to ride tomorrow."

"Reckon you're right." I unbuckled my gunbelts and laid them beside my bedroll, and H'landa did the same with his sword, tucked away in its scabbard. As he began to strip off his uniform's tunic, I reached over to the sword, wanting to give it a closer look. Before I could even lay a finger on it, however, his own hand shot out and grabbed me by the wrist, twisting it. "Hey...*ow,* dammit! Quit it!" I yelled, and jerked out of his grip. "What the Hell was that for?"

"You do not touch that," H'landa said, pointing at the sword. "*Ever.*"

"Why not? You've had your grimy paws all over my guns..."

"That was different. Your *trit bakido* are just machines. Complicated machines, *kai,* but nothing more." He dropped his tunic next to his bedroll and picked up the scabbard. "They do not compare to the power contained within this blade."

I rubbed my sore wrist, muttering, "It's just a damn sword."

"Wrong. This is not just any sword," he explained, "it is a *legend*, passed down over the centuries by my ancestors. The line of *H'landa* is its protector, keeping it from falling into the hands of those who would use it for evil intents." He unsheathed it and held the blade over the fire -- the flames seemed to be drawn towards the black metal, twisting and flowing along its etched surface. "The stories say it was forged from pure darkness, and that not even Avisar has the power to dull its edge." He then removed the sword from the flames and pointed it towards me. "This sword helped give birth to nations," the lawman said, "and has drawn blood from people far more important than you, so when I tell you not to touch it, *you will obey*."

"All right, I promise I won't touch it," I told him, leaning back as far as I could to get away from it. Surprisingly, despite its time in the fire, I couldn't feel any heat coming from it. I didn't know why, but that oddity scared me more than the sword itself.

Perhaps H'landa picked up on that, because when he finally withdrew the sword and sheathed it again, there was a grim sort of smile on his face. He placed the scabbard on top of his tunic before lying down. "Sleep well, Taran," he said, pulling the blanket over himself.

"Easy for you to say," I answered.

CHAPTER 12

I was awakened rather abruptly the next day: Pietruvek had his hands on my shoulders and was attempting to shake my brains right out of my head. "Get up, Reshard," he kept saying. "Please, wake up."

Groaning, I worked my way into an upright position, silently wishing that Arkans had something equivalent to coffee. I briefly entertained the idea of trying to invent it, then decided that it sounded like too much work and scrapped the whole notion. "Somebody had better be trying to kill us, kid," I said in English, my eyes still closed.

"*Lermekt* H'landa is gone."

I rubbed my eyes and looked over to where the lawman had been sleeping. His bedroll was still spread out, and his mount and ours were still tied to a nearby tree -- the only things missing besides him were his sword and tunic. "Was he already gone when you got up?" I asked the boy.

He nodded. "I called out for him, but no answer."

"Well, most of his stuff's still here, so I don't think he deserted us." I tossed off my blanket and got up myself. "Maybe we got lucky and a bear came along and ate him so we can go home now," I suggested.

Pietruvek looked confused. "Bare...naked?"

"No, not 'bare-naked', I mean a...forget it." I paced around the campsite, wondering where H'landa had gone. Maybe back to the church? I scratched at my cheek -- my whiskers were getting long again, and it made my face itch.

Wait a minute...Good Lord, Richard, you can be so dense sometimes. "Don't worry, Peter," I said, "I know where he is, or at least what he's doing."

"*Kai?*"

"Yeah. Why don't you start fixing up breakfast or something, I'll go get him." I began to walk downstream beside the bank, hoping I'd picked the right direction. After a few minutes, I spotted the lawman kneeling next to the stream, mirror in one hand and razor in the other. His tunic and belts were draped over a large rock nearby. "You know, you could have left a note or something," I said as I approached. "You scared the Hell out of the kid with your disappearing act."

He stopped shaving and glanced back the way I'd come. "Is he still at camp?"

"Don't worry, your secret's safe," I answered, taking a seat on the ground next to him. "You plan on doing this your whole damn life?"

"I have been doing it for fifteen years," he said, "and I never had any problems until *you* came along." He angled his chin upward and dragged the blade over the hairs beneath. "Sometimes I think your only reason for being in this world is to give me trouble."

"That's my best talent: makin' trouble." I watched as he meticulously shaved off a bit of stubble he'd missed along his jawline. I scratched my own whiskers again and asked, "You think I could borrow that later, maybe? Just so I don't look like a complete slouch when we get to Dak-Taorin."

"I will think about it," he said, which I figured meant "no".

Once he was done, he tucked his shaving kit into a little leather pouch, then leaned over the stream and splashed water on his now-bare cheeks. After the evidence of his Taran nature had been washed away to his satisfaction, he began to tie back his long black hair in the usual Arkan manner, muttering under his breath when it tangled. As he fussed, I saw a glint of metal beneath his unfastened shirt collar. "What's that around your neck?" I asked.

He paused, pressing a hand to his chest, right over the object underneath his shirt. "An amulet of protection. It belonged to my *padra*. He used to tell me that the *kroz* had the power to shield one's *kahn* from evil."

"*Kroz*? I don't know that word."

"Not surprising. My *padra* was the only person I have ever heard speak it." He slipped his hand down the front of his shirt to pull out the amulet, saying, "I have long thought the word to be nonsense, but he insisted that was its proper name." As I looked upon the object dangling from the silver chain wrapped around his fingers, I tried to not let the shock show on my face.

It wasn't a *kroz*, it was a *Cross*. A Celtic one, at that. The whole thing wasn't more than two inches long, and intricately crafted of gold and silver. It appeared to have taken a bit of a beating over the centuries, and the bottom of it had snapped off entirely, but there was no mistaking it. There was also no mistaking that H'landa had no clue about the Cross's origin in my world: considering his general attitude about me and, of course, his own ancestry, I doubted that he would be very keen on wearing it if he'd known what it really was. I briefly considered telling him, but then I realized that, if I couldn't even get him to understand the concept of a church, explaining Christianity was going to be a lot tougher. "Did he ever say where he, um...where that *kroz* came from?" I asked as casually as I could.

"*Nee*, he only showed it to me a few times before he died," he said, gazing at the Cross for a moment before slipping it back beneath his shirt. "Where it came from is not important to me. The important thing is that it belonged to my *padra*. As long as I have it, a part of him will always be with me." The lawman looked out over the water and said, "You probably think that is quite silly."

"No, I understand completely." I reached into my pocket and pulled out my own good-luck charm: my pocket watch. "My father gave this to me when I was seven, right before he went off to the War. He told me...he told me to hold onto it until he got back." My head hung low as I looked at the watch cradled in my hands, my heart breaking a little more from the memory of that day. "He died a couple of years later," I said quietly.

"You never mentioned that your *padra* was a soldier."

"He wasn't...I mean, he wasn't like *you*. Being a soldier wasn't his whole life, he was just a man who thought he should help his country, that's all." I fiddled with the winding stem. "That was just the sort of guy he was: always trying to help people, especially the sort that couldn't help themselves."

H'landa nodded. "My *padra* was like that, as well," he said, then stood up and began to put on the rest of his uniform.

I slipped the watch back into my pocket, saying, "Reckon we've got more in common than I thought, cousin."

He'd been in the middle of buckling down his sword belt when I spoke. He stopped, brow furrowed and said, "I have been trying to figure out that word for some time now, but I cannot."

"What word is that?"

"'Cousin.'" He adjusted one of the belts. "I have noticed that you only seem to use it in regards to me, so I hope it is not some sort of Taran insult."

"Well, *you* might think it is. It means...Hell, it just means 'cousin'. I don't think I've ever heard an Arkan equivalent." I mulled it over for a minute. "Let's say that your father's brother -- his *k'nosh* -- had a child."

"My father had no brothers," he interrupted.

"Okay...but let's pretend that he *did*. If your father's brother had a child, that child would be your cousin. You get it? It's somebody that's related to you, but not directly."

Understanding suddenly dawned in his eye. "Ah, you mean a *kanitu*...someone who is related to you by bloodline."

"Yeah, that sounds about right."

"So you are saying that, since I had a Taran ancestor, you and I are *kanituiben*. 'Cousins'."

I shrugged. "You never know, we could be."

"Hmm...I am not sure what to think of that." H'landa looked me over, saying, "To be sure, there is no family resemblance between us."

"You're right about that." I stood up and gave him a once-over as well. "Matter of fact, I'd say the odds of us actually being related are slim to none."

"*Kai*, very slim," he replied, then smirked. "And personally, I find that very comforting."

"Same here. Being friends with you is enough of a burden on me."

The lawman cocked an eyebrow. "Oh, so you think we are friends now, Taran?"

"Well, 'friends' in a 'tolerate-each-other's-presence' sort of way." I hitched a thumb towards the campsite. "C'mon, let's get back before the kid thinks we killed each other or something."

* * * * * *

We broke camp less than an hour later. H'landa was insistent that, if we hit the trail as soon as possible, we could probably reach the Kana-Semeth stronghold by dark. I didn't know about Pietruvek, but the prospect of sleeping in a warm bed that night certainly made me move a little faster. The lawman also insisted that I put on his cloak for the time being, with the hood pulled up so as to hide my face once we left the forest. "The people of Betedek may have grown used to the sight of you," he explained, "but I am not sure how the people of Dak-Taorin will react." I grumbled about it -- the day felt too warm to be wearing his heavy black cloak -- but I agreed that the less attention we attracted, the better.

It was nearly midday by the time we rode out of the forest proper. According to H'landa, we still had about thirty-four *kalem* (or roughly eleven miles, by my figuring) to go until we reached the outer border of Dak-Taorin. "The city is quite large," he said, "even without the King's private lands and the Kana-Semeth holdings. We shall have to ride through the heart of it before heading to the training grounds."

"Training grounds?" I echoed, puzzled.

"The capital city is where the Kana-Semeth train their people, at least for this area," Pietruvek chimed in. "A friend of mine became a *s'kuro* last year, when he came of age."

The lawman seemed intrigued by this bit of information. "Really? Did he make it through his first year?"

"*Kai*, but it was not easy. He wrote me that all they ever seem to do is exercise and listen to lectures. No excitement at all."

"They do that for a reason: to cut out the ones that joined for the excitement. The Kana-Semeth are keepers of the peace, not warmongers, and peace can sometimes be quite dull. We do not want officers who will make trouble simply because they are bored."

I could agree with that sentiment: a bored soldier or lawman could sometimes be a lot more dangerous or cruel than his criminal counterpart. Sheriff Walker seemed a good example of that. "Just how many people do you have cooped up in this stronghold, anyhow?" I asked. "Must be quite a few if you're housing cadets or *s'kuro* or whatever along with your regular troops."

H'landa shrugged -- not an easy bit of body language to read when you're bouncing around on a *vessek*. "Depends on how many soldiers we have out on field duty, like myself. A station that size usually has about five or six hundred officers and *s'kuro* running it, inside and out." He pointed a finger at me, saying, "And before you go and make a *bruhzod* of yourself in front of the wrong person, let me give you a little advice: if you see a Kana-Semeth with any marks on their collar, *keep your mouth shut*. Those are the high officers, and they do not take kindly to the sort of remarks that usually slide off your tongue. Be *doubly* respectful if you see silver."

"What's so special about silver?"

"The *Y'meer*," he said in a tone that bordered on reverence. "They are the very spirit of the Kana-Semeth, acting as keepers and interpreters of the Laws. Every major judgment must be approved by a *Y'meer*."

"I'm probably going to be running into quite a few of these *Y'meer*, aren't I?"

"*Kai,* unfortunately, so mind what I say about your behavior." His gaze shifted to Pietruvek. "Both of you."

The boy pulled away from him a little, shifting in the saddle until his back was pressed against my chest. I couldn't blame him, the lawman had said that last part a bit too harshly. Then again, we were about to tread upon his home soil, so to speak -- he probably just wanted to make sure we didn't embarrass him in front of his peers.

A couple of hours later, we caught our first glimpse of the city. While I'd seen much bigger places back in my world, the sight of Dak-Taorin was rather impressive: large buildings of both wood and stone sprawled out before us for a good mile or so in either direction, each one seeming to fit snugly amongst the others, like pieces of a puzzle. Despite what I'd been told, I had still expected it to be no more than three times as large as Betedek and, of course, just as primitive-looking, but now that I saw it, I couldn't believe that I'd had such thoughts. Nina had called it "the King's city", and it showed.

The road we traveled on broadened as it joined with two others branching in from either side of us -- after the juncture, the surface changed from trampled, rutted earth to smooth cobblestones. Tall wooden poles flanked our path, many with Arkan words and symbols carved into them, and each one helping to support a crisscrossing of deep green and yellow banners fluttering above our heads. According to H'landa, these were the colors of the royal family, whose palace could be seen in the distance at the eastern edge of Dak-Taorin. "We shall be riding northwest, however, once we pass through the gate," he said, referring to an ancient-looking archway that lay ahead of us, marking the southern entrance to the city. The gate was more symbolic than functional, though, as the city had no wall around it. A pair of Kana-Semeth stood watch beside it, looking more than a little unhappy with their assignment as they slouched against the archway. When they saw H'landa, however, they scrambled to stand at attention -- the *lermekt* shook his head and muttered something under his breath as we passed them. I imagined that those two might find themselves cleaning out stables or doing some other nasty job tomorrow.

Once we were past the gate, the sights and sounds and smells of countless people and livestock and things I couldn't even identify closed in around us. The streets were broad but crowded, so we rode along single-file, with H'landa leading the way. A few people watched us as we made our way through it all, but most seemed too preoccupied with their own business to notice. Occasionally, someone would trot up and pull on the leg of my trousers, then proceed to try and talk me or Pietruvek into buying something. The items ranged from jewelry and fabrics to live animals and food (I swear to God, one guy tired to sell me a fried lizard on a stick), and it finally got so ridiculous that the kid and I began to holler *"Nee!"* at anybody who even looked in our direction. They didn't even try to pawn anything off on the lawman.

Unlike Betedek, few of the buildings in Dak-Taorin were smaller than three stories, and many of them were constructed completely of stone, or at least had a white, stone-like exterior. As we neared the heart of the city, I saw some that appeared to be about five stories tall, with small walkways suspended between the roofs of the closely-built structures. Neither Pietruvek nor I could figure out the purpose, so the boy caught H'landa's attention and inquired about them. "Living quarters," he answered. "They put the paths in-between so the people do not have to come down to street level to visit their neighbors."

"Is it safe, being up so high?" Pietruvek asked.

"I suppose. You could never get me up on those things, though. I hate heights."

Not long after, the crowds began to thin as we neared the outskirts of the Kana-Semeth stronghold, I could see a large stone wall looming at the end of the street we were traveling on, as well as two Kana-Semeth riding our way at a casual pace: a *karrel* and a *damekt*, if I understood H'landa's explanations of rank correctly. They nodded to us as they passed, and we each returned the gesture, but when the lower-ranking *damekt* got a glimpse of my face beneath the cloak's hood, his expression went from good-natured friendliness to open-mouthed shock. The *karrel* appeared to take note of me as well, but nowhere near as blatantly.

Pietruvek and I exchanged glances, and I could tell by his own expression that we were both thinking the same thing. "The cat's out of the bag, H'landa," I called out in English.

"*Ke?*" He turned around in his saddle.

I jerked a thumb at the duo behind us. The higher-ranking officer gave his partner a sharp smack on the back of the head as the younger man pointed back at me and said something in Arkan. I didn't understand all of it, but one word stood out amongst the rest as clearly as my own name: *Taran*. As judging by the looks I was now getting from some of the civilians on the street with us, I wasn't the only one who heard it.

H'landa cursed and looked at me with a grim expression. "Ride fast," he said.

I nodded and wrapped an arm tightly around the boy's chest. "Hold on, Peter," I told him, "this is gonna get bumpy."

We doubled our pace up the street, the hooves of our *vessekiben* clattering on the cobblestones. Luckily, everyone ahead of us was kind enough to get the Hell out of our way when they heard us coming. The buildings ended a good hundred feet away from the wall, leaving an open avenue of earth and stonework between the Kana-Semeth stronghold and Dak-Taorin proper. We reined in our mounts once we reached the open area, then looked back the way we'd come: quite a few people were looking in our direction now, but whether it was due to our sudden passing or the loudmouth that spotted me, we weren't sure. "How much trouble do you think that jackass is going to cause us?" I asked H'landa as I pushed back the hood -- it obviously wasn't doing me any good to wear it anymore.

"Depends on how many citizens out there already know." He walked his animal up to the tall gates of the stronghold. Unlike the gate at the southern end of the city, this one wasn't for show: the gates were made of thick banded metal, and the stone wall itself stretched upward nearly twenty feet, with narrow slots at the top every five feet or so. "We need to get you inside, and quickly, just in case there is trouble," H'landa said, then turned his attention towards the top of the wall and called out in Arkan, "Watcher of the Gates! I ask that you grant admittance to myself and my charges!"

No answer. Pietruvek and I sidled up beside him for a better look, but there appeared to be no one manning the gates. "How long to we have to wait?" the boy asked.

"Until they answer, unfortunately." He began to take a deep breath to call out again when a figure came into view through one of the slots. I then realized that there were about a half-dozen more peering at us from behind the wall...and a few of them had those *gautteng* things like H'landa's pointed at us.

"Who asks?" the shadowed figure called down.

"I am *Lermekt* Jamin H'landa, current Station Officer for the village of Betedek."

"And what of them?"

The lawman gestured towards the boy. "This is Pietruvek Bannen, also of Betedek," he said, and then he pointed at me. "And this is..."

"Richard Corrigan, of the United States of America!" I yelled in English, my hands cupped around my mouth.

H'landa shot me an "I'll get you later for that" look before continuing to speak to the guard in Arkan. "We are expected by *H'drek* Sela. It is urgent that we meet with her as soon as possible."

There was a pause before the figure called down, "A moment, *d'ho-lermekt*," and disappeared from view. We could hear the clanking of metal on the other side of the wall as some kind of mechanism was engaged. Shortly afterwards, the gates slid open, two soldiers on either side pushing them clear of our path. Beyond the gates lay an open courtyard, some smaller buildings, and of course, more Kana-Semeth. H'landa nudged his mount forward to trot beneath the archway, stopping only when he realized the boy and I weren't following. He looked back towards me, one eyebrow cocked.

Pietruvek was puzzled as well. "What the matter?" he asked me in English.

"Just a feeling," I answered as I stared at the inside of the stronghold. "A really, *really* bad feeling." About what, I couldn't exactly say, but it certainly didn't disappear once we rode through the gates and I heard them shut behind us with a heavy *clang*.

* * * * * *

"So, you are the man who has come into our midst and caused all this trouble."

"I suppose I am, *d'ho-h'drek*." I settled back into my chair, a slight smile on my face. H'landa had taken us straight up to *H'drek* Sela's office as soon as he found someone to take care of our mounts and our gear. A few of the officers that we passed on the way stared at me like the one out in the street had, but most of them didn't even give me a second glance, as if seeing a Taran was a commonplace occurrence for them.

The office was located in the main building of the compound, and its furnishings reflected what I'd seen in the rest of the Kana-Semeth's holdings: they had money, more than most Arkans, and they poured it into items that were both functional and flashy. The chairs we sat in, for example, were finely carved and lacquered, but you could also see that they had probably been made a century ago, and would more than likely still be in use for another century or two. The appearance of *H'drek* Sela herself surprised me a bit: even though H'landa had told me so before, I still couldn't entirely believe that his commanding officer was a woman. Back home, a woman in the military or law enforcement was...well, there just *wasn't*. Not like this. But H'landa didn't seem to have a problem with it, and Sela carried herself like she could handle anything just as well as any man could, so I tried to ignore my misgivings and just think of her as another lawman...er, lawwoman...whatever.

She regarded me from behind her desk, her slender hands clasped before her and resting on the dark polished wood. She smiled a little herself and said in Arkan, "I must admit, I was not expecting you to look so...normal."

I almost asked her just what the Hell she *was* expecting when Pietruvek said, "If I may, *d'ho-h'drek*, Arkans and Tarans share many physical traits. If not for the differences in color, you would be hard-pressed to tell them apart from us at a glance."

"*Kai*, that pink skin definitely makes him stand out," she answered, still smiling. I gritted my teeth at that -- I didn't appreciate being talked about like I wasn't there -- but she didn't seem to notice. "I certainly wish he *did* look more like the rest of us," she continued. "It would make my job much easier."

"Something has happened," H'landa said, more as a statement than a question.

Her expression became grave. "Quite a lot has happened since you left, *d'ho-lermekt.* Despite being paid quite handsomely to remain silent, the man who first informed us of the Taran's arrival has been relating his story to others, and word has been spreading far too quickly for us to control anymore." She shook her head. "It was bad enough when the lower ranks in the stronghold began passing rumors, but when the general public found out..."

I glanced at Pietruvek, but he seemed as confused as me. I cleared my throat and asked her in Arkan, "Um, excuse me...who told you I was here? In Arkhein, I mean."

H'drek Sela finally gave me her full attention. "A traveler happened to be passing through Betedek when you arrived. He saw the whole thing, and was apparently so terrified that he left the village immediately. Luckily, one of our officers heard him relating his tale in a local tavern and took it seriously. It took a few days to get the truth out of him, but once we did..." She gestured towards H'landa.

"And now the whole city knows," I said. "But no one seemed to notice me until that one soldier pointed me out."

"They probably have no idea what a Taran actually looks like," Pietruvek chimed in. "Even *Padra* and I were surprised at your true appearance."

Sela nodded, saying, "Many of the citizens are also treating the news the way they treat most rumors: they dismiss it as false, or they simply do not care. It is the ones who *do* care that are causing us concern."

Uh-oh. "Why? What are they doing?"

She picked up a sheaf of papers lying on the desk, flipping through them. "Well, one woman came to us and offered to bear your children so the Taran race would not die out again," she said. "Another woman told us she was *already* pregnant with your child, and therefore you were legally her husband. We have also had three separate people claim to be Taran themselves and demand to see you, despite the fact that none of them could back up their stories."

"Jesus, you've got to be kidding me," I muttered in English. "Don't these people have anything better to do?"

Sela looked at my two companions. "What did he say?"

Smirking slightly, H'landa answered in Arkan, "He wants to know if the first woman is pretty." He was sitting beside me, so I kicked him in the shin.

"This is not a joke, *d'ho*-Corrigan," she said as she glared at me, "these are just the lesser disruptions we have experienced. There have also been more than a few protests regarding your presence amongst us, some of which have led to near-riots. We have five officers in the infirmary, thanks to you."

I leaned forward in my chair. "I hope you are not going to try and hold me accountable for this nonsense."

"Not directly, but you *are* the source of these disruptions, and that is the reason why we had *Lermekt* H'landa bring you into custody."

I whipped my head around towards the lawman, growling in English, "You lying sonovabitch..."

He held up his hands. "I told you the truth, Richard, I swear upon the memory of my *padra*!" He then said to his commander, "*D'ho-h'drek*, there must be some misunderstanding. you wrote that *d'ho*-Corrigan was not to be a prisoner..."

"And he is *still* not a prisoner," she answered. "In fact, technically, he is not anything. According to the Laws, he does not even exist."

"What?!?" The three of us nearly fell out of our chairs at that.

"The Laws were written for Arkans, pertaining to Arkhein and Arkhein alone. Until a month ago, Tarahein was a myth, a legend connected to a time that few people want to remember." She fixed her gaze upon me again. "The people who have been protesting your arrival believe

Tarans are responsible for the Great Plague, did you know that? They think you have come back to destroy the world."

"The Tarans were victims as well!" Pietruvek said. "To be honest, neither side was truly responsible for what happened."

"The truth is not the issue here, it is perception," she replied. "One half of the population does not believe that Tarans are real, and the other half believes them to be a threat to our very existence. In the midst of that, you have the *Y'meer* trying to decide if a race that can cause such division should be granted the same rights as all Arkans. They have spent close to a month debating this, as well as having to explain to the King and his advisors why these outbursts keep happening. This has gotten too far out of hand." She leaned back in her chair, saying, "Until this matter is resolved, the Taran is to remain here in the stronghold. It is hoped that, in a few months, the public will forget all about this and..."

"A few *months*? Are you *out* of your *mind*?" I stood up, fighting the urge to jump over the desk and grab her. "Look, I am sorry about everything that has happened, but I will not let you people hide me away until you think of a better option."

"The decision has already been made," she said calmly, "and quarters have been prepared for you. Any resistance you put up will be met with equal force, I assure you."

"I'll show you 'equal force', you two-faced little..." I spat back in English, and started to draw one of my guns. Before I even cleared leather, though, H'landa was on his feet, the blade of his sword pressed against my throat.

Dead silence filled the room, or at least it seemed that way: my heart was pounding too loudly in my ears to hear anything clearly. The two of us stared at each other, neither willing to back down an inch. H'landa wasn't exactly in a safe position, either: he stood on my right side, and that was the gun I had half-drawn. Another three inches or so, and I could shoot him in the belly at point-blank range. I let him know about his mistake by cocking the hammer. He didn't flinch. Brave soul.

"Do not do this, Richard," the lawman said in English.

"Don't give me a reason to."

"This is just a misunderstanding. Put away the weapon, sit down, and we will figure this out."

"You first, traitor."

"Pietruvek, please get up and take Richard's *trit bakido* from him."

The kid sounded as stunned as I felt. "*D'ho-lermekt*, I cannot..."

"If you do not," H'landa continued, "and anyone is harmed by the Taran's actions, you will be held accountable as well. If anyone should die..."

"For Christ's sake, he's just a boy," I said. "You can't force him to make a choice like that."

"He is also a boy that you would never let come to harm," the lawman replied, "or have I misjudged you?"

He had me there. I lowered the hammer and let the gun fall back into its holster, then stared straight ahead at *H'drek* Sela, who hadn't moved from her spot behind the desk the whole time. That in itself was quite surprising, considering that nothing the three of us said would have made any sense to her.

H'landa didn't lower his blade until after Pietruvek had removed both my gunbelts and my knife from my reach. The guilt in the boy's eyes as he did it was almost painful, and I didn't blame him: we'd been betrayed, and now he had no choice but to add to that betrayal. Once the task was done, the lawman forced me back down into my chair and leaned over me, saying in an even tone, "I am as disgusted with all of this as you are, but violence will only worsen this situation. Now, be still and let me try to salvage this."

I didn't answer him, I just sat there with a clenched jaw and balled fists as he turned to face his commander. "Is everything under control, *d'ho-lermekt*?" she asked.

Switching back to Arkan, he said, "With all due respect, *d'ho-h'drek*, I have to object to the way the Kana-Semeth are handling this entire incident. To hold *d'ho-*Corrigan against his will simply because the *Y'meer* refuse to make a decision is absurd. Do they truly think if they hide him, the problem will simply disappear?"

"Do not be *bruhzod*. We are not hiding him, we are merely trying to ensure his safety."

"He was safe in Betedek."

"For how long, though? It is only a matter of time before someone traces those stories back to Betedek. If that happens, there is no way we could possibly prevent harm coming to the Taran if he remained out there unguarded."

"And what of Betedek itself, then?" he asked. "You make this sound inevitable, yet you leave the citizens there unprotected."

"Not for long. As soon as the *Y'meer* have finished interviewing you and *Bannen-su* about the incident," she said, referring to Pietruvek by the honorific used for children, "you shall return to the village as permanent Station Officer, at least until we have decided that the potential for any sort of disturbance has passed."

H'landa's lips moved, but no sound came out. He looked at me, the guilty expression on his face now -- if he was in Betedek, I'd be completely at the mercy of his superiors. "I...I cannot let you do this, *d'ho-h'drek*," he finally managed to say. "So long as the question of *d'ho-*Corrigan's status remains unanswered, I will not abandon him. He has rights, no matter what the Laws say."

She regarded him levelly for a moment. "You seem to be forgetting your rank, *d'ho-lermekt*. I see no silver on your collar, nor will I ever if you continue to act like this. In fact, you almost seem to be taking the *Y'meer's* decision personally."

The lawman paled. "Forgive me, *d'ho-h'drek*," he said, his voice shaky, "I am merely concerned for the Taran's welfare."

"Understandable. He has been in your charge for quite some time." She got up and came around the desk to stand beside him. "If you wish, you may escort him to his quarters and inspect them yourself, to ease your conscience."

"K'sai, d'ho-h'drek." He bowed slightly.

"We have quarters prepared for you as well, of course, *Bannen-su*," she said, turning to the boy. "But first, I would like to look over these artifacts your *padra* was so kind as to send to us."

Pietruvek remained rooted to his chair, his hands twisting my gunbelts still lying in his lap. His eyes darted from Sela to me, as unsure of his own fate as I was of mine. He really didn't have much to worry about, though: he was undoubtedly Arkan. "Do what she says," I mouthed.

"I will watch over him for as long as I can," H'landa said to me in English, his voice low. "We should go now." I stood up without a word, glaring at him so hard he wouldn't look me in the eye. "I truly did not expect this," he continued. "I will do my best to change their minds, but the *Y'meer* can be difficult."

"Don't try to do me *too* many favors, cousin," I snarled.

He turned pale again. "Please, do not call me that anymore."

I leaned close to his ear and said, "I wonder what they'd do to *you* if they found out the truth. Maybe we could get adjoining rooms."

"Be quiet," he hissed. That old look of hatred was returning to his face: hatred of me, of Tarans, of that small, alien part of himself. Now, however, he had a real reason to hate it: if his superiors decided that I wasn't worth giving any basic human rights to, who knows what they'd do to a half-breed like him. "You promised me, *not a word.*"

"I'll take it to the grave, H'landa," I replied, "but *you're* the one who's gonna have to live with where that grave's gonna be, and when."

"I am sorry about all this, Richard."

"Yeah...so am I."

CHAPTER 13

"Okay, Richard, time to take stock of all the ridiculous things you've had to go through this past month." My voice sounded worn thin, almost to the point of breaking, even to my own ears. "You've been shot in the head, locked up, beat up, had a vision of your own death, shot a *dead person*, were nearly torn to shreds by some demonic *thing*, been exiled to another world, poisoned, locked up *again*, beat up *again*, had the very nature of your existence called into question more times than you can count, and now, to top it all off, you've been locked up *for a third fuckin' time* and didn't even *do* anything this time 'round to deserve it. Dear God, just kill me now, 'cause I don't want to see how much worse my life can get."

I paced around the room, retracing the same pattern I'd been making for three days now: eight steps from the door to the window, four from the window to the bed, six from the bed back to the door. It seemed stupid, but there was nothing else for me to do in there, save look out the window at the soldiers marching below in the courtyard or sleep. The view had gotten boring real fast, and as far as sleeping goes, I hadn't been doing much of that: every time I tried, my dreams would degenerate into a mass of dark, jumbled images that I couldn't even remember clearly when I woke up, but would nevertheless leave me feeling shaken and scared and even more restless than I'd been before. I couldn't stand it anymore, I *had* to get out of there. Where I'd go, I had no idea, but I was going to lose my mind if I spent any more time cooped up.

I paused when my path brought me back to the glass-fitted window, and inspected it for the hundredth time since being locked away: narrow frame barely wide enough for a man to pass through, no ledge, three-story drop to an open courtyard...not impossible, but with five hundred or so Kana-Semeth around, it would definitely be tough.

"Quit kidding yourself," I muttered. "They'd cut you down without a second thought if you pulled a stunt like that." I'd been talking to myself quite a bit lately -- that's what happens when you don't sleep for three days straight. I figured that, pretty soon, my brain would be so wasted from insomnia that the idea of escape wouldn't seem so far-fetched after all, and I'd probably just jump out the window and hope for the best.

I leaned forward, rested my head against the glass, and closed my eyes. Too much aggravation, that's why I couldn't sleep. Too many things beyond my control. Too many people smiling and telling me how honored they were to meet me and take care of me and fulfill my every need but don't you *dare* set one foot outside this nice room with its lush carpets and comfy chairs and the softest bed you've ever laid on *too damn bad you can't sleep for more than ten minutes a night you worthless Taran why didn't you save us all some trouble and drop dead the moment you got here...*

The door behind me opened, but I didn't bother to turn around, figuring that it was either Zanam or Zoram dropping off lunch. They were the two low-ranking Kana-Semeth assigned to guard my door and attend to anything I might want (so long as it didn't involve me leaving the room, of course). I tended to ignore them or act like I didn't understand Arkan whenever they came in, and when I did have to acknowledge them, I'd intentionally mix up their names, which was about the only source of amusement I had open to me. So imagine my surprise when I heard a very familiar voice say my name. I turned and saw Pietruvek standing in the doorway, my bodyguards lurking behind him in the hall, along with another Kana-Semeth I wasn't familiar with. The boy wore what looked like the fanciest clothes he owned: a nicely-cut black tunic and matching breeches, a dark red shirt, and a high sheen on his usually scuffed-up boots. His expression seemed quite dour. "Alright, who died?" I quipped in English.

He smiled a little, then ran up and threw his arms around me -- kind of strange, but I hadn't seen him since I'd left *H'drek* Sela's office, so I didn't pry him off right away. "Thou looks terrible," he said when he finally let go.

"I feel worse than I look," I answered, trying to make a joke out of it. "Where have you been? I've been asking to see you, but those guys out there kept stonewalling me." I motioned over to a set of chairs on one side of the room, and we each took a seat.

"They have kept me busy answering questions," he said. "About thee, thy world, the Crossroad, my family...always questioning, but I do not think they hear everything. I feel..." He put his fists together and made a twisting motion.

"Wrung out?"

"*Kai.* First *H'drek* Sela, then another *h'drek*, then the *Y'meer*...all the same *bruhzod* questions. Like a forest full of *vekaiben*, all twittering at once."

"At least they let you out." I told him about the last few days, staring at the same four walls. "This is worse than a jail cell, Peter. At least there, they don't pretend that they like you."

"Not sure thou will like this, either: the *Y'meer* wish to speak with thee. Took a lot of convincing, but *Lermekt* H'landa made them see that they should meet with thee first before passing judgment."

"Well, it's the least that bastard could do for me." Actually, I was surprised H'landa had kept his word: I figured the potential of being exposed as part-Taran had scared him too much to act on my behalf. "Why didn't he come here himself?"

"He did not think thou would speak to him."

"Damn straight. You think J'nath can hold a grudge...Hell, he ain't got nothin' on me, the way I feel lately." I rubbed my bloodshot eyes. "All right, give me some time to clean up, then I'll go and talk to these high-and-mighty *Y'meer*." Pietruvek relayed the message to his escort, who graciously let me have perhaps five minutes to make myself presentable before he insisted that we head on out.

The guards led me and Pietruvek down what seemed like an endless series of hallways until we reached the "courtroom", for lack of a better term. Looks-wise, it was the best way to describe it: the room was laid out similarly to the meeting hall in Betedek, but with fewer windows and benches. A long, curved judge's bench was set back against the wall, behind which sat nine Kana-Semeth -- six men and three women -- all with the silver on their uniforms that H'landa warned me about. The sight of all those *Y'meer* staring down at me as I entered the room was pretty damned intimidating, which is why I'm sure they set themselves up there like that. Zanam and Zoram led me to a partially-enclosed dais standing in the open area before the *Y'meer*, while Pietruvek's escort sat down with him on one of the benches -- I spotted H'landa sitting out there was well, one of maybe a dozen or so regular Kana-Semeth in attendance. From what I could tell, there were no civilians present to witness what could possibly be my last act as a free man.

"Taran Reshard Corrigan," the *Y'meer* in the centermost seat addressed me in Arkan, "do you *kedda* why you have been brought before us?"

"More or less," I answered. "You are trying to decide if I am 'worthy' enough to live amongst Arkans."

"That is a rather rough way to state it," one of the female *Y'meer* said. "We are merely trying to do what we always do: protect the people from harm."

"I have not intentionally harmed anyone."

"Your *presence* has caused harm," another *Y'meer* chimed in. "Because of that, we need to determine what sort of long-term influence you may have on our people...for good or for ill."

"So far," the first *Y'meer* said, "what we have learned of you is not encouraging. According to reports from both *H'drek* Sela and *Lermekt* H'landa, as well as observations from others, you have a tendency towards violence, a great disrespect for authority, and you show little regard for anyone besides yourself."

I looked down at the floor, saying, "That is not entirely true." But enough of that *was* true, and that certainly didn't help my case. I had to think of a way to defuse this.

"You disagree with our statements?" one of them asked after a moment.

I lifted my head and did my best to look each of them in the eye in turn. "I am not a bad person by nature, but you have to look at all this from my point of view. I have been torn from my home and thrown someplace I never could have imagined to exist. Every night I dream of a world I will never see again, and every day I have to deal with people and things that I can barely relate to sometimes. If you were in my situation, how would you react to it all? Sensibly? Or would you perhaps become a little violent and disrespectful as well?"

That seemed to stop them cold for a bit. The first *Y'meer* leaned over to confer with the one sitting next to him, and I noticed a couple others doing the same with their neighbors. *Good,* I thought, *maybe I knocked a little sense into these yahoos.* When they turned their attention back to me, I half-expected them to apologize and let me go on the spot. Boy, was I wrong.

"*D'ho*-Corrigan, are you implying that you want revenge for ending up in this situation?"

I gaped at them. "I did not say..."

"Are you planning on forcing your Taran customs upon our citizens in an effort to recreate your world?"

"Why would I do..."

"Do you believe that you can ignore the Laws since you came here unwillingly?"

I grasped the rail encompassing the dais and dug my nails into the wood as they continued to pelt me with their ridiculous assumptions. I soon realized that it didn't matter what I said or how well I said it, they would still tear it apart until they found the tiniest fragment that smacked of sedition or corruption and throw it back at me. I did my best to keep my temper in check through it all, just so I wouldn't give them the pleasure of some *real* ammunition to use against me, but it wasn't easy.

About an hour or so into this farce, the lack of sleep began to pull at me. The world felt fuzzy, and my legs ached from standing still for so long, but I just kept on answering questions. *Come on, Richard,* I told myself, *they'll get bored eventually and let you go back to your room. Just hang on until then.* I closed my eyes for a moment and took a few deep breaths to clear my head. It helped a little, but when I opened my eyes again, I felt even worse than before.

My old buddy, the mystery man in the black cloak, was standing in front of me, his back to the *Y'meer.* An odd choking noise came out of my throat when I saw him, and I tried to back away, but my legs wouldn't obey me. All I could do was stand and stare at the figure that had picked now, of all times, to come back and haunt me. He stepped towards me without a sound, closing the gap between us with three graceful strides. As before, the hood of his cloak hid his features from me, but I could still make out a smooth, hairless chin beneath those shadows, and for the first time, I noticed how pale and ashen his complexion appeared to be. "You're Arkan," I gasped, lapsing back into English. "That's why you've been hiding your face, isn't it? You didn't want me to know you were Arkan!"

"I am not Arkan," the figure replied. "Not like you think." As he said the words, he came around and stepped up onto the dais, his hand creeping out from beneath his cloak.

D-don't...don't touch me...please..." I somehow managed to sputter as his gloved fingers came up towards my face. The last time he touched me, it felt like my brain was going to explode, and I was terrified of what might happen now.

"I am sorry, Richard," he said, "but we cannot wait for you to come around of your own accord any longer." I could see the seams on the glove hovering inches from my face. "We need you now."

"No, don't do this."

"Stop fighting us. You..."

"D'ho-Corrigan!"

My head snapped up to see all the *Y'meer* glaring at me from behind the bench. *"D'ho*-Corrigan, did you even hear what I just said?" one of them asked.

"Wh...what..." I looked around the dais, then the rest of the courtroom, searching for the mystery man, but I couldn't see him. "Where did he go?" I asked in Arkan, albeit shakily.

"Where did *who* go?" The last *Y'meer* narrowed his eyes at me. "Is there something wrong with you?"

"I'm beginning to think so," I muttered in English, rubbing a trembling hand over my face. Dear God, I'd nodded off in the middle of my interrogation...what was happening to me? I glanced behind me at Pietruvek and H'landa, both of whom looked just as worried about me as I was. Turning once more to the bench, I switched to Arkan again and said, "Forgive me, *d'ho-Y'meer*, but I think I need some time to rest. If you could permit me to return to my room for a while, I may be able to continue later."

The group conferred for a moment before the centermost *Y'meer* spoke. "Very well. If you feel this is necessary, we can continue after Fifth Light today."

Judging by the angle of the light coming through the windows, the sun was already in its midday or Fourth

Light position, which gave me two to three hours to get my head on straight again. As Zanam and Zoram escorted me back to my quarters, I found that the further I got from the courtroom, the better I felt. I'd nearly convinced myself in the past month that my first two dreams of the mystery man had been just that: *dreams*. There had been no prophecies, no real-life connections, just a couple of stupid nightmares, and I kept telling myself as I walked down the corridor that today's incident had just been more of the same. Besides, my waking life was strange enough already without adding on that sort of thing.

Once the guards admitted me back into my room, Zoram asked, "Do you need anything at the moment?"

"Yeah," I said in English. "A shot, a beer, and a naked redhead with huge breasts." I held my hands about ten inches from my chest. "'Bout to here will do." They, of course, responded with their usual blank looks, so I shrugged and said, "Okay, forget the beer," then closed the door on their stoic faces. With a sigh, I leaned my back against the door and shut my eyes so I wouldn't have to look at that godawful room. Two hours. That was roughly how long I had before I'd have to go back to that nonsense with the *Y'meer*, and I knew there was no way I could get any decent rest in that period of time. *Dammit, I really wish I could have a drink,* I thought. *Just enough to loosen up, then maybe I could finally get some sleep.*

"There is no time for that, Richard Corrigan. You have a job to do."

My bloodshot eyes flew open. The mystery man stood literally toe-to-toe with me, his dark cloak filling my vision. *Oh Jesus I'm asleep again I'm asleep I'm asleep,* my mind babbled. *I fell asleep standing up and this isn't real you're not real for God's sake don't touch me!*

He laid a hand over my face, his fingertips barely grazing my skin. "Forgive me," he whispered.

Suddenly, the entire world seemed engulfed by a blaze of light -- I tried to close my eyes to block it out, but they remained fixed open as the light burned into my skull, blinding me. *What's happening?!?* I screamed in my mind as I felt myself fall away into the light. Then, just as suddenly, the light was gone, and I crashed to the ground. Though I still couldn't see, I could inexplicably feel dirt and short grasses beneath my palms. "Damn you, what did you do to me?" I hollered in the darkness. "Where am I?"

"Still in your room," the mystery man said from somewhere, "just deeply asleep. At least, your body is: your mind and soul are here, with us, and will remain here until you finally choose to see what you *must* see."

"You *blinded* me, you bastard! I can't see *anything*!"

"You blinded *yourself.* We tried to open your eyes, but you are so stubborn that you undo our work at every turn. That is why we brought you here, as dangerous as it is." The man's voice seemed closer now, but I still couldn't pinpoint it. "If we cannot make you see here, our worlds are damned."

"See what?" I pushed myself up to a sitting position. "It's been a month since you bothered me, and you didn't show me anything then."

"We tried to show you some, but it was evident that you needed more time to adjust...which we once thought we had. This is all happening much faster than we expected: we planned on spending *years* preparing you, but we underestimated him, and now we have *days*. Do you understand that? The longer you fight us, the stronger he becomes."

"What are you talking about? Who's stronger?"

"Beterion."

Just like that, he spat it out. The name of the monster that nearly killed me and kept me from ever going home again. The source of the near-extinction of the Arkan race. The demon-king of the Crossroads. I squeezed my blinded eyes shut and shook my head in denial -- I still wasn't clear about all this, but that one tiny nugget of information was enough for me to want out.

Matter of fact, it made me want to crawl under a rock and hide for the rest of my life.

"I know you are afraid," the voice continued, intimately close now. "I was afraid once, as well. I thought that I did not have the strength to do the task required of me, but that was before I understood what I am...and what *you* are. Look past what the world has forced you to become. You have the potential to be more than you ever dreamed, but first, you must open your eyes and see what we need you to see." His voice sounded so different from the cold, distant way he usually spoke to me. I could hear real emotion there, an almost pleading tone, and I began to think that he was pretty damn scared himself, despite what he said.

I crossed my arms over my chest as vague memories of pain danced through my mind. "Beterion came close to tearing me to shreds once," I told him. "I'm not about to let it have another shot at me."

"What about the others who have suffered? The ones who *are* suffering because you keep turning your back on the truth? Ignoring it will not make it go away, it will just prolong their agony until the sky turns black with ash and the landscape withers and dies and *you* will be all that remains. Stop denying what you have seen in your dreams and accept the truth, while we still have time."

Slowly, inevitably, his words wore down whatever barriers my mind had built up over the past month, and all those half-remembered nightmares came forth in full clarity, overwhelming me with images of death and pain. People choking on blood and bile. Doors spattered with white paint as a shaking hand drew that strange funeral-symbol on it. Bodies unceremoniously dumped on the *idiayo,* their faces shriveled and black. The faces I saw were the worst part of it all, because *I knew those faces.* I had passed them in the street, talked with them, worked with them, made awkward jokes with them. God help me, I was watching Betedek die. "Why?" I moaned. "For the love of God, *why?*"

"Open your eyes and you will see why."

I did as he asked, and found myself kneeling in front of the Crossroad. The grass surrounding it had become yellowed, and the earth looked dry and crumbly. Beyond it stretched the path to Betedek, and though it was too far away to see anything distinctly, I knew that it was now as dead as that town in New Mexico had been. I had *seen* it, I had *felt* it...

"No, it is not dead," the mystery man told me, "but it *is* dying, and quickly." He towered over me, a swath of darkness in the light of midday. "The people of Betedek know what is happening, but they do not have the strength left to stop it. So they gather together, just as the people of Hadley had done on your world, and they wait for the end."

"This...this can't be happening. This can't be the plague, it's *gone*, the Crossroad's sealed up here."

"Is it?"

I gaped at the man, then stared down at the Crossroad: it looked the same as always, the piece of the Heart of Avisar at its center unharmed. No, wait...the sunlight bouncing off its facets didn't look right. I leaned forward, careful not to touch the stone itself, and gazed into its beautiful blue-green depths, the colors swirling and pulsing and...fracturing. Black, cancerous lines were eating away at the center of it, polluting the once-unblemished crystal. *The Heart's strength lies in its size*, that's what J'nath had told me. Any imperfections weakened the whole, and a handful of shards were less powerful than one large, fist-sized piece. But how... "Oh God," I said aloud, pushing myself away from the Crossroad. "Oh dear God, I did this, didn't I? When I crossed over, I broke it, just a little, and now it's...oh God, this is all my fault."

"We did not foresee this happening," the mystery man said. "But then, no one could have. The Heart of Avisar is not a natural component of the Crossroad. We had no way of knowing how it would react when the portal was opened, so we simply hoped for the best. We were wrong."

"J'nath checked it." My voice sounded flat, worn out. "I *saw* him, he *checked* it. Why didn't he see the problem? Why didn't anything happen until *now*?"

"The damage must have been microscopic. A flaw too tiny for his eyes to see, and one we were too blind to notice. But Beterion saw...and he *pushed*. When the Heart splintered enough, he slithered through the cracks and sought out the smallest sparks of the Light: the weakest souls, the creatures he could kill with the least amount of effort."

"Those things in the barn, the *zemezi*," I whispered, "they didn't die from poison...Beterion got a hold of them. And then it killed that guy...he had a weak heart, J'nath told me." I looked up at him, eyes wide. "You tried to talk to me at his funeral, didn't you? But I blocked you out, just like I've been blocking out my dreams."

He nodded. "We had no suspicions until Darus Mederi was taken from us. By then, Beterion had grown stronger, and was poised to pull even more victims into his maw, but to do that, he had to be unopposed."

"I can't believe this. Are you saying that I'm so damned 'important' that Beterion waited until I left Betedek to do all this?" I asked, waving a hand towards the silent village. "Come on, J'nath knows more about the Crossroads and Beterion than..." I stopped cold as I was struck dumb by realization, bits of conversation springing up in my brain:

"Pardon my saying so, but you look like Hell."

"He kept getting headaches, for the last four or five days..."

"It looks merely like a case of Winter's chill, but that should not cause him to lose consciousness."

"J'nath...it killed J'nath," I choked. "Sweet Jesus, what am I going to tell Peter?"

"Do not fear, for J'nath Bannen is strong," the man said. "He fights on, despite what Beterion has done to him, but he is weakening. Once his heart gives out and his body dies, he will be beyond our reach."

"Then save him, dammit!" I reached out, still on my knees, and grabbed a handful of the man's cloak. "Stop wasting time jabbering at me and *save him!*"

"My battle lies elsewhere. The one in Betedek, unfortunately, is yours alone."

"Quit saying things like that, God damn you!"

His gloved hand darted out and slapped me across the mouth, knocking me backward. "Never...*never* say that word, especially here." He stood over me, fists clenched. "You say it like it means nothing, but it is the most horrible curse you could ever utter. You think *yourself* damned by God, unaware that *no one* should ever suffer that fate, especially by inviting it upon themselves."

I glared up at him, rubbing a hand across my mouth -- I thought I could taste blood. "You don't know me, 'cause if you did, then you'd know that I'm damned already. I'm an *outlaw*. I'm a *murderer* and a *thief*. I'm going to Hell when I die and I *deserve* to, because God and I both know that I'm absolutely *worthless*."

The man looked down at me, his expression hidden by shadows. "If God truly thought you were worthless, He would not have brought you here and charged you with this task."

I felt as if I'd been struck again. "Whuh...what did you say?"

"Your mind does not accept the words, but in your soul, I can see joy...and relief." He bent down on one knee beside me, saying, "For too long, you have thought of yourself as abandoned: first by your family, then by the world, and even by God. You fear rejection so much that you almost try and *make* people hate you just to save yourself potential grief, yet the loneliness that follows drives you to attempt suicide at times. I can see that, even now, you are regretting the feelings that had begun to grow in your heart towards Betedek and J'nath's family. You wish that you had never let down your guard once again." He laid a hand upon my shoulder. "You should never torture yourself like that, Richard Corrigan, nor should you deny the fact that God has never forsaken you."

I opened my mouth to speak, shut it, and then stared down at the ground for a while. How do you respond to something like *this*? The man must have seen the rough time I was having, and silently waited as I put my thoughts in order. When I finally looked back up at him, tears had begun to well up in my eyes. "You've got...you've got the wrong guy," I said. "You need a savior, not...not *me*. I'm nothing. I'm not a hero."

"You are mistaken," he replied, his voice soft. "We do not need a hero, we need a *n'toku-rejii*. That is what you truly are, beneath all the blood and the pain and the scars. It is the one glorious, shining gift that no one can ever beat from you, which no bullet or blade can tear from you. It is the reason why you were chosen, and why you now must return to Betedek with no fear in your heart."

"B-but the Kana-Semeth...the *Y'meer*...I'm under lock and key."

"Speak with the *h'landa*. In this matter, he can be trusted. Though his role in the coming battle shall be small, he will understand it well. You must speak with the boy on this matter, also. Now that his father has fallen, his knowledge shall be invaluable."

"They'll never believe me."

"Yes, they will. Have faith, and remember what you see in the Light." He laid a hand over my face again, and the world was once more awash in brilliant white light, only this time there was no pain when it came over me. When the light faded, I felt like I was floating in nothingness -- it took some time to reconnect with reality, to remember how to see and hear and feel. Actually, feeling came back first: impossible as it seemed, my mouth still ached from being slapped, and I reached up and clumsily touched the spot with partly-numb fingers.

"Perhaps he is not dead, after all," I heard a voice say in Arkan. H'landa's voice.

I opened my eyes, and though my vision was a bit hazy, I could still tell that the blurry figure hovering over me was indeed the *lermekt*, who looked quite relieved. He turned away from me, telling someone, "I believe he will recover, but send for a *z'kira*, just in case."

"Forget...forget that," I said in English, my tongue feeling heavy and foreign in my mouth. "Be fine. Have to talk. Now."

"You sound far from 'fine'," he replied. "Now lay still, you may have hit your head when you fell over."

I frowned, confused, until I realized that I could feel carpet beneath me -- I must have collapsed on the floor during my "conversation", just as I'd done when I had the vision at the funeral. "How long?" I asked him.

H'landa shrugged. "Depends on how busy the *z'kira* is, I suppose."

"No, no...how long was I unconscious?"

"Oh. Not too long, I think. The guards heard you fall shortly after they had left you alone in here. They ran into me on the way to fetch the *z'kira*, which was lucky for you, because they told me that they could not find the pulse-beat in your neck. They kept looking for it here by mistake." He pressed his fingers on a spot behind my right ear, near my neckbone -- the typical spot for an Arkan, but certainly not for a regular human.

"Must've scared the piss out of 'em," I muttered as I propped myself up on my elbows and looked towards the open door. Zanam and Zoram were standing there as always, alternately looking in on the two of us and speaking with one of the *Y'meer* out in the hallway. "Where's Peter? I need to talk to him, too." I waved a hand at the other Kana-Semeth. "Don't tell them anything, though. I want this conversation to remain private."

H'landa cocked an eyebrow at me. "You must be feeling better than you look. You are already trying to order me around again."

"Listen, we don't have time for jokes. Get the kid in here and I'll explain everything...or at least I'll *try* to."

"Just how do you expect me to do this when they will not allow you visitors?"

"I dunno, you're the big bad Kana-Semeth guy. I'm sure you'll think of something."

He grunted, then stood up and went over to his fellow lawmen gathered out in the hall. "I have checked him over. There is no need for a *z'kira*, just give him some more time to rest," he told them in Arkan.

"Are you sure?" Zanam asked. "Upon my Oath, he seemed dead."

"He was just...he had a fainting spell. *Kai*, a very common problem for Tarans. They get overexcited, they stop breathing, and then..." H'landa spread out his hands. "Flat on the floor. I have seen him do it quite a few times."

The two guards peered around his shoulder as I got to my feet, doing my best to act like I wasn't listening. "A fainting spell?" Zoram repeated, sounding unconvinced.

The *lermekt* nodded. "Trust me. You give him a big enough scare, and he goes over like a *dirruk* on a fencepost." I had no clue what that meant, but they all seemed to think it was pretty damn funny. Turning to the *Y'meer*, H'landa then said, "With your permission, I would like to bring *Bannen-su* in to see him, just to reassure the boy that we are not mistreating the Taran."

"If you are certain this will not cause him further harm, I suppose we can allow it," he answered. "Do you think he is well enough to continue questioning?"

"I think it would be best to wait until tomorrow, *d'ho-Y'meer*," H'landa said. "He still seems a little out of sorts."

More than you know, cousin, I thought, sitting down on the bed. I hung my head and did my best to look exhausted as the lawman pulled the door shut, still talking to his superior. As soon as I heard it latch, I jumped up and pressed my ear to the wood -- the conversation wasn't perfectly clear, but I heard enough to know that they'd bought the story.

Now I just had to hope that, when H'landa got back with Pietruvek, I could make them buy the story that *I* had to tell.

*   *   *   *   *   *

"...and then I woke up on the floor with H'landa leaning over me."

We sat in a tight circle, me on the edge of the bed and the two of them in chairs clustered in front of me. It had taken a few harsh words from H'landa in order to convince the guards to give us some privacy, and once that door was shut, I'd gathered up my courage and told them the reason I so desperately needed to speak with them. Neither had said a word as I spilled my guts about what I'd seen and heard in my dreams, starting with the one I'd had in the jail cell in Barrelhead (minus the cell, of course). It took a few minutes for me to get comfortable talking about all of it, but I felt that, if I was going to convince them I wasn't kidding, they had to know everything...well, *almost* everything.

The boy took it the way I thought he would: he looked like I'd punched him in the gut. His eye were wide, his jaw slack, and his whole expression begged me to tell him that this was a joke. I would have given anything to tell him it was. The lawman, surprisingly, seemed to be taking the news a little better. "So," he said in English once I was through, "the Taran now claims to have conversations with God."

"I didn't say he was God, or at least he never gave me that impression," I told him. "He struck me more as...somebody relaying a message. I don't know who or what he was, but when he talked, he usually said 'we', which leads me to believe that the words he spoke weren't always his own."

"Somebody who speaks for God," H'landa muttered, then got out of his chair and walked over to the window. "You never saw his whole face?" he asked me, gazing down upon the courtyard below. "He never told you his name?"

"No, nothing like that."

"Are you sure you left out no details about him, no matter how minor? For Avisar's sake, did you at least see his eyes?"

"For all I know, he doesn't *have* eyes. Listen, it isn't the messenger that concerns me right now, it's the message: Beterion is loose again, and I'm supposed to stop it somehow."

"But why you? Two months ago, you did not know Arkhein even existed." H'landa pointed towards the courtyard. "I could go down there, grab any soldier by the collar, and they would be a hundred times better suited for this than you."

"Perhaps Avisar does not want soldiers," Pietruvek said quietly. "Soldiers answer to other soldiers, not to God."

The lawman's expression turned icy. "What is that supposed to mean, boy?"

"I think he means the Kana-Semeth have their own agenda," I said. "Hell, look at how they've handled me showing up so far. Imagine how they'd react to this new bit of information: by the time they could agree on a course of action, half of this world would probably be dead."

"The system works better than it appears. It just was not made to handle *this*...and *you*..." He waved his hands in the open air, and then at me. "This all keeps coming back to you. Had you never come here, we would all be better off, I think."

I looked at Pietruvek, still sitting in front of me. "You probably think the same thing by now, huh?"

The boy stared down at his hands lying in his lap. "I do not feel like thinking at the moment," he said. "All I know is that I do not want my *padra* to die."

"He isn't going to die," I told him, "not if I can help it."

H'landa shook his head. "This must be a mistake. I can believe that *perhaps* Avisar is using you to warn us all -- makes sense, since you probably *did* cause this -- but the idea that *you* are the key to stopping it?" He let a couple of Arkan curses fly.

"I didn't ask for the damn job, cousin. Matter of fact, I turned it down about a half-dozen times, but the guy insisted that I was the one they wanted. 'You are a *n'toku-rejii*', he kept telling me." I snorted. "Like I have any clue what *that* nonsense is supposed to mean."

"He called you...what?" The lawman's face had gone so pale, he looked nearly white. He reached out and grasped the window frame to steady himself, repeating, "He called you *what*?"

"A *n'toku-rejii*. I think that's how he said it." I glanced from him to Pietruvek, who looked rather surprised himself. "Let me guess, it's a curse word."

"*Nee*," the boy said, "it actually does not mean *anything* that I am aware of. I have only seen the word written in one of the old texts. It was just a fragment of a passage...the rest had been torn out." He then intoned in Arkan, "'We fear not the Darkness, for the *n'toku-rejii* watches over us with God's own eyes.'" He bit his lip before telling us in English, "I always thought it was part of an old prayer to Avisar."

"Not a prayer...a statement. About one of His emissaries," H'landa said. "Everything else you told us I could write off as hallucination, but that word..." He narrowed his eyes at me. "*You could not know that word.*"

"This can't get any worse," I groaned, cradling my head in my hands. "I used to be a normal guy, what the

Hell happened? Out of all the people to grab onto and drag into this mess, why did God pick me?"

"God gets strange ideas, sometimes," the lawman replied. "Whether His reasons for choosing you are sound or not, you are all we have. We shall have to make do."

"But what *are* we doing?" Pietruvek asked. "Reshard is still confined...do we tell the *Y'meer* what has occurred and pray they release him?"

"Like Hell they would." I looked up at H'landa. "I think you and Peter are gonna have to break me out of here, the sooner the better."

He nodded, but I didn't like the look on his face -- he was probably seeing his entire Kana-Semeth career go up in flames. "But when we do this," he said, "you will do as I say. No questions, no backtalk, or I will crack your skull, Word of God or not."

"Agreed. Before we take off, though, I want to get my guns back from the *Y'meer*. And we'll need horses...*vessekiben*, I mean...and supplies for the trip back. We can't afford to make any stops."

"I can take care of the last two things," the boy said, "but I may need some money."

"Then let me contribute to the cause." I reached into my pocket and pulled out the coins Dimi had given me before we left. "Remind me to thank that man when we get home," I said as I dropped them into Pietruvek's hand. "Now, on the subject of getting home..."

In about an hour, we had a bare-bones plan sketched out, most of it depending on H'landa, seeing as how the stronghold was his territory. We all agreed that it would be easiest to do this at night, and decided on Full Dark, when the moon (only a sliver that night, luckily) would be at its highest position. I would just have to sit tight until then, and be ready to move out when the time came.

Not long after H'landa and Pietruvek left to prepare, the guards brought me my evening meal. As always, it looked and smelled wonderful, even better than anything Nina had ever prepared for me, but I had no appetite that night. My mind was on anything but food at the moment. After a while, though, I made myself eat, simply because I didn't know when my next chance would be.

Last Light came and went. Torches were lit in the courtyard, though few people passed through it now. I couldn't see the moon very well from my room, so I stood at the window and watched for the lawman or the kid instead. After about three hours (I'd wound and set my watch at sunset, just to have something else to go by), I left my post and started to circle the room, occasionally peeking out at the courtyard. Despite my best efforts to remain calm, I was wound as tight as my watch from all the waiting, not to mention the thought of what I'd be facing once we got back to Betedek. "How am I even supposed to stop this nightmare?" I whispered, looking up at the ceiling. "Lord, if what that guy said is true, if You really did pick me to do this, then You made a *huge* mistake. I mean, You should have at least picked somebody that still goes to church on a regular basis. You *do* know what I tried to do the last time I was in a church, right?" I stopped pacing, half-hoping for a reply of some sort. Nothing happened.

"I never stopped believing in You, Lord," I continued, "not even after that. I reckon I just thought You stopped believing in me. I mean, I'd...you know..." My voice faded, not wanting to speak aloud what I'd done in the past, and I sat down on the edge of the bed. After a minute, I said, "Dammit, if You really are responsible for me coming here and seeing all this stuff, why did You wait so long to talk to me? Did You even care about me before I got here, or did You just ignore me until You needed me? Can You even *hear* me right now?" I fell back against the bed, my eyes still fixed upon the ceiling. "Were You really even speaking to me in the first place?"

I lay very still, waiting for an answer, but nothing came. *Stupid*, I thought. *What right do you have to make demands of God?* Then I heard something...not the Word of God, mind you, but voices in the hall. I jumped off the bed and rushed to the door, pressing my ear to the wood. While the voices were indistinct, I could tell one of them belonged to H'landa. Suddenly, someone or something banged against the door, and I stepped back, unsure of what was going on out there. One word carried through the thick wood quite well -- "*Narras! Narras!*" -- followed by a couple more bangs before all fell silent again. After a moment or two, I could hear someone unlocking the door -- real brass locks on this one, not an elaborate slide-bolt like in Betedek -- so I set my feet and clenched my fists just in case the wrong guy had come out on top.

The door swung open, revealing H'landa cautiously stepping over an unconscious Zanam -- they only posted one guard at night, and I reckoned he must've drawn the short straw. "Took some time to find these," he said in English, and tossed at me a bag he'd been carrying. "Getting into the private chamber of the *Y'meer* is not easy."

I opened it up and saw my guns, along with my knife and a few other items they'd pulled off of me. I also found a small glass bottle and a wet rag. "What's this?" I asked, uncorking the bottle -- it gave off a pungent smell.

"Sadrin's oil. Do not breathe it in," he explained as he took hold of the guard's shoulders and dragged him into the room. "I do not want to carry you out of this place."

"You gave him a dose of ether, didn't you?" I said. "Smart idea."

"Well, I *would* rather not end up in the workhouse when all this is done." He pulled down the blankets on the bed, saying, "The fewer people we harm during all this, the better off we will be. Now, help me get him up here."

We hoisted Zanam onto the bed, then H'landa used the leather hand-restraints off the guard's own belt to bind him before pulling the blankets over the poor guy's head -- I was immediately reminded of Reeves doing nearly the same thing when he sprung me from jail in Barrelhead. "Quickly, put those belts of yours on," the lawman told me. "We have to get out before they notice anything is wrong." I did as he asked, glad to be wearing my guns again, then he took the bottle and rag and stuffed them in my coat pocket, saying, "We may need it later." After checking on the unconscious guard one last time, he asked me, "Are you ready to do this?"

"Ready as I'll never be."

"*Ke?*"

"Forget it, let's just go already."

We stepped out into the hall, H'landa locking the door behind us. No torches had been lit in the corridor, the only light source being a small oil lamp hung next to the door for the guard to see by. I was about to pick it up to bring along with us when the lawman whispered, "*Nee*, blow it out. Best if no one sees a moving light."

I snuffed it, saying, "What, can you see in the dark now?"

He grabbed my wrist and began to pull me down the hall. "No questions, no backtalk, remember? Be quiet and stay close."

We crept down the hall, shadows amongst shadows, every once in a while turning down a new passage or heading down a narrow stairway. Sometimes we'd approach an outer wall and have to duck under windows, just in case someone should look up and see us passing by. The real trick, though, was traversing the ground floor: most of the corridors were well-lit, and more than a few Kana-Semeth were still milling about. "Kitchens on one end, infirmary on the other, with a common area in the middle," H'landa explained as we huddled in a dark doorway. "It is never empty."

"Should we really try to get through here, then?" I watched as a woman walked by, oblivious to our presence, and headed towards the infirmary -- she was wearing a green smock or apron, similar to one I'd seen *Z'kira* Kali wear on a few occasions, so I supposed she must have been a doctor.

"Here is no better than anywhere else, really, but this is closer to the west gate, and that is our way out." He poked his head out of the doorway and looked about. "It is clear now. Time to go."

By some miracle, we managed to make it out of the building undetected, though the mad sprint we'd done across an open-but-empty lobby to reach them should have sunk us for sure. "Do you think maybe we're getting a little extra help?" I whispered to H'landa as we paused in the building's shadow.

"What are you talking about?"

"You know..." I pointed up at the starlit heavens. "Help."

He looked up, then repeated my gesture, saying, "What is this supposed to mean?"

I tried not to groan. "Never mind." We proceeded across the compound, spotting no one, but remaining cautious anyway. As we approached the west gate, H'landa suddenly stopped and yanked me back behind the corner of a building we'd just rounded. "What? What's wrong?" I asked.

"We have a problem."

I carefully peered around the corner at the west gate about fifty feet away. It was about half the size of the one we'd originally entered, with two guards on post -- I watched as one of them knelt down beside a large, dark bundle on the ground. "Big deal," I muttered. "One for you, and one for me."

"Not them," he hissed, "the *baouth*."

"What's a..." I started to say, but stopped cold when the bundle stood up on four legs and shook itself. It looked like some bizarre offspring of a German shepherd and a lion: roughly three feet high at the shoulder, thick brindled hair covering a lean, muscled body, and massive paws. It yawned, and I caught a glimpse of sharp teeth filling its long muzzle.

"The Kana-Semeth breed them," H'landa told me, leaning over my shoulder. "We use them for tracking, mostly. Very fast, very powerful. If it scents us..."

"You bring anything we can bait it with? Like maybe side of beef or a small infant?" I joked, trying to hide how nervous the sight of that thing made me.

"That would not work. They are too well-trained."

I pulled out my gun, saying, "Then I guess we'll have to risk a little noise."

"Put that away. The other soldiers may not know the sound, but it will still attract them." He leaned against the wall, lost in thought. "We cannot outrun it, cannot outfight it..." he muttered as he looked at me. I could practically see the wheels turning in his skull. "Give me your shirt."

"Say again?"

He grabbed my coat and began to pull it off me. "Your shirt, I need it."

"Fine, fine." I shrugged off my coat and took off my shirt. "What are you gonna do?"

"I...by Avisar, what happened to you?" He stared at the scars on my back in the dim moonlight.

"Hey, you don't ask me about my back, and I won't ask you about your eye," I said as I tossed the shirt at him, putting my coat back on over my bare torso. "Agreed?"

"*Kai.*" He folded my shirt in half and wrapped it around his left forearm. "Get out the Sadrin's oil," he said. "If we are lucky, I might be able to drug the *baouth* into submission."

"And if we're *not* lucky?"

He took the bottle from me and poured the stuff all over my shirt, careful to hold his arm away from his face. "Then it will probably tear my arm off." Given the expression he wore, I don't think he was exaggerating. He set the empty bottle on the ground. saying, "No matter what happens to me, you knock out the guards, go out that gate, and run south. *Kedda* that? You run *no matter what.*"

I nodded, and we stepped around the corner together, the lawman in the lead. We tried not to run at first so we wouldn't attract attention, but the closer we got to the gates, the faster we moved. When the guards finally noticed us, we charged, with H'landa heading straight for the *baouth*, his wrapped arm held at chest level. The guard nearest the animal barked some order, and it leapt right at H'landa -- he shoved his arm forward and lodged it in the beast's jaws, then tangled his free hand in its mane. They both went down with a thud.

Meanwhile, I rammed straight into one of the guards, knocking him flat on his back before he could even draw his sword. He seemed stunned, but he recovered quickly and began to shove me off of him, so I so I gave him a hard right to the jaw. That worked a little better. I was winding up for another one when the second guard grabbed my arm and pulled me off his semi-conscious partner. *"M'taka Taran!"* he spat at me.

"Same to you, fella," I said, and drove my other fist into the guy's crotch. He made a funny gurgling noise as he collapsed. *Thank God we're both built the same below the waist*, I thought. I made sure they were both out before getting up, amazed at how easy that was...until I heard a deep growl behind me.

I spun around and saw that the *baouth* had H'landa pinned, its back claws digging into the ground as the lawman struggled to get the monster off his chest. Ignoring all of our previous efforts to be quiet, I shouted his name, but he didn't respond. I called out again, moving towards them as I did so -- I had no idea what I was going to do, but I knew that I couldn't leave him like that. Before I could reach them, though, the *baouth's* back legs began to slip, leaving little furrows in the earth. After a few more moments the animal shuddered and slumped forward onto H'landa. The lawman grunted under the weight as he tried to push it off, but he just couldn't manage, so I raced over and grabbed a handful of its pelt, tugging at it until he worked his way free. His face was covered in sweat and stray animal hairs, and his uniform had ripped in a half-dozen places. "Told you...run," he gasped, not even looking at me.

"Since when do I listen to you?" I helped him to his feet, careful of his left arm -- blooms of deep red were spreading across my ruined shirt. "That broken?" I asked.

He flexed his fingers tentatively and shook his head.

"Gonna fuckinpuke?"

He smiled a little at that. "I might," he answered. "We need to go. Too much noise."

I dragged the guards out of sight as H'landa unbarred the gate. Neither one of us wanted to touch the *baouth*. Once outside, we ran south down a rutted dirt road paralleling a sparsely wooded field -- I guessed that this must have been the very edge of Dak-Taorin. Just as we cleared the shadow of the Kana-Semeth stronghold, I spotted Pietruvek beneath a stand of trees, a pair of *vessekiben* behind him. "Best I could do under the circumstances," he explained to me, "but I did manage to sneak out most of our belongings." He gave me an odd look as he noticed my bare chest. "Where is thy shirt?"

"A *baouth* ate it." I swung up into the saddle and helped the boy up as well.

"Better the shirt than my arm," the lawman added, mounting up on the other *vessek*. "Come now. First Light will be here before we know it."

We turned our mounts south and galloped off towards what could very well be our deaths.

CHAPTER 14

We paused in our mad dash to Betedek around dawn, still within that stretch of woodland we'd camped out in just a few days before. Our mounts had been driven almost to the point of exhaustion, and they drank gladly when we led them to the edge of the stream. The three of us were feeling a bit worn out as well, both from worry and lack of sleep, but we knew we couldn't linger there. It wouldn't take long for the Kana-Semeth to figure out which way we were headed, and we needed to keep as much distance between us and them as possible.

As I dug through the satchels trying to find a shirt, Pietruvek helped H'landa bind the wounds on his arm. The *baouth's* teeth had punctured the skin, but luckily hadn't done much damage beyond that -- the neat little holes ringing his arm cleaned up nicely. The blood he'd lost worried me, though. "I feel somewhat light-headed," he admitted, "but it will pass."

"I would have never been able to do that," Pietruvek said, carefully winding a strip of cloth around the lawman's arm. "I saw one of those things while we were in the stronghold. Monsters."

"They can be docile when we want them to be. My family keeps a few as pets."

"You'd be safer with a pet grizzly bear," I muttered in English. I found a suitable replacement for my old shirt and slipped it on, then said to H'landa in Arkan, "You had mentioned that there was another village off this road. How far?"

"About eight or nine *kalem* from the crossing, I suppose. Why?"

"We should switch mounts before these two collapse on us. Perhaps we can find a quicker route to Betedek, as well."

The lawman was hesitant at first, but finally agreed after we'd remounted, as it was obvious that the animals' breathing was becoming labored. We drove them on anyways, flying out of the woods and down the road to Vel K'noshiben Hala. Eventually, we reached a small house about a half-mile from the village that had a corral out back, and despite his near-constant glances in my direction, the owner seemed more than willing to let us trade with him. "Always happy to help the Kana-Semeth," he said as he led us to the corral's gate. "My sister, she thinks you have no business doing what you do, but I say you people are what keeps this world together." The man coughed, cleared his throat, and hacked a gob of spit on the ground. "I should not speak ill of her, though. Poor girl has been sick lately...been taking care of her." The man never shut up the whole time, just kept talkin' and spittin' and talkin' some more while he and H'landa picked out two strong-looking *vessekiben*. Pietruvek and I remained outside the corral, unloading the gear from our old mounts, which looked thankful to be relieved of their burden.

After they'd brought over the fresh animals, I said to H'landa, "Did you ask him about the road? Is there a faster way to Betedek from here?"

"The road twists around too much," the man told me as he helped slip a bridle over the head of the animal I was gearing up -- this *vessek* didn't like me any more than the others and had been fighting me. "Best bet is overland, due south, until you hit this small trail. That will take you the rest of the way in." He looked me over once again. "Why are you in such a hurry to get there?"

I glanced at the lawman, who simply said, "Private business," then went back to buckling down his own mount. Once we'd finished transferring our gear, H'landa thanked the man, adding that we'd bring the animals back as soon as possible.

"Oh, there is no rush. As I said before, I am glad to help." The man started to cough again, the worst spell yet. He bent over with hands on his knees until it passed, then spat out a gob that looked like it was more blood than spittle. "Grass fever," he explained, wiping at a speck of blood on his chin. "Always get it in the spring once the plants start to bloom. Never this bad, though."

Pietruvek made an odd noise in the back of his throat and took a couple steps away from the man. I followed the boy's lead, saying in Arkan, "We...um...we need to go. Wasting daylight."

"*Kai*, we definitely need to go," H'landa echoed. The three of us quickly mounted up and began to head south once more. Once we were well away from that place, the lawman said what was on all our minds: "Do you think that was the plague?"

"Could be," I replied. "Probably."

"It was," Pietruvek said. "Avisar save us all, *it was*. The blood was dark, like the old texts say."

H'landa looked hard at the boy, saying, "What about us? Does this mean we are infected now, as well?"

"I do not know! I never studied the Great Plague that deeply. It never seemed that important." I could feel Pietruvek begin to shake as he sat in front of me. "None of this was ever supposed to happen again."

The lawman opened his mouth to say something else, but I cut him off. "Not another word, H'landa. Peter's got enough things to worry about without you making him feel guilty." We rode on in silence after that, galloping over open fields until we finally reached the trail. When it led us into the woods on the northern end of Betedek, we slowed our pace so as to keep an eye out for anything unusual.

A few minutes after we'd entered the woods, Pietruvek told us to stop. "That cannot be normal," he said to us, and pointed at a tree to the left of the trail. Clustered around the base of it were about seven or eight dead birds, and just beyond them, if we looked carefully, we could spot more scattered around the forest floor, broken wings sticking up like tiny headstones. The corpses of some other small animals also lay about here and there, bringing to my mind again all those dead *zemezi* the boy and I had found in the grain bin a month ago.

"Most of them appear to be facing away from Betedek," H'landa noted. "Even when dying, those creatures had more sense than us."

"Yeah, but we can end this," I said, and nudged my *vessek* forward -- now that we'd stopped, the poor animals wanted to *stay* stopped, and I couldn't blame them. We eased on down the trail, which ended not too far from the village livery. The doors stood open, and the smell of the dead animals inside was horrendous, even with the ventilation. We forced our mounts into a pair of empty stalls, not even bothering to remove the saddles and other gear -- none of us wanted to risk getting gored or having our teeth kicked in.

"I have to get home," Pietruvek said in Arkan once we'd finished at the stable. "I have to see *Padra*, I have to..." He sounded close to panic as he began to head up the street.

"Your *padra* will have to wait," H'landa told him, blocking his path. "No one is going near that Crossroad until we find out what is happening here in the village."

"The two of you can do that without me. I want to go and see *Padra*."

"Not alone," I said in English. "Trust me, the last thing you want to do right now is walk off by yourself." I came up beside him and laid a hand on the boy's shoulder. "Look, Peter, I want to go check on your father, too, but we *have* to stick together."

"But he is *dying*...thou said so before. *Please*, Reshard, I must see him before he leaves this world."

That hit a nerve. "I...I promised your mother I'd keep you safe," I said, then pointed towards where the

Crossroad lay. "And at the moment, that place ain't safe."
Never mind that the whole damn village isn't safe, I
thought. "But I swear to you, when we're done here..."

An indistinct voice echoed down the empty street
from the direction of the square. We all turned towards
the noise, then looked at each other -- we'd each hoped
that there were people still alive, of course, but to actually
hear evidence of life in this place was startling. H'landa
recovered first, calling out, "Who is there?" No one
answered, but we heard something fall over, so we ran
towards the square until we found the source of the noise:
a filthy, naked woman laying face-down in the middle of
the street. It appeared that she'd tripped over some pieces
of lumber that were littering the path -- I hadn't noticed
until then that, just like in Hadley, some of the doors and
windows on the nearby buildings were boarded up.

As we approached, the woman tried to pick herself
up, but she couldn't seem to make her limbs work
properly, and after watching her for a few seconds, I
realized why. H'landa began to reach out to her, but I
grabbed his arm and pulled him back, saying in English,
"For God's sake, don't touch her!"

"What is wrong with you? She needs help."

"I think she's a little beyond our help." I pointed
at her back, which was the most visible in her prone
position. Her ashen skin had paled until it had become a
transparent bluish membrane, mottled with huge black
lesions -- the dirt and dust that coated her obscured most of
it at first glance, but not all of it.

The lawman fought hard to keep his face
expressionless, but enough of his revulsion showed
through to let me know that he wasn't as tough as he
wanted people to think. "You...you are sure that she
is...that *it* is..." he stammered, unable to turn his gaze away
from the poor creature.

Just then, the woman managed to work one
twisted arm beneath herself, lifting her torso up enough to
reveal a half-rotted chest cavity. Her head turned in our

general direction, but I think she was going more off sound than sight, as her dead-white eyes rolled about in bloody sockets, focusing on nothing. Her other arm reached out towards us, the hand dangling limply from the wrist as her mouth fell open and a sound of some sort came out. Pietruvek made a sound of his own and stumbled backward, nearly falling over himself as he tried to put some distance between himself and the nightmare before us. To his credit, H'landa didn't retreat, but he didn't seem sure of what to do, either, so I took care of the problem the best way I knew how: I pulled out my gun and shot the thing between the eyes. The body immediately keeled over onto its side and lay still. "Nobody touch it. Nobody even go *near* it," I ordered.

Neither of them objected, at least not aloud. Pietruvek stared silently at me, as if he couldn't comprehend how I could be so cold-blooded about it. H'landa simply nodded, whether in agreement or just approving of the way I'd dispatched the thing, I didn't bother to ask. We gave the corpse a wide berth and continued on up the street, with myself in the lead, Pietruvek behind me, and H'landa taking up the rear, his sword now drawn in case we should cross paths with any more corpse-things. We did pass a couple of unmoving bodies, and the boy insisted on at least covering their faces before we moved on, even going so far as to remove his tunic when he couldn't find a rag or blanket. "I should give them the Mark of Path's End, as well," he said, "but I have nothing to do it with."

"What do you mean?" I asked.

He pointed at one of the nearby doors, the symbol I'd seen on the funeral shroud hastily painted upon it -- we'd passed quite a few like it on our way up the street. "It is to keep the *kahn* from rejoining the body. It tells it to prepare to move on." Pietruvek looked up at me with a pained expression. "We should have done that with the first body, to be sure." I almost told him that what he wanted to do was a moot point in this case, but I held my tongue, saying instead that we should keep moving. Midday had already passed, and I didn't want to be roaming around this place once the sun had set.

When we reached the village square, it was like entering the proverbial eye of the storm: a scene of maddening calm, relatively untouched by the chaos of debris and death we'd passed through to get here. Doorways stood open all around the square, and while we found a few items inside those buildings strewn about, there was still a sense of order to it all. However, the dry-goods store had been picked clean, and quite a few things had apparently been taken from *Z'kira* Kali's offices. "They still had enough sense in them to take supplies," H'landa said to me in English, "but where did they go? Some ended up in Vel K'noshiben Hala, obviously, but what about the ones too sick to travel?"

"You got me there, boss. The guy in my dream only said they were gathering together, he didn't say *where*." My eyes scanned the square, hoping for a clue. "We might have to search every damn building until...oh, for Chrissakes." I slapped my forehead. "Do Arkans have a word for somebody that misses what's painfully obvious?"

The boy nodded. "*K'neget*," he answered, looking confused. "Why?"

"'Cause that's what we all are, a bunch of damn *k'negetiben*." I started walking over to the far end of the square, towards the only building with closed doors. "They're in the meeting hall!"

They each got their own looks of "Why the Hell didn't I think of that?" plastered across their faces before following me. As I got closer to the building, I could see the lower parts of the windows had been blocked off from the inside, and all the glass panels near the bottom had been shattered as well. *More money for H'landa to shell out*, I thought absently, then ran up to the doors and tried to open them. They didn't budge, of course. "Hey, can anybody hear me?" I yelled, banging my fist on the thick wood. "Say something, make some noise, anything!"

The lawman stepped up beside me, saying, "It might help if you did not speak Taran to them." He rapped on the door himself, calling out in Arkan, "This is *Lermekt* H'landa, we have come to help!" He paused, listening for any sort of response, but none came. "If you do not answer, we *will* break this door down!" he said.

"What if they cannot answer?" Pietruvek asked.

"Do not start talking like that," I told him, and started pounding again, with the boy and H'landa joining in after a moment. We shouted out names, words of encouragement, anything we could think of to get a response. I was about to give up and suggest working on one of the windows instead when I felt something thump against the door from the inside. The three of us stopped cold and stared at each other, unsure if we'd imagined it or not.

H'landa recovered first, giving the door three quick knocks. After a pause, three knocks came back, then a voice: "Please...give us some time to clear the door..."

"How many people do you have in there?" H'landa asked, leaning in close.

There was an even longer pause, broken only by the occasional thud against the door. "Sixty...perhaps sixty-five..." the voice finally answered.

"Jesus Christ," I moaned, and turned away from the door. There were at least two hundred people living in Betedek, perhaps more, not to mention all the folks living on farms just outside the village. How many of them had fled, and how many had died? I rubbed a hand over my eyes, then looked out at the empty square. At least, it *used* to be empty. "Tell 'em to move faster, H'landa," I whispered in English.

He turned around, his mouth open to ask me why, but the words never made it out. Pietruvek saw it now as well, and managed to sputter out, "Avisar save us."

Four of the corpse-things had crept into the square, probably attracted by all the noise we'd been making. These ones moved a lot better than the first one we'd seen -- they easily skirted the few obstacles between them and the meeting hall -- but then again, who knew how many times they'd already been here, banging on the doors like we had done, knowing that the building was filled with warmth and life? I drew my other gun and slowly, cautiously moved down the steps. "Stay close to the doors, don't move," I told my companions as quietly as I could. "I don't think these things can see too good."

As if to prove my point, one of the corpse-things bumped into another, just barely grazing its arm, but that was enough for them to latch onto each other violently -- memories of that corpse in Hadley grabbing hold of Reeves when he leaned over it suddenly filled my mind. We watched as bony fingers clawed at slack-jawed faces, their embrace falling somewhere between horrific and passionate, the latter aspect enhanced by the fact that they appeared to have been a man and a woman in life. As they tussled, the other two stopped advancing on the building and turned towards them, seeming to forget about their original goal entirely. After a few seconds, the "amorous" pair somehow realized their mistake and pushed away from each other, one of them clearly saying in Arkan, "All cold...all gone..."

Cold sweat ran down my back as I stood at the foot of the steps, guns cocked and raised, but scared to death of moving another inch. The merry quartet before us appeared to have the attention span of gnats, and I sure as Hell didn't want to remind them that I was standing less than fifteen feet away. One of them started to advance again, but it didn't seem aware of me...and it definitely hadn't noticed that I'd slowly leveled one of my pistols at its head. I held off on firing, though, since the noise would just catch the attention of the other three. I chanced a glance back at the door: H'landa had pushed Pietruvek behind him and now stood at the ready, sword raised and a steely look in his eye reminiscent of the one Reeves would get right before a job. The lawman seemed wary of lashing out directly against these creatures as well -- better to wait them out and let them wander away when they lost interest rather than provoke them.

The one I had in my sights stopped about four feet away from me, just close enough for me to get a whiff of the stench rolling off of it. Part of its face had been torn away, revealing decaying teeth and bone beneath tattered strips of skin. It turned its head towards me, blind eyes staring at nothing as its mouth dropped open slightly and a black, viscous fluid oozed out from between its lips. *Go away*, I thought as loudly as I could. *Go on, take off, there's nothing for you here!*

Just then, the door to the meeting hall swung open. One of the men inside began to beckon us in, but that was before he caught sight of the corpse-things. He let out a yelp and tried to slam the door shut, but Pietruvek managed to wedge himself in the frame. All the commotion was just enough to wake up our new friends, who turned towards the door simultaneously, their faces coming alive with hunger.

I pumped two bullets into the head of the one in front of me before it could take its first step. "Don't let 'em touch you!" I hollered at the lawman, who was rushing the two closest to him. He brought his sword down in a wide arc, slicing one of them open from chest to groin. It let out an unearthly howl as it staggered away from the blade, while the second corpse-thing rushed forward before H'landa could raise his sword again. I shouted a warning and took aim, but H'landa beat me to it: he spun around, swinging his foot up, and kicked the creature square in the jaw. It sprawled flat on its back, the lower half of its face a good three inches out of joint.

As the lawman finished dispatching his pair, I opened fire on the last one, who seemed oblivious to what had befallen its companions -- I emptied one gun before I landed a good enough head-shot to make it drop. The dirty work done, we ran inside the meeting hall, slamming the door shut behind us. I leaned against it for a minute, eyes shut as I tried to make my hands stop shaking. Eventually, though, I had to open my eyes and see what the people of Betedek had been reduced to.

All of the benches inside the hall had been stacked up in front of the windows and, of course, against the door. Blankets, clothing, supplies, and personal items of every sort were scattered about the floor, covering nearly every square inch. Families clustered here and there in the middle of all this mess, most of them staring at us with weary eyes and haggard faces. A few were crying, children and adults. About a third of them were visibly sick: deathly pale, feverish, black lesions forming on the skin, not to mention the smell. I recognized it from my time in Hadley, and had even smelled it at the funeral, and on the corpse-things outside.

The smell of the Great Plague.

"You should have stayed away," one of the men said as they began to block the door again. "This is a place of death now. Avisar has turned His eyes from us."

The words stunned me in a way I never would have thought possible. Before I could come up with a good reply, though, I heard Nina call out from the back of the room. Pietruvek whipped around at the sound of his mother's voice, and then vaulted over every obstacle between the two of them until he fell into her waiting arms. She held him tightly, sobbing over and over, "Little one, my little one," rocking a bit with each word.

Three older men approached H'landa and I amongst all the chaos: Yaved N'dahl and two others I recognized as members of Betedek's *tehr-hidmon*. Despite everything that had happened so far, the old social order appeared to be intact. "It is a miracle you made it here," one of them told H'landa, "and we are grateful for your offer of help, but I do not think there is anything you can do." He wrung his hands together. "No medicine can stop the Great Plague, and the Crossroad, it...we cannot destroy it."

"Cannot, or will not?" H'landa pressed.

"Maybe a little of both," I said to him in English. "Most of them are probably too weak to do it any damage, and the rest...well, would *you* want to mess with it, if you were one of them?"

"But destroying the Crossroad would save them, *all* of them!"

"Yeah, but look at these people. Do you really think anybody besides us is thinking clearly right now?" I turned to the *tehr-hidmon* and said in Arkan, "I know it does not seem possible, but I have come to stop the plague. I have...I have faith that it can be done. Just give me some time to..."

Something thunked hard against the back of my skull. I grunted and stumbled forward, clutching my head, then a second blow connected between my shoulder blades and sent me to my knees. I could hear someone yelling, but it took a moment for me to focus enough to make it out: "Plague-bearer! Murderer! You are the one that should die!" I looked up to see who was making all the fuss and saw H'landa holding back a blond-haired man with a crazed expression. The lawman was also holding a short plank of wood, presumably the loon's weapon of choice. "Why did you come back here?" the man continued to rant at me. "To mock us, to spit upon our dead faces?"

"That is enough!" H'landa snarled.

The man jerked free of his grip, then backed away, pointing at the lawman and yelling, "This man has no authority here! He is in league with the Taran, he protects the fiend in exchange for his life! That is why they left our village, so the plague would not touch them!"

I got to my feet, muttering in English, "You're out of your mind, pal."

His eyes widened, and he threw his arms up in front of his face, screaming, "*Nee!* I will not let you curse

me like you did my poor Ari!" When he said that, I
realized who he was: Noren, the guy who wanted my head
on a stick for drunkenly assaulting his wife. I barely
recognized him, the man's face was so gaunt -- I probably
wouldn't have been far off in assuming that he was getting
rather sick himself. "He placed the plague upon her when
she refused him," Noren continued, looking about at those
gathered nearby. "*D'ho*-Bannen angered him as well, so
he cursed him and stole his son. Everyone he has ever
touched will die! He is a monster!"

Murmurs of assent rippled through the room,
especially among those who appeared to be in the first
stages of sickness like Noren. Some nodded and pointed
at me, each of them finding reasons to blame me for their
plight:

"He lingered outside my store two days in a row."
"I saw him talk to my husband once."
"He followed my children home, I *know* he did."
"He cursed us *all* during Halitova, not just Ari and
J'nath!"

I faced them all, holding my hands up for calm.
"Please, I did nothing to hurt *anyone*," I said in Arkan, but
no one seemed to hear. I spotted Dimi, huddled nearby
with his family. The man returned my gaze for a moment,
then turned away from me and pulled his youngest
daughter closer to him. She was only six, and pale as
death.

H'landa tried to come to my defense. "You
people are being ridiculous," he told them. "The Taran is
not a plague-bearer and you know it."

That was about as far as he got before Noren came
up on his blind side and jumped on his back, one arm
wrapping around the lawman's throat. "No more lies! No
more death!" the man screamed as the two of them
tumbled to the ground. H'landa tried to push him off, but
Noren had the strength of a madman. Then someone else
grabbed my arms and twisted them behind me -- I tried to
break free, but only succeeded in wrenching my shoulder.

The *tehr-hidmon* backed away from us, probably afraid that they'd be next. "There is only one way to stop this," the loon went on. "We have to give the demon out there what it wants: blood." He sat on H'landa's back, grinding his face into the floor. "We will take these two out to the Crossroad, cut their throats over the stone, and leave their bodies for the Dead Ones." Noren looked past me to where Nina and Pietruvek stood, then said, "The boy, as well."

The moment Nina's cry of terror passed her lips, every vestige of "civilized behavior" I'd managed to build up around myself in the past month shattered. I let out a roar I didn't even know I was capable of making as I snapped my head back, smashing the nose of the man holding me. He loosed his grip with a howl of his own, and I bashed him in the face with my forearm for good measure, then leapt at Noren, knocking him off H'landa. I proceeded to punch, claw, kick, and swear at the man in at least two languages before someone bashed me in the head again, filling my vision with stars. People crowded around me, pulling me off Noren, but I kept fighting, even going so far as to start biting when they managed to tie my hands behind me. The whole room seemed to be nothing but shouts now -- me in English, them in Arkan. Someone reached down and ripped off my gunbelts, tossing them out of reach before they began to drag me towards the door as others cleared the debris aside again. I fought them as hard as I could, but between the blows to the head and the lack of sleep over the past week, I was quickly running out of steam.

A shot rang out, almost ear-splitting in that confined space. The crowd stopped fighting, a few people screamed, and we all turned to see *Lermekt* H'landa standing in the center of the room, uniform ripped, face bruised, and both of my Peacemakers in his hands. He leveled them at my captors. "Let. Him. Go." He sounded surprisingly calm.

No one moved, probably more out of fear than defiance. H'landa aimed over our heads and let off another shot, this one ricocheting off the brass plaque his Kana-Semeth forebears had put above the door. "The next one," he told the crowd, "will go in someone's head."

"Y-you cannot do that," one of the men holding me stammered. "The Laws forbid..."

H'landa pointed one of the guns directly at the man's face. "I *am* the Laws, you worthless *m'taka*," he hissed through gritted teeth, his single blue eye glittering like hard ice. "Not that you people seem to care about them. Do you really think that sacrificing the Taran will save you all? This is *Beterion*! He does not care *who* dies, just so long as we *all* die! He will devour the world once again if we keep standing around and blaming one another instead of solving the problem. Do you want that?" In lieu of answering, they all stared at the ground or at each other, and H'landa said, "I ask again: *Do you all want to die?*"

Slowly, the ones holding me let go and began to disperse. I staggered over to the lawman, trying not to show how badly shaken I was by the whole thing. He tucked one of my guns under his belt so he could loosen my bonds, then he pointed the other at Noren, who cowered near the door. "Now, as for you, you miserable excuse for an Arkan..." H'landa started to say as he advanced on him. The man gulped and tried to run, but there was nowhere to go. That, and he wasn't moving very fast after the whuppin' I'd given him. H'landa caught up to him easily, smacking him across the face with the butt of the gun and sending him sprawling into a pile of filthy blankets, then the lawman leaned over him, grabbed him by his shirtfront and snarled, "I ought to drag you out there and feed *you* to those things!" Noren trembled in the grip of the lawman, who suddenly let go of Noren's shirt and stood up straight. "Unlike *someone* I know, however," H'landa continued in a more even tone as

Noren wiped blood and snot off his face, "I have respect for life and the Laws. Consider yourself under arrest."

He gave the man a moment to compose himself before dragging him to his feet and marching him towards the office. As they passed me, H'landa paused and handed over my guns. "You may want to reload these," he said in English before continuing on. Sure enough, when I checked the cylinders, they were both empty. I smirked and shook my head, then retrieved my gunbelts and began to replace the bullets while I kept a wary eye on the dispersing villagers.

As I put the belts back on, someone nearby said in Arkan, "You are bleeding." I looked up and saw *Z'kira* Kali, her silvery hair barely contained in her braid. The age-lines on her face appeared deeper than when I'd last seen her nearly a week ago. "The back of your head," she continued. "It does not appear serious, but you should let me make sure, considering..." She gestured vaguely to the chaos around us.

I nodded and let her lead me to where she'd left her medicine box, sitting me down. "When did it start?" I asked her, both of us aware without speaking of what "it" I meant.

She knelt behind me, gently pushing my hair aside as she searched for the wound. "Hard to say. Looking back, I can see some of the clues I missed the first time, but those people are gone now, so I will never know for certain. I *was* sure with *d'ho*-Vohra, though."

"Eveth Vohra? Kalo Gorin's wife?" I asked, turning my head to look at her. "Is she..."

"*Kai*, the night before you left." She placed her hands on either side of my head and forced me to look forward again. "He tracked me down not long after I treated *d'ho*-Bannen. He told me that she had been ill off and on for days, but they had both dismissed it as *zi-maia oudur*."

My brow furrowed at the words. "*Nee kedda.* Did you just say 'mother's belly'?"

"They were trying to have a child," she explained. "They thought her sudden illness meant they had succeeded, but as it progressed, *d'ho*-Gorin became worried." She pulled her hands away and fell silent -- when I turned around again, she didn't object. "I never fully believed that Beterion was real," she said finally, "not even after you appeared. This idea that a sickness can be...intelligent...calculating..." She shook her head in denial. "Eveth did not have the same symptoms as J'nath, not completely, but neither did anyone else before that. It *knows* not to make an obvious pattern, not until we can do nothing about it."

The implications of what she was saying took a moment to sink in. *Maybe that's why that town in New Mexico seemed to die off so quickly,* I thought. *It looked like a bunch of isolated incidents instead of one huge nightmare.*

"I spent the rest of the day with her," the doctor continued. "She was fading so fast, nothing helped. By nightfall, she had passed on. Her husband was terribly shaken, as was I, so I decided to stay at their house for the night, for both our sakes. He insisted on standing vigil in their bedroom with her, but I was so exhausted, I fell asleep in front of their hearth." She shut her eyes, her lips pressed together until they became a pale, thin line. "Kalo...he started screaming around dawn, woke me up from a sound sleep. By the time I got to the bedroom, she...he was..."

"She had gotten a hold of him," I finished for her, remembering what that corpse-thing had tried to do to Reeves.

"There was not a mark on him, but she had killed him. Just by touching him. Then she tried to touch me, so I..." Her hands shook as she said, "Avisar forgive me...I am supposed to *save* lives, not *take* them."

"You helped her," I said, having no idea if that was really true. "Better that you ended her suffering there than to let it take you, as well."

"I ended nothing. So many people have died, even after I told the *tehr-hidmon* what was happening." Her watery blue eyes met mine. "Beterion cannot be stopped," she said, looking just as lost as everyone else in the room.

I laid my hands over her hers, saying, "I can end this, Beva." I'd never called her by her first name before. "Do not ask me how I know this, but I will find a way to kill this thing and save Betedek." I smirked and added, "Whether these people like it or not, I can help them. Do not lose hope just yet."

She turned her head away for a moment, and when she looked at me again, she seemed more composed, even managing a weak smile. "*K'sai*, Reshard, for listening. For someone who speaks Arkan so poorly, you know just what to say."

"I guess at it a lot," I answered.

*   *   *   *   *   *

"We cannot waste any more time," Jamin H'landa said, leaning against the desk in the Kana-Semeth's office as he looked around the room. His gaze fell upon everyone present in turn: myself, *Z'kira* Kali, the three remaining *tehr-hidmon*, Pietruvek, and Nina, who had barely let the boy out of her sight since we'd arrived. She had insisted on joining us in our little meeting, no matter how much it pained her to leave J'nath's side. "Last Light is rapidly approaching," the lawman continued, "and if the *z'kira* is correct, many of these people may not live through the night."

Including J'nath, I thought. After she'd finished cleaning up the gash on my head, Beva and I had gone to J'nath's bedside, and I could barely contain my shock over his appearance: his skin had become white as chalk, with dark smudges around his closed eyes. Every breath seemed a struggle, shaking his frail form like a death rattle, and despite all the blankets piled on top of him, he remained cold to the touch -- I could actually feel the heat leach out of my hand when I wiped sweat from his brow. When the doctor said it was a miracle that he'd lasted for so long, I had to bite my lip.

N'dahl took the lead for the other *tehr-hidmon,* saying to H'landa and me, "What do you propose we do?"

I pressed my back up against the wall and shoved my hands into my pockets. "We have to smash the Crossroad to bits, leave nothing intact."

N'dahl turned to glare at me. "Do you think that we have not tried that already? Everyone that has gone out to do so has died in the attempt."

"The Crossroad cannot be broken," Pietruvek said matter-of-factly. "It has existed for over five centuries without so much as a crack or a chip marring its surface."

"Then we will pry it off of its foundation," I countered. "They had started to do that in my world..."

"But it still functioned, obviously," H'landa said, "or else you would not be here. We need to be sure that the Crossroad is closed permanently." He looked over at the boy. "How did they close the others, back during the Great Plague?"

Pietruvek's brow furrowed, which made him look very much like his father. "I cannot recall anything in the texts about that. The closest thing I remember is a passage that went something like 'The Will of Avisar was thrust into the stone, and both Arkhein and its shadow shook from its passing.'" He shrugged. "That could be *anything.*"

"It's too bad you guys don't have dynamite," I said in English. "That'd take care of it for sure."

"What does that mean, 'die-of-might'?" H'landa asked.

"*Dyna*mite," I corrected. "It's a kind of explosive. Real dangerous stuff if you're not careful, but if you want something blown to kingdom come, that's the way to go."

"Can you make it?"

"Hell no! I wouldn't even know where...oh, wait, of course!" I turned to the *tehr-hidmon* and said to them in Arkan, "We need blasting powder, like for a cannon."

"Are you *mad*?" one of them gaped. "We do not have a cannon!"

"We do not *need* a cannon, just the powder. Are you telling me no one in this village has ever had to clear a big stump out of a field or something?"

The lawman stepped forward. "What are you suggesting, Richard?"

"We dig a shallow trench, all around the Crossroad, maybe dig a little under it as well. Then we pack it full of blasting powder, light it..." I smacked my hands together. "*BANG!* The whole things blows sky-high."

"Do you think that will work?"

"I honestly do not know, but I think we should try. At the least, it may weaken the stone enough that you people can break it apart."

H'landa cocked his head, saying, "What do you mean by 'you people'? What will *you* be doing?"

"With any luck, I will be on the other side doing the same thing." I glanced at all those faces staring at me in disbelief. "I thought about this the whole way back here: while Betedek has only been suffering through this for a few days, the Crossroad on my world has been wide open for at least a month-and-a-half. No one there knows what it is, or that it even exists, and God knows how many people have died there already because of that." I gestured north, to where the Crossroad lay. "If we shut that thing down and I stay here, I am going to wonder for the rest of my life if everyone in America is dead. I have a hard enough time sleeping at night without having something like that on my conscience."

"You *are* mad," H'landa said. "You will most likely kill yourself in the process."

"I have tried killing myself before, but at least this time, it would be for much less selfish reasons. Besides, I have a plan." The lawman had a look of doubt in his eye. "No, I honestly do," I reassured him, "but it will be no good if we cannot get the blasting powder."

H'landa considered my words for a moment, then looked over to the *tehr-hidmon*. "Well? Do you have any or not?" he said.

"We will...ask around," one of them replied.

"Best start now," H'landa told them, pointing at the door. "Quietly, please."

The elders left the office, obviously displeased with the task laid before them -- they seemed content with just laying down and dying as opposed to fighting this. After they had gone, Pietruvek said, "It will not work." He and his mother were sitting on what was left of the cot -- all the bedding had been stripped away, leaving nothing but naked wooden slats.

"If you have a better idea than blowing it up, now is the time to say it," I told him.

"The blasting powder may destroy it," the boy replied, "but you will not be able to open the Crossroad."

"Why not?" Instead of answering, he turned his head and looked at the wall. I asked again, but he still said nothing. "Dammit, boy, this isn't a game!" I shouted in English as I grabbed him by his shirt and pulled him to his feet. Nina cried out, but I ignored her and gave the kid a good shake, saying, "Why won't you tell me?"

"Because I do not want thee to die," Pietruvek sobbed. "*Lermekt* H'landa is correct: if thou enters the Crossroad, Beterion will kill thee. Thou knows this, *Padra* told thee." He looked up at me, his eyes red as he pleaded, "Just stay here. Forget Tarahein and *stay here*."

"Do you have any idea what you're asking me to do? You want me to sacrifice millions just to save my own miserable hide. Well, let me tell you something, kid: *I'm not worth it.* Not one life, and certainly not millions, no matter what...what *they* say." Even in English, there were a few words I was wary of saying aloud -- we hadn't told anyone else about my dreams. "I don't belong here, and I never will. Hell, I'm not really sure *where* I belong, but if I do this, and if...I said *if*...I die, at least I'll have died doing something good for once." I let go of him and said, "So, are you gonna help us, or do we have to fumble around in the dark?"

He snuffled and rubbed at his nose as he stared down at the floorboards. "In the cellar," he said finally, "there is a sealed brass container. According to the texts, the contents must be placed in the center of the Crossroad for it to open...but thou cannot do that without removing the Heart of Avisar."

"I was gonna do that anyways."

Pietruvek's head snapped up, the words lodged in his throat coming out clear on his face. Even the lawman behind me made a strangled noise, but I held up a hand. "Trust me, and for God's sake, don't say anything about this in Arkan." They obviously still weren't satisfied, and I could see that, even with us speaking in English, Nina and *Z'kira* Kali knew something was up. But none of that was my concern at the moment, we had a dozen other things to take care of first.

One of the *tehr-hidmon* found someone that had a stash of blasting powder about a half-hour away from the meeting hall, which meant it'd be dark for sure by the time our little operation got underway. H'landa decided to go with the men heading out to fetch it, and as a precaution, I loaned him my left-hand gunbelt. "It's fully loaded," I told him, "and there's a dozen more bullets on the belt, but try not to use it unless you have to."

"You certainly are trusting with these all of the sudden," he said, buckling it around his waist backwards so he could still reach his sword.

"You seemed to know what you were doing earlier. Besides, this way, you can keep some distance between you and the corpse-things." I clapped him on the shoulder and said, "You watch your back out there."

"And you watch your own in here," he answered as he walked over to the rest of his party. After the incident earlier, I'd been surprised that we had found anybody willing to help us in this task, but a few people had a change of heart once they'd seen those of us who weren't ready to give up yet. I was glad of that: it let me know I wasn't doing all this for nothing.

Good Lord, what *was* I doing? I only had a vague idea, not the grand plan that I kept hinting at. *This isn't really within my realm of expertise*, I thought as I stood in the middle of the meeting hall, looking around the room. *I'm faking it, mostly, just to keep everybody else's confidence up.* My gaze fell upon Nina and Pietruvek, kneeling beside J'nath. The boy held his father's hand and spoke to him, but no response ever came. *My fault...it's all my fault*, I thought, then turned away and began to walk towards the office, just so I wouldn't have to see the mess I'd created anymore.

Once I was inside, I closed the office door and collapsed behind the desk. The desire to simply break down right then and there was overwhelming, but I couldn't, especially not with that bastard Noren locked up in the cell a few feet away. I tried to make my mind go blank, but I couldn't stop thinking about J'nath, and about all the Hell I'd put him through ever since I'd arrived here. He didn't deserve this, not one bit, nor did I deserve one speck of kindness that he'd ever shown me. He'd treated me like a human being, not a criminal...and he deserved to know the truth before I ran out on him.

Without really thinking about it, I rummaged around the lawman's desk until I found some paper, ink, and a stylus. I stared at them for a moment, not having any idea of what I wanted to say, or at least how to say it. Then slowly, I began to scratch out a couple of words, which soon poured out of me in a torrent:

> *J'nath ~*
> *First, even though this sounds fake, I'm sorry for everything. You people have been waiting a long time for someone to pop through that Crossroad,*

*and all you got was me. You should have gotten
somebody smart or important, but I'm neither, I'm
just a thief and a murderer. It's the truth.
Everybody hates me back home. I tried to be good
here, but trouble follows me. I wish I could have
been what you needed, but I don't know how to be.
All I seem capable of doing is bringing people
death and pain.
I'm going to try harder to be good now, because of
you. If I make it through this alive, I swear I
won't hurt anyone ever again. I don't like being a
bad person. No one's ever let me be anything
else, just you. Thank you.
I'm going to miss you. I'm scared (don't tell Peter
that) I just hope you'll be okay. I don't know how
Arkans pray but could you pray for me? I need a
lot of help.
I'm sorry I lied please forgive me.*

~ Richard A. Corrigan

I sat back and looked over what I'd spewed onto
the page. *It's not enough,* I said to myself, but I couldn't
think of anything else to say. I folded the letter into thirds
and wrote J'nath's name on the backside in Arkan, then
picked up the lit candle from its holder on the desk. After
dribbling wax onto the edge of the folded paper, I reached
into my pocket and pulled out one of my American coins:
a nice, hefty silver dollar. I pressed the front side of it into
the blob of wax I'd made, and then carefully peeled it off,
leaving behind a perfect backwards image of the Goddess
of Liberty, staff in hand and shield at her side -- it was no
brass seal, but it somehow seemed right.

Sitting back in the chair, I flipped the coin around
between my fingers, watching the candlelight slide across
the edges as I thought about what I'd soon have to do out
at the Crossroad. *I'm not sure if I have the guts to go
through with this. This isn't about money this time, this is*

for the world, both mine and theirs. This is...this is big, so much bigger than me. And if I mess this up...

The coin slipped out of my hand and clattered onto the desktop, tails up. As I picked it up again, I could plainly see the words *IN GOD WE TRUST* stamped above the eagle's head. Cocking an eyebrow, I looked up at the ceiling and said, "Is that supposed to be a message or something? A little divine encouragement?" I stuffed the silver dollar back into my pocket. "Can't blame a guy for being terrified."

Someone knocked on the door not long afterward, and a young woman poked her head into the office. "Forgive me, *d'ho*-Corrigan," she said in Arkan, "but the Kana-Semeth has returned and is asking for you."

I told her that I'd be out in a moment, and once the door had closed, I looked up at the ceiling again and said in English, "Well, I guess there's no backing out now, huh?"

No response.

"Yeah, that's what I figured." I stood up, grabbed the letter off of the desk, and walked over to the door.

Time to get down to business, Richard, I thought.

CHAPTER 15

"Christ, this is all of it?" I picked up a small clay container weighing about two pounds -- H'landa and the others had brought back six of them, all filled to the brim with blasting powder and ready to be fitted with fuses. "Doesn't leave much room for mistakes," I said to the lawman in English.

"Will it be enough to take care of both sides?" he asked.

"Gonna have to be." I handed him the pot. "Get these things prepped, then round up some shovels and picks, along with as many torches and oil lamps as you can find. We're gonna want as much light out there as possible."

"And what will you be doing?"

"I get the hard job," I said as I began to walk over to where J'nath lay. "I gotta say goodbye to Nina and Peter."

Nina had stepped away from her husband's bedside for a moment, but their son hadn't moved an inch -- he didn't even look up when I sat down on the floor next to him. "Time for me to go, little bird," I told him.

Pietruvek said nothing, he just kept clasping his father's hand, as if his will alone could make J'nath better.

"Look, I'm sorry I yelled at you earlier," I continued, "but you've got to understand: what either of us wants right now doesn't matter. This is the worst time to be selfish, Peter. If we're going to save your father or anybody else tonight, we all have to be willing to make sacrifices."

"Dost thou have to be one of them?" he said finally.

I sighed. "I have no intention of going down easy, if that's what you mean. I plan on making it through the Crossroad, doing the deed, and walking away unscathed...I'll just be doing it under blue skies, is all. Besides, in the end, it's for the best. Look at all the trouble I've caused just by being here. Once I'm gone, everything will go back to normal."

"I do not *want* it back to normal, and neither would *Padra*," he replied, his voice strained. "Before thou came to us, Tarahein was just strange words in old books, some relics locked away in the cellar. Did thou know some people made fun of our family? Said we sat watch over ghosts." He turned to me, saying, "Thou art not a ghost. Thou art *real*, and when thou leaves, all we will have is ghosts again."

"Do you really believe that? After all we've been through?" The boy started to turn away, but I put an arm around his shoulders and pulled him close, our foreheads almost touching. "Listen, those 'ghosts' are the reason I'm alive and talking to you right now. Your family saved me, sheltered me, gave me hope when I needed it the most. You couldn't have done that for me without them, and because of that, I want you to keep watching over those ghosts, no matter what people say. I want you to tell your kids about them, and about the crazy Taran that turned your life upside-down for a while." I laid my other hand over J'nath's and his own. "And I want your father to be there, too, and the best way I can ensure that is by leaving. I think J'nath will understand that...but right now, I need *you* to understand that, Pietruvek."

He stared at me, stammering, "My name...thou said my name..." A smile broke out on his face, lighting up the darkness that permeated the meeting hall. "Thou finally said it right!"

"Yeah, well, it only took me a month." I gave him a lopsided smile of my own. "Reckon it doesn't really matter now, but you know I did it." He nodded, and I could see he was beginning to tear up again. "Aw, jeez, don't start that. Everything's gonna be fine, I swear, just hold yourself together."

"I am trying."

"Well, try harder." I pulled my bandana out of my pocket and handed it to him. "Here, clean yourself up."

He wiped his eyes, saying, "Why does life have to be like this?"

I shrugged. "Dunno. When I find out, I'll let you know," I told him, then got to my feet. "I have to get going. I'm sorry." Pietruvek stood as well, holding out the bandana to me -- he seemed so helpless, so young. "Keep it," I said, "and stop looking at me like that." It came out a bit harsher than I wanted, and he jerked back, his mouth twisting. I turned away from him then, not wanting to make it any worse.

I found Nina speaking with *Z'kira* Kali, who began to move away when she saw me coming. "No, stay a moment, please," I said to her in Arkan. "I suppose I should say goodbye to you, as well."

"So, you are really going through with this?" the doctor asked.

"I have no choice."

"There are always choices. They just may not be the proper ones...or easy ones." The doctor laid a hand upon my shoulder. "I am glad to have known you, no matter how short the time was."

I thanked her, and she stepped away to go tend to her patients. "And what of you?" I asked Nina. "Glad to see me go, I am sure."

"A month ago, perhaps, but not now. Not like this." Her vividly-blue eyes were clouded over with sadness. "When you first arrived in our world, you terrified me, even before you woke up. Then I began to see how terrified *you* were. Like a lost child." Nina smiled slightly. "I know: you are a strong, brave man, you know nothing of fear...but I have seen that brave mask slip away more than once."

"And how is it today?"

"Holding up better than mine, I think."

I wrapped my arms around Nina, not knowing what to say or how to say it even if I did. Her small hands gently clasped my back, and we just stood there, silent and still, doing our best to hold each other up. After a minute or two, I whispered to her, "Remember me. For the little bit of good that I *did* accomplish here, remember me."

"And you remember us," she answered, "when the nights become too dark for you to bear alone."

"Every day." My voice cracked, and I tried to cover it up by clearing my throat.

"J'nath will be proud of you. I will tell him you stood like Ilan at the gates of Madurah when the arrows rained down." She looked up at me. "And I will remind everyone that you saved us even after they turned their backs upon you."

"*K'sai*, Nina Kandru," I said, then, without thinking twice about it, I put my hand beneath her chin and quickly kissed her on the lips. Her eyes widened in astonishment, but she made no complaint as I let go of her and walked away without another word.

*   *   *   *   *   *

It was the longest walk of my life. Betedek, which had seemed scary enough in the daylight, became a true nightmare when lit only by torches. Every shadow loomed closer, every noise a precursor to death. I led the party down the street, Peacemaker drawn, straining to see what may or may not have been lurking ahead. None of the corpse-things approached us, but we could all hear them shuffling about. I'd heard some of the Arkans call them "the Dead Ones" earlier: a straightforward name for something unimaginable to me just a couple of months before.

"Why do they hold back?" one of the men wondered aloud -- five had volunteered to head out with H'landa and myself. "Do they fear the fire?"

"They watch us," another said. "Beterion has taken their eyes for its own use, it can see what they see...it *knows* what we are doing!"

"Then go back," I replied, "and let us do our job." We'd passed the last of the buildings that made up Betedek proper, and had begun to trek across the open field that lay between the village and the Bannen home.

The second man hesitated, nearly dropping away from the group before increasing his pace, saying, "Best that we stay together. We will all be safer that way."

"And you as well, of course," H'landa added, putting his hand on the man's back and shoving him forward.

The slivered moon cast little light for us to see by, but it did help us pick out some movement near the edge of the woods that ran alongside the field: three corpse-things, ambling along parallel to us about twenty yards away. They moved in a jerky fashion, sometimes stumbling right into one another, but they never seized at each other like that pair had done in the square. *Are they trying to ambush us?* I wondered. *Wouldn't that take more thinking than they're capable of?* Once we got in sight of the Crossroad, however, I saw that I'd severely underestimated them: blocking our path were nearly a dozen of the corpse-things, their blank, bloody eyes staring directly at us. The three that had been following us lined up with them, forming a wall of rotting flesh in front of the Crossroad.

We all stopped dead in our tracks. "I told you," our not-so-confident companion whimpered. "Beterion knows, *they* know, and now...and now..." He backed up a few paces, then turned and ran for the village.

"Berin, no!" one of the men cried as he reached out to stop him, but only managed to grab the pack he'd been carrying. The strap ripped, and Berin went on running, the torch in his hand flying away after a moment.

He didn't get very far: a hand darted up out of the tall grass we'd just passed through and dragged him down.

Berin let out a scream I didn't know people were capable of making, while five more corpse-things stood up out of the knee-high grass and turned towards us in unison -- they'd been hiding there the whole time, waiting patiently for us to pass by so they could block off our escape route.

"Backs together, everyone!" H'landa pulled out the gun I'd loaned him. "Grab a weapon and brace yourselves!"

Packs dropped, torches were planted in the earth. Pietruvek had managed to smuggle H'landa's *gautteng* out of the stronghold, and the lawman had given it and the other weapons stored in his office to the volunteers capable of using them. Others were armed only with simple farm implements: a man beside me whispered what sounded like a prayer as he held a shovel in a white-knuckle grip. I thumbed back the hammer on my pistol and whispered, "Dear God, please don't let me run out of bullets."

As one, the corpse-things came after us, running as best as decaying muscle would allow. I opened fire, fighting the urge to shoot blindly and instead picked my targets with great care: head shots only, quick and dirty. I'd taken out four before reloading, and managed to finish that seconds before they hit us. Hands reached out and tore at whatever they touched. Teeth snapped at warm flesh. Shouts, human and inhuman, blended together into a wall of noise. I ignored it all and kept on shooting. When the gun was empty again and I couldn't reload, I flipped it back into its holster and pulled out my knife, cutting deep into dead flesh. The smell of blood filled my nostrils, and I didn't know or care whose it was, I just kept fighting until I could barely lift my arms. Then one of the corpse-things got hold of me and yanked me to the ground, ripping my shirt and tangling its skeletal fingers in my hair. I knew what it was trying to do, so I wedged my arm between its face and mine as it forced me closer, ever closer, its desiccated lips parting in anticipation. I wanted to cry out for help, but I was too afraid of what might happen if I opened my mouth.

Then someone grabbed the corpse-thing and tore it off me with such force that its arms disconnected from its body. I shook them off with revulsion as the monster screamed and flailed just a few feet away until its skull got smashed in by a bootheel. Only then did it go limp, finally, truly dead. I wiped blood from my face and stared up at my savior -- I was expecting it to be H'landa, but it was one of the volunteers, shaking and covered in gore like myself. "I think that is the last one," he gasped.

I got to my feet, swaying, and surveyed the battlefield: myself, H'landa, and the man who saved me were the only ones left standing. Bodies and parts of bodies were scattered everywhere across the field, a few of the things struggling to get back up. The lawman walked slowly amongst the carnage, pausing occasionally to dispatch those who wouldn't stay still -- a quick thrust downward with his sword was usually all it took. The remains of the other men who'd come with us were mixed in with our attackers, but they were indistinguishable now...and most likely just as dangerous.

I turned to the man beside me and said in Arkan, "Are you injured?"

He looked down at his bloodied self. "I cannot tell."

I nodded. The pain coming from any wounds we'd suffered would be felt later, once the shock wore off. One thing that I *could* feel at the moment, and I was sure the others were feeling as well, was the cold: a deep, down-to-the-bone numbness all over my body, like I'd been plunged into an icy river. I'd experienced a milder version of it before, when I'd touched J'nath. *That's how Beterion gets you*, I thought. *It just sucks you dry of life until you're just a cold hunk of meat.* "What is your name?" I asked the man.

He stared at me with glassy eyes, rubbing his arms in an effort to warm up. For a moment, he looked just like

Reeves did in Hadley when I found him sitting on the boardwalk. Then he finally replied, "Gavas."

"Good. Now, Gavas, I need you to focus on the task before us." I waved a hand at the carnage, saying, "Do not look at this. It is behind us now. We need to finish what we came out here to do, so this will never happen again. *Kedda*?"

"*Kai*," he answered, nodding slowly. He seemed coherent enough, but I had my doubts as to how long it would last. My own thought processes still appeared to be clear, thankfully. I just hoped they stayed that way.

We split up and began to gather the equipment that had been strewn across the field. By some miracle, none of our clay "bombs" had been broken in the struggle. Most of our illumination had been snuffed out, but that was easy enough to remedy with a couple of matches. As we placed some torches in a circle around the Crossroad, I noticed three corpse-things hanging back beneath the shelter of the woods. "Hey, H'landa, we've got some more over thisaway," I called out in English as I reloaded my gun.

He sidled up and took a look for himself. "I saw two more back there. They did not advance, even when I took a few steps towards them."

"Do you really think Beterion's steering them around?"

"How else would you explain it? Overwhelming us did not stop us, so now he holds them back until another idea presents itself." He patted the gun on his hip. "We could easily hit them from here."

"Good idea," I said, holding up my own weapon, "but I've only got three bullets left. How about you?" Turned out that, between the gunbelt and the cylinder, he was down to eight. I shook my head, saying, "Forget it. Once we run out of ammunition, these guns will be nothing but cast-iron clubs. If those things want to sit under the trees, I say let 'em sit for now, and blow their heads off when they become lively."

H'landa reluctantly agreed, and we divvied up the remaining bullets: five for him, six for me. Despite everything that had happened so far, the dearth of bullets worried me the most. No guns meant no distance, and with our numbers so greatly reduced, another mad rush like we'd experienced before could wipe us out with ease. *And yet that monster holds its troops back*, I thought as we walked over to the Crossroad so we could get to work. *What is it waiting for?*

Gavas had already started digging, although it had taken quite a lot of persuading from us for him to do so. Since our workforce had been cut in half, we decided on making three small holes around and beneath the stone, just big enough to wedge the blasting powder loads in, then pack them in with dirt to direct the blast upward. Hopefully, the force of it would at least crack the rock. As we dug, we each stole glances at the woods, making sure our silent observers kept their distance. They all did, despite our vulnerability. "Maybe Beterion's too damn scared to do anything now," I joked.

"I doubt it," H'landa answered, "but one can hope."

Beterion's influence had leached the soil around the stone of all life. The dry, crumbly earth gave way easily to our shovels, yet it still managed to hold up the Crossroad as we hollowed out the underside. We dug in as far as we dared, then set in our bombs, trailing the long fuses out of the holes. Despite this, the Dead Ones stayed away, and I found myself wishing that they *would* do something just to get it over with.

As we finished packing in the loads, I realized that I had forgotten a very important element to this whole mission. I cursed under my breath and grabbed an oil lamp. "Back in a minute, fellas," I said in English.

"Where in Avisar's name are you going?" H'landa asked.

"The cellar." I jerked a thumb at J'nath's house. "I gotta get that thing the kid talked about."

"You are most certainly not going alone."

"What are you talking about?" Gavas asked in Arkan. "What is going on?"

"Nothing," I snapped, "keep working." I turned back to the lawman and said in English, "You do the same. Going back to New Mexico is my risk, not yours, so I'm going in the cellar. You two stay out here and make sure our 'friends' keep away from the Crossroad."

H'landa narrowed his gaze. "They have already ambushed us once. What if there are some in the house waiting for you?"

I drew my gun and waggled it at him, saying, "Well, as long as there ain't more than six of 'em, I reckon I'll be alright." I turned towards the house. "Don't do nothin' until I get back."

The corpse-things didn't even stir as I tramped across the yard, which surprised me: I expected them to try something as soon as I broke away from the others. That made me doubly cautious when I pushed open the front door. There was nothing there that I could see, so I gave the door a good kick, hard enough for it to slam against the wall, in the hopes that the noise would scare anything out of hiding. Still nothing. *Fine by me*, I thought as I stepped into the house proper and did a quick search of the rooms, relaxing only once I found everything in order. Now all I had to do was hope nothing was hiding down in the cellar.

I pulled open the trapdoor, then lay flat on my belly and lowered in the lamp -- the view wasn't the best, but at least I could see that there wasn't anything to see, thank God. The place was still a mess, though, and I had to tread carefully once I'd dropped down there. I soon began to make a mess of my own as I shoved artifacts aside while searching for the container. "C'mon, where is it?" I muttered. "Christ, J'nath, did you give it to the junk man by mistake or something?" I finally found it on a high shelf, dusty and blackened with age, with a simplified Crossroad design etched into the brass. A waxen seal filled the seam between container and lid. I pierced it with a grimy thumbnail, and was greeted with the pungent smell of bone meal as I removed the lid. There appeared to be a few crystalline fragments mixed in as well, but that smell told me something I should have suspected ever since I'd first collapsed on that stone in New Mexico: to open the path between our worlds, you needed a sacrifice of blood. *I wonder if J'nath has any clue how dirty his "good magic" really is,* I thought as I replaced the lid.

Just one more thing to do. Turning towards the table in the center of the room, I set down the lamp and pulled the letter out of my coat pocket, laying it on top of the pile of books and maps littering the surface. In the dim lamplight, I could see that the exterior of the letter now bore smears of blood from the battle out in the field, a grim counterpoint to the information contained within. "Just another artifact for you to file away, J'nath," I said, then picked up the lamp and headed for the ladder.

I clutched the container to my chest as I ran back to the Crossroad, afraid that something may have happened in my absence. Everything still appeared to be in order, though. "Could you perhaps have taken a little longer?" H'landa quipped in English. "Sitting out in the open like this is making me nervous."

"*You're* nervous? You aren't the one jumping in there. Speaking of which, did you tell him what's going on?" I nodded towards Gavas, who was pacing around the field in a tight circle, constantly eyeing the woods.

"*Kai.* He says it is a terrible idea, but he is not about to try and head back alone to get away from here." The lawman smiled. "He called you a very brave fool."

"Damn right I am. Here, hold onto this." I gave him the container. "You and Gavas might want to back up a bit while I pry out the crystal."

H'landa stared hard into my eyes, saying, "You can still stay here, Richard. No one will think less of you." He swallowed hard. "Once you break that seal, though, we will have no barrier to protect us."

"I know...God help me, I know." I put a hand on his shoulder and pushed. "Now, step back."

The lawman finally did as I asked, with he and Gavas moving about thirty feet away from the Crossroad before deeming it "safe". None of us had any real clue as to what would happen once I removed the crystal -- for all we knew, we could be struck dead on the spot. Despite this, I approached the stone, a river of cold sweat rolling down the back of my neck, and carefully knelt down on its broad, black surface. If there had been a way to do this without actually touching the thing, I would have, but there were no such options. I propped myself up with one hand, noting how warm the stone felt even though the sun had been down for hours, then ran a finger along the edge where the crystal was set into it. There was only a hair's breadth between the two, certainly not enough room to wedge something in and pop the crystal out intact.

"Only one way," I said under my breath, and pulled out my Bowie knife. As Bowies go, it had a rather short blade -- only about eight inches or so -- but what it lacked in size, it made up for in beauty: the handle was pure ivory with silver fittings, including a smooth, rounded pommel on the butt of the knife. I'd used that pommel before as an impromptu hammer, and it always stood up to the abuse, now I just had to hope that it was sturdy enough to break crystal. I centered the knife over my target, blade up, then drew my arm back and slammed it down with as much force as I could muster. The crystal gave away with a sharp crack, and then...nothing. No flash of light, no Armageddon, just a busted rock. I stared at it, waiting for something to happen, only to realize that I'd been holding my breath for a good thirty seconds. I gulped down air, letting it out with a nervous laugh as I thought, *Well, that's one obstacle out of the way. On to the next one.*

After H'landa and Gavas returned to my side, they brought something disturbing to my attention: the corpse-things were becoming restless. "The moment after your arm went down, I could hear them moving about," H'landa said in Arkan. "I think Beterion may have more control over them now. We may not be able to turn them away again."

"I do not think that will be a problem," I replied as I gathered up the shards of crystal. "J'nath told me that a small piece of the Heart of Avisar is enough to keep the plague at bay, at least for one person. If that is the case, it may also help to keep those things off of us." I held the shards out to them. "Each of you take a piece, a big one."

The lawman picked one out, saying, "I take it this is the 'plan' you kept talking about."

"More or less. J'nath told me there was no safe way to send me home without a piece of the Heart for protection." I closed my hand around the remaining crystals. "Now I have three times as much as what I originally traveled here with."

I cut the drawstring closures from a few of our now-empty packs so we could hang the shards around our necks, though I had to wrap my handful in a piece of my shirttail first. After we'd slipped them on, I noticed that the coldness I'd felt before was dissipating, and that Gavas seemed more alert. *You almost had us, didn't you?* I thought. *You sonovabitch...figure the plague will get us if the corpse-things don't.*

"I think...I think we are ready now," I told them, realizing that the time had arrived, no more playing around.

"Almost," H'landa said. "Gavas, go and check the fuses."

"*D'ho-lermekt*, I am sure..."

"Check them," he repeated, more firmly this time. Gavas didn't question him any further. "I did not want to have him asking about what we are saying," the lawman explained in English once Gavas was gone.

"And what *are* we saying?" I prodded.

"That I was wrong about you, and about a few other things. If Avisar truly has guided you here, then He has chosen wisely, for you are willing to go where I would never dare. For that, I will always admire you...cousin."

"I couldn't have done half of it without you, *kanitu*," I said, then reached down and clasped his hand in mine, which drew a puzzled look from him. "This is how they say 'goodbye' where I...where *we* come from," I explained as I gave him a firm handshake.

He returned the gesture as best he could before letting go, saying, "I will try to remember that." H'landa then helped me slip on my pack, making sure the cargo within was still secure -- the last thing I needed was to reach the other side only to find that the bombs had fallen out during the trip. As I steeled myself for what I was about to face, he asked me, "How will we know when you have made it across?"

"You won't know," I replied. "As soon as the Crossroad closes, I want you to light the fuses and get as far away from here as you can. No hesitation, just light 'em up and run, okay?"

Before the lawman could answer, we heard Gavas cry out a warning. We looked over and saw that our friends were on the move again for sure -- two were already past the tree line and were slowly making their way towards us. I started to pull leather, but H'landa grabbed my arm, telling me, "Save your bullets and get going!"

"We can take them out first, then..."

"This world is no longer your concern." He shoved the brass container with its grisly contents into my hands. "We each have our own roles to play here. This is mine," he said as he drew his sword. "Go and take care of yours." Grim-faced, I headed towards the Crossroad, while H'landa turned towards the corpse-things, shouting in Arkan, "I know you can hear me, demon, and see me as well. You should have turned back as soon as you saw my face." He swung the sword in a wide arc. "You should have known that no H'landa shall ever let you win so long as one of us still lives!"

Gavas stared at me dumbfounded as I stepped onto the Crossroad and opened the container. "What are you doing? The Dead Ones are..."

"Keep them away from me until I am finished," I ordered. "Once I am gone, blow this cursed thing up."

"I...I will," he stammered, then reached over to one of the lit torches, his hand trembling, and pulled it out of the ground. I continued my work on the Crossroad, crouching over the stone's now-open center and filling it with the ancient, sacrificial remains of God-knows-what -- the smell assaulted me worse than anything else that night. I had no idea how much it would take to open the portal, so I dumped in the brownish powder until it brimmed the hole, then tossed the empty container away and waited.

Nothing happened. *Maybe the stuff's too old*, I thought. *Oh God, what if there's something else I have to do?* Panicked, I slammed my fist onto the stone, screaming, "Open up, damn you! We ain't got time for this!" In the midst of my fit, I heard Gavas let out a shout of defiance, and I snapped my head up in time to see him strike a corpse-thing in the face with his torch -- it staggered back with a shriek, and Gavas gave chase. I hollered for him to come back, but my words were drowned out by the roaring noise growing beneath my feet.

"Oh Jesus, it's happening," I gulped as I looked down, not really wanting to. A strange blue-white light had ignited in the center of the stone and was quickly snaking outward, spreading through the Crossroad sigils like floodwater rushing through a canyon. I could feel the heat it gave off radiating through the soles of my boots. I almost stepped off of the stone, but I fought common sense and stayed rooted to the spot, daring only to rise to a standing position. A steady, familiar thrum grew beneath me as the light became more intense, washing out the world around me. I threw up my hands, straining to catch a final glimpse of Arkhein through my splayed fingers before the Crossroad pulled me in, but I could see nothing except the light.

Then without warning, the world dropped out from beneath my feet, and for a second time, I plummeted into Hell.

*   *   *   *   *   *

Think of a pond in winter. That's what J'nath had first said when trying to explain the Crossroads to me. He probably had no idea how appropriate that analogy was: traveling through the space between our worlds was like being swept along by a fast current, only there was no water to tread. I flailed my arms about, trying to right myself, then realized this place had no sense of "up". In fact, it had nothing at all: a reddish-black expanse stretched off in all directions, punctuated here and there by searing-bright arcs of lightning that seemed to have no beginning or end, flashing into existence and burning out just as quickly. I saw no land, no horizon, so I had little perspective on how big this place was or what direction I was being pulled in. What little depth I could perceive was due to some bits of debris just...hanging in the nothingness. Chunks of wood and stone floated about, some spinning end over end in lazy circles, completely ignoring the notion of gravity. A few manmade objects had found their way into this realm as well. I observed a leather shoe, its owner nowhere in sight, pass within arm's length of me. Without thinking, I reached out to grab it, and my hand connected with, then passed through, some kind of barely-tangible barrier. Only then did I realize the speed at which I was moving...and it was certainly faster than that shoe. I missed what looked like an easy grab by a foot or two (pardon the pun) as I flew past it, and the shoe soon dropped out of sight behind me. I gritted my teeth as my outstretched arm buffeted against the barrier, causing a rippling wake of light up and down the shaft I appeared to be traveling in, and I only managed to pull it free after a supreme effort.

Okay, I thought, rubbing my sore arm, *don't do that again.* The only good thing about the experience was that the wake I'd caused helped me get my bearings on which direction I was heading. It appeared that I was racing towards a bright spark of light in the distance. I twisted my body around a little so that I was facing it, thinking, *End of the line. Two or three more minutes of this, and then I'll be back home.* Curious as to how far I'd traveled, I looked behind to see if I could find a corresponding spot of light for Arkhein.

That was when I finally saw Beterion in all its maddening glory. A black, amorphous shape filled my entire view, sliding around the shaft of light generated by the open Crossroad. It had no discernible head or body, but I could make out dark ribbon-like tendrils all across its surface -- they writhed with a life of their own, some twisting their way down the outside of the shaft towards me at alarming speeds. As they drew closer, they began to braid together, their forms melting into one another until they became large tentacles, each tipped with four razor-sharp pincers. When the pincers opened, they took on the appearance of diamond-shaped jaws, which snapped at me with insatiable hunger from the other side of the barrier. For all their ferocity, they seemed incapable of piercing the barrier, bouncing off it every time they made to strike. Despite this, I drew myself up into a fetal position and wrapped my hands around the packet of crystals hanging around my neck as I continued to be swept towards the other Crossroad. *Lord, you've protected me this far*, I silently prayed, *so please don't abandon me now.*

Beterion finally realized that it was getting nowhere, and I watched in growing horror as the tentacles withdrew, then entwined until they had formed a limb thicker than my torso. This new appendage reared back, then rammed down with enough force to rupture the barrier and send me flying out of the shaft. Beterion pulled away from me as soon as I was outside the barrier, the end of the massive tentacle smoking and dripping ichor from coming into contact with the Heart of Avisar. It drew the injured limb towards itself, merging it back into the whole of its mass as if it had never existed.

I hung in emptiness, all my forward momentum gone and my body aching from the double impact with both Beterion and the barrier. I tried to draw a breath, but found that the air outside the shaft was almost nonexistent. *Don't panic, Richard*, I told myself. *The shaft of light is still there, it's still intact, you just need to get back inside of it. As long as you've got the crystal, Beterion won't be able to...*

A new limb came out of nowhere and smashed into me, knocking me even further away from where I needed to be. Once again, it injured itself in the attempt, and I couldn't figure out why it kept attacking me like that when it obviously couldn't touch me for long. Then I remembered what J'nath had told me about the shard of crystal that had crossed over with me: it had disintegrated due to prolonged contact with Beterion. "Shit...oh shit..." I gasped in the thin air as I stared up at the black cloud hanging above me. A portion of the surface appeared to be bubbling, then it melted away to reveal a pair of misshapen eyes crudely positioned above a gaping, twisted mouth brimming with teeth -- the features seemed lit from within by a reddish light that mirrored the environment around us. *No, the rest of that is Beterion too*, I realized. *This whole place is a part of it...the space between Arkhein and Tarahein isn't just a prison, it's the prisoner as well.*

The mouth opened wider, if such a thing was possible, and it let out a noise akin to the squeal of emergency brakes on a train -- metal grinding on metal, neither willing to give in to the force applied to them. I clapped my hands over my ears as it roared, the force of its cries actually pushing me back. My heart was pounding so hard, both from fear and lack of air, that I could swear I felt it hitting my ribcage. Another limb began to form before my eyes, and I suddenly knew that Beterion would keep smacking me around like a cat toying with a mouse until all the crystals that protected me had disintegrated...and then the real fun would start. I had to get out of this place fast, especially since I didn't know how long it would be before the Crossroads shut down again. Unfortunately, I could only think of one way to get where I needed to be, and it certainly wasn't going to be easy.

As the massive appendage came crashing down on me, I wrapped my arms around it, trying not to think twice about how insane an action it was. I could feel the shards heating up against my chest as Beterion attempted to pull away, but I just dug my fingers deeper into the writhing mass. Tiny thorn-like projections formed out of the monster's flesh and sank into my own skin as it tried to make me let go, and when that didn't work, it began to flail me about, hurling its limb at larger chunks of debris. Despite its best efforts, I held on tight, ignoring Beterion's banshee cries and the growing numbness in my body from being in such close contact with it for so long. "Come on...that the best...you've got?" I rasped, trying to keep an eye out for my intended target. It finally came into view just as Beterion began to swing its appendage in a downward arc. I waited for the right moment, then pushed off and sailed away from it. Just as before, Beterion immediately drew the damaged limb back into itself...then howled even louder as it realized that it had given me enough momentum to carry me back towards the Crossroads' light-shaft.

I hit the shaft feet-first and was dragged along half-in, half-out for a few seconds before my whole body was sucked in by the current. I could hear the monster's rant as I raced away from it, back on course, but it didn't make another attempt to stop me. I leaned back as I was swept along, gulping air into my oxygen-starved lungs and trying to shake some feeling back into my numb hands. Then my speed seemed to increase, and I found myself engulfed by blinding light, just as I had been when I first entered the Crossroad. I could feel my body being pushed straight up, and it took a moment to realize that I was feeling what "up" was once again. I also became reacquainted with "down" when I landed face-first on solid ground.

I rolled onto my side and laid there, body aching, head ringing, and deliriously happy. "I made it," I said aloud, then laughed. "Holy Christ, I made it back." I took a few moments to savor my view of the beautiful blue sky before getting up to finish what I had started. It appeared to be about midday, which was fine by me. Something in my pack clinked as I shifted about, and I could smell gunpowder as well. At least one of the clay containers had busted while Beterion whipped me around. "Doesn't matter," I said as I slipped off the pack and rested it on the ground, "I'll fix it later. I'm home now, I'm safe." I climbed slowly to my feet, looking about the pit where the Crossroad lay. Nothing had changed, really: tools and materials were still scattered about, although more than a few had become partially buried under dried mud, courtesy of the storm that had rolled through the day I'd fallen into the Crossroad. I finally turned towards the Crossroad itself, which was still open and shooting a fountain of light into the clear blue sky. Despite knowing what lay within it, I found the display quite breathtaking. At the same time, I wondered again how long it would take before it shut down -- I couldn't do a damn thing to the stone while the portal was open like that. I decided to work on repairing the broken bomb while I waited and reached down to pick up my pack.

That was when I saw the slim black tendrils sliding out over the rim of the Crossroad like the shadows of snakes.

CHAPTER 16

Every muscle in my body locked in place, trapping me in a half-crouched position with my hand hovering over the pack of homemade bombs. I couldn't take my eyes off the Crossroad's edge as a living darkness radiated outward from all sides, pouring over the sun-baked earth of New Mexico. It never blocked the beam of light shooting upward from the center of the stone, choosing instead to squeeze itself out *around* the offending obstacle. *It can't do that,* I thought. *Nobody said Beterion could physically leave the Crossroad!* About then it occurred to me that no one specifically said Beterion *couldn't,* either.

A black ring, about six inches wide and nearly as tall, had formed around the Crossroad. Miniature versions of those diamond-mouthed tentacles I'd seen earlier began to sprout up, swaying slightly as their jaws opened and closed, sometimes brushing against each other and merging to make larger monsters. The big ones dragged their "heads" along the ground, occasionally flicking out something that looked like a tongue but functioned like another appendage, wrapping around rocks or hard clumps of earth to hold them in place until the jaws snapped shut around them. *It can't see, at least not yet,* I thought. *Maybe it's too small right now, or the light's blinding it.* The why didn't really matter to me right then, just the fact that it couldn't see where I was. It took all the will I could muster, but I somehow got myself moving again, wrapping my hand around one of the pack's shoulder straps and lifting it as I slowly straightened up.

Then some of the broken pottery inside shifted about and clinked together. Two of the larger "heads" nearby shot forward like enormous rattlesnakes, clamping onto the pack with their pincers. The rest of the black mass flowed towards my position as I struggled to pull the pack away, my arms feeling like they were coming loose from my shoulders. Beterion was growing before my eyes, the two limbs grasping the pack thickening and sprouting smaller spiky tendrils that dug into the rough-woven cloth. "Let...go, you bastard..." I spat out, then sprawled backward as the strap I was pulling on tore away. I landed hard on my ass, momentarily stunned. The tug-of-war over, Beterion shredded the pack in no time flat, gunpowder spraying all over me and the pit like confetti, then it tossed what little remained to the side. The monster towered over me now, a writhing dark mass nearly eight feet tall, a quartet of pincers bigger than pickaxes snapping at the air...and a blood-red eye bulging out on either side of its mouth. It let out that horrible metal-on-metal shriek again before it lunged at me, jaws wide.

I rolled out of the way, just missing being impaled by inches, then scrambled to my feet as Beterion tore at the dirt in anger. Smaller tentacles literally nipped at my heels, nearly tearing off one of my boots, but I somehow managed to reach the edge of the pit and climb out of the cursed thing intact. I turned to my right, towards the northern end of town, and had started to run when a black sickle shot out of the pit and slashed down into my path, digging a furrow into the street. I stopped short, backpedaled, then turned left, only to find another sickle coming down in front of me, this time close enough for me to feel it pass in front of my face. I jumped back again, then headed westward, opposite the pit -- a boarded-up building lay just ahead, and I threw myself at the front door, hoping to at least put some obstacles between myself and that monster, but the damn door refused to budge. "Oh God oh shit oh God," I panted as I rammed my shoulder against the unyielding door. "Open up oh shit *open up!*"

An ebony spike embedded itself in the door, missing my head by mere inches. Before I even had a chance to react, a dozen more surrounded me, digging into the sandblasted wood of the building and cutting off any avenue of escape. I froze once again, still facing the door, my eyes wide and my voice gone. There was a smell of rot and decay filling the air around me, as well as a sound like something slick and wet sliding around in thick mud. I could feel no breath on my neck, but I knew Beterion was right behind me, within arm's reach. With a shaking hand, I reached up and felt for the crystals hanging around my neck -- the bit of shirttail I'd wrapped them in was still there, but it gave off no heat like before. *They're all used up*, I thought, *it's over*. Swallowing the rock that had formed in my throat, I turned around slowly and faced Beterion.

A vision of madness greeted me. Tentacles slithered about, twisting around nearby awning supports and tugging at loose planks on the boardwalk. A thick midsection anchored them all to the Crossroad, which still stood wide open -- Beterion seemed unable to completely separate itself from its prison, thank God. The massive set of jaws that I'd evaded earlier now loomed in front of me, pincers quivering, the red eyes on either side of it seeming to stare into my soul. Its black "skin" started to bubble like I'd seen it do earlier, the eyes sliding into a more frontal position as pincers turned inward and multiplied, the whole of the mouth sinking downward and elongating. A crude brow and jawline formed, as well as an opening for a nasal cavity. Once it had finished its transformation, Beterion leered at me with the appearance of an oversized, exaggerated skull, black as pitch and lit from within by unholy red fire as teeth the size of railroad spikes gnashed at the air between us. Tendrils trailed back from its brow, some merging with the midsection, others flicking about the face like stray locks of hair. One of them reached out towards my own face, its tip curling and growing thinner as it approached. I jerked back, slamming my head against the door in an effort to get away from it, but there was nowhere to go. The tendril stretched until it became thinner than a single hair, barely visible. It waved about in front of my eyes for a second, then darted down and slid behind me, tickling the nape of my neck. *It's going to choke me to death*, I thought, unable to fathom what this thing was really capable of.

The tendril drove itself into the base of my skull, sending waves of pain crashing through my head and straight down my spine. I couldn't stop the scream that tore out of my throat. I tried to reach up and yank the tendril out, but two new claws shot forward, pinning my arms to the door. I thrashed about in its grip as Beterion worked its way deeper into me, slipping between cells and tapping into veins. Blood began to dribble out of my ears as I thought, *Dear God, what is this thing trying to do to me?*

Just making it easier for us to talk, a voice...*my own voice* echoed in my head. Or, at least, it was a close imitation of my voice: it sounded rumbly, vicious, like someone on the verge of exploding in anger. Rage punctuated every syllable, infested every pause. I didn't think I'd ever sounded that angry in my entire life, even on my worst day. I focused as best I could on Beterion, the black death's-head hovering inches from my face. "Wh...why do you..." I struggled to say.

Because this is the only way a stupid piece of meat like you can understand me, it said, each word like a drop of venom in my mind. ***A certain level of intimacy is required, you see, if we're to have anything resembling a meaningful conversation. Besides, I know J'nath has told you quite a bit about me...so now I want to learn all about you. The REAL you.***

It pushed itself further into me, beyond the physical, and into the deepest recesses of my mind. I squeezed my eyes shut in a vain effort to block out the memories that it dredged up from within me. Moments of pain, of weakness, of failure. Deaths that I caused, deaths that I couldn't stop. Snatches of the past that I'd tried to tell myself never happened, locking them away in the darkest corners of my soul, but now those places had been torn open and laid bare before me. I wanted to cry out, to expel at least of a fraction of my agony, but my tongue felt like it was plastered to the roof of my mouth.

Oh, what a priceless creature you are, it said as it finally eased up on me. *A suicidal outlaw with crippling feelings of guilt and a fondness for the drink. You're probably the best example of why this sick joke called "The Universe" is such a waste of time. I don't even know why you're bothering to fight against me. I'd be doing you a favor by killing you.*

"Go to..." The rest of the sentence was lost in a cry of pain.

Ah, now it starts: the posturing, the grand delusion that you're not the insignificant maggot that you truly are. Its head tilted slightly, regarding me like some rare specimen. *Come now, these are your last moments of consciousness on this plane. Is that really the best you can do?*

I somehow managed to draw my gun, but I couldn't muster the strength to point it at its head -- the claw holding my arm against the door was as unbreakable as an iron manacle. In my head, I heard a laugh eerily similar to my own, but my ears picked up a sound that vaguely resembled the echo of a rockslide. *You think you can actually hurt me with that thing?* it mocked. *Do you have any notion of the power I wield? I can crack the very foundation of reality, and you threaten me with A TOY!* Beterion tightened its grip on my arms and slammed me against the door. Black thorns sprung up from its limbs, cutting through my coat and shirtsleeves, sliding across my skin like coils of barbed wire. Earlier, Beterion's touch had made me feel numb, but when those thorns began to tear into my bared flesh, it felt like my blood had been set on fire. Just like the first tendril, these thorns just kept burrowing deeper into me, and soon, more darkness was flowing across the surface of my arms and up my shoulders, drawing blood wherever it went. Another pair of tendrils began to snake around my boots, slicing into my trousers as they worked their way up my legs. My balls crept up into my stomach as I feared the worst. "Don't...don't do that," I pleaded. "For the love of God, don't..."

HOW DARE YOU SAY THAT! The darkness contracted everywhere it touched flesh -- I heard the bones in my left forearm snap, but my nerves were so overloaded that I couldn't feel it. *How dare you speak of "love" and "God" to me! Your "God" is the reason I have to use meat like you! If you say that name again...if you even THINK it...I'll feed you your eyes!* Tiny black ribbons crawled up the sides of my face, tugging at the soft tissue around my eyes to emphasize the point. *Perhaps I should, anyways, just to make sure you know I'm not bluffing.* A larger tentacle hovered before me, its tip razor-sharp. *I must admit, the eyes are my favorite part. Your kind are just so vulnerable without them. And they're so easy to damage. Just...one...flick...* The tentacle snapped at my face like a whip, and I turned my head out of instinct. It made a gouge along the right side of my jaw, just deep enough to draw blood -- the wound burned like acid, but I clamped my mouth shut and tried to swallow this new pain along with all the rest. My silence couldn't hide what I really felt from Beterion, though. *Go ahead*, it taunted, *let it out. Raise your voice to the heavens and show the Other how miserably you've failed.*

Other? I thought, too exhausted to speak aloud. *Other what?*

My opposite number. Your so-called "God". It spat out the name like a curse. *I don't expect you to fully understand, since you're basically a bag of meat that's learned to talk: the circles we travel in are a bit over your head. Suffice it to say, when one of us surges ahead, the other falls behind...and let me tell you, this little mistake you've made with the Crossroads has definitely put me on top again. You see, for every one of you that I take back, the less brightly the Other shines. If I take back enough of you, the Other won't be able to maintain order, and then the darkness will creep back in. MY darkness.*

What do you mean, "take back"? What do you need us for?

The red glow of Beterion's eyes flared up as a new spike of pain raced through my head. ***BECAUSE THE OTHER CARVED ME UP TO MAKE PUTRID LITTLE SOFT THINGS LIKE YOU! THE OTHER TORE FROM ME WHATEVER IT COULD, THEN BURIED THE REMAINS AND HOPED THAT I WOULD DIE! THE ONLY REASON ANYTHING EXISTS IS BECAUSE OF ME!*** It snapped its jaws at me, the ragged rows of teeth nearly brushing my skin before it pulled back slightly. ***But that doesn't matter anymore. Soon, all will be as it should once more, thanks to you stupid meat-bags. If those men hadn't reopened the Crossroad, I'd still be trapped. Do you want to see how I repaid them for their kind act? Do you?***

It never gave me a chance to respond, the images simply exploded to life within my mind, blinding me with the final memories of everyone that died in Hadley. The ones who'd actually shattered the crystal were the first to be infected, though they didn't know it, and within three days, nearly a quarter of the townsfolk had the plague. Within a week, those people were dead, and twice as many were showing signs of the illness. For every six people that died, one of them would be transformed into a living corpse: rotting, inhuman, the remains of their soul wracked by pain and hungry for anything warm and alive. Full-on panic set in on the seventh day as many of the townsfolk barricaded themselves in their homes, praying to God to deliver them from what they saw as the end of the world. Some people fled, only to die in the desert, choking on their own blood. One man made it all the way to Barrelhead, but he passed away before he could tell anyone about the horrors he'd seen -- by the day of our botched bank robbery, four people in Barrelhead were plague-ridden. Sheriff Walker and Doc Ayers had somehow managed to put a lid on any possible rumors to maintain order, not that it helped in the end: Barrelhead had become a ghost town as well, occupied only by the corpse-things.

From there, Beterion spread across New Mexico like a phantom wildfire, fueled by terrified people trying to escape flames that had already consumed them. How long before the Great Plague reached a major city? Perhaps it already had, and Beterion just didn't bother to show me. Not that it needed to, the Hell that it laid bare before me was enough: over one hundred people dead in the two weeks before Reeves and I had stumbled across the dead town of Hadley, and more than three times as many had fallen into Beterion's maw since then...and I could feel the torment of every single soul the monster had claimed. They were shackled to that madness now, giving it strength and form, everything those people *were* merging with it so that *their* thoughts, *their* memories became *Beterion's* -- whatever its victims knew, it now knew as well. A choked sob somehow managed to escape my throat, a sound that didn't begin to convey the anguish which the hundreds...no, *millions* of imprisoned souls within Beterion experienced: a living Hell, with no hope of salvation.

Grotesque laughter echoed through my mind again. ***Don't think that I forgot about your friends back in Betedek, either. For them, I have a special token of appreciation.*** New Mexico melted away before my eyes, and I found myself looking at Arkhein, but from a vantage point much higher then I was used to. I suddenly realized that I was seeing the world through Beterion's own eyes: it had grown powerful enough to be in two places at once, shaping a second head from the formless mass that dwelled between worlds and forcing itself through Betedek's now-open Crossroad. It was in that moment I finally saw the world the way Beterion saw it.

I could see the Light.

It lay just beneath the surface of everything, making the night shine brighter than midday. It rippled through the ground, up the trees, and spread out into the sky. Living things like plants seemed to give off a warmer, more intense Light than the soil or the rocks did, and even a few of the mangled bodies I glimpsed held tiny embers within, flickering and pulsing ever dimmer. I looked upon it all with a sense of awe, amazed that this sight had been hidden from...

I'M NOT SHOWING YOU THIS SO YOU CAN ENJOY THE VIEW, OUTLAW! My whole body convulsed as Beterion screamed in my mind, fresh blood trickling from my ears, and now from my nose as well. Despite all this, the vision never faded, though it did shift as Beterion turned its head, and I saw Gavas lying on the ground, two corpse-things huddled around his prone form. His body threw off Light like a search beacon, but I could sense that it wasn't as strong as it should be. He kept trying to pull himself along the ground in an effort to escape, but the corpse-things never let him get far: they'd grab his legs and yank him back, Light surging up from his body and across theirs before fading out.

What are they doing to him? I asked, bracing for more pain.

Softening him up. A black sickle, like the one Beterion had used to block my path, came into view. It loomed over the poor man's back, then thrust down and pierced him between the shoulder blades -- a fountain of Light gushed up from the wound, and was quickly swallowed up by Beterion's black void. It lifted him off the ground, the sickle protruding from Gavas's chest as he jerked about like a worm on a hook, his body giving off less and less Light until he was as dim as the corpse-things. Having finished with Gavas, Beterion flung the cold, dark body to the ground, where its minions dove upon him, not realizing yet that there was nothing left to feed upon.

You drained out his soul, I thought, *that's why the Light's gone. You just tapped him like a keg and drank him dry.*

Suddenly, the vision snapped off, and I was seeing with my own eyes again. Beterion's face was still intimately close to my own, still staring at me from behind that death's-head image, but it had changed somehow. It looked afraid.

"You...messed up...didn't you?" I panted, trying to concentrate on the words and not the blood trickling down the back of my throat. "You were trying to...scare me some more, but...you showed me something...didn't want me to see..."

Shut up, it hissed. *You're mine now, you see what I want you to see! You're just meat! And so is he!* Arkhein formed before my eyes again, this time showing me *Lermekt* H'landa, ragged and bloody. A dark spot covered the left side of his face, but from the right came a steady, rhythmic pulse of Light as blood flowed out of a wound beneath his hairline. His back was pressed against a tree, his sword held out and downward -- a strange reddish glow rippled across the blade, reminding me of when he'd held it over the campfire. All around his feet, Beterion's tentacles slithered like a nest of vipers. One of them reared up and lashed out at him, only to be cut down by his sword. Another attacked from the other side and suffered the same fate. With every strike, I could see a blue-green spark flash high upon his chest, so intense that it appeared as if his uniform had caught fire somehow. *The Heart of Avisar*, I thought. *He's still got his piece of the Heart. Gavas must have lost his, but H'landa's still protected.*

Don't be so sure. Five tentacles reached out for the lawman at once, and despite his speed, one got past his defenses and impaled his left thigh. The Heart flared, then dimmed suddenly as the crystal fractured. *I may not be able to kill him yet, but I can make him suffer*, Beterion told me. *His family has gotten in my way too many*

times, but not this time. The line of H'landa ends here.
It struck at him again, a dark blade slicing through boot
leather and into his right calf. He howled in pain and fell
to his knees, leaning on his sword like an old man with a
cane as blood poured freely from the crippling wounds.
With gritted teeth, he raised his head and stared straight
into Beterion's (and, consequently, my own) eyes, then
pursed his lips and spat a blood-tinged gob at its face.
"*Nee bakhen,*" he said. *No surrender.*

"Doesn't go down easy, does he?" I taunted.

I grow tired of your prattling, Beterion answered
as H'landa slipped away from view, my vision returning to
normal again. *You really shouldn't talk to me so, not
when I can do whatever I please to your miserable
carcass.* A barbed tongue slid out of its mouth and lapped
at my gore-streaked face. *So, what sort of end would you
like? I could drag you back down into the void with me,
or I could pull off your limbs like fly's wings and leave
you for the buzzards...there are so many options!* A thin
membrane of black began to cover my right hand, which
still held my gun. *Or perhaps I should go with one
you're more familiar with.* The membrane coated every
finger like a second skin, flexing muscles that had gone
numb, then my arm rose up, completely out of my control,
and nestled the gun barrel behind my right ear. *I know
you put it in your mouth last time, but I think this will
work even better. More direct.*

My entire body felt cold, the only sensations left
being the movement of my eyes, the beating of my heart,
and the pressure of the gun barrel. Even my voice was
gone now: the darkness had trickled over my throat and
chilled it to the core. The monster had taken over my
body, it had cracked open my mind like an eggshell, and
once it made me pull the trigger, it would have my soul. I
somehow managed to shut my eyes, not wanting to see
that hideous face in front of me as I died -- if I had to
spend the rest of eternity as part of this bastard, I wanted to
have at those last few moments of freedom to myself.

Beterion manipulated my thumb, pulling back the hammer. I thought of all the times I wanted to die, the times where I'd tried to kill myself to escape the pain I felt. I'd always thought of death as some sort of release, perhaps even a proper punishment for the terrible things I've done, but now it had become prelude to a never-ending nightmare. I wondered what it would feel like, my soul flowing from this body to Beterion's...would I even notice the transition? We were already connected to each other on such an intimate level, so maybe...

Wait a minute. If we're already connected, why would it need a gun to kill me?

What? Beterion stopped moving my fingers, my grip on the trigger relaxing minutely.

My eyes flew open, and I could see the look of fear back on Beterion's face. *You heard me,* I spoke in my mind. *You've already gotten into my brain, you've got a stranglehold on my body...why the Hell do you have to shoot me?*

It said nothing, nor did it apply pressure to the trigger again.

You asked me earlier how I wanted to die. Well, I've decided: I want you to rip my soul right out of my body. Right now. No guns, no nothing, just take it.

Do you really want me to do that? it snarled. **If you thought the pain you felt before was unbearable...**

Oh, I have no doubt that it hurts, I just don't think that you can do it to me. When I saw the world through your eyes earlier, I could see the power that holds the world together, what Arkans call the Light. I didn't really understand what they meant by that until you killed Gavas. That's why you took the vision away: you didn't want me to understand, but you couldn't prevent me from seeing the Light any more than I could keep you out of my mind.

I do believe the threat of death has made you delusional, outlaw.

Like Hell I am. I think this the clearest my mind's been in years. Deep within me, I could feel *something* begin to grow, pulsing with a warmth that reminded me of when I held the Heart of Avisar in my hand...but this wasn't from the crystal, this was from *me*. I focused on it, urging it on as I spoke in my mind, *The Light touches everything, it IS everything, save for you and the corpse-things. You can absorb it, though: you can siphon off enough Light with one touch to make somebody go numb. But what happens if you try to gulp down too much at once? Does the Light absorb you instead?*

You're forgetting your place, meat. I own you now, I'm your lord and master. The words were punctuated by sharp waves of pain, but they didn't seem so deadly now. In fact, some of the barbs were sliding out of my skin as the feeling within me engulfed my heart and began spreading through my veins like wildfire.

What's the matter, getting too hot for you? I taunted as I concentrated on my gun hand -- slowly, the darkness receded to the point where I could pull it away from my head. *What exactly do you see when you look at me, anyways? Gavas and H'landa were almost blinding to look at, so what must I look like to you? Ten times brighter? A hundred? That's the real reason I managed to cross over the first time, isn't it? You figured if I died in your realm, the Light inside me might tear you apart, so instead you threw me at the sealed Crossroad like a battering ram and hoped that you'd inflicted enough damage on me that I'd die in Arkhein.*

I'LL GUT THE HALF-BREED RIGHT NOW! A very un-demonic note of panic had crept into its voice. ***THE HEART ONLY BURNS FOR A SHORT WHILE, THE PAIN WILL BE WORTH IT TO WATCH THE H'LANDA DIE!***

Even when I didn't have a clue, I still held enough power within me to hurt you. And now that I'm aware of it, it's like stoking a furnace, and it's burning your poison right out of me. That's what the man in my dreams has been trying to tell me: You can tear apart my mind, you can cripple my body, but... "But you...can never...touch my soul," I gasped aloud as the tendrils melted away from my face and throat -- the warmth had spread to every inch of my body now, inside and out, forcing Beterion to pull away from me as fast as it could. The only place it still held onto me was at the base of my skull, and even that felt tenuous now.

Despite the fact that it was literally losing its grip on me, Beterion refused to admit defeat, screaming in my mind, *IT'S A LIE! YOU'RE NOTHING! JUST MEAT!*

"You're wrong," I said, reaching behind my head with my left hand -- the splintered bones in my forearm ground together as I did it, but compared to how I'd felt a few minutes ago, that pain was heavenly. I grabbed hold of that last tendril and yanked it out, barely feeling it. "I am a *n'toku-rejii*, and I'm going to send you back to Hell." I pointed the gun at Beterion, pressing the barrel between its eyes, and unloaded the whole cylinder in its face.

At such a close range, even that monster couldn't withstand the force of the bullets. Its head collapsed in on itself as it let out a shriek so loud I thought my eardrums might burst. The claws it had sunk into the building tore at the lumber spasmodically, weakening the whole structure. I ducked under its flailing limbs and dove for the safety of the street just as the whole mess came crashing down. My left arm whacked against the ground when I rolled away, sending blinding white pain shooting from my fingers to my shoulder, but I swallowed it as best I could and kept moving, holstering my gun to free up my good hand and stumbling to my feet as I tried to get away from Beterion's rapidly-reforming jaws. I was pointed north, so that was the direction I ran, tentacles lashing at me the whole time but never able to get a firm grip as I sprinted down the street, my busted arm pressed tightly to my chest.

I was nearly in front of the shop where I'd last seen Reeves when I realized I wasn't being chased anymore. Common sense told me not to stop, but I had to see why Beterion was no longer on my ass. I skidded to a halt and turned around, ready for anything but what I saw:

Beterion's form swarmed all over the street, crawled up the sides of buildings...and came to a dead stop less than twenty-five feet away from me. It bore its misshapen teeth at me and stretched its tendrils until they became wispy as spiderwebs, but it simply couldn't close the gap between us. Apparently, its physical reach in the real world was quite short, and I'd exceeded it.

Now it was *my* turn to laugh. It sounded awful and it hurt like Hell, but I couldn't help myself. I slowly sank to my knees, pointing and cackling while Beterion tore apart a storefront in a fit of anger, tossing debris everywhere -- I had to dodge a chunk of lumber the size of a railroad tie that it threw in my direction. "Sorry, pal," I called out after I got the laughter out of my system, "but I don't wanna play with you no more. I'm too tired."

The darkness bristled as Beterion shrieked at me, its cries shattering what few windows were still intact. Massive claws ripped at the ground, straining to pull itself even an inch closer to me, but it was getting nowhere fast.

"If you think I'm gonna let you get hold of me again, you're sadly mistaken!" I hollered, still kneeling in the middle of the street. "You can't kill me, so just go home, you ugly shit!"

Beterion paused in its rant, its head dipping down to my level and its eyes narrowing to red slits -- it actually seemed to be considering what I'd said. And why not? As long as I was alive, I'd keep fighting until the Crossroad was destroyed. It could never win here.

Then I caught the look in those narrowed eyes, and remembered what it had said it wanted to do to H'landa, along with what it had *already* done to him. Once he was gone, Beterion could take Arkhein with little effort, especially if it was no longer splitting its attention between two worlds. Cold, dead fear engulfed my heart and squeezed as the tendrils began to retract into the dark mass, leaving behind scarred earth and piles of rubble. Beterion shifted slowly backward as it returned to the Crossroad, its eyes never leaving mine the whole time.

"Bastard...leave them alone. *Just leave them alone!*" I tried to get back on my feet, but my body had taken too much abuse that day, and I nearly ate dirt as my legs buckled. It didn't matter anyways, there was nothing I could do to stop this monster from destroying Arkhein, it knew that as well as I did. Beterion let out another roar, mocking and triumphant at the same time, as the darkness retreated behind a building and out of my view. A few minutes later, silence enveloped the town as the Crossroad finally shut down. I broke the silence with an inarticulate cry of horror and anger, keeling forward and slamming my good fist on the ground. *I failed them all*, I thought. *My world will live, but Arkhein will die, and I can't stop it.* "Why are You doing this to me?" I said aloud, my face inches from the ground. "This is *impossible*! I can't save both worlds by *myself*!" I lifted my head and screamed at the clear blue sky, "I *told* you I couldn't do this, and *now* look at what's happened! *I've killed them!* Is *that* what you wanted?"

Gauzy white clouds drifted across the blue. I saw no answer in them. "So I'm a *n'toku-rejii*, and Beterion can't steal my soul. So what? I still can't be in two places at once, and even if I could, the Crossroad's closed again!" I waved a bloodied fist at the sky. "Why the Hell won't You tell me what to do? I don't know how to...stop..." My voice faded out as I stared at my upraised fist, at the blood spattered across my skin.

"Oh God...oh my God, I'm so stupid," I said, and lowered my hand, my eyes still fixed on the heavens above me -- for the first time in the twenty years I'd drawn breath, I really *looked* at the sky, and I now felt like I could never see enough of it. "Please forgive me, Lord. I've been so afraid of messing up that I wasn't thinking straight." I tapped a finger against my temple. "You told me before that I don't think with my mind often enough, and I reckon this was almost one of those occasions."

My gaze fell to the ground, and I said quietly, "I'm not sure if I can fix all this as well as it needs to be, but I'm gonna try, because...because You asked me to." I squeezed my eyes shut, bracing for the pain that I knew would come when I tried to get up again. "Please, Lord, just give me the strength to finish this."

*   *   *   *   *   *

The town's general store had been well barricaded when I'd first passed through, but Beterion's little tantrum eliminated that problem: the beast had ripped the front wall wide open, exposing what few sundries remained inside. I only hoped the items I had in mind were amongst them. After ducking under the sagging awning and stepping through the hole in the wall, I decided that I'd better do something about my busted arm first. I gingerly peeled off my coat, then took a couple of small pieces of wood that used to be part of the building and made a splint, tying it on over my shirtsleeve to keep it from abusing my skin any more than it already had been. It still hurt like a sonovabitch, but at least my left arm was semi-usable again. Now it was time to go shopping.

A battered satchel lay forgotten behind the clerk's counter. I tossed the strap around my neck and proceeded to scour the store for my targets. The first lay behind the counter as well: bullets. A few boxes had been overlooked by those who had looted the store before fleeing town, but only one contained the .45-caliber cartridges I needed. I reloaded my pistol and the loops on my gunbelt, then tossed the remainder in the bag. After a moment's thought, I added the other bullets as well, thinking I might make use of them later on somehow. As I began to step out from behind the counter, I spied an old cavalry saber mounted above it on the wall, still in its scabbard. Perhaps the shopkeeper had been a veteran of the War, or had simply bought it for a conversation piece. How it had ended up there didn't really matter to me, but its presence seemed important. Even though I'd never held a sword in my life, I pulled it off the wall and jammed the scabbard beneath my belt before moving on.

I walked through the store, sifting through the items the townsfolk had decided weren't worth hauling off. I stuffed into the satchel a few things that were far from necessary, but I liked to think of as last-minute souvenirs: a couple of periodicals, a near-full box of cigars (real expensive-lookin' ones, too), and a bottle of whiskey that had somehow escaped the chaos unscathed. That little gem got wrapped up in my coat before going in the bag. I put an end to my impromptu scavenger hunt, however, when I found in the back room what I'd been truly searching for, the one thing more important to me at the moment than bullets or booze: a crate of dynamite. It's probably not right to thank God for high explosives, but I did anyways as I fell to my knees and ripped off the lid to reveal...seven sticks.

"That's it?" I said, looking about the room in the vain hope that there may be another crate nearby. There wasn't. "*That's fucking it?*" I said again and slapped my palm against the crate. Seven sticks of dynamite might be enough to take care of both Crossroads -- barely -- but I was hoping to have some leftover to toss at Beterion. After seeing what a bullet at close range was capable of doing, I figured something with a higher yield could really rip through it. Now I'd have to hold that bastard back with just my guns. I cursed and smacked the crate again, then got up and checked the back room one more time, tossing junk aside in frustration. I nearly tripped over an ugly, faded-red chair laying on the floor, so I gave it a good kick, snapping off one of the wooden legs, and went back to searching.

Then I stopped, turned back, and looked down at the busted chair...and then at the crate of dynamite...and then at the chair again...

Ten minutes later, I was running back to the Crossroad, listing to the left thanks to the weight of my overloaded satchel. As I made my way, I took in all the damage done to the town during Beterion's retreat -- if I had seen it without knowing what really happened, I would have thought a tornado ripped the place to shreds. No building within its reach had been untouched, and the ones closest to the pit were no longer standing. A few desiccated bodies lay amongst the shattered boards and wisps of tarpaper, their hiding places having been torn asunder. Mounds of earth had sprung up all over the formerly hard-packed street, making passage difficult. When I finally reached the pit, I found it half-filled with dirt and debris, as if Beterion had intentionally tried to bury the stone once more. The stone itself remained clear, though the path to it certainly wasn't. Slowly, I made my way down into the pit, ever mindful of where I stepped -- between the debris, my broken arm, and how much I'd been torn up in general, I'd be in trouble if I took a bad tumble.

When I finally reached the edge of the Crossroad, I stood before it on weakening legs, wobbling like a drunkard. I could see that the crowbars the townsfolk had wedged beneath the broad black stone were still in place, lifting one side clear of the ground by a few inches. I knelt down by the gap and pulled out four sticks of dynamite, fused and ready to go. I spaced them out beneath the stone as far as I could, then braided the fuses together and snaked them out and over the top of the stone. The other sticks remained in the satchel, destined for Arkhein...if I made it back. *Now is not the time to be thinking like that, Richard,* I told myself, and ran my good hand over my face, wiping away a mixture of blood, dirt, and cold sweat. I stood up and stepped onto the Crossroad, then crouched over its center, above the hole big enough to shove your fist into. A memory suddenly burst forth in my mind of a Psalm I'd learned as a child, back when my life was much more simple and the world made perfect sense. I couldn't remember the whole thing anymore, but what I could seemed appropriate, and I recited it as I began to work:

"I will say of the Lord, He is my refuge and my fortress: my God...in Him will I trust."

With my right hand, I reached down and unsheathed my knife.

"He shall cover thee with His feathers, and under His wings shalt thou trust: His truth shall be thy shield and buckler. Thou shalt not be afraid for the terror by night...nor the arrow that flieth by day...nor for the pestilence that walketh in darkness...nor for the destruction that wasteth at noonday."

I held my left hand over the hole and pressed the tip of the blade into my open palm, carving a small crescent into my skin. The blood flowed out immediately, the volume increasing as I flexed my fingers.

"A thousand shall fall at thy side, and ten thousand at thy right hand...but it shall not come nigh thee."

I sheathed the knife and thrust my bloody hand into the hole. My spilt blood had opened it once before by accident, but that had only been some stray spatters from my gunshot wounds. This was much more direct, and given willingly.

"For He shall give His angels charge over thee, to keep thee in all ways." My voice rose as the Crossroad began to roar to life, the light literally pulling at my fist when I drew it out of the hole. "Thou shalt tread upon the lion and the adder: the young lion and the dragon shalt thou trample under feet."

I'd stashed a few matches in my trouser pocket earlier, and I pulled one out, struck it against the heel of my boot, then lit the fuses as the sigils started to blaze with blue-white fire. I turned my face to the sky, screaming the words now to be heard over the earsplitting noise, truly believing in the old verse for the first time in years. It had become a declaration to Heaven above me, and a battle cry to Hell below. "He shall call upon me, and I will answer Him: I will be with Him in trouble...I will deliver Him, and honor Him! With long life will I satisfy Him, *and show Him my salvation!*"

The portal opened wide, and I tumbled into Beterion's realm once again, broken, bleeding...but no longer afraid. I had no reason to be. I twisted about until I was facing towards Arkhein -- in the distance, Beterion's form still swarmed about the Crossroad's open gate. It took a moment for the monster to realize that I'd reentered its world, and when it did, it tried to stop me the same way as before: small tendrils braided together until they'd become a limb large enough to break into the shaft I was speeding through. This time, however, Beterion probably wouldn't be content with knocking me about its prison, and would most likely smother me or tear my head off the second it got hold of me, consequences be damned.

Lucky for me, the dynamite charges went off before it even had a chance to penetrate the barrier. The explosion seemed to amplify the force that already propelled me, so that I could now really feel just how fast I was going. My teeth rattled in my head as I sped along, and I hoped that I didn't run headlong into anything when I exited the Crossroad. I chanced a look behind me and saw my back trail quickly being engulfed in a mass of blinding, crackling, blue-white energy. Beterion shrieked in what sounded like utter terror as it tried to avoid the approaching maelstrom. The darkness dissolved (or perhaps just pulled back) wherever it came into contact with the intense pulse of energy that blossomed outward from the shaft, a blue-green haze marking where the two forces collided.

I rapidly approached the other Crossroad unimpeded, the few remaining tentacles that still reached through the opening not so much as twitching in my direction as I flew past them. And I do mean "flew": the speed at which I reentered Arkhein was enough to fling me a good eight feet into the air before gravity took hold of me once again. I braced for it this time, and managed to land a few feet away from the portal, keeping my footing and moving away as soon as I touched the ground. Surprisingly, Beterion still didn't try and grab me, but then again, the destruction of the New Mexico stone appeared to have dealt it a devastating blow. The dark mass on this side was much smaller, though still impressive, and it seemed less cohesive, almost runny in parts -- even the features of its face were adrift as it stared me down.

"Didn't think I'd come back, did you?" I said, standing a good distance away from Beterion. "Well, I just couldn't resist, what with the way you threatened my friend's life and all." I cast a quick glance around the yard. The light from the Crossroad continued to pulse out, obliterating all shadows, but I didn't see the lawman anywhere. "Where is he, you monster?"

Beterion silently leered at me, then like a magician unveiling his final trick, it lifted up a human-sized chunk of itself and let the darkness slide back to reveal H'landa from the chest up, his head lolling back. If he was still conscious, it wasn't by much: the man's face was slack and bone-white, and the leather patch that normally covered his left eye had been ripped off, exposing the mangled, scarred flesh over the empty socket. I barely had time to register the sight before ice-cold hands wrapped around my throat from behind -- one of the corpse-things was still running about, it seemed. Startled but unafraid, I reached behind me, grabbed a handful of stringy hair clinging to its head, and pulled forward until the neckbone gave way with a dry snap, the body collapsing in a heap. Another came shambling towards me, but I pulled leather and shot it in the head before it even got close. I turned back to the death's-head and croaked, "You certainly are full of surprises today, aren't you? That's alright, 'cause I've got one for you." I dropped my gun back into its holster as I reached into the satchel with my injured hand. Though tightening my grip was painful, I managed to get hold of what I wanted. I flashed a grin at Beterion as I held up a bundle of red sticks bound together with strips of rag, a long fuse dangling from one end. "A smart fella like you knows what dynamite is, right? Hell, you oughta: I just used some a few minutes ago to blow the other Crossroad to kingdom come!"

Tentacles lashed out towards me as Beterion let out a shriek of anger. I easily backpedaled out of its reach -- all of its terrifying speed was gone -- then I paused to scoop up one of the torches. It had fallen over and was on the verge of sputtering out, but it still had enough spark left to light a fuse. "Reckon you might want to start backing off, pal," I said, and brought the torch within inches of the bundle. "You come any closer, and I'll toss this right into the Crossroad. I noticed on the way back that you and high explosives don't mix well, so I know you don't want me to do that."

One of the tentacles receded, reaching instead for H'landa's exposed face. The message was pretty clear: the monster was daring me to make a move while it literally held the lawman's life in its hands.

"You really think you've got me, don't you? You figure there's no way in Hell I'm gonna do anything that might get him killed." My grin widened. "Hate to tell you this, 'Betty', but I ain't bluffing, and you know it. You've been in my head, you've dug through my memories." I took a couple of steps towards the Crossroad, saying, "Did you come across what I did three years ago in Saundersville?"

The tentacles shuddered before they shrank back, both from me and H'landa's face.

"You're a fast learner," I said, "but that's not good enough. I want you to let him go...mind, soul, *and* body."

The death's-head bared its teeth and started to pull the lawman into itself again, scant portions of him still visible through the darkness.

"Fine!" I hollered as I brought the torch closer to the fuse. "I guess you *want* to burn!"

It shrieked again, but its defiance was brief. The darkness rippled, then shrank away as it disgorged H'landa onto the ground just a few feet away from where I stood -- his good eye was open but blank, staring at nothing, the only sign of life being the steady rise and fall of his chest. I wanted to drop everything and run to his side, but this standoff was far from over.

Beterion's face dipped down to my level, positioning itself between me and the Crossroad, then it thrust out a limb resembling a mangled claw. I gestured towards it with the bundle, saying, "I suppose you want me to give this to you."

Beterion rumbled assent.

"Okay...here you go!" I lit the fuse, dropped the torch, and tossed the bundle into my right hand. As the claw shot forward to grab me, I threw the bundle as high and as far as possible, hoping my aim was true. I watched as it arced over the demon's grasping limbs, flying right into the shaft of light above the Crossroad -- the speed at which it was pulled down into the portal was so fast, it seemed like it had never been there. Then the darkness hit me like a battering ram, melting around my body and squeezing me in its vise-like grip, black talons digging at my throat. "Not...very smart," I gasped. "Only got...less than a minute...'til it blows. Kind of...divided your attention."

A look of doubt crept onto Beterion's face. I was sure that, at that same moment, the part of it still in the Crossroad was racing furiously to break into the shaft of light and grab that bundle, but it just kept falling short. Not enough strength, not enough power, it just needed a little more...

The demon roared in anger and tossed me to the side, towards the woods. I smacked into the base of a tree, and I lay there in a heap as Beterion slid back into the Crossroad, pulling every last tendril down into the abyss with it. Once the portal was clear of obstacles, the Crossroad shut down, leaving only a ringing in my ears and a blotchy afterimage hanging in front of my eyes. Groaning, I scrambled to my feet and ran as best I could over to the stone, feeling heat rolling off of it in waves like a desert rock at noonday. "Gullible little cuss, ain'tcha?" I muttered, then reached into my satchel and pulled out a second bundle...the *real* bundle of dynamite. "You can't even tell the difference between a stick of dynamite and a bunch of red-stained chair legs."

Once again, I knelt down on the Crossroad, only this time, I wasn't about to give it any more blood than it had already taken from me. I wedged the explosives into the central hole, fuse up, struck a match, and touched the flame to the end of the fuse. It sputtered, and for a moment, I thought it wouldn't light, then it suddenly sparked to life -- by my figuring, I now had a little over thirty seconds 'til all Hell broke loose. I damn-near jumped off the stone and ran over to H'landa, who was still sprawled out where Beterion had dropped him. I fell to my knees and slapped his cheek in an effort to rouse him, saying, "C'mon, cousin, get up! We've gotta move!"

The lawman's good eye, still open, still blank, stared right through me, but his mouth moved as some part of his brain attempted to wake up. Unfortunately, the only sounds that came out were utter nonsense to me. I cursed and tossed one of his arms over my shoulders, hauling him to his feet. We somehow managed to stay upright, though I had my doubts as to how far we could get as we stumbled towards the tree line. *We're gonna be too close*, I thought. *After all this Hell, we're gonna get killed by a few sticks of dynamite and some low-grade gunpowder.*

We were only a couple feet shy of the woods when the explosives went off, the concussion knocking us flat. I landed on top of H'landa and stayed there, eyes squeezed shut as I waited for the shrapnel, but nothing hit us. Confused, I lifted my head and looked back at the Crossroad. The same blue-white energy I'd seen after the first blast now loomed over the portal...and it was growing, spilling out from the Crossroad's perimeter and rolling across the ground like fog, with jagged arcs of lightning snapping out ahead of it. I raised my arm in a vain attempt to block out the searing light, but it was no use. *What happens when it reaches us?* I thought, only to realize that

I'd have my answer in a few seconds. I braced myself for God-knows-what, but it turned out to be a moot point: the energy wave suddenly reversed direction with such force that I felt it tug at me, and for a second I thought I might get swept up in it. Then a huge, deafening crack rang out as it collapsed in on itself, all that power funneling back into the Crossroad, leaving only an eight-foot-wide crater in the yard. The entire area was strangely free of debris, save for a fine white layer of ash where the stone had once been, perfectly outlining the dimensions of the portal.

As I sat in the long, trampled grass, staring at the crater, I felt a hand fall on my arm, and I looked over to see H'landa laying there, looking back at me. A dazed expression was the best he could manage, but that was fine by me, I was just glad he was still around to give me *any* sort of expression. "You...you get him?" he croaked.

"And then some," I answered. "Sonovabitch got what he deserved."

He smiled and patted my arm weakly. "*N'toku-rejii*," he said, his hand dropping down and his good eye slipping closed as he passed out again. I decided that he had a pretty good idea and collapsed next to him, staring up at the night sky. At that moment, I wanted nothing more than to crawl into someplace dark and warm and sleep for about a thousand years, but that spot would do for now.

I closed my eyes and let my mind drift away, feeling more at peace than I'd ever been in my life.

CHAPTER 17

When the dream came to me once again, there was no confusion, no struggle. I welcomed it, accepting the vision as reality, which I was beginning to believe it was on some level that I didn't completely understand yet, though part of me had certainly tapped into.

Knowledge drifted through my head out of nowhere, giving me insight that seemed more like memories than new information: I knew that the path I walked upon had once run through the same woods that H'landa and I had tracked down that *lissur* in, even though the trees here looked sparser, younger. The church we'd found lay at the end of the path, unmarred by age, the bronze panels on its doors gleaming in the dappled rose light. The low wall surrounding the building was made of finely carved stone, barely reaching past my waist as I walked through the open gateway. The church doors swung open before me, inviting me to cross the threshold. I could smell incense and candle wax, and I could feel the warmth of the light streaming through the windows. I strode up the aisle as I'd done a few days before, only now my boots trod across polished hardwood, and I was flanked by rows of richly-embroidered cushions where I'd expected to see pews. The ruined statues I'd seen before were whole again, their stone garments painted with vibrant hues -- there were eight in all, four on either side, and they looked down upon me as I walked past in my own torn and bloody clothes.

The altar had been draped in silks, tall iron candelabras standing at either end. Behind it, near the back wall of the church, was another statue. It was larger than the others, taller than me even, and pure alabaster white. It depicted a person in heavy robes and a hood pulled so low that nothing of the face could be seen. The arms were spread wide with the palms turned upward, as if it were beckoning me to come forward, but I couldn't bring myself to do so, choosing instead to kneel before the altar. It didn't seem right to approach that pristine figure while I was covered in gore and filth, though I wanted to so badly. I wanted to fall into those outstretched arms, and I knew they would enfold me and hold me up, and then there would be no more pain, no more nightmares, just peace.

"What holds you back?" asked a voice beside me.

I didn't even look, I had no need. "You don't see this?" I said to the man in the black hooded cloak, and held up my bloodstained hands, the spot where I'd cut open my left palm visible despite the layers of filth.

"It washes away, given time," he replied, "and more easily if you choose not to add to what already covers you. Fortunately, time is something we have once again, thanks to you."

I turned and looked up at him where he stood. "So I really did it? It worked?"

He gave me a barely perceptible nod, saying, "The Crossroads are no more, and the doors to Beterion's prison are locked tight once again. The threat of the Great Plague is over."

"What about the people that are already sick? Is J'nath..." I couldn't say it, couldn't *think* it.

"Beterion can no longer touch them, but damage has been done. Some may recover, some may not."

"Why can't you ever give me a straight answer?" I demanded as I stood up to face him. "I just went toe-to-toe with the Devil, for lack of a better term, so I think I deserve something more than vague riddles!"

"I have no answer to give. To those whom Beterion hurt, we are blind. We see them, but not *into* them, not *beyond* them. In time, we will again, but not now." His shoulders seemed to sag beneath his cloak, making him look tired, like he was the one who'd gone through Hell and back instead of me. "For now, we have to do what we did long ago: wait and hope."

"That's not *good* enough, dammit! If you can save them, then do it. I mean, you're some sort of emissary from God, right? Why can't God just wave His hand and fix all this?"

He sighed. "With Beterion, it is never that simple. Avisar does what He can, and the *n'toku-rejii* take care of the rest."

"Oh no, don't start with that line again." I poked him in the chest with my finger. "You always say it like it explains everything. Well, maybe to *you* it does, but it means very little to *me*, so I advise that you think of another way to say whatever the Hell it is you're saying, or else I'll clock you upside the head the next time I hear that word."

He reached up and grabbed my filthy hand, pulling it away from his chest with barely any force. A long, painful silence passed between us, my hand still clasped by his, before he finally said, "Do you understand why Beterion could not kill you?"

"I think so. My soul is...I don't know, too big, I guess. Too much to take all at once."

"And do you know why that is?" he asked, but continued before I could even bluff an answer. "Every person born, anywhere in the Infinite, has nestled within them a tiny portion of the Light. You call it a soul, Arkans say *kahn*, but it is the same thing: a connection to all that exists, past, present, and future. Each one contains a vast amount of power that continues to grow as time passes and it weaves itself through life after life. For some, though -- those rare and special few -- no time is needed, and they are born with the ability to shake the world with a single step. In the old Holy Words, those people were called *n'toku-rejii* -- the Voice of the Infinite -- because they were believed to speak and act directly under the orders of Avisar Himself. Not all of them do, however, only the ones who are needed." He eased my hand down until it hung at my side. "You were needed, Richard Corrigan, and you still are...if you are yet willing."

I raised my hand again after a moment, pressing it this time against my own chest, as if I could reach into myself and pull out this strange thing within me so I could look it over to see if he was telling the truth. Since I couldn't, I instead asked the only question that came to mind: "Why me?"

"Why *not* you?"

"The first time you came to me, I was lying unconscious in a jail cell after robbing a bank and killing a little boy, and you *still* can't see why I'm a bad choice?"

"Unlike you, I see all your paths, not just the one you constantly have your eyes fixed upon. Even killers have hearts, hidden though they may be. You just have to stop staring down at the ruin beneath your feet and see everything else you are capable of." He leaned close to me, his shadowed face so near but still indistinct. "The path you have been treading was never your own. It was forced upon you, and you always knew that, yet you never stopped following it. Even when you manage to leave it, you always look back and think you belong there. You could not be more wrong."

"Then where *do* I belong? Arkhein?"

"For now," he said, pulling away slightly. "Your true path -- the one we have put you back upon -- has brought you here, to Betedek. It does not end here unless you wish it."

"I thought you said you still needed me?"

"We do, but now that you have a better understanding of the situation, we will not force you to blindly obey us. A choice must be made. If you choose to turn away, then Betedek will become your home, and I must..." Again, there was a sense of tiredness about him. "We will find another way."

"And what if I accept this *n'toku-rejii* thing? What then?"

"Then you will also have to accept that your life is no longer entirely your own. There will be times when you may be compelled to do something and not fully understand why, or you may be asked outright by us to perform a task and you have no desire to comply, but in both cases, *you will have no choice*. That is our burden: we must sometimes cast aside our own free will in order to preserve the greater good." His gaze went to the statue behind the altar, and I could see a warm, placid smile shine out from beneath his dark hood. "But there will also be times when it all falls into place, and you will *see*, and you will *understand*...those are the times when it all becomes worthwhile." He turned towards me again. "These are things you need not concern yourself with yet, though. You need to heal first, as does Betedek. Afterward, you will need to prepare for when your time comes."

"Prepare how? And for what?"

"That is where your connection to the Light comes in. Now that you are aware of it, its presence should be much more evident at times, perhaps even overwhelming. Learn to recognize when it happens and why, so you can bring it forth whenever you wish."

"You mean I can do to you what you've been doing to me? Seeing things and stuff like that?"

"You are a long, *long* way from that," he said, shaking his head. "I mean you can use it to gain insight, to help you see and hear things that your normal senses cannot perceive. I know telling you to just sit down sometimes and...open yourself up sounds ludicrous, but I suggest you start doing it. If you do not, preparing you for your next task will take even longer, and we would rather not cut things so closely again."

I narrowed my eyes a bit and said, "Remember what I told you before about being vague? You're doing it again. Wouldn't it be easier for all concerned if you just spoke plainly?"

"No."

"*That's it?* Just 'No', and I'm supposed to be satisfied?"

"You will have to be, for now. The things you want me to tell you are still too much for you to handle." He gently placed his hands on my shoulders, saying, "I can make you a promise, however: one day, you and I will sit together like old friends, and I will answer any questions that remain. No more shadows, just truth and light. Until then, I can give you nothing but my word."

I stared as hard as I could into the depths of the man's cowl, straining to see more of him than the curve of his ashen jaw and the thin line of his mouth, but even that was denied me. "What about your name?" I asked. "If you can't reveal anything to me, not even your face, can you at least tell me your name?"

"Why does it matter?"

"Consider it...a gesture of goodwill."

The man's gaze returned to the similarly-cloaked statue behind the altar, and I had the distinct impression that perhaps he and I didn't see the same thing standing there. "If I tell you, then you must swear to never speak it to another, not until we meet in the proper manner." I agreed, and he fixed his gaze upon me once again, saying, "My name is Kavek, though I hear it very little these days."

"Why is that?"

"There is no one left to speak it," he replied -- a rather ambiguous answer, but those seemed to be his stock in trade -- then took a few steps back. "You had best be returning now, before they think you dead once again."

"Who are you...oh," I gasped, and clapped a hand over my mouth. "Oh, Jesus, I'd almost forgotten. What am I going to tell them?"

"Not a word," he said, his tone dead serious. "Let the *h'landa* take care of it. Those people may call themselves 'Guardians of the Light', but I prefer to keep them in the dark on some things."

"I wouldn't know where to begin anyways. This whole journey feels like it's taken years, but it's only been...a month? Maybe a month-and-a-half? I can't tell anymore."

"I am sorry to tell you that part will become no easier...but you need not concern yourself about that just yet. For now, I want you to go back to Betedek, heal your wounds, and learn to live again while you prepare yourself for what lies ahead. When you are ready to move on, we will let you know."

"I'll do my best 'til then, I guess."

"You always do." He gave me that placid smile again -- for all his infuriating mystery, that smile seemed like something about him I could trust. "Remember every word I have told you, and believe in them as I believe in you."

I nodded. "I'll try...Lord knows, I'll try."

His smile broke wider. "He certainly does," he said, and like the Cheshire Cat, that smile was the last I saw of him. Bright white light flooded my view, dissolving the world around me and letting me drift along for a moment before the sensations of reality began to filter back in: ugly, heavy smell of blood filling my nostrils and coating the back of my throat, torn muscle and shattered bone screaming in my left arm...and voices. They came at me from everywhere, but one sounded close, just inches from my ear. I focused on it until the words made sense. "Do not be dead," it pleaded over and over in Arkan. "Avisar hear me, do not let him be dead."

The voice sounded familiar, so I attempted to respond to it properly, croaking out, "Dimi..."

For my trouble, my broken body was quickly gathered up in a bear hug that didn't let up until I managed to let out a pitiful mewling sound. "Please forgive me, Reshard," Dimi said once he'd backed off. "I should have stood by your side, but my girls...my little one..." I heard a funny click as he swallowed hard.

I waved my good hand in a gesture of dismissal as I looked up at him through half-open eyes -- dawn had finally broken out over this world, and the sunlight was a bit too intense for me. "Is your daughter well again?" I asked, carefully pushing myself upright with his help.

"Her fever has broken, but she has not awakened. *Z'kira* Kali thinks the worst has passed for her, though."

"That is why you decided to accompany the Kana-Semeth out here," I said matter-of-factly.

He gaped at me. "How did you know they..." he sputtered, but I just waved my hand again, then turned to look around the yard. A quick head-count revealed four civilians and six soldiers, including *H'drek* Sela, who was giving out orders like she saw this sort of nightmare all the time. Two men were moving H'landa onto a hastily-made stretcher comprised of tree branches and a tied-down blanket, which I recognized as the one that usually lay on J'nath and Nina's bed. Another man nearby was readying a stretcher for me, ironically using the blanket off of *my* bed -- this struck me as funny for no good reason, and I let out a weak chuckle. Nearly everyone in the yard stopped and turned towards me when they heard it, a strange, upbeat sound in the midst of all the death and chaos Beterion had wrought.

H'drek Sela approached, glaring down at me. "I am glad you are amused by the mess you have made," she said.

"Forgive me, *d'ho-h'drek*," I answered, getting myself back under control. "It has been a long day."

I didn't think it was possible for her to look angrier than she did already, but she managed quite well. "You can expect them to become much longer, once we are through with you."

"What do you mean?" Dimi asked, obviously puzzled. "You make it sound like he was wrong to save us all."

"He knows what I refer to," she said. "Tell him, *d'ho*-Corrigan, about how you assaulted my officers, and corrupted *Lermekt* H'landa." She pointed behind her to where the lawman lay, and he stirred a little at the sound of his name. "I am sure it was easy to sway Bannen-*su* -- he is only a child, after all -- but what could you offer a Kana-Semeth that would make him betray his Oath?" I didn't dignify her with an answer, and she threw up her hands. "It does not matter. You are back in our custody now, and you will more than likely never leave it again."

"Oh, I think not," I told her, and placed my hand on the butt of my gun as I climbed unsteadily to my feet. She took a step or two back, signaling to the other officers as she did so -- swords came out as they began to close in on me, and the villagers present, Dimi included, tried to get out of the way. I knew fighting back against them was insane: I could barely stand up straight, much less shoot straight, but I wasn't about to let them put me back under lock and key. The circle of soldiers grew tighter around me, and I began to pull leather, thinking, *Forgive me, Lord. Old habits die hard...*

"Stop! I command you, *stop this!*"

The soldiers hesitated at that, yet still stood at the ready. Some of them, as well as *H'drek* Sela and myself, turned towards the voice, confused as to who the Hell was barking orders, only to see H'landa propped up on one elbow and giving us all his patented "kill-you-with-a-glance" look. His face was still far too pale, and it looked like a stiff breeze would knock him flat back onto the stretcher, but he'd somehow mustered enough strength to make himself heard. "You have no right to hold this Taran against his will," he continued, his voice straining to get the words out. "He has broken no Law, and no charge has been made against him."

His commander didn't even falter. "He is charged with the assault of three officers, as are you, *d'ho-lermekt*." She said his rank with a note of contempt.

"And what of *before* that? Show me the Law that allows us to arrest someone on the basis of their bloodline." A low murmur passed among many of those present upon hearing that.

"We did no such thing..."

"You did *worse* than that!" he yelled, spittle flying from his lips. "Both you and the short-sighted *Y'meer* decided that the Laws did not apply to him: a rational being no different than any man or woman standing here, save for his place of birth." He managed to sit up and looked about the yard at the villagers gathered there. "All of you have seen Richard since he arrived in this world. Some of you have come to know him quite well. At any time, did you ever think him to be soulless creature? Did you ever doubt that Avisar laid His hand upon the brow of every Taran and gave them the same sort of heart and mind as every Arkan?" He turned to me, and in a much more sedate tone said, "I thought those things and more, for over half my life, but I can no longer do so. We are *kanituiben*, his blood is mine." He looked back to his commander with a glare. "And if you condemn one Taran, *d'ho-h'drek*, then you must condemn us all."

"What sort of nonsense is that?" she answered, almost laughing. "Are you claiming to be Taran *yourself*, now?"

H'landa said nothing more, just reached up and scratched beneath his chin...at a full day's worth of stubble. We'd been going nonstop since the night before last, and for the first time in his life, shaving behind closed doors must have slipped his mind. Frankly, I hadn't even noticed until he pointed it out. Neither had anyone else, from what I could tell, and who could blame them for missing it? There were a helluva lot more important things to pay attention to in that yard than whether or not H'landa had a few whiskers on his jaw. The realization of it, though -- or maybe just the sight of it on him -- made Sela blanch, her eyes widening so much I thought they'd fall right out of her head. "Not possible," was all she could manage to say, and rather quietly at that. "This cannot be possible..."

"I assure you, it is quite possible," the lawman told her, "and I know of at least three people who can verify it, two of them being Kana-Semeth with very bright collars, shall we say. I can also assure you that, while it may be thin these days, the line of Taran blood runs the length of the H'landa name...*the full length*." Those last three words, which meant nothing to me, visibly shook the *h'drek* to the core. "Promise me you will tell the *Y'meer* that when you go back to Dak-Taorin empty-handed, then ask them to look a little harder at the Laws they claim to know so well."

Flustered beyond belief, she stared at him for a couple seconds before recovering herself. She turned to the nearest soldier and said, "I want these two bound and put under constant watch, no exceptions." The soldier looked at us, but didn't move. "You heard me, *damekt!*" she barked at him, not even bothering with the honorific. "Take them into custody!"

I thought the guy was about to buckle, but he stood firm. "With all respect, *d'ho-h'drek*...this is a mistake. We are supposed to protect the people, and if *Lermekt* H'landa speaks the truth..."

"Nothing is true until the *Y'meer* say it is!" She pointed at a soldier closer to me and repeated her order -- he took a couple steps toward me, then Dimi stepped in front of him.

"If you arrest these men," Dimi said firmly, "then you had best do the same with me."

"Fine," *H'drek* Sela said, "take him as well."

Another one of the villagers stepped forward to stand beside Dimi -- I remembered working with the guy during the barn-raising -- and the rest quickly followed suit, making a half-circle around H'landa and myself. The first soldier joined our group, as well two others, who took up position next to the lawman in a show of support for their fellow officer.

H'drek Sela stared at us all. Outnumbered and outgunned, she'd have no choice but to concede defeat, especially once word reached everyone back at the meeting hall that the Kana-Semeth seemed to be making up new rules. "What in Avisar's name has gotten into you people?" she said.

I gave her a shrug and replied in English, "Reckon Avisar's on *my* side."

* * * * * *

None of Beterion's victims recovered immediately. Once we returned to the meeting hall, I found that some had actually gotten worse, which took me a while to make sense of. Eventually I figured that when we'd been fighting back against the demon (and especially when it had been losing), it must've siphoned off these poor people's souls even harder than before, wringing them dry like dishrags to give itself strength. In the first couple of days after our victory, eight more people died. They just didn't have anything left, and we were all scared of who might follow them. I was concerned for each and every one of them, but the majority of my worries were for J'nath. Though the plague had technically dissipated the moment the Crossroad was destroyed, he still looked like he was caught in the throes of it, his face gaunt and a reedy whistle escaping his lips with every breath. *Some may recover, and some may not*, the man I now knew as Kavek had told me. *Wait and hope*. Wouldn't you know it, those were the two hardest things for me to do, but dammit, I did my best. I spent every spare moment at J'nath's bedside, talking to him, begging him to wake up, promising him a thousand stupid things if he'd only open his eyes and say something. There were times when I couldn't help but wonder just how badly Beterion had hurt him, and when I looked across the bed at Nina sitting on the other side, I would often see the same question in her eyes. Even the middle of the night, I would wake up and find her there, one hand clasping J'nath's while the other held Pietruvek close as he slept, his head nestled in the hollow of his mother's shoulder, looking more like the boy he was then the man he wanted to be. One glance at her was all it took to learn J'nath's condition, and whether or not anything had changed. Nothing ever did.

On the upside, the Kana-Semeth became downright reasonable as the days passed. It didn't take long for *H'drek* Sela to realize all the shit about my "status" was just that compared to helping Betedek put itself back together. First thing she did was send one of her soldiers back to Dak-Taorin to inform the Y'meer that the situation had become a bit more complicated (and to relay H'landa's revelation, I'm sure). The rest were partnered up with villagers and assigned to various places that needed "repair", which was the euphemism that quickly sprang up for any spot possibly containing dead bodies along with actual physical damage. For example, the field around the Crossroad needed *a lot* of "repair". Though I was hampered by my broken arm, I volunteered to help out with that task: I had caused the mess out there, and it didn't feel right having other people take care of it without me at least being present to take some blame for it. So I bore the stench and helped haul bodies and prayed that, whatever may lay ahead on the path God had in mind for me, it wouldn't include any more scenes like this. Once was enough, I felt.

Late on the second day, one of the victims finally awoke: Ari, the woman I'd been accused of "cursing" by her husband Noren. She was still quite weak, and her voice could not rise above a whisper, but she was coherent...and most importantly, she'd come back from whatever abyss Beterion had tried to drag her into, and we hoped that meant others would soon follow. A sense of relief washed over everyone at the thought of that, myself included, burning away the darkness that had engulfed our hearts from constant worry. We could all see now that Betedek would survive this, despite the scars, and even *H'drek* Sela begrudgingly admitted to me that perhaps -- just perhaps -- all the trouble I'd caused with my breakout could be overlooked, considering the "miracle" I'd pulled off here.

H'landa had become rather quiet since his speech out in the yard, though I figured he was just sulking because *Z'kira* Kali was making him take it easy. The wounds he'd sustained from Beterion trying to tear him apart, coupled with a significant loss of blood (and maybe some of his soul), would probably keep him off his feet for weeks -- that's an awful blow for somebody who's used to being in the thick of it. It also probably didn't help his mood much to see me walking around with just a few cuts and bruises and my arm in a sling, but the truth was I felt better with every passing day. Sure, I was far from being in top shape, and every once in a while I had a dizzy spell, but other than that I was fine. Beterion had marred my body, but my soul had come out of this stronger than before, and it showed. Sometimes H'landa would give me an odd look, and I'd swear he was jealous about what happened to me, but he never broached the subject. I wouldn't have known what to tell him if he had: *Oh yeah, God says I'm to be His earthbound enforcer, so I guess that makes me...what? A prophet? An angel? Completely nuts? Please, cousin, help me get a handle on this.*

When the two of us did talk, it was pretty mundane stuff. He usually asked how things were progressing outside the meeting hall, since he'd been confined to one of the makeshift beds. We also discussed what may or may not happen to us once everything was back to normal. "At worst, we will spend time in the workhouse," he said. "We may get your adjoining rooms after all." When I told him about *H'drek* Sela's comment, he damn-near laughed himself silly. "Oh, I must have truly terrified her if she is saying things like that! I wish I could see the faces of the *Y'meer* when they hear about all this." A wistful look came into his eye. "All this time, I kept the truth hidden, and now it may be the only thing that saves us."

"I don't get it. Are you talking about telling Sela you're part Taran? How's that help?"

He smiled at me. "I would not expect you to know...and I suppose very few people outside of the Kana-Semeth even know. For all who wear the uniform, however, it is one of the first lessons learned: the founder of the Kana-Semeth, the man who wrote the Laws the *Y'meer* cling so tightly to, was my ancestor and namesake. I am the last of a line of soldiers that runs three hundred years long."

I stared at him, dumbfounded, as I tried to puzzle out just what he was implying. "So, if the H'landa bloodline was started by a Taran," I ventured, "then that means the Laws were written by someone who was part Taran, and were enforced by his descendants for centuries..."

"And if the *Y'meer* declare that Tarans have no rights under Arkan Laws," he finished for me, "then they must also declare that those same Laws are void because the man who wrote them was of Taran ancestry." He drew a circle in the air with his finger. "As we say back in Nevasile: They have woven a rope that has no ends."

I shook my head. "You've got to be shitting me."

"I shit you not."

We both sat there silent for a moment, and then burst out laughing. I doubted it was going to be as cut and dry as H'landa made it out to be, but some of the weight had been lifted off my shoulders. The Kana-Semeth would have to tread lightly if they made any charges against us, for fear of negating their own existence. I hoped they were really squirming back in Dak-Taorin over this whole debacle, but also that they wouldn't take forever to get back to us.

Around the fifth day, a small semblance of normality returned to the village as those who were well enough began to return to their homes. The doors to the meeting hall stood open all the time now, the warm Spring air wafting in and clearing the place of the smell of death.

Riders set out to the surrounding villages to let the
refugees know that Betedek was safe once again, though
none of us knew if they would be willing to return. If they
did, we'd welcome them all back without question. About
half of the victims had awakened by then, and the others
were looking better and would probably recover soon.
The lone exception was J'nath, who seemed to look worse
every day, although *Z'kira* Kali said I was imagining it. I
didn't tell her or anybody else about the horrible notion
growing in my mind: since Beterion couldn't kill me and
I'd pulled H'landa from its clutches, it had taken all its
anger out on J'nath, tearing out his soul and leaving us
nothing but a breathing, mindless husk. I had no idea if it
was possible for that monster do to such a thing, but
whenever I saw J'nath lying there, still as a corpse, it
seemed *very* possible.

By the time the Kana-Semeth reinforcements
arrived, most of the major problems around the village had
been taken care of, but they rode their mounts into the
main square like they were our saviors anyhow. The
Y'meer had seen fit to send us a dozen soldiers, for all the
good they'd do us now. I was happier to see the supplies
and two additional doctors they'd brought along. H'landa
and I were sitting on the front steps of the meeting hall
sharing a smoke when they rode up -- he'd talked *Z'kira*
Kali a few days before into letting him move around on a
pair of crutches, and he used them to hobble over to the
newcomers as they dismounted. Not surprisingly, they
were taken aback by his appearance: barefooted, banged-
up, in a borrowed shirt and breeches to replace his ruined
uniform, and sporting a full, neatly-trimmed beard that
was coming along nicely for only being a week or so old.
"*Dandoa, d'ho-tekarrel*," he said to the lead officer,
leaning forward on his crutches as best he could, "and
welcome to the village of Betedek, from one officer to
another."

"Are you *Lermekt* Jamin H'landa?" the officer
asked, looking doubtful.

"I am Jamin H'landa, but whether I still hold my rank depends on what word you bring from the *Y'meer*." He nodded his head in my direction, and I got off the steps and began to walk over to them, cigar clamped between my teeth. "We hope they have come to a decision about us, for our patience has grown thin," he continued.

"I do have orders," the *tekarrel* said, "but I am to give them to *H'drek* Sela, not..."

"Do not worry, we will see that she receives them." He held out his hand, saying, "Unless you have been told otherwise, I am still Station Officer here. I have just as much right to see them as the *h'drek*."

The officer grumbled, but eventually produced a message cylinder from one of his saddlebags and handed it over. H'landa broke the seal and spent a minute or two looking over the papers, occasionally flipping back to another page. When I couldn't take it anymore, I blurted out in English, "Well, are we going to jail or what?"

"I have been suspended for disobedience and -- I love this part -- 'withholding information'. Fifty days, starting when I return to Dak-Taorin." He smiled and added, "That should be more than enough time for me to fully recover."

"Hooray for you. What does it say about *me*?"

H'landa ignored me and began to roll up the letter. "There was a packet being delivered along with this," he said to the *tekarrel* in Arkan. "Do you have it?"

The officer went back into the saddlebag and produced a small leather portfolio. When he held it out, H'landa told him to give it to me instead. I took it, somewhat confused, and propped it in the crook of my injured arm so I could rifle through it with my good hand. All it contained was three sheets of heavy paper filled with column after column of Arkan text -- at the bottom of every page were nine embossed seals, a name printed beside each one. Unfortunately, my inability to read Arkan well had once again become one Hell of a snag.

"Okay, I give up," I told H'landa. "I can tell it's about me, but not whether it's good news or bad."

"It is neither." He gave the cylinder back to the officer, then plucked each page out of my hand as he explained their meaning. "The first letter verifies you as a true Taran and tells of your arrival in our world. The second declares you to be a full citizen in all the Guarded Lands of Arkhein, granting you all rights and binding you to all Laws, present and future. The third is a Right of Descent for the bloodline of 'Korrigan': it renders these documents valid for as long as your name carries on. Each of these has been endorsed by the *Y'meer*, which makes it just as binding as the Laws they watch over." He tucked them back into the portfolio with great care before giving them back to me. "This packet, for good or ill, contains the rest of your life, along with the lives of all that may follow you."

"So that's it, then?" I asked in disbelief. "I'm a free man, just like that?"

"You are more than that, you know," he answered, and I gave him a look out of the corner of my eye, wondering if he was referring to what I thought he was referring to. Instead, he laid a hand on my shoulder and said, "You are an Arkan. Not born of this land, but you are a part of it now."

"I suppose I am." It had taken more than three pieces of paper to make me that, though. Having people who cared about me no matter what, along with a willingness to do anything to help those people when they needed me...that's what really made me part of this place. To me, I became an Arkan the moment I returned here of my own free will, and I didn't need the Kana-Semeth to tell me what I'd figured out more than a week ago.

Later on, H'landa and I broke the news about us being mostly off the hook to *H'drek* Sela, and it didn't take a mind reader to know that she wasn't happy about it. She probably felt we'd made a fool of her...and I didn't feel the least bit bad about that, not after how she'd tried to lock me away. Nina and Pietruvek, however, we overjoyed to hear that the whole matter had been settled in my favor. I had the boy read the papers aloud twice -- once in Arkan and again in English -- as the three of us sat in a tight cluster around J'nath's bed. I listened intently to his translation, making sure there were no hidden loopholes anywhere in the documents. In fact, I was so focused on Pietruvek's voice that I jumped a little when Nina suddenly told her son to stop reading. We looked over and saw her leaning close to J'nath's face, her eyes squeezed shut in concentration. "What is wrong?" I asked in Arkan. "Should I get one of the *z'kira*?"

She opened her eyes and sat up, her expression landing somewhere between elation and confusion. "I think...I think he is trying to speak, but the word makes no sense to me."

"What does it sound like?"

Her brow furrowed. "'Saith'...is it a Taran word? 'Saith'?"

Rather than tell her no, I bent forward myself, placing my ear inches away from J'nath's mouth -- I could feel his breath on the side of my face, but that was all. *She imagined it*, I thought. *He must have gotten one of those funny rattles in chest again, and she thought he was talking.* I was trying to think of a good way to tell her so when J'nath drew in a quick, sharp breath and let it out slowly, carrying with it one clear syllable:

Safe.

I jerked my head up, my eyes meeting Nina's. I gave her a brief nod, and one hand flew up to her mouth while the other wrapped around the slim fingers on J'nath's right hand. I bent down again and whispered in his ear, "That's right, J'nath, I'm safe now. Everyone's safe. But we've all been really worried about you, especially Nina." I glanced up at her and said in Arkan, "Can you squeeze her hand, show her you are back with us?"

He responded almost immediately, grasping her hand with just enough strength to let us know he really heard me. The tears began to run down Nina's cheeks not long after that as she pulled him gently into her arms, never letting go of his hand the whole time. Pietruvek dropped the papers on the floor and damn-near knocked me over trying to get past me to his father. He grabbed J'nath's other hand and whispered something, then let out a shout a moment afterward as J'nath finally opened his eyes.

All the commotion had drawn a few spectators, including one of the Kana-Semeth doctors. I stepped up and asked them all to stay back for now, to which the doctor objected until I explained that he'd been unconscious for half a month. "What J'nath needs at the moment is his family," I said. "They are the reason he came back from the brink of death."
She agreed with me, as did all the other people gathered round, so we stood there quietly as the three of them huddled together, crying with relief.

CHAPTER 18

"Well, here we are again, saying our goodbyes." H'landa and I were standing at the foot of the meeting hall's steps, doing our best to stay out of the way of the Kana-Semeth filing in and out. It'd been more than a month since the Crossroad's destruction, and the powers-that-be had decided there was little more these soldiers could do here. Orders had arrived the day before to pack up and return to Dak-Taorin, minus one man they'd chosen to serve as Station Officer for a time. Obviously, that wasn't H'landa. "You sure you don't want to stick around?" I asked him in English. "I can think of worse places to sit out your suspension."

He shook his head. "I have to stay in the stronghold for the duration. Besides, I want some time to myself. I have some things I need to sort out in my mind."

"You're not thinking about quitting, are you?"

"Not exactly." He shifted on his crutches. His legs, while healing fine, were still kind of weak -- he'd be going back to Dak-Taorin in a wagon, not a saddle. "It is just that, in the past couple of months, too many things I knew as truth have changed."

"Yeah, I know what you mean."

"*Nee*, you do not. I hope you never do, and as soon as I am well enough, I plan on making sure you never will."

"What are you talking about?"

He shot me that jealous look again, and I still didn't know why. "Will you do something for me, as a friend and *kanitu*?"

"Depends on what it is."

"Stay in Betedek. Until I send word to you, do not go beyond the borders of this village, even if *he* tells you to do so."

I had a pretty good idea which "he" H'landa was referring to. "I can't promise you that. I'm kind of obligated, I think."

He muttered something under his breath before responding, "Can you promise then that you will not follow this man blindly? If he gives you an order that feels wrong, do not obey it." His good eye locked onto mine. "Remember, he may speak for God, but that does not mean he is delivering the correct message."

"Alright, I promise." I didn't have any problem with that, being the sort of person who questions everything already...including why H'landa was acting like this.

Before I could ask him about his odd behavior, however, one of the officers coming down the steps stopped beside H'landa and tapped him on the shoulder, saying that it was time to leave. "What about that bundle I gave you?" H'landa asked in Arkan. "If you lose that sword..."

"All has been taken care of, I swear," the officer reassured him. One of the villagers had found his sword and my second gun while we'd been clearing out the field around the Crossroad. I'd offered to let the lawman keep the revolver after I'd cleaned all the dirt and muck out of the mechanisms, but he turned it down -- while he found it to be a useful weapon, it was too loud for his tastes. He did, however, admire the cavalry sword I'd brought back with me, but I wasn't about to give him that.

The officer said he'd help H'landa up into the wagon, and H'landa gave the poor guy a glare that clearly said he'd get on board when he was damn good and ready. "Keeps treating me like an old man," he muttered in English, watching the officer walk over to one of the wagons, climb in, and root around the items on board until he picked up a bundle about the right size for the lawman's sword. He carefully laid it back down in an obvious spot.

"Admit it, you like the attention," I said with a grin.

"The sooner I can stand on my own, the happier I will be." He turned to look up the steps and into the now-empty hall -- the last of the victims had been moved out a week ago. Those who had survived the ordeal, including J'nath, were all now safe in their homes, surrounded by warmth and family. "What we accomplished here is worth the pain, though. We defended the Light and held back the Darkness, just as we always swore we would."

"'We' swore?"

"My family, as well as the Kana-Semeth. Part of the Oath every officer must recite has us swear to defend the Light with our last dying breath." He squared his shoulders and intoned in Arkan, "If we succumb to the Darkness, so shall the world."

One of the officers nearby called back, "Our faith shall never falter!"

"And our strength shall never fade!" said another, picking up the thread. Both of them gave H'landa a salute I'd seen a few times in the stronghold: the thumb and first two fingers on the left hand laid over the Kana-Semeth emblem by the right shoulder, then brought up to touch the center of the forehead, and finally drawn down before them, making a vertical line in the air.

Even though he wasn't in uniform, H'landa returned the gesture, a slight smile on his face. I could tell right then and there that he was born to be a soldier and nothing else. "I hold dear every word of that, as well," he told me in English. "Even when I was helping you escape, I kept my Oath in mind, and I am mindful of it now as I leave you. Always remember, Richard, to do what is best for the world, not just yourself." He then held out his right hand rather stiffly, and when I didn't respond immediately, he said, "This is what you showed me, is it not?"

I blinked, then laughed and gave him a good firm handshake. When I did so, I felt something shift under my left arm, and I said, "Oh, I almost forgot to give you this." I handed him an oblong package wrapped in cloth. "Just a little goodbye gift, straight from New Mexico."

He unwrapped it and stared at the item in confusion. "What is it?"

"Good ol' American whiskey. I figure since you can't drink any Arkan booze either, this will take real good care of you."

"You do not want to keep this?"

"Nah, I kind of gave up the stuff a couple of months ago. Bad for my health."

He laughed, then rewrapped the bottle and said, "I have nothing to give you in return."

"Forget it. You send me a note every once in a while, let me know how my favorite cousin is doing, and we'll call it even. *Kai?*"

"*Kai.*" We shook hands again, and he made his way over to the wagon, shrugging off help when it was offered. Once he'd settled in, the mounted officers began to file out of the square and head for the main road leading away from Betedek. The wagons landed up somewhere in the middle, and I waved to H'landa before he passed out of my sight. He waved back from his seat next to one of the doctors, smiling and holding aloft the whiskey bottle.

Damn, I wish I could be there to see him get soused on that stuff, I thought.

*   *   *   *   *   *

Learn to live again. Every day, I was reminded of what Kavek told me, for it didn't just apply to me, but to all of Betedek. We all wanted things to be normal again, but it didn't seem right for us to go on like we had before the plague. Some of it was guilt as well as grief, I'm sure, an inability to deal with the fact that we'd survived while so many had not. I saw quite a few people in the village with thin, white cloth ribbons wound around their left palm and wrist, usually marked with Arkan symbols. I recalled seeing some during the funeral I'd attended months earlier, and when I asked Nina about it, she explained they were tokens of mourning, worn to honor family members who'd passed away. As Spring changed over to Summer, I saw the ribbons less and less, and the pall that had fallen over Betedek slowly began to lift.

Harmony returned to our household much quicker than others, probably because no great loss had befallen us personally. That's not to say we were unaffected, for J'nath had emerged from the Great Plague a changed man: he tired easily, and his whole personality seemed only a shadow of what it had been before. Every once in a while, though, the old J'nath would resurface, and make us briefly forget the man who tended to nod off in front of the hearth before Last Light, wrapped in blankets to ward off a chill no one else felt. It pained me to watch him struggle through his bad days, but I just kept reminding myself that the worst was over, there was nothing left to worry about.

I couldn't have been more wrong.

* * * * * *

The day started simply enough: Pietruvek and I took care of some chores around the yard and in the barn before running some errands over in Betedek. A couple of people inquired about J'nath, and I was glad to tell them that he was having one of his better days. "You should bring him along next time you come by," one of the shopkeepers told me. "I never see him anymore." I said that I'd do my best, but privately thought that, if he missed J'nath so much, he should come to the house instead of making J'nath wear himself out with the trip.

We headed for home ourselves about an hour before midday, splitting between us what few sundries we'd picked up. As we walked, I cast my eyes about the field where I had fought to save this world only a couple of months before. No signs of the battle remained, save for a slight depression in the earth that marked the Crossroad's previous location. Many of the villagers had talked of putting a memorial of some sort on the spot, but I'd been happy with filling it in with dirt and letting the grass grow over it. When we neared the spot, I noticed J'nath in the distance, sitting on the bench that ran alongside the barn. I raised a hand and called out to him, but oddly, he didn't acknowledge us until we were almost to the house, and even then all he did was stand up and watch as we approached. When we drew closer, I could see something thin and flat in J'nath's hand, and he kept tapping it against his leg in a nervous gesture. "Good to see you getting some sun," I told him in Arkan. "You have been hiding in the house too often lately."

He looked up at me briefly, saying nothing, and then turned to Pietruvek. "Go inside, my son," he said. "Reshard and I have some things to discuss."

I was about to ask him what the big deal was when I finally realized what he kept tapping against his leg: a folded sheet of paper, speckled with dried bloodstains and bearing J'nath's name in shaky Arkan script. A wave of numbness seized my heart, then spread up to my face and down my arms...I couldn't believe this was happening, I couldn't believe I'd *forgotten* that!

Without a word, I handed Pietruvek the bundle of goods I'd been carrying. His eyes met mine, and I'm sure he saw the distress I was in, although he'd have no idea why -- he didn't leave right away, just looked at me for a moment, then his father, before heading inside. As soon as the boy was through the door, I opened my mouth to speak, not sure of what I was going to say, or even if I could find my voice, but J'nath cut me off before I had a chance. "Not out here," he said, pointing to the open barn door. Somehow, I managed to move my legs in the right direction. I stopped short when I reached the entrance, though: I caught a glimpse of a rope hanging down from the loft, and for a moment I thought I saw a noose at the end of it. Once I'd convinced myself it was merely a rope, I stepped inside. J'nath came in behind me and pulled the door partway shut, the narrow shaft of light pouring in through the crack emphasizing how thin he'd become -- Nina had hemmed most of his clothes to fit his new, slimmer build, but they still tended to hang on him at odd angles. A beat-up wooden crate lay not far from the doorway, and J'nath sat down on it, while I drifted to the other side of the barn, trying my best to sink into the shadows there.

"I went down into the cellar today," he said in English. "I have not been down there since I fell ill. I do not remember making the mess that I found, but I did my best to clean it up. I stopped cleaning when I got to the table." He then held up the letter, the broken seal quite visible. "I presume thee made a mistake, leaving it there?"

"Not at first," I answered, my voice barely above a whisper. "I just...I thought you had a right to know."

"Did I have none before? Was it easier to tell me thinking I may die, and knowing thou would be long gone?"

"Yes."

He sat up a little straighter at that, temporarily silenced by my bluntness. When he recovered, the words came out more slowly: "If Beterion had not...resurfaced...if all this had not happened...would thou have ever told me?"

I rubbed my palm over my left forearm. The bandage was gone, the bones fully healed, but I could sometimes still feel the break, just as the scar that monster had given me across my jaw would sometimes ache like a fresh wound. "I don't know," I said, "maybe...it just didn't seem like a smart move at the time, okay?"

"And what of now? Canst thou tell me now?"

"Tell you *what*? You *know* already, the proof's in your hand."

"I know nothing, Reshard. What this paper says and what I have seen are two different things." He gave the letter a good shake. "*This* speaks of a man who has no reason to trust or care about anyone, a man who believes himself to be less than nothing. I have seen shadows of this man, *kai*, but mostly my eyes have seen a man who has suffered many pains, yet still stands while others fall. *That* man has a sense of worth, for if he did not, he would have given up and died long ago."

If only you knew, I thought, but said nothing.

"I am not trying to judge thee," he continued. "I only want to *kedda* how someone who seems so good in his heart could do these terrible things. Please, just tell me the truth, and I will never ask thee again."

"You wouldn't understand," I said, turning away from him. I couldn't bear to see his face, and I was growing ashamed to show him mine. "I just sort of...fell into it, and I couldn't pull myself back out. I tried to, but it was hard. *It was too damn hard.*" I stepped deeper into shadow, to the barn's back wall, and stared off into the corner. "It's kind of like treading water, I guess: you keep kicking and hoping somebody will come along to pull you up, but you tire out and the water gets deeper, and you start to realize nobody's coming, and then you think, 'Why the Hell am I even trying? I should just give up and drown.'" I let out a long, shuddering sigh as I leaned against the wall, still facing the corner. "I've been drowning for ten years now, give or take. I've cheated, lied, stole...when I started to kill, the water got *real* deep. Despite it all, there were still times when I could keep my head above water, stay on the straight and narrow -- sometimes a couple months, usually only a day -- and then something would happen, and I'd slip right back under, but dammit, I kept on trying and trying and *it was never good enough*!" I slammed the side of my fist against the wall, tears starting to roll down my cheeks. "The last time I tried was about a year ago. I wanted out so badly, but Reeves...he ruined it, and I almost killed him, and then Stewart...Stewart died. He was still a kid, for Christ's sake, he never...I tried to save him, but I couldn't do it, and he..."

I lifted my hands up, only to let them drop in a gesture of defeat. "I stopped giving a damn about myself after that. Whenever I wasn't planning a job, I'd either get dead drunk or try to kill myself, 'cause I knew by then there was no way out of that life. Doesn't matter how far you run, or how much good you do, or that God Himself comes down and says, 'This guy messed up, but in the end he's alright'...it always catches up with you." I sniffled, rubbed the back of my hand under my nose, and said, "Look, if you just...if you could just give me the night to get some things together, I'll be out of here by morning. I swear, you'll never see me again."

"I never asked thee to leave," J'nath replied.

"Not yet, but you will. You'd be crazy not to."

"And why is that? Art thou truly a dangerous man? Is thy soul as black as thou seems to think it is?"

"*I don't know!*" I screamed at him. "Stop asking me stuff like that, 'cause I don't know *what* I am anymore!"

"Then tell me what thou *wants* to be. Not a murderer, that is certain, for it appears to pain thee as badly as thy victims."

"Some people...some of them I *wanted* to kill, but the rest...there's times when I close my eyes, and I can see them, and it...it's like a knife in my guts...gives me nightmares." I looked over at him, still sitting on the crate, leaning forward with his forearms resting on his knees. "Don't you get it?" I said. "It doesn't matter what I want, that shit's always going to be there, and as soon as everybody else finds out about this, that's all they'll see when they look at me."

He shook his head, saying, "I saw more than that. I would not have allowed *Lermekt* H'landa to make me thy *gama* if I had not."

"That doesn't count, you didn't know back then." But then I saw the look in his eyes, and I realized I wasn't the only one keeping secrets all this time. "You found the wanted poster I had in my pocket, didn't you?" I asked breathlessly. "You've known exactly what I was ever since I got here."

"Again, I knew only what the paper told me," he explained, "and like thy letter, I found it quite by accident: when thou arrived, thy clothes were soaked with both blood and water, so we emptied thy pockets to dry them out. When I came across the paper, it took me some time to puzzle out what it was, for thy written language has changed somewhat in five hundred years, just as thy spoken form has. Once I translated it fully, I was quite shocked."

"I'm sorry, J'nath," I said, turning away again. "I'm sorry I didn't..."

"Let me finish. That paper spoke of a dangerous creature, just as this one does, but at the time, all I saw was an injured man -- possibly a *dying* man -- and Arkans do not believe any wicked deed warrants death."

"'No life shall ever be valued over another, and no death shall ever be acceptable'," I recited in Arkan.

He cocked an eyebrow in surprise. "*Kai*, that is the First Law," he continued in English. "I did not feel thy alien origins should exempt thee from it, and I certainly did not feel it was proper to judge thee solely by what I had read. Mostly, though, I wanted that information to be *wrong*. Thy presence justified a centuries-long vigil, something both I and my ancestors had long hoped for, but to have those hopes fulfilled by a...a criminal..." He flushed a little and cast his eyes to the floor, saying, "For me, pride overtook common sense. I thought that, even if thou were a criminal, I could control thee, but I lost my patience after our argument on Halitova, and cast thee unto the mercy of the Kana-Semeth. I did not even realize until thou came to me in the square days later how poorly I had been treating thee."

"How poorly *you* treated *me*? What're you..."

"I treated thee like an *object*, Reshard, not a person. I had been looking upon thee as another artifact to be studied and shown off, barely considering thy thoughts and feelings until thou became...how does thou say it...'riled up'. Had thou not lashed out at me during the festival, I may have never stopped." He held up the letter again and said, "Thou wrote of thy wish to be what I needed, but in truth, *I* wish I had been what *thee* needed, and not a self-centered man, near-blind to the fears of a lost soul. I let my own expectations get in the way whenever I looked at thee, and it was not until thou tried to apologize to me that I saw the true Reshard Corrigan, stripped of all his anger and bluster. Despite what I knew, I saw no killer there, no criminal. Looking back, I believe I caught a glimpse of what Avisar must see within thee: vast potential, slowly withering away from years of neglect." I stared at him, speechless, as he explained, "Pietruvek told me of thy visions, or at least what he knows of them, and of how Avisar guided thee to defeat Beterion. I think I may have even seen some of the battle in my fever-dreams, but they have become rather hazy. But I do not need to recall them to know that there is something inside of thee that, if allowed to flourish, could become a grand sight to behold. Before that can happen, though, I think thou needs to face who thou used to be, and I do not believe thou should have to do that alone."

J'nath fell silent after that, and I didn't bother to fill that silence, I just let it hang between us as I thought about all he said, and what Kavek had said as well. Since the beginning of this whole ordeal, all I'd been able to see was death and destruction, because that's what I was accustomed to seeing. Even when I was trying to reform myself, I was only thinking of it as a means of escaping death, nothing more. But now, the truth became clear: this was never about death, only life. Saving lives, changing lives...

My life.

I could feel fresh tears trickling down my face as I realized that God didn't just bring me to Arkhein to save others, but also to save *me*, to remove me from an environment that was destroying me. The end of one life,

the beginning of another. The outlaw had to die so the
n'toku-rejii could live. Kavek had tried to tell me that the
first time I'd met him, but I'd been too stupid to
understand. I had to learn a new language first, a new way
to see, or else I never would have been able to do what
was needed. But bringing me here was only part of
solution: if I wanted to fully live up to what was expected
of me, I had to shake the last bits of dirt and dust from that
old life out of my soul...and J'nath was right, I shouldn't
do it alone. "It's going to take a long time," I said to him
hoarsely. "This isn't just one little incident we're talking
about."

"I have time," he answered with a hint of a smile.
"Tell me what thou can, however long it takes. I only
wish to help thee, not judge thee."

"But you will, I think. You won't be able to stop
yourself, and once you know it all, I don't think you'll be
able to forgive me."

"I can never grant thee forgiveness," he said, then
stood up and crossed the distance between us, stepping out
of the band of sunlight and into the shadows surrounding
me. "Whatever thy crimes, only Avisar can truly forgive
them...and by bringing thee to us, I believe He has begun
to do that."

I wiped my eyes as I tried not to break down
again. I felt weak and sick but, strangely enough, better.
The secrets were gone now...well, almost gone.
"Don't...please, don't tell..." I gestured vaguely towards
the house and Betedek.

"No one else shall know unless thou wishes it."
He placed his hands on my shoulders and looked up at me
-- I could see numerous white roots in his dark hairline
where there used to be none. "Nor shall we speak of this
unless thou speaks first. I shall not force thee anymore."

"*K'sai*," I said, and swallowed hard. "Can
we...can we go in the house now? I need some time to...to
figure out how to..." I couldn't put my need into words,
but he understood. He stepped aside and let me lead the

way out of the shadows and back into the strong light of midday. I squinted at the brightness, but the warmth felt good on my face.

It took a long time, but eventually, he did hear it all. I started with the bank robbery in Barrelhead a lifetime ago, then just let things spill out when they came to mind, relaying my experiences in random order. I told him about all the death I'd seen, all the scars I'd collected...the more I spoke, it seemed, the more I remembered. J'nath barely questioned me during those times, just letting me ramble on until I was finished with whatever I was trying to say. Sometimes it would take me a few minutes, sometimes hours, but he never complained. Once, after telling him about what I felt was a rather cold-blooded incident, I asked him if he thought I was (at least back then) an evil man. He sat quietly for a few minutes before answering, "Once, I may have agreed with that, but now I have seen true evil. We both have, and we have both been at the mercy of true evil. The evil wrought by men is nothing compared to what Beterion has wrought, for an evil man can still find redemption, as thou has."

Until the day I die, I'll love J'nath for saying that.

EPILOGUE

Not fair it's not fair I was so close!
    Its talons clawed in vain at the spots where the
holes once opened, misshapen teeth champing at nothing.
The explosions had not killed it, no, nothing could do that,
but they burned, almost as badly as that accursed Heart
burned. It would take years to repair the damage the
Outlaw had done to its being, but even after it finished
healing itself, it would still be trapped. In its twisted mind,
it could hear the Other laughing at its pain. The Outlaw
and the H'landa laughed as well, believing themselves
superior to an entity that had existed for billions of years.
And the Priest...no, he would not laugh, not aloud. He
knew the consequences of open mockery.
    This isn't the end, it thought, turning away from
the sealed portals and gathering together the frayed
remnants of itself, concentrating on reforming and
strengthening all of its parts back into the whole. *Let the
Other have its reprieve. Let the meat-bags have their
"victory". There are other ways out of this prison.
Longer, slower ways, but the path has become twice as
easy as of late. I will be free again.*
    And we will have our revenge.

ACKNOWLEDGEMENTS

Right of the bat, I want to thank the team that helped me put this book together once I decided to go into self-publishing: Kerrie Moyer for editing the manuscript in every form it's taken (including handwritten lines on looseleaf paper), Bill Steveling for always helping out when I ran into computer trouble, Matt Erkhart for all the beautiful art he supplied (as well as thinking up Beterion's lovely nickname), and Stan Timmons for supplying the cover blurb. I also want to thank the people who read the manuscript in its various stages over the years, gave me advice when I got stuck on something, or just encouraged me to keep on writing no matter what: Jennifer King, Lysha Fetty, Johanna O'Bryan, Chantell Brettell Steveling, Mike Bodie, Father Robert Slaton, Jimmy Palmiotti, the gang at Idlewilder.proboards.com, all the members of the "Wild Bunch" (you know who you are), my Mom, my husband, Dad & Charlotte, and my in-laws LaDonna & Ricky. If I left somebody off the list, please remember that I have a brain like a sieve...anybody who knows me should be well aware of that by now.

Last but not least, I want to thank you, dear reader, for picking up this book and giving it a chance. It's been a long, hard road getting *Swords & Sixguns* out into the world for all to see, but we made it, and I hope you'll stick around to see where Richard goes next.

ABOUT THE AUTHOR

At the age of five, Susan Hillwig decided she wanted to be a cartoonist when she grew up. By her twenties, she realized she was a much better writer than an artist (though she's still known to doodle when the mood strikes). Somewhere in between, she developed an unladylike obsession with comic books, sci-fi/fantasy, horror, and Westerns, as evidenced by her blog, *One Fangirl's Opinion* (susanhillwig.blogspot.com), and her occasional articles for the online 'zine *DC in the '80s* (dcinthe80s.blogspot.ca/p/home-page.html).

Swords & Sixguns: An Outlaw's Tale is her first novel, with more to come. Go to her blog as well as facebook.com/SwordsAndSixguns for news about upcoming releases and appearances, and you can contact her at swordsandsixgunsnovel@gmail.com. Susan and her husband live in Michigan amongst a mountain of books, DVDs, and toys.

Made in the USA
Middletown, DE
15 March 2019